THE ALPHA SERIES
HAS TWO CRITERIA ONLY:

1. Literary excellence

2. And importance to the *genre*.

"The main intent of the *Alpha* series is to assemble groups of stories that give pleasure by demonstrating the richness and variety of the science-fiction form. Quality of storytelling is the touchstone . . . [These stories] show the reader visions he has not previously had, and send him away transformed and enlarged. Go thou and read. Go and be changed."

—Robert Silverberg

ALPHA
4

Edited by

Robert Silverberg

BALLANTINE BOOKS • NEW YORK

Contents

INTRODUCTION

This is the fourth annual *Alpha* collection. The years since the first volume of the series was compiled have seen a steady increase in public recognition of science fiction as a stimulating and rewarding subspecies of literature; indeed, with the science-fiction novels of Kurt Vonnegut and Michael Crichton on the best-seller lists, with such films as *A Clockwork Orange, Planet of the Apes,* and *THX 1138* drawing large audiences, with science-fictional themes infiltrating the world of rock music, with courses in science fiction sprouting in hundreds of high schools and colleges, it sometimes seems as if science fiction is Taking Over.

Whether such a takeover is a desirable end is something that even the most devout science-fictionist might wish to question: s-f is not the whole of literature, and I for one would regret such a universalization of science fiction that all writers felt obliged to turn their gaze to Betelgeuse and Proxima Centauri, and the new novels of Messrs. Updike, Bellow, Mailer, Roth, Malamud, and Beckett dealt exclusively with the events of the thirtieth century and beyond. But it is comforting to have emerged from obscurity and disrepute, at any rate, and to enjoy some of the rewards, financial and otherwise, that writers in less specialized fields enjoy.

One odd aspect of the current science-fiction boom, however, is its neglect of the science-fiction professional, the writer who, laboring for years or decades at cent-a-word rates, helped to forge the body of ideas and images that constitutes the s-f achievement. Few of those professionals have shared in the recent bonanzas. Arthur Clarke is one, thanks largely to the success of the Kubrick-Clarke movie, *2001;* Frank Herbert is another, and Robert Heinlein a third, as a result of the adoption of their novels *Dune* and *Stranger in a Strange Land* as totems of the youth culture. Isaac Asimov's television appearances and ubiquitous non-fiction output have helped to keep his s-f popular; Ray Bradbury's acceptance by literary critics as a major short-story writer swells the sales figures of his early Martian fantasies. For most others, though, the only impact of the science-fictionalizing of America has been a barely perceptible increase in standard paperback royalties. The *Alpha* series is intended, in part, to draw attention to some of these neglected writers, whose work is often the equal in vision and artistry of those who have become household names. The Vonneguts, the Crichtons, the Bradburys, and others whose national reputations have already been made will not often appear in these pages; we prefer to concentrate on the no less gifted but rather more obscure writers who toil patiently in the same vineyard. May the jackpot of public fancy one day be theirs; meanwhile, the good fortune of experiencing their work is yours.

ROBERT SILVERBERG

CASABLANCA

Thomas M. Disch

Here is a story of the very near future—comic and terrifying both at once, like most true nightmares, and brilliantly executed. Thomas Disch, Iowa-born, Minnesota-reared, more recently a cosmopolitan sort who turns up now in Istanbul, now in New York, now in Rome, now in London, is the author of several novels, including **The Genocides** and the much-acclaimed **Camp Concentration.** His best short stories, elliptical and disturbing, have been brought together in a collection entitled **Fun With Your New Head.**

In the morning the man with the red fez always brought them coffee and toast on a tray. He would ask them how it goes, and Mrs. Richmond, who had some French, would say it goes well. The hotel always served the same kind of jam, plum jam. That eventually became so tiresome that Mrs. Richmond went out and bought their own jar of strawberry jam, but in a little while that was just as tiresome as the plum jam. Then they alternated, having plum jam one day, and strawberry jam the next. They wouldn't have taken their breakfasts in the hotel at all, except for the money it saved.

When, on the morning of their second Wednesday at the Belmonte, they came down to the lobby, there was no mail for them at the desk. "You can't really expect them to think of us here," Mrs. Richmond said in a piqued tone, for it had been her expectation.

3

"I suppose not." Fred agreed.

"I think I'm sick again. It was that funny stew we had last night. Didn't I tell you? Why don't *you* go out and get the newspaper this morning?"

So Fred went, by himself, to the news-stand on the corner. It had neither the Times nor the Tribune. There weren't even the usual papers from London. Fred went to the magazine store nearby the Marhaba, the big luxury hotel. On the way someone tried to sell him a gold watch. It seemed to Fred that everyone in Morocco was trying to sell gold watches.

The magazine store still had copies of the Times from last week. Fred had read those papers already. "Where is today's Times?" he asked loudly, in English.

The middle-aged man behind the counter shook his head sadly, either because he didn't understand Fred's question or because he didn't know the answer. He asked Fred how it goes.

"Byen," said Fred, without conviction, "byen."

The local French newspaper, *La Vigie Marocaine,* had black, portentous headlines, which Fred could not decipher. Fred spoke "four languages: English, Irish, Scottish, and American." With only those languages, he insisted, one could be understood anywhere in the free world.

At ten o'clock, Bulova watch time, Fred found himself, as though by chance, outside his favourite ice cream parlour. Usually when he was with his wife, he wasn't able to indulge his sweet tooth, because Mrs. Richmond, who had a delicate stomach, distrusted Moroccan dairy products, unless boiled.

The waiter smiled and said, "Good morning, Mister Richmon." Foreigners were never able to pronounce his name right for some reason.

Fred said, "Good morning."

"How are you?"

"I'm just fine, thank you."

"Good, good," the waiter said. Nevertheless, he looked saddened. He seemed to want to say something to Fred, but his English was very limited.

It was amazing, to Fred, that he had to come halfway around the world to discover the best damned ice cream sundaes he'd ever tasted. Instead of going to bars, the young men of the town went to ice cream parlours, like this, just

as they had in Fred's youth, in Iowa, during Prohibition. It
had something to do, here in Casablanca, with the Moslem
religion.

A ragged shoe-shine boy came in and asked to shine Fred's
shoes, which were very well shined already. Fred looked out
the plate glass window to the travel agency across the street.
The boy hissed *monsieur, monsieur,* until Fred would have
been happy to kick him. The wisest policy was to ignore the
beggars. They went away quicker if you just didn't look at
them. The travel agency displayed a poster showing a pretty
young blonde, rather like Doris Day, in a cowboy costume.
It was a poster for Pan-American airlines.

At last the shoe-shine boy went away. Fred's face was
flushed with stifled anger. His sparse white hair made the
redness of the flesh seem all the brighter, like a winter sunset.

A grown man came into the ice cream parlour with a
bundle of newspapers, French newspapers. Despite his lack
of French, Fred could understand the headlines. He bought
a copy for twenty francs and went back to the hotel, leaving
half the sundae uneaten.

The minute he was in the door, Mrs. Richmond cried out,
"Isn't it terrible?" She had a copy of the paper already spread
out on the bed. "It doesn't say *anything* about Cleveland."

Cleveland was where Nan, the Richmonds' married
daughter, lived. There was no point in wondering about their
own home. It was in Florida, within fifty miles of the Cape,
and they'd always known that if there were a war it would be
one of the first places to go.

"The dirty reds!" Fred said, flushing. His face began to
cry. "God damn them to hell! What did the newspaper say?
How did it start?"

"Do you suppose," Mrs. Richmond asked, "that Billy and
Midge could be at Grandma Holt's farm?"

Fred paged through *La Vigie Marocaine* helplessly, looking for pictures. Except for the big cutout of a mushroom
cloud on the front page and a stock picture on the second of
the president in a cowboy hat, there were no photos. He tried
to read the lead story but it made no sense.

Mrs. Richmond rushed out of the room, crying aloud.

Fred wanted to tear the paper into ribbons. To calm himself he poured a shot from the pint of bourbon he kept in the

dresser. Then he went out into the hall and called through
the locked door to the W.C.: "Well, I'll bet we knocked hell
out of *them* at least."

This was of no comfort to Mrs. Richmond.

Only the day before Mrs. Richmond had written two
letters—one to her granddaughter Midge, the other to
Midge's mother, Nan. The letter to Midge read:

December 2

Dear Mademoiselle Holt,

Well, here we are in romantic Casablanca, where the old
and the new come together. There are palm trees growing
on the boulevard outside our hotel window, and sometimes it
seems that we never left Florida at all. In Marrakesh we
bought presents for you and Billy, which you should get in
time for Christmas if the mails are good. Wouldn't you like
to know what's in those packages! But you'll just have to
wait till Christmas!

You should thank God every day, darling, that you live in
America. If you could only see the poor Moroccan children,
begging on the streets. They aren't able to go to school, and
many of them don't even have shoes or warm clothes. And
don't think it doesn't get cold here, even if it is Africa! You
and Billy don't know how lucky you are!

On the train ride to Marrakesh we saw the farmers plow-
ing their fields in *December*. Each plow has one donkey and
one camel. That would probably be an interesting fact for
you to tell your geography teacher in school.

Casablanca is wonderfully exciting, and I often wish that
you and Billy were here to enjoy it with us. Someday, perhaps! Be good—remember it will be Christmas soon.

Your loving Grandmother,
"Grams"

The second letter, to Midge's mother, read as follows:

Dec. 2, Mond. afternoon

Dear Nan,

There's no use my pretending any more with *you!* You saw it in my first letter—before I even knew my own feelings. Yes, Morocco has been a terrible disappointment. You wouldn't believe some of the things that have happened. For instance, it is almost impossible to mail a package out of this country! I will have to wait till we get to Spain, therefore, to send Billy and Midge their Xmas presents. Better not tell B & M that however!

Marrakesh was terrible. Fred and I got *lost* in the native quarter, and we thought we'd never escape! The filth is unbelievable, but if I talk about that it will only make me ill. After our experience on "the wrong side of the tracks" I wouldn't leave our hotel. Fred got very angry, and we took the train back to Casablanca the same night. At least there are decent restaurants in Casablanca. You can get a very satisfactory French-type dinner for about $1.00.

After all this you won't believe me when I tell you that we're going to stay here two more weeks. That's when the next boat leaves for Spain. Two more weeks! ! ! Fred says take an airplane, but you know me. And I'll be d——ed if I'll take a trip on the local railroad with all our luggage, which is the only other way.

I've finished the one book I brought along, and now I have nothing to read but newspapers. They are printed up in Paris and have mostly the news from India and Angola, which I find too depressing, and the political news from Europe, which I can't ever keep up with. Who is Chancellor Zucker and what does he have to do with the war in India? I say if people would just sit down and try to *understand* each other, most of the world's so-called problems would disappear. Well, that's my opinion, but I have to keep it to myself, or Fred gets an apoplexy. You know Fred! He says, drop a bomb on Red China and to H—— with it! Good old Fred!

I hope you and Dan are both fine and *dan*-dy, and I hope B & M are coming along in school. We were both excited to hear about Billy's A in geography. Fred says it's due to all the stories he's told Billy about our travels. Maybe he's right for once!

Love & kisses,
"Grams"

Fred had forgotten to mail these two letters yesterday afternoon, and now, after the news in the paper, it didn't seem worthwhile. The Holts, Nan and Dan and Billy and Midge, were all very probably dead.

"It's so strange," Mrs. Richmond observed at lunch at their restaurant. "I can't believe it really happened. Nothing has changed here. You'd think it would make more of a difference."

"God damned reds."

"Will you drink the rest of my wine? I'm too upset."

"What do you suppose we should do? Should we try and telephone to Nan?"

"Trans-*Atlantic?* Wouldn't a telegram do just as well?"

So, after lunch, they went to the telegraph office, which was in the main post office, and filled out a form. The message they finally agreed on was: IS EVERYONE WELL QUESTION WAS CLEVELAND HIT QUESTION RETURN REPLY REQUESTED. It cost eleven dollars to send off, one dollar a word. The post office wouldn't accept a travellers' cheque, so while Mrs. Richmond waited at the desk, Fred went across the street to the Bank of Morocco to cash it there.

The teller behind the grill looked at Fred's cheque doubtfully and asked to see his passport. He brought cheque and passport into an office at the back of the bank. Fred grew more and more peeved, as the time wore on and nothing was done. He was accustomed to being treated with respect, at least. The teller returned with a portly gentleman not much younger than Fred himself. He wore a striped suit with a flower in his buttonhole.

"Are you Mr. Richmon?" the older gentleman asked.

"Of course I am. Look at the picture in my passport."

"I'm sorry, Mr. Richmon, but we are not able to cash this cheque."

"What do you mean? I've cashed cheques here before. Look, I've noted it down: on November 28, forty dollars; on December 1, twenty dollars."

The man shook his head. "I'm sorry, Mr. Richmon, but we are not able to cash these cheques."

"I'd like to see the manager."

"I'm sorry, Mr. Richmon, it is not possible for us to cash your cheque. Thank you very much." He turned to go.

"I want to see the manager!" Everybody in the bank, the tellers and the other clients, were staring at Fred, who had turned quite red.

"I am the manager," said the man in the striped suit. "Good-bye, Mr. Richmon."

"These are American Express travellers' cheques. They're good anywhere in the world!"

The manager returned to his office, and the teller began to wait on another customer. Fred returned to the post office.

"We'll have to return here later, darling," he explained to his wife. She didn't ask why, and he didn't want to tell her.

They bought food to bring back to the hotel, since Mrs. Richmond didn't feel up to dressing for dinner.

The manager of the hotel, a thin, nervous man who wore wire-framed spectacles, was waiting at the desk to see them. Wordlessly he presented them a bill for the room.

Fred protested angrily. "We're paid up. We're paid until the twelfth of this month. What are you trying to pull?"

The manager smiled. He had gold teeth. He explained, in imperfect English, that this was the bill.

"Nous sommes payée," Mrs. Richmond explained pleasantly. Then in a diplomatic whisper to her husband, "Show him the receipt."

The manager examined the receipt. *"Non, non, non,"* he said, shaking his head. He handed Fred, instead of his receipt, the new bill.

"I'll take that receipt back, thank you very much." The manager smiled and backed away from Fred. Fred acted without thinking. He grabbed the manager's wrist and prised the receipt out of his fingers. The manager shouted words at him in Arabic. Fred took the key for their room, 216, off its hook behind the desk. Then he took his wife by the elbow and led her up the stairs. The man with the red fez came running down the stairs to do the manager's bidding.

Once they were inside the room, Fred locked the door. He was trembling and short of breath. Mrs. Richmond made him sit down and sponged his fevered brow with cold water. Five minutes later, a little slip of paper slid in under the door. It was the bill.

"Look at this!" he exclaimed. "Forty dirham a day. Eight dollars! That son of a bitch." The regular per diem rate for the room was twenty dirham, and the Richmonds, by taking it for a fortnight, had bargained it down to fifteen.

"Now, Freddy!"

"That bastard!"

"It's probably some sort of misunderstanding."

"He saw that receipt, didn't he? He made out that receipt himself. *You* know why he's doing it. Because of what's happened. Now I won't be able to cash my travellers' cheques here either. That son of a bitch!"

"Now, Freddy." She smoothed the ruffled strands of white hair with the wet sponge.

"Don't you now-Freddy me! I know what I'm going to do. I'm going to the American Consulate and register a complaint."

"That's a good idea, but not today, Freddy. Let's stay inside until tomorrow. We're both too tired and upset. Tomorrow we can go there together. Maybe they'll know something about Cleveland by then." Mrs. Richmond was prevented from giving further counsel by a new onset of her illness. She went out into the hall, but returned almost immediately. "The door into the toilet is padlocked," she said. Her eyes were wide with terror. She had just begun to understand what was happening.

That night, after a frugal dinner of olives, cheese sandwiches and figs, Mrs. Richmond tried to look on the bright side. "Actually we're very lucky," she said, "to be here, instead of there, when it happened. At least, we're alive. We should thank God for being alive."

"If we'd of bombed them twenty years ago, we wouldn't be in this spot now. Didn't I say way back then that we should have bombed them?"

"Yes, darling. But there's no use crying over spilt milk. Try and look on the bright side, like I do."

"God-damn dirty reds."

The bourbon was all gone. It was dark, and outside, across the square, a billboard advertising Olympic Bleue cigarettes (C'est mieux!) winked on and off, as it had on all other nights of their visit to Casablanca. Nothing here seemed to have been affected by the momentous events across the ocean.

"We're out of envelopes," Mrs. Richmond complained. She had been trying to compose a letter to her daughter.

Fred was staring out the window, wondering what it had been like: had the sky been filled with planes? Were they still fighting on the ground in India and Angola? What did Florida look like now? He had always wanted to build a bomb shelter in their back yard in Florida, but his wife had been against it. Now it would be impossible to know which of them had been right.

"What time is it?" Mrs. Richmond asked, winding the alarm.

He looked at his watch, which was always right. "Eleven o'clock, Bulova watch time." It was an Accutron that his company, Iowa Mutual Life, had presented to him at retirement.

There was, in the direction of the waterfront, a din of shouting and clashing metal. As it grew louder, Fred could see the head of a ragged parade advancing up the boulevard. He pulled down the lath shutters over the windows till there was just a narrow slit to watch the parade through.

"They're burning something," he informed his wife. "Come see."

"I don't want to watch that sort of thing."

"Some kind of statue, or scarecrow. You can't tell who it's meant to be. Someone in a cowboy hat, looks like. I'll bet they're Commies."

When the mob of demonstrators reached the square over which the Belmonte Hotel looked, they turned to the left, toward the larger luxury hotels, the Marhaba and El Mansour. They were banging cymbals together and beating drums and blowing on loud horns that sounded like bagpipes. Instead of marching in rows, they did a sort of whirling, skipping dance step. Once they'd turned the corner, Fred couldn't see any more of them.

"I'll bet every beggar in town is out there, blowing his horn," Fred said sourly. "Every god-damn watch pedlar and shoe-shine boy in Casablanca."

"They sound very happy," Mrs. Richmond said. Then she began crying again.

The Richmonds slept together in the same bed that evening for the first time in several months. The noise of the demonstration continued, off and on, nearer or farther away, for several hours. This too set the evening apart from other evenings, for Casablanca was usually very quiet, surprisingly so, after ten o'clock at night.

The office of the American Consul seemed to have been bombed. The front door was broken off its hinges, and Fred entered, after some reluctance, to find all the downstairs rooms empty of furniture, the carpets torn away, the mouldings pried from the walls. The files of the consulate had been emptied out and the contents burned in the centre of the largest room. Slogans in Arabic had been scrawled on the walls with the ashes.

Leaving the building, he discovered a piece of typing paper nailed to the deranged door. It read: "All Americans in Morocco, whether of tourist or resident status, are advised to leave the country until the present crisis is over. The Consul cannot guarantee the safety of those who choose to remain."

A shoe-shine boy, his diseased scalp inadequately concealed by a dirty wool cap, tried to slip his box under Fred's foot.

"Go away, you! *Vamoose*! This is your fault. I know what happened last night. You and your kind did this. Red beggars!"

The boy smiled uncertainly at Fred and tried again to get his shoe on the box. "*Monsieur, monsieur,*" he hissed—or, perhaps, "*Merci, merci.*"

By noonday the centre of the town was aswarm with Americans. Fred hadn't realised there had been so many in Casablanca. What were they doing here? Where had they kept themselves hidden? Most of the Americans were on their way to the airport, their cars piled high with luggage. Some said they were bound for England, others for Germany. Spain, they claimed, wouldn't be safe, though it was probably safer than Morocco. They were brusque with Fred to the point of rudeness.

He returned to the hotel room where Mrs. Richmond was waiting for him. They had agreed that one of them must always be in the room. As Fred went up the stairs the manager tried to hand him another bill. "I will call the police," he threatened. Fred was too angry to reply. He wanted to hit the man in the nose and stamp on his ridiculous spectacles. If he'd been five years younger he might have done so.

"They've cut off the water," Mrs. Richmond announced dramatically, after she'd admitted her husband to the room. "And the man with the red hat tried to get in, but I had the chain across the door, thank heaven. We can't wash or use the bidet. I don't know what will happen. I'm afraid."

She wouldn't listen to anything Fred said about the Consulate. "We've got to take a plane," he insisted. "To England. All the other Americans are going there. There was a sign on the door of the Con—"

"No, Fred. No. Not a plane. You won't make me get into an airplane. I've gone twenty years without that, and I won't start now."

"But this is an emergency. We have to!"

"I refuse to talk about it. And don't you shout at *me*, Fred Richmond. We'll sail when the boat sails, and that's that! Now, let's be practical, shall we? The first thing that we have to do is for you to get out and buy some bottled water. Four bottles, and bread, and——No, you'll never remember everything. I'll write out a list."

But when Fred returned, four hours later, when it was growing dark, he had but a single bottle of soda, one loaf of hard bread, and a little box of pasteurised process cheese.

"It was all the money I had. They won't cash my cheques. Not at the bank, not at the Marhaba, not anywhere." There were flecks of violet in his red, dirty face, and his voice was hoarse. He had been shouting hours long.

Mrs. Richmond used half the bottle of soda to wash off his face. Then she made sandwiches of cheese and strawberry jam, all the while maintaining a steady stream of conversation, on cheerful topics. She was afraid her husband would have a stroke.

On Thursday the twelfth, the day before their scheduled sailing, Fred went to the travel agency to find out what pier their ship had docked in. He was informed that the sailing had been cancelled, permanently. The ship, a Yugoslav freighter, had been in Norfolk on December 4. The agency politely refunded the price of the tickets—in American dollars.

"Couldn't you give me dirham instead?"

"But you paid in dollars, Mr. Richmond." The agent spoke with a fussy, overprecise accent that annoyed Fred more than an honest French accent. "You paid in American Express travellers' cheques."

"But I'd *rather* have dirham."

"That would be impossible."

"I'll give you one to one. How about that? One dirham for one dollar." He did not even become angry at being forced to make so unfair a suggestion. He had been through this same scene too many times—at banks, at stores, with people off the street.

"The government has forbidden us to trade in American money, Mr. Richmond. I am truly sorry that I cannot help you. If you would be interested to purchase an airplane ticket, however, I can accept money for that. If you have enough."

"You don't leave me much choice, do you?" (He thought: *Betty will be furious.*) "What will it cost for two tickets to London?"

The agent named the price. Fred flared up. "That's highway robbery! Why, that's more than the first-class to New York City!"

The agent smiled. "We have no flights scheduled to New York, sir."

Grimly, Fred signed away his travellers' cheques to pay for the tickets. It took all his cheques and all but 50 dollars of the refunded money. His wife, however, had her own bundle of American Express cheques that hadn't even been touched yet. He examined the tickets, which were printed in French. "What does this say here? When does it leave?"

"On the fourteenth. Saturday. At eight in the evening."

"You don't have anything tomorrow?"

"I'm sorry. You should be quite happy that we can sell you these tickets. If it weren't for the fact that our main office is in Paris, and that they've directed that Americans be given priority on all Pan-Am flights, we wouldn't be able to."

"I see. The thing is this—I'm in rather a tight spot. Nobody, not even the banks, will take American money. This is our last night at the hotel, and if we have to stay over Friday night as well. . . ."

"You might go to the airport waiting room, sir."

Fred took off his Accutron wristwatch. "In America this watch would cost $120 wholesale. You wouldn't be interested. . . ."

"I'm sorry, Mr. Richmond. I have a watch of my own."

Fred, with the tickets securely tucked into his passport case, went out through the thick glass door. He would have liked to have a sundae at the ice cream parlour across the street, but he couldn't afford it. He couldn't afford anything unless he was able to sell his watch. They had lived the last week out on what he'd gotten for the alarm clock and the electric shaver. Now there was nothing left.

When Fred was at the corner, he heard someone calling his name. "Mr. Richmond. Mr. Richmond, sir." It was the agent. Shyly he held out a ten dirham note and three fives. Fred took the money and handed him the watch. The agent put Fred's Accutron on his wrist beside his old watch. He smiled and offered Fred his hand to shake. Fred walked away, ignoring the outstretched hand.

Five dollars, he thought over and over again, *five dollars.* He was too ashamed to return at once to the hotel.

Mrs. Richmond wasn't in the room. Instead the man in the red fez was engaged in packing all their clothes and toilet articles into the three suitcases. "Hey!" Fred shouted. "What do you think you're doing? Stop that!"

"You must pay your bill," the hotel manager, who stood back at a safe distance in the hallway, shrilled at him. "You must pay your bill or leave."

Fred tried to prevent the man in the red fez from packing

the bags. He was furious with his wife for having gone off—
to the W.C. probably—and left the hotel room unguarded.

"Where is my wife?" he demanded of the manager. "This
is an outrage." He began to swear. The man in the red fez
returned to packing the bags.

Fred made a determined effort to calm himself. He could
not risk a stroke. After all, he reasoned with himself, whether
they spent one or two nights in the airport waiting room
wouldn't make that much difference. So he chased the man
in the red fez away and finished the packing himself. When
he was done, he rang for the porter, and the man in the red
fez returned and helped him carry the bags downstairs. He
waited in the dark lobby, using the largest of the suitcases
for a stool, for his wife to return. She had probably gone
to "their" restaurant, some blocks away, where they were
still allowed to use the W.C. The owner of the restaurant
couldn't understand why they didn't take their meals there
any more and didn't want to offend them, hoping, perhaps,
that they would come back.

While he waited, Fred occupied the time by trying to remember the name of the Englishman who had been a supper
guest at their house in Florida three years before. It was a
strange name that was not pronounced at all the way that it
was spelled. At intervals he would go out into the street to
try and catch a sight of his wife returning to the hotel.
Whenever he tried to ask the manager where she had gone,
the man would renew his shrill complaint. Fred became
desperate. She was taking too long. He telephoned the restaurant. The owner of the restaurant understood enough
English to be able to tell him that she had not visited his
W.C. all that day.

An hour or so after sunset, Fred found his way to the
police station, a wretched stucco building inside the ancient
medina, the non-European quarter. Americans were advised
not to venture into the medina after dark.

"My wife is missing," he told one of the grey-uniformed
men. "I think she may be the victim of a robbery."

The policeman replied brusquely in French.

"My wife," Fred repeated loudly, gesturing in a vague
way.

The policeman turned to speak to his fellows. It was a piece of deliberate rudeness.

Fred took out his passport and waved it in the policeman's face. "This is my passport," he shouted. "My wife is missing. My wife. Doesn't somebody here speak English? Somebody *must* speak English. *Ing-glish!*"

The policeman shrugged and handed Fred back his passport.

"My wife!" Fred screamed hysterically. "Listen to me— my wife, my wife, my wife!"

The policeman, a scrawny, moustached man, grabbed Fred by the neck of his coat and led him forcibly into another room and down a long, unlighted corridor that smelled of urine. Fred didn't realise, until he had been thrust into the room, that it was a cell. The door that closed behind him was made not of bars, but of sheet metal nailed over wood. There was no light in the room, no air. He screamed, he kicked at the door and pounded on it with his fists until he had cut a deep gash into the side of his palm. He stopped, to suck the blood, fearful of blood-poisoning.

He could, when his eyes had adjusted to the darkness, see a little of the room about him. It was not much larger than Room 216 at the Belmonte, but it contained more people than Fred could count. They were heaped all along the walls an indiscriminate tumble of rags and filth, old men and young men, a wretched assembly.

They stared at the American gentleman in astonishment.

The police released Fred in the morning, and he returned at once to the hotel, speaking to no one. He was angry but, even more, he was terrified.

His wife had not returned. The three suitcases, for a wonder, were still sitting where he had left them. The manager insisted that he leave the lobby, and Fred did not protest. The Richmonds' time at the hotel had expired, and Fred didn't have the money for another night, even at the old rate.

Outside, he did not know what to do. He stood on the kerbside, trying to decide. His pants were wrinkled, and he feared (though he could not smell it himself) that he stank of the prison cell.

The traffic policeman in the centre of the square began

giving him funny looks. He was afraid of the policeman, afraid of being returned to the cell. He hailed a taxi and directed the driver to go to the airport.

"Où?" the driver asked.

"The airport, the airport," he said testily. Cabbies, at least could be expected to know English.

But where was his wife? Where was Betty?

When they arrived at the airport, the driver demanded fifteen dirhams, which was an outrageous price in Casablanca, where cabs are pleasantly cheap. Having not had the foresight to negotiate the price in advance, Fred had no choice but to pay the man what he asked.

The waiting room was filled with people, though few seemed to be Americans. The stench of the close air was almost as bad as it had been in the cell. There were no porters, and he could not move through the crowd, so he set the suitcases down just outside the entrance and seated himself on the largest bag.

A man in an olive-drab uniform with a black beret asked, in French, to see his passport. *"Votre passeport,"* he repeated patiently, until Fred had understood. He examined each page with a great show of suspicion, but eventually he handed it back.

"Do you speak English?" Fred asked him then. He thought, because of the different uniform, that he might not be one of the city police. He answered with a stream of coarse Arabic gabbling.

Perhaps, Fred told himself, *she will come out here to look for me.* But why, after all, should she? He should have remained outside the hotel.

He imagined himself safely in England, telling his story to the American Consul there. He imagined the international repercussions it would have. What had been the name of that English man he knew? He had lived in London. It began with *C* or *Ch*.

An attractive middle-aged woman sat down on the other end of his suitcase and began speaking in rapid French, making sharp gestures, like karate shops, with her well-groomed hand. She was trying to explain something to him, but of course he couldn't understand her. She broke into tears. Fred couldn't even offer her his handkerchief, because it was dirty from last night.

"My wife," he tried to explain. "My—wife—is missing. My wife."

"Bee-yay," the woman said despairingly. "Vote beeyay." She showed him a handful of dirham notes in large denominations.

"I wish I could understand what it is you want," he said.

She went away from him, as though she were angry, as though he had said something to insult her.

Fred felt someone tugging at his shoe. He remembered, with a start of terror, awakening in the cell, the old man tugging at his shoes, trying to steal them but not understanding, apparently, about the laces.

It was only, after all, a shoe-shine boy. He had already begun to brush Fred's shoes, which were, he could see, rather dirty. He pushed the boy away.

He had to go back to the hotel to see if his wife had returned there, but he hadn't the money for another taxi and there was no one in the waiting room that he dared trust with the bags.

Yet he couldn't leave Casablanca without his wife. Could he? But if he did stay, what was he to do, if the police would not listen to him?

At about ten o'clock the waiting room grew quiet. All that day no planes had entered or left the airfield. Everyone here was waiting for tomorrow's plane to London. How were so many people, and so much luggage, to fit on one plane, even the largest jet? Did they all have tickets?

They slept anywhere, on the hard benches, on newspapers on the concrete floor, on the narrow window ledges. Fred was one of the luckiest, because he could sleep on his three suitcases.

When he woke the next morning, he found that his passport and the two tickets had been stolen from his breast pocket. He still had his billfold, because he had slept on his back. It contained nine dirham.

Christmas morning. Fred went out and treated himself to an ice cream sundae. Nobody seemed to be celebrating the holiday in Casablanca. Most of the shops in the ancient

medina (where Fred had found a hotel room for three
dirham a day) were open for business, while in the European
quarter one couldn't tell if the stores were closed permanently or just for the day.

Going past the Belmonte, Fred stopped, as was his custom, to ask after his wife. The manager was very polite and
said that nothing was known of Mrs. Richmond. The police
had her description now.

Hoping to delay the moment when he sat down before
the sundae, he walked to the post office and asked if there
had been any answer to his telegram to the American Em-
bassy in London. There had not.

When at last he did have his sundae it didn't seem quite
as good as he had remembered. There was so little of it! He
sat down for an hour with his empty dish, watching the
drizzling rain. He was alone in the ice cream parlour. The
windows of the travel agency across the street were covered
up by a heavy metal shutter, from which the yellow paint
was flaking.

The waiter came and sat down at Fred's table. *"Il pleuve,
Monsieur Richmon. It rains. Il pleuve."*

"Yes, it does," said Fred. "It rains. It falls. Fall-out."

But the waiter had very little English. "Merry Christmas,"
he said. *"Joyeuse Nöel.* Merry Christmas."

Fred agreed.

When the drizzle had cleared a bit, Fred strolled to the
United Nations Plaza and found a bench under a palm tree
that was dry. Despite the cold and damp, he didn't want to
return to his cramped hotel room and spend the rest of the
day sitting on the edge of his bed.

Fred was by no means alone in the plaza. A number of
figures in heavy woollen djelabas, with hoods over their
heads, stood or sat on benches, or strolled in circles on the
gravel paths. The djelabas made ideal raincoats. Fred had
sold his own London Fog three days before for twenty
dirham. He was getting better prices for his things now that
he had learned to count in French. The hardest lesson to
learn (and he had not yet learned it) was to keep from
thinking. When he could do that, he wouldn't become angry,
or afraid.

At noon the whistle blew in the handsome tower at the

end of the plaza, from the top of which one could see all of Casablanca in every direction. Fred took out the cheese sandwich from the pocket of his suit coat and ate it, a little bit at a time. Then he took out the chocolate bar with almonds. His mouth began to water.

A shoe-shine boy scampered across the gravelled circle and sat down in the damp at Fred's feet. He tried to lift Fred's foot and place in on his box.

"No," said Fred. "Go away."

"Monsieur, monsieur," the boy insisted. Or perhaps, *"Merci, merci."*

Fred looked down guiltily at his shoes. They were very dirty. He hadn't had them shined in weeks.

The boy kept whistling those meaningless words at him. His gaze was fixed on Fred's chocolate bar. Fred pushed him away with the side of his foot. The boy grabbed for the candy. Fred struck him in the side of his head. The chocolate bar fell to the gravel, not far from the boy's calloused feet. The boy lay on his side, whimpering.

"You little sneak!" Fred shouted at him.

It was a clear-cut case of thievery. He was furious. He had a right to be furious. Standing up to his full height, his foot came down accidentally on the boy's rubbishy shoe-shine box. The wood splintered.

The boy began to gabble at Fred in Arabic. He scurried forward on hands and knees to pick up the pieces of the box.

"You asked for this," Fred said. He kicked the boy in the ribs. The boy rolled with the blow, as though he were not unused to such treatment. "Little beggar! Thief!" Fred screamed.

He bent forward and tried to grasp a handhold in the boy's hair, but it was cut too close to his head, to prevent lice. Fred hit again in the face, but now the boy was on his feet and running.

There was no use pursuing him, he was too fast, too fast.

Fred's face was violet and red, and his white hair, in need of a trim, straggled down over his flushed forehead. He had not noticed, while he was beating the boy, the group of Arabs, or Moslems, or whatever they were, that had gathered around him to watch. Fred could not read the expressions on their dark, wrinkly faces.

"Did you see that?" he asked loudly. "Did you see what that little thief tried to do? Did you see him try to steal . . . my candy bar?"

One of the men, in a long djelaba striped with brown, said something to Fred that sounded like so much gargling. Another, younger man, in European dress, struck Fred in the face. Fred teetered backward.

"Now see here!" He had not time to tell them he was an American citizen. The next blow caught him in the mouth, and he fell to the ground. Once he was lying on his back, the older men joined in in kicking him. Some kicked him in the ribs, others in his head, still others had to content themselves with his legs. Curiously, nobody went for his groin. The shoe-shine boy watched from a distance, and when Fred was unconscious, came forward and removed his shoes. The young man who had first hit him removed his suit coat and his belt. Wisely, Fred had left his billfold behind at his hotel.

When he woke up he was sitting on the bench again. A policeman was addressing him in Arabic. Fred shook his head uncomprehendingly. His back hurt dreadfully, from when he had fallen to the ground. The policeman addressed him in French. He shivered. Their kicks had not damaged him so much as he had expected. Except for the young man, they had worn slippers instead of shoes. His face experienced only a dull ache, but there was blood all down the front of his shirt, and his mouth tasted of blood. He was cold, very cold.

The policeman went away, shaking his head.

At just that moment Fred remembered the name of the Englishman who had had supper in his house in Florida. It was Cholmondeley, but it was pronounced *Chum-ly*. He was still unable to remember his London address.

Only when he tried to stand did he realize that his shoes were gone. The gravel hurt the tender soles of his bare feet. Fred was mortally certain that the shoe-shine boy had stolen his shoes.

He sat back down on the bench with a groan. He hoped to hell he'd hurt the god-damned little son of a bitch. He hoped to hell he had. He grated his teeth together, wishing that he could get hold of him again. The little beggar. He'd kick him this time so that he'd remember it. The god-damn dirty little red beggar. He'd kick his face in.

DIO

Damon Knight

The sensuous and crystalline prose of Damon
Knight is seen all too infrequently these days; he
was never an extraordinarily prolific writer, but the
period when we could count on at least two or
three new Knight stories a year seems forever
gone, now that he occupies his time editing anthologies and running writers' workshops. The long
story here, dating from his most productive period
—the mid-1950s—makes one hope that his insti-
tutional duties will not keep him much longer away
from his own art. This vivid and moving vision of a
world of immortals, this poignant parable of a
dying god, is science fiction at its finest.

I

It is noon. Overhead the sky like a great silver bowl
shimmers with heat, the yellow sand hurls it back; the distant ocean is dancing with white fire. Emerging from underground, Dio the Planner stands blinking a moment in the
strong salt light; he feels the heat like a cap on his head,
and his beard curls crisply, iridescent in the sun.

A few yards away are five men and women, their limbs
glinting pink against the sand. The rest of the seascape is
utterly bare; the sand seems to stretch empty and hot for
miles. There is not even a gull in the air. Three of the figures
are men; they are running and throwing a beach ball at one

23

another, with far-off shouts. The two women are half reclining, watching the men. All five are superbly muscled, with great arched chests, ponderous as Percherons. Their skins are smooth; their eyes sparkle. Dio looks at his own forearm: is there a trace of darkness? is the skin coarsening?

He drops his single garment and walks toward the group. The sand's caress is briefly painful to his feet, then his skin adapts, and he no longer feels it. The five incuriously turn to watch him approach. They are all players, not students, and there are two he does not even know. He feels uncomfortable, and wishes he had not come. It isn't good for students and players to meet informally; each side is too much aware of the other's goodnatured contempt. Dio tries to imagine himself a player, exerting himself to be polite to a student, and as always, he fails. The gulf is too wide. It takes both kinds to make a world, student to remember and make, player to consume and enjoy; but the classes should not mix.

Even without their clothing, these are players: the wide, innocent eyes that flash with enthusiasm, or flicker with easy boredom; the soft mouths that can be gay or sulky by turns. Now he deliberately looks at the blonde woman, Claire, and in her face he sees the same unmistakable signs. But, against all reason and usage, the soft curve of her lips is beauty; the poise of her dark-blonde head on the strong neck wrings his heart. It is illogical, almost unheard-of, perhaps abnormal; but he loves her.

Her gray eyes are glowing up at him like sea-agates; the quick pleasure of her smile warms and soothes him. "I'm so glad to *see* you." She takes his hand. "You know Katha of course, and Piet. And this is Tanno, and that's Mark. Sit here and talk to me, I can't move, it's so hot."

The ball throwers go cheerfully back to their game. The brunette, Katha, begins talking immediately about the choirs at Bethany: has Dio heard them. No? But he must; the voices are stupendous, the choir-master is brilliant; nothing like it has been heard for centuries.

The word "centuries" falls carelessly. How old is Katha —eight hundred, a thousand? Recently, in a three-hundred-year-old journal, Dio has been surprised to find a reference to Katha. Evidently he had known her briefly, forgotten her completely. There are so many people; it's impossible to remember. That's why the students keep journals; and why the players don't. He might even have met Claire before, and forgotten . . . "No," he says, smiling politely, "I've been busy with a project."

"Dio is an Architectural Planner," says Claire, mocking him with the exaggerated syllables; and yet there's a curious, inverted pride in her voice. "I told you, Kat, he's a student among students. He rebuilds this whole sector, every year."

"Oh," says Katha, wide-eyed, "I think that's absolutely fascinating." A moment later, without pausing, she has changed the subject to the new sky circus in Littlam—perfectly vulgar, but hilarious. The sky clowns! The tumblers! The delicious mock animals!

Claire's smooth face is close to his, haloed by the sun, gilded from below by the reflection of the hot sand. Her half-closed eyelids are delicate and soft, bruised by heat; her pupils are contracted, and the wide gray irises are intricately patterned. A fragment floats to the top of his mind, something he has read about the structure of the iris: ray-like dilating muscles interlaced with a circular contractile set, pigmented with a little melanin. For some reason, the thought is distasteful, and he pushes it aside. He feels a little light-headed; he has been working too hard.

"Tired?" she asks gently.

He relaxes a little. The brunette, Katha, is still talking; she is one of those who talk and never care if anyone listens. He answers, "This is our busiest time. All the designs are coming back for a final check before they go into the master integrator. It's our last chance to find any mistakes."

"Dio, I'm sorry," she says. "I know I shouldn't have asked you." Her brows go up; she looks at him anxiously under her lashes. "You should rest, though."

"Yes," says Dio.

She lays her soft palm on the nape of his neck. "Rest, then. Rest."

"Ah," says Dio wearily, letting his head drop into the crook of his arm. Under the sand where he lies are seventeen inhabited levels, of which three are his immediate concern, over a sector that reaches from Alban to Detroy. He has been working almost without sleep for two weeks. Next season there is talk of beginning an eighteenth level; it will mean raising the surface again, and all the forceplanes will will have to be shifted. The details swim past, thousands of them; behind his closed eyes, he sees architectural tracings, blueprints, code sheets, specifications.

"Darling," says her caressing voice in his ear. "You know I'm happy you came, anyhow, even if you didn't want to. *Because* you didn't want to. Do you understand that?"

He peers at her with one half-open eye. "A feeling of power?" he suggests ironically.

"*No.* Reassurance is more like it. Did you know I was jealous of your work? . . . I am, very much. I told myself, if he'll leave it, now, today—"

He rolls over, smiling crookedly up at her. "And yet you don't know one day from the next."

Her answering smile is quick and shy. "I know, isn't it awful of me: but *you* do."

As they look at each other in silence, he is aware again of the gulf between them. *They need us,* he thinks, *to make their world over every year—keep it bright and fresh, cover up the past—but they dislike us because they know that whatever they forget, we keep and remember.*

His hand finds hers. A deep, unreasoning sadness wells up in him; he asks silently, *Why should I love you?*

He has not spoken, but he sees her face contract into a rueful, pained smile; and her fingers grip hard.

Above them, the shouts of the ball throwers have changed to noisy protests. Dio looks up. Piet, the cotton-headed man, laughing, is afloat over the heads of the other two. He comes down slowly and throws the ball; the game goes on. But a moment later Piet is in the air again: the others shout angrily, and Tanno leaps up to wrestle with him. The ball drops, bounds away: the two striving figures turn and roll in midair. At length the cotton-headed man forces the other down to the sand. They both leap up and run over, laughing.

"Someone's got to tame this wild man," says the loser, panting. "I can't do it, he's too slippery. How about you, Dio?"

"He's resting," Claire protests, but the others chorus, "Oh, yes!" "Just a fall or two," says Piet, with a wide grin, rubbing his hands together. "There's lots of time before the tide comes in—unless you'd rather not?"

Dio gets reluctantly to his feet. Grinning, Piet floats up off the sand. Dio follows, feeling the taut surge of back and chest muscles, and the curious sensation of pressure on the spine. The two men circle, rising slowly. Piet whips his body over, head downward, arms slashing for Dio's legs. Dio overleaps him, and, turning, tries for a leg-and-arm; but Piet squirms away like an eel and catches him in a waist lock. Dio strains against the taut chest, all his muscles knotting; the two men hang unbalanced for a moment. Then, suddenly, something gives way in the force that buoys Dio up. They go over together, hard and awkwardly into the sand. There is a surprised babble of voices.

Dio picks himself up. Piet is kneeling nearby, whitefaced, holding his forearm. "Bent?" asks Mark, bending to touch it gently.

"Came down with all my weight," says Piet. "Wasn't expecting—" He nods at Dio. "That's a new one."

"Well, let's hurry and fix it," says the other, "or you'll miss the spout." Piet lays the damaged forearm across his own thighs. "Ready?" Mark plants his bare foot on the arm, leans forward and presses sharply down. Piet winces, then smiles; the arm is straight.

"Sit down and let it knit," says the other. He turns to Dio. "What's this?"

Dio is just becoming aware of a sharp pain in one finger, and dark blood welling. "Just turned back the nail a little," says Mark. "Press it down, it'll close in a second."

Katha suggests a word game, and in a moment they are all sitting in a circle, shouting letters at each other. Dio does poorly; he cannot forget the dark blood falling from his fingertip. The silver sky seems oppressively distant; he is tired of the heat that pours down on his head, of the breathless air and the sand like hot metal under his body. He has a sense of helpless fear, as if something terrible had already happened; as if it were too late.

Someone says, "It's time," and they all stand up, whisking sand from their bodies. "Come on," says Claire over her shoulder. "Have you ever been up the spout? It's fun."

"No, I must get back, I'll call you later." says Dio. Her fingers lie softly on his chest as he kisses her briefly, then he steps away. "Goodbye," he calls to the others, "Goodbye," and turning, trudges away over the sand.

The rest, relieved to be free of him, are halfway to the rocks above the water's edge. A white feather of spray dances from a fissure as the sea rushes into the cavern below. The water slides back, leaving mirror-wet sand that dries in a breath. It gathers itself; far out a comber lifts its green head, and rushes onward. "Not this one, but the next," calls Tanno.

"Claire," says Katha, approaching her, "it was so peculiar about your friend. Did you notice? When he left, his finger was still bleeding."

The white plume leaps, higher, provoking a gust of nervous laughter. Piet dances up after it, waving his legs in a burlesque entrechat. "What?" says Claire. "You must be wrong. It couldn't have been."

"Now, come on, everybody. Hang close!"

"All the same," says Katha, "it was bleeding." No one hears her; she is used to that.

Far out, the comber lifts its head menacingly high; it comes onward, white-crowned, hard as bottle glass below, rising, faster, and as it roars with a shuddering of earth into the cavern, the Immortals are dashed high on the white torrent, screaming their joy.

Dio is in his empty rooms alone, pacing the resilient floor, smothered in silence. He pauses, sweeps a mirror into being on the bare wall; leans forward as if to peer at his own gray face, then wipes the mirror out again. All around him the universe presses down, enormous, inexorable.

The time stripe on the wall has turned almost black: the day is over. He has been here alone all afternoon. His door and phone circuits are set to reject callers, even Claire—his only instinct has been to hide.

A scrap of yellow cloth is tied around the hurt finger. Blood has saturated the cloth and dried, and now it is stuck tight. The blood has stopped, but the hurt nail has still not reattached itself. There is something wrong with him; how could there be anything wrong with him?

He has felt it coming for days, drawing closer, invisibly. Now it is here.

He remembers that moment in the air, when the support dropped away under him. Could that happen again? He plants his feet firmly now, thinks, *Up*, and feels the familiar straining of his back and chest. But nothing happens. Incredulously, he tries again. Nothing!

His heart is thundering in his chest; he feels dizzy and cold. He sways, almost falls. It isn't possible that this should be happening to him. . . . Help; he must have help. Under his trembling fingers the phone index lights; he finds Claire's name, presses the selector. She may have gone out by now, but sector registry will find her. The screen pulses grayly. He waits. The darkness is a little farther away. Claire will help him, will think of something.

The screen lights, but it is only the neutral gray face of an autosec. "One moment please."

The screen flickers; at last, Claire's face!

"—is a recording, Dio. When you didn't call, and I couldn't reach you, I was very hurt. I know you're busy, but— Well, Piet has asked me to go over to Toria to play skeet polo, and I'm going. I may stay a few weeks for the flower festival, or go on to Rome. I'm sorry, Dio, we started out so nicely. Maybe the classes really don't mix. Goodbye."

The screen darkens. Dio is down on his knees before it. "Don't go," he says breathlessly. "Don't go." His last courage is broken; the hot, salt, shameful tears drop from his eyes.

The room is bright and bare, but in the corners the darkness is gathering, curling high, black as obsidian, waiting to rush.

II

The crowds on the lower level are a river of color, deep electric blue, scarlet, opaque yellow, all clean, crisp and bright. Flower scents puff from the folds of loose garments; the air is filled with good-natured voices and laughter. Back from five months' wandering in Africa, Pacifica and Europe, Claire is delightfully lost among the moving ways of Sector Twenty. Where the main concourse used to be, there is a maze of narrow adventure streets, full of gay banners and musky with perfume. The excursion cars are elegant little baskets of silver filigree, hung with airy grace. She gets into one and soars up the canyon of windows on a long, sweeping curve, past terraces and balconies, glimpse after intimate glimpse of people she need never see again: here a woman feeding a big blue macaw, there a couple of children staring at her from a garden, solemn-eyed, both with ragged yellow hair like dandelions. How long it has been since she last saw a child! . . . She tries to imagine what it must be like, to be a child now in this huge strange world full of grown people, but she can't. Her memories of her own childhood are so far away, quaint and small, like figures in the wrong side of an opera glass. Now here is a man with a bushy black beard, balancing a bottle on his nose for a group of laughing people . . . off it goes! Here are two couples obliviously kissing. . . . Her heart beats a little faster; she feels the color coming into her cheeks. Piet was so tiresome, after a while; she wants to forget him now. She has already forgotten him; she hums in her sweet, clear contralto, "Dio, Dio, Dio. . . ."

On the next level she dismounts and takes a robocab. She punches Dio's name; the little green-eyed driver "hunts" for a moment, flickering; then the cab swings around purposefully and gathers speed.

The building is unrecognizable; the whole street has been done over in baroque façades of vermilion and frost green. The shape of the lobby is familiar, though, and here is Dio's name on the directory.

She hesitates, looking up the uninformative blank shaft of the elevator well. Is he there, behind that silent bulk of marble? After a moment she turns with a shrug and takes the nearest of a row of fragile silver chairs. She presses "3"; the chair whisks her up, decants her.

She is in the vestibule of Dio's apartment. The walls are faced with cool blue-veined marble. On one side, the spacious oval of the shaft opening; on the other, the wide, arched doorway, closed. A mobile turns slowly under the lofty ceiling. She steps on the annunciator plate.

"Yes?" A pleasant male voice, but not a familiar one. The screen does not light.

She gives her name. "I want to see Dio—is he in?"

A curious pause. "Yes, he's *in*. . . . Who sent you?"

"No one *sent* me." She has the frustrating sense that they are at cross purposes, talking about different things. "Who are you?"

"That doesn't matter. Well, you can come in, though I
don't know when you'll get time today." The doors slide
open.

Bewildered and more than half angry, Claire crosses the
threshold. The first room is a cool gray cavern: overhead are
fixed-circuit screens showing views of the sector streets. They
make a bright frieze around the walls, but shed little light.
The room is empty; she crosses it to the next.

The next room is a huge disorderly space full of machinery
carelessly set down; Claire wrinkles her nose in distaste.
Down at the far end, a few men are bending over one of
the machines, their backs turned. She moves on.

The third room is a cool green space, terrazzo-floored,
with a fountain playing in the middle. Her sandals click
pleasantly on the hard surface. Fifteen or twenty people are
sitting on the low curving benches around the walls, using
the service machines, readers and so on: it's for all the world
like the waiting room of a fashionable healer. Has Dio taken
up mind-fixing?

Suddenly unsure of herself, she takes an isolated seat and
looks around her. No, her first impression was wrong, these
are not clients waiting to see a healer, because, in the first
place, they are all students—every one.

She looks them over more carefully. Two are playing chess
in an alcove; two more are strolling up and down separately;
five or six are grouped around a little table on which some
papers are spread; one of these is talking rapidly while the
rest listen. The distance is too great; Claire cannot catch any
words.

Farther down on the other side of the room, two men
and a woman are sitting at a hooded screen, watching it
intently, although at this distance it appears dark.

Water tinkles steadily in the fountain. After a long time
the inner doors open and a man emerges; he leans over and
speaks to another man sitting nearby. The second man gets
up and goes through the inner doors; the first moves out of
sight in the opposite direction. Neither reappears. Claire
waits, but nothing more happens.

No one has taken her name, or put her on a list; no one
seems to be paying her any attention. She rises and walks

slowly down the room, past the group at the table. Two of the men are talking vehemently, interrupting each other. She listens as she passes, but it is all student gibberish: "the delta curve clearly shows . . . a stochastic assumption . . ." She moves on to the three who sit at the hooded screen.

The screen still seems dark to Claire, but faint glints of color move on its glossy surface, and there is a whisper of sound.

There are two vacant seats. She hesitates, then takes one of them and leans forward under the hood.

Now the screen is alight, and there is a murmur of talk in her ears. She is looking into a room dominated by a huge oblong slab of gray marble, three times the height of a man. Though solid, it appears to be descending with a steady and hypnotic motion, like a waterfall.

Under this falling curtain of stone sit two men. One of them is a stranger. The other—

She leans forward, peering. The other is in shadow; she cannot see his features. Still, there is something familiar about the outlines of his head and body. . . .

She is almost sure it is Dio, but when he speaks she hesitates again. It is a strange, low, hoarse voice, unlike anything she has ever heard before: the sound is so strange that she forgets to listen for the words.

Now the other man is speaking: ". . . these notions. It's just an ordinary procedure—one more injection."

"No," says the dark man with repressed fury, and abruptly stands up. The lights in that pictured room flicker as he moves, and the shadow swerves to follow him.

"Pardon me," says an unexpected voice at her ear. The man next to her is leaning over, looking inquisitive. "I don't think you're authorized to watch this session, are you?"

Claire makes an impatient gesture at him, turning back fascinated to the screen. In the pictured room, both men are standing now; the dark man is saying something hoarsely while the other moves as if to take his arm.

"Please," says the voice at her ear, "*are* you authorized to watch this session?"

The dark man's voice has risen to a hysterical shout— hoarse and thin, like no human voice in the world. In the screen, he whirls and makes as if to run back into the room.

"Catch him!" says the other, lunging after.

The dark man doubles back suddenly, past the screen; then the room is vacant; only the moving slab drops steadily, smoothly, into the floor.

The three beside Claire are standing. Across the room, heads turn. "What is it?" someone calls.

One of the men calls back, "He's having some kind of a fit!" In a lower voice, to the woman, he adds, "It's the discomfort, I suppose . . ."

Claire is watching uncomprehendingly, when a sudden yell from the far side of the room makes her turn.

The doors have swung back, and in the opening a shouting man is wrestling helplessly with two others. They have his arms pinned and he cannot move any farther, but that horrible, hoarse voice goes on shouting, and shouting. . . .

There are no more shadows: she can see his face.

"Dio!" she calls, getting to her feet.

Through his own din, he hears her and his head turns. His face gapes blindly at her, swollen and red, the eyes glaring. Then with a violent motion he turns away. One arm comes free, and jerks up to shield his head. He is hurrying away; the others follow. The doors close. The room is full of standing figures, and a murmur of voices.

Claire stands where she is, stunned, until a slender figure separates itself from the crowd. That other face seems to hang in the air, obscuring his—red and distorted, mouth agape.

The man takes her by the elbow, urges her toward the outer door. "What are you to Dio? Did you know him before?"

"Before what?" she asks faintly. They are crossing the room of machines, empty and echoing.

"Hm. I remember you now—I let you in, didn't I? Sorry you came?" His tone is light and negligent; she has the feeling that his attention is not really on what he is saying. A faint irritation at this is the first thing she feels through her numbness. She stirs as they walk, disengaging her arm from his grasp. She says, "What was wrong with him?"

"A very rare complaint," answers the other, without pausing. They are in the outer room now, in the gloom under the bright frieze, moving toward the doors. "Didn't you know?" he asks in the same careless tone.

"I've been away." She stops, turns to face him. "Can't you tell me? What *is* wrong with Dio?"

She sees now that he has a thin face, nose and lips keen, eyes bright and narrow. "Nothing you want to know about," he says curtly. He waves at the door control, and the doors slide noiselessly apart. "Goodbye."

She does not move, and after a moment the doors close again. "What's *wrong with him?*" she says.

He sighs, looking down at her modish robe with its delicate clasps of gold. "How can I tell you? Does the verb 'to die' mean anything to you?"

She is puzzled and apprehensive. "I don't know . . . isn't it something that happens to the lower animals?"

He gives her a quick mock bow. "Very good."

"But I don't know what it is. Is it—a kind of fit, like—" She nods toward the inner rooms.

He is staring at her with an expression half compassionate, half wildly exasperated. "Do you really want to know?" He turns abruptly and runs his finger down a suddenly glowing index stripe on the wall. "Let's see . . . don't know what there is in this damned reservoir. Hm. Animals, terminus." At his finger's touch, a cabinet opens and tips out a shallow oblong box into his palm. He offers it.

In her hands, the box lights up; she is looking into a cage in which a small animal crouches—a white rat. Its fur is dull and rough-looking; something is caked around its muzzle. It moves unsteadily, noses a cup of water, then turns away. Its legs seem to fail; it drops and lies motionless except for the slow rise and fall of its tiny chest.

Watching, Claire tries to control her nausea. Students' cabinets are full of nastinesses like this; they expect you not to show any distaste. "Something's the matter with it," is all she can find to say.

"Yes. It's dying. That means to cease living: to stop. Not to be any more. Understand?"

"No," she breathes. In the box, the small body has stopped moving. The mouth is stiffly open, the lip drawn back from

the yellow teeth. The eye does not move, but glares up
sightless.

"That's all," says her companion, taking the box back.
"No more rat. Finished. After a while it begins to decom-
pose and make a bad smell, and a while after that, there's
nothing left but bones. And that has happened to every rat
that was ever born."

"I don't *believe* you," she says. "It isn't like that; I never
heard of such a thing."

"Didn't you ever have a pet?" he demands. "A parakeet,
a cat, a tank of fish?"

"Yes," she says defensively, "I've had cats, and birds.
What of it?"

"What happened to them?"

"Well—*I* don't know, I suppose I lost them. You know
how you lose things."

"One day they're there, the next, not," says the thin man.
"Correct?"

"Yes, that's right. But why?"

"We have such a tidy world," he says wearily. "Dead
bodies would clutter it up; that's why the house circuits are
programmed to remove them when nobody is in the room.
Every one: it's part of the basic design. Of course, if you
stayed in the room, and didn't turn your back, the machine
would have to embarrass you by cleaning up the corpse in
front of your eyes. But that never happens. Whenever you
saw there was something wrong with any pet of yours, you
turned around and went away, isn't that right?"

"Well, I really can't remember—"

"And when you came back, how odd, the beast was gone.
It wasn't 'lost,' it was dead. They die. They all die."

She looks at him, shivering. "But that doesn't happen to
people."

"No?" His lips are tight. After a moment he adds, "Why
do you think he looked that way? You see he knows; he's
known for five months."

She catches her breath suddenly. "That day at the beach!"

"Oh, were you there?" He nods several times, and opens
the door again. "Very interesting for you. You can tell people
you saw it happen." He pushes her gently out into the vestibule.

"But I want—" she says desperately.

"What? To love him again, as if he were normal? Or do you want to help him? Is that what you mean?" His thin face is drawn tight, arrow-shaped between the brows. "Do you think you could stand it? If so—" He stands aside, as if to let her enter again.

"Remember the rat," he says sharply.

She hesitates.

"It's up to you. Do you really want to help him? He could use some help, if it wouldn't make you sick. Or else— Where were you all this time?"

"Various places," she says stiffly. "Littlam, Paris, New Hol."

He nods. "Or you can go back and see them all again. Which?"

She does not move. Behind her eyes, now, the two images are intermingled: she sees Dio's gorged face staring through the stiff jaw of the rat.

The thin man nods briskly. He steps back, holding her gaze. There is a long suspended moment; then the doors close.

III

The years fall away like pages from an old notebook. Claire is in Stambul, Winthur, Kumoto, BahiBlanc . . . other places, too many to remember. There are the intercontinental games, held every century on the baroque wheel-shaped ground in Campan: Claire is one of the spectators who hover in clouds, following their favorites. There is a love affair, brief but intense; it lasts four or five years; the man's name is Nord, he has gone off now with another woman to Deya, and for nearly a month Claire has been inconsolable. But now comes the opera season in Milan, and in Tusca, afterwards, she meets some charming people who are going to spend a year in Papeete. . . .

Life is good. Each morning she awakes refreshed; her lungs fill with the clean air; the blood tingles in her fingertips.

On a spring morning, she is basking in a bubble of green glass, three-quarters submerged in an emerald-green ocean.

The water sways and breaks, frothily, around the bright disk of sunlight at the top. Down below where she likes, the cool green depths are like mint to the fire-white bite of the sun. Tiny flat golden fishes swarm up to the bubble, turn, glinting like tarnished coins, and flow away again. The memory unit near the floor of the bubble is muttering out a muted tempest of Wagner: half listening, she hears the familiar music mixed with a gabble of foreign syllables. Her companion, with his massive bronze head almost touching the speakers, is listening attentively. Claire feels a little annoyed; she prods him with a bare foot: "Ross, turn that horrible thing off, won't you please?"

He looks up, his blunt face aggrieved. "It's *The Rhinegold.*"

"Yes, I know, but I can't understand a word. It sounds as if they're clearing their throats. . . .Thank you."

He has waved a dismissing hand at the speakers, and the guttural chorus subsides. "Billions of people spoke that language once," he says portentously. Ross is an artist, which makes him almost a player, really, but he has the student's compulsive habit of bringing out these little kernels of information to lay in your lap.

"And I can't even stand four of them," she says lazily. "I only listen to opera for the music, anyhow, the stories are always so foolish; why is that, I wonder?"

She can almost see the learned reply rising to his lips; but he represses it politely—he knows she doesn't really want an answer—and busies himself with the visor. It lights under his fingers to show a green chasm, slowly flickering with the last dim ripples of the sunlight.

"Going down now?" she asks.

"Yes, I want to get those corals." Ross is a sculptor, not a very good one, fortunately, nor a very devoted one, or he would be impossible company. He has a studio on the bottom of the Mediterranean, in ten fathoms, and spends part of his time concocting gigantic menacing tangles of stylized undersea creatures. Finished with the visor, he touches the controls and the bubble drifts downward. The waters meet overhead with a white splash of spray; then the circle of light dims to yellow, to lime color, to deep green.

Beneath them now is the coral reef—acre upon acre of

bare skeletal fingers. A few small fish move brilliantly among the pale branches. Ross touches the controls again; the bubble drifts to a stop. He stares down through the glass for a moment, then gets up to open the inner lock door. Breathing deeply, with a distant expression, he steps in and closes the transparent door behind him. Claire sees the water spurt around his ankles. It surges up quickly to fill the airlock; when it is chest high, Ross opens the outer door and plunges out in a cloud of air bubbles.

He is a yellow kicking shape in the green water; after a few moments he is half obscured by clouds of sediment. Claire watches, vaguely troubled; the largest corals are like bleached bone.

She fingers the memory unit for the Sea Pieces from *Peter Grimes,* without knowing why; it's cold, northern ocean music, not appropriate. The cold, far calling of the gulls makes her shiver with sadness, but she goes on listening.

Ross grows dimmer and more distant in the clouding water. At length he is only a flash, a flicker of movement down in the dusky green valley. After a long time she sees him coming back, with two or three pink corals in his hand.

Absorbed in the music, she has allowed the bubble to drift until the entrance is almost blocked by corals. Ross forces himself between them, levering himself against a tall out-cropping of stone, but in a moment he seems to be in difficulty. Claire turns to the controls and backs the bubble off a few feet. The way is clear now, but Ross does not follow.

Through the glass she sees him bend over, dropping his specimens. He places both hands firmly and strains, all the great muscles of his limbs and back bulging. After a moment he straightens again, shaking his head. He is caught, she realizes; one foot is jammed into a crevice of the stone. He grins at her painfully and puts one hand to his throat. He has been out a long time.

Perhaps she can help, in the few seconds that are left. She darts into the airlock, closes and floods it. But just before the water rises over her head, she sees the man's body stiffen.

Now, with her eyes open under water, in that curious blurred light, she sees his gorged face break into lines of pain.

Instantly, his face becomes another's—Dio's—vividly seen through the ghost of a dead rat's grin. The vision comes without warning, and passes.

Outside the bubble, Ross's stiff jaw wrenches open, then hangs slack. She sees the pale jelly come bulging slowly up out of his mouth; now he floats easily, eyes turned up, limbs relaxed.

Shaken, she empties the lock again, goes back inside and calls Antibe Control for a rescue cutter. She sits down and waits, careful not to look at the still body outside.

She is astonished and appalled at her own emotion. It has nothing to do with Ross, she knows: he is perfectly safe. When he breathed water, his body reacted automatically: his lungs exuded the protective jelly, consciousness ended, his heartbeat stopped. Antibe Control will be here in twenty minutes or less, but Ross could stay like that for years, if he had to. As soon as he gets out of the water, his lungs will begin to re-absorb the jelly; when they are clear, heartbeat and breathing will start again.

It's as if Ross were only acting out a part, every movement stylized and meaningful. In the moment of his pain, a barrier in her mind has gone down, and now a doorway stands open.

She makes an impatient gesture, she is not used to being tyrannized in this way. But her arm drops in defeat; the perverse attraction of that doorway is too strong. *Dio,* her mind silently calls. *Dio.*

The designer of Sector Twenty, in the time she has been away, has changed the plan of the streets "to bring the surface down." The roof of every level is a screen faithfully repeating the view from the surface, and with lighting and other ingenious tricks the weather up there is parodied down below. Just now it is a gray cold November day, a day of slanting gray rain: looking up, one sees it endlessly falling out of the leaden sky: and down here, although the air is as always pleasantly warm, the great bare slabs of the building fronts have turned bluish gray to match, and silvery insubstantial streamers are twisting endlessly down, to melt and disappear before they strike the pavement.

Claire does not like it; it does not feel like Dio's work. The crowds have a nervous air, curious, half-protesting, they

look up and laugh, but uneasily, and the refreshment bays
are full of people crammed together under bright yellow
light. Claire pulls her metallic cloak closer around her throat;
she is thinking with melancholy of the turn of the year, the
earth growing cold and hard as iron, the trees brittle and
black against the unfriendly sky. This is a time for blue skies
underground, for flushed skins and honest laughter, not for
this echoed grayness.

In her rooms, at least, there is cheerful warmth. She is
tired and perspiring from the trip; she does not want to see
anyone just yet. Some American gowns have been ordered;
while she waits for them, she turns on the fire-bath in the
bedroom alcove. The yellow spiky flames jet up with a
black-capped *whoom,* then settle to a high murmuring curtain of yellow-white. Claire binds her head in an encapsulat-
ing scarf, and without bothering to undress, steps into the
fire.

The flame blooms up around her body, cool and caressing;
the fragile gown flares and is gone in a whisper of sparks.
She turns, arms outspread against the flow. Depilated, refreshed, she steps out again. Her body tingles, invigorated
by the flame. Delicately, she brushes away some clinging
wisps of burnt skin; the new flesh is glossy pink, slowly paling
to rose-and-ivory.

In the wall mirror, her eyes sparkle; her lips are liquidly
red, as tender and dark as the red wax that spills from the
edge of a candle.

She feels a somber recklessness; she is running with the
tide. Responsive to her mood, the silvered ceiling begins to
run with swift bloody streaks, swirling and leaping, striking
flares of light from the bronze dado and the carved crystal
lacework of the furniture. With a sudden exultant laugh,
Claire tumbles into the great yellow bed: she rolls there, half
smothered, the luxuriant silky fibers cool as cream to her
skin; then the mood is gone, the ceiling dims to grayness;
and she sits up with an impatient murmur.

What can be wrong with her? Sobered, already regretting
the summery warmth of the Mediterranean, she walks to the
table where Dio's card lies. It is his reply to the formal
message she sent en route: it says simply:

THE PLANNER DIO WILL BE AT HOME.

There is a discreet chime from the delivery chute, and fabrics tumble in in billows of canary yellow, crimson, midnight blue. Claire chooses the blue, anything else would be out of key with the day; it is gauzy but longsleeved. With it she wears no rings or necklaces, only a tiara of dark aquamarines twined in her hair.

She scarcely notices the new exterior of the building; the ascensor shaft is dark and padded now, with an endless chain of cushioned seats that slowly rise, occupied or not, like a disjointed flight of stairs. The vestibule above slowly comes into view, and she feels a curious shock of recognition.

It is the same: the same blue-veined marble, the same mobile idly turning, the same arched doorway.

Claire hesitates, alarmed and displeased. She tries to believe that she is mistaken: no scheme of decoration is ever left unchanged for as much as a year. But here it is, untouched, as if time had queerly stopped here in this room when she left it: as if she had returned, not only to the same choice, but to the same instant.

She crosses the floor reluctantly. The dark door screen looks back at her like a baited trap.

Suppose she had never gone away—what then? Whatever Dio's secret is, it has had ten years to grow, here behind this unchanged door. There it is, a darkness, waiting for her.

With a shudder of almost physical repulsion, she steps onto the annunciator plate.

The screen lights. After a moment a face comes into view. She sees without surprise that it is the thin man, the one who showed her the rat. . . .

He is watching her keenly. She cannot rid herself of the vision of the rat, and of the dark struggling figure in the doorway. She says, "Is Dio—" She stops, not knowing what she meant to say.

"At home?" the thin man finishes. "Yes, of course. Come in."

The doors slide open. About to step forward she hesitates again, once more shocked to realize that the first room is also unchanged. The frieze of screens now displays a row of gray-lit streets; that is the only difference; it is as if she were looking into some far-distant world where time still had meaning, from this still, secret place where it has none.

The thin man appears in the doorway, black-robed. "My name is Benarra," he says, smiling. "Please come in; don't mind all this, you'll get used to it."

"Where is Dio?"

"Not far. . . . But we make a rule," the thin man says, "that only students are admitted to see Dio. Would you mind?"

She looks at him with indignation. "Is this a joke? Dio sent me a note. . . ." She hesitates; the note was noncommittal enough, to be sure.

"You can become a student quite easily," Benarra says. "At least, you can begin, and that would be enough for to-day." He stands waiting, with a pleasant expression; he seems perfectly serious.

She is balanced between bewilderment and surrender. "I don't—what do you want me to do?"

"Come and see." He crosses the room, opens a narrow door. After a moment she follows.

He leads her down an inclined passage, narrow and dark. "I'm living on the floor below now," he remarks over his shoulder, "to keep out of Dio's way." The passage ends in a bright central hall from which he leads her through a doorway into dimness.

"Here your education begins," he says. On both sides, islands of light glow up slowly: in the nearest, and brightest, stands a curious group of beings, not ape, not man: black skins with a bluish sheen, tiny eyes peering upward under shelving brows, hair a dusty black. The limbs are knob-jointed like twigs; the ribs show; the bellies are soft and big. The head of the tallest comes to Claire's waist. Behind them is a brilliant glimpse of tropical sunshine, a conical mass of what looks like dried vegetable matter, trees and horned animals in the background.

"Human beings," says Benarra.

She turns a disbelieving, almost offended gaze on him. "Oh, no!"

"Yes, certainly. Extinct several thousand years. Here, another kind."

In the next island the figures are also black-skinned, but taller—shoulder high. The woman's breasts are limp leathery bags that hang to her waist. Claire grimaces. "Is something wrong with her?"

"A different standard of beauty. They did that to themselves, deliberately. Woman creating herself. See what you think of the next."

She loses count. There are coppery-skinned ones, white ones, yellowish ones, some half naked, others elaborately trussed in metal and fabric. Moving among them, Claire feels herself suddenly grown titanic, like a mother animal among her brood: she has a flash of absurd, degrading tenderness. Yet, as she looks at these wrinkled gnomish faces, they seem to hold an ancient and stubborn wisdom that glares out at her, silently saying, *Upstart!*

"What happened to them all?"

"They died," says Benarra. "Every one."

Ignoring her troubled look, he leads her out of the hall. Behind them, the lights fall and dim.

The next room is small and cool, unobtrusively lit, unfurnished except for a desk and chair, and a visitor's seat to which Benarra waves her. The domed ceiling is pierced just above their heads with round transparencies, each glowing in a different pattern of simple blue and red shapes against a colorless ground.

"They are hard to take in, I know," says Benarra. "Possibly you think they're fakes."

"No." No one could have imagined those fierce, wizened faces; somewhere, sometime, they must have existed.

A new thought strikes her. "What about *our* ancestors—what were they like?"

Benarra's gaze is cool and thoughtful. "Claire, you'll find this hard to believe. Those were our ancestors."

She is incredulous again. "Those—absurdities in there?"

"Yes. All of them."

She is stubbornly silent a moment. "But you said, they *died*."

"They did; they died. Claire—did you think our race was always immortal?"

"Why—" She falls silent, confused and angry.

"No, impossible. Because if we were, where are all the old ones? No one in the world is older than, perhaps, two thousand years. That's not very long. . . . What are you thinking?"

She looks up, frowning with concentration. "You're saying it happened. But how?"

"It didn't happen. We did it, we created ourselves." Leaning back, he gestures at the glowing transparencies overhead. "Do you know what those are?"

"No. I've never seen any designs quite like them. They'd make lovely fabric patterns."

He smiles. "Yes, they are pretty, I suppose, but that's not what they're for. These are enlarged photographs of very small living things—too small to see. They used to get into people's bloodstreams and make them die. That's bubonic plague"—blue and purple dots alternating with larger pink disks—"that's tetanus"—blue rods and red dots—"that's leprosy"—dark-spotted blue lozenges with a crosshatching of red behind them. "That thing that looks something like a peacock's tail is a parasitic fungus called *streptothrix actinomyces*. That one"—particularly dainty design of pale blue with darker accents—"is from a malignant oedema with gas gangrene."

The words are meaningless to her, but they call up vague images that are all the more horrible for having no definite outlines. She thinks again of the rat, and of a human face somehow assuming that stillness, that stiffness . . . frozen into a bright pattern, like the colored dots on the wall. . . .

She is resolved not to show her disgust and revulsion. "What happened to them?" she asks in a voice that does not quite tremble.

"Nothing. The planners left them alone, but changed us. Most of the records have been lost in two thousand years, and of course we have no real science of biology as they knew it. I'm no biologist, only a historian and collector." He rises. "But one thing we know they did was to make our bodies chemically immune to infection. Those things"—he nods to the transparencies above—"are simply irrelevant now, they can't harm us. They still exist—I've seen cultures taken from living animals. But they're only a curiosity. Various other things were done, to make the body's chemistry, to put it crudely, more stable. Things that would have killed our ancestors by toxic reactions—poisoned them—don't harm us. Then there are the protective mechanisms, and the paraphysical powers that *homo sapiens* had only in potential. Levitation, regeneration of lost organs. Finally, in general we might say that the body was very much more homeostatized than formerly, that is, there's a cycle of functions which always tends to return to the norm. The cumulative processes that used to impair function don't happen—the 'matrix' doesn't thicken, progressive dehydration never gets started, and so on. But you see all these are just delaying actions, things to prevent you and me from dying prematurely. The main thing—" he fingers an index stripe, and a linear design springs out on the wall—"was this. Have you ever read a chart, Claire?"

She shakes her head dumbly. The chart is merely an unaesthetic curve drawn on a reticulated background; it means nothing to her. "This is a schematic way of representing the growth of an organism," says Benarra. "You see here, this up-and-down scale is numbered in one-hundredths of mature weight—from zero here at the bottom, to one hundred per cent here at the top. Understand?"

"Yes," she says doubtfully. "But what good is that?"

"You'll see. Now this other scale along the bottom, is numbered according to the age of the organism. Now: this sharply rising curve here represents all other highly developed species except man. You see, the organism is born, grows very rapidly until it reaches almost its full size, then the curve rounds itself off, becomes almost level. Here it declines. And here it stops: the animal dies."

He pauses to look at her. The word hangs in the air; she says nothing, but meets his gaze.

"Now this," says Benarra, "this long shallow curve represents man as he was. You notice it starts far to the left of the animal curve. The planners had this much to work with: man was already unique, in that he had this very long juvenile period before sexual maturity. Here: see what they did."

With a gesture, he superimposes another chart on the first.

"It looks almost the same," says Claire.

"Yes. Almost. What they did was quite a simple thing, in principle. They lengthened that juvenile period still further, they made the curve rise still more slowly . . . and never quite reach the top. The curve now becomes asymptotic, that is, it approaches sexual maturity by smaller and smaller amounts, and never gets there, no matter how long it goes on."

Gravely, he returns her stare.

"Are you saying," she asks, "that we're *not* sexually mature? Not anybody?"

"Correct," he says. "Maturity in every complex organism is the first stage of death. We never mature, Claire, and that's why we don't die. We're the eternal adolescents of the universe. That's the price we paid."

"The price . . ." she echoes. "But I still don't see." She laughs.

"Not *mature*—" Unconsciously she holds herself straighter, shoulders back, chin up.

Benarra leans casually against the desk, looking down at her. "Have you ever thought to wonder why there are so few children? In the old days, loving without any precautions, a grown woman would have a child a year. Now it happens perhaps once in a hundred billion meetings. It's an anomaly, a freak of nature, and even then the woman can't carry the child to term herself. Oh, we *look* mature; that's the joke—they gave us the shape of their own dreams of adult power." He fingers his glossy beard, thumps his chest. "It isn't real. We're all pretending to be grown-up, but not one of us knows what it's really like."

A silence falls.

"Except Dio?" says Claire, looking down at her hands.

"He's on the way to find out. Yes."

"And you can't stop it . . . you don't know why."

Benarra shrugs. "He was under strain, physical and mental. Some link of the chain broke, we may never know which one. He's already gone a long way up that slope—I think he's near the crest now. There isn't a hope that we can pull him back again."

Her fists clench impotently. "Then what good is it all?"

Benarra's eyes are hooded; he is playing with a memocube on the desk. "We learn," he says. "We can do something now and then, to alleviate, to make things easier. We don't give up."

She hesitates. "How long?"

"Actually, we don't know. We can guess what the maximum is; we know that from analogy with other mammals. But with Dio, too many other things might happen." He glances up at the transparencies.

"Surely you don't mean—" The bright ugly shapes glow down at her, motionless, inscrutable.

"Yes. Yes. He had one of them already, the last time you saw him—a virus infection. We were able to control it; it was what our ancestors used to call 'the common cold'; they thought it was mild. But it nearly destroyed Dio—I mean, not the disease itself, but the moral effect. The symptoms were unpleasant. He wasn't prepared for it."

She is trembling. "Please."

"You have to know all this," says Benarra mercilessly, "or it's no use your seeing Dio at all. If you're going to be shocked, do it now. If you can't stand it, then go away now, not later." He pauses, and speaks more gently. "You can see him today, of course; I promised that. Don't try to make up your mind now, if it's hard. Talk to him, be with him this afternoon; see what it's like."

Claire does not understand herself. She has never been so foolish about a man before: love is all very well; love never lasts very long and you don't expect that it should, but while it lasts, it's pleasantness. Love is joy, not this wrenching pain.

Time flows like a strong, clean torrent, if only you let things go. She could give Dio up now and be unhappy, perhaps, a year or five years, or fifty, but then it would be over, and life would go on just the same.

She sees Dio's face, vivid in memory—not the stranger, the dark shouting man, but Dio himself, framed against the silver sky: sunlight curved on the strong brow, the eyes gleaming in shadow.

"We've got him full on antibiotics," says Benarra compassionately. "We don't think he'll get any of the bad ones.

. . . But aging itself is the worst of them all. . . . What do you say?"

IV

Under the curtain of falling stone, Dio sits at his workbench. The room is the same as before; the only visible change is the statue which now looms overhead, in the corner above the stone curtain: it is the figure of a man reclining, weight on one elbow, calf crossed over thigh, head turned pensively down toward the shoulder. The figure is powerful, but there is a subtle feeling of decay about it: the bulging muscles seem about to sag; the face, even in shadow, has a deformed, damaged look. Forty feet long, sprawling immensely across the corner of the room, the statue has a raw, compulsive power: it is supremely ugly, but she can hardly look away.

A motion attracts her eye. Dio is standing beside the bench, waiting for her. She advances hesitantly: the statue's face is in shadow, but Dio's is not, and already she is afraid of what she may see there.

He takes her hand between his two palms; his touch is warm and dry, but something like an electric shock seems to pass between them, making her start.

"Claire—it's good to see you. Here, sit down, let me look." His voice is resonant, confident, even a trifle assertive; his eyes are alert and preternaturally bright. He talks, moves, holds himself with an air of suppressed excitement. She is relieved and yet paradoxically alarmed: there is nothing really different in his face; the skin glows clear and healthy, his lips are firm. And yet every line, every feature seems to be hiding some unpleasant surprise; it is like looking at a mask which will suddenly be whipped aside.

In her excitement, she laughs, murmurs a few words without in the least knowing what she is saying. He sits facing her across the corner of the desk, commandingly intent; his eyes are hypnotic.

"I've just been sketching some plans for next year. I have some ideas . . . it won't be like anything people expect." He laughs, glancing down; the bench is covered with little gauzy boxes full of shadowy line and color. His tools lie in disorderly array, solidopens, squirts, calipers. "What do you think of this, by the way?" He points up, behind him, at the heroic statue.

"It's very unusual . . . yours?"

"A copy, from stereographs—the original was by Michelangelo, something called 'Evening.' But I did the copy myself."

She raises her eyebrows, not understanding.

"I mean I didn't do it by machine. I carved the stone myself—with mallet and chisel, in these hands, Claire." He holds them out, strong, calloused. It was those flat pads of thickened skin, she realizes, that felt so warm and strange against her hand.

He laughs again. "It was an experience. I found out about texture, for one thing. You know, when a machine melts or molds a statue, there's no texture, because to a machine granite is just like cheese. But when you carve, the stone fights back. Stone has character, Claire, it can be stubborn or evasive—it can throw chips in your face, or make your chisel slip aside. Stone fights." His hand clenches, and again he laughs that strange, exultant laugh.

In her apartment late that evening, Claire feels herself confused and overwhelmed by conflicting emotions. Her day with Dio has been like nothing she ever expected. Not once has he aroused her pity: he is like a man in whom a flame burns. Walking with her in the streets, he has made her see the Sector as he imagines it: an archaic vision of buildings made for permanence rather than for change; of masonry set by hand, woods hand-carved and hand-polished. It is a terrifying vision, and yet she does not know why. People endure; things should pass away. . . .

In the wide cool rooms an air whispers softly. The border lights burn low around the bed, inviting sleep. Claire moves aimlessly in the outer rooms, letting her robe fall, pondering a languorous stiffness in her limbs. Her mouth is bruised with kisses. Her flesh remembers the touch of his strange hands. She is full of a delicious weariness; she is at the floating, bodiless zenith of love, neither demanding nor regretting.

Yet she wanders restively through the rooms, once idly evoking a gust of color and music from the wall; it fades into an echoing silence. She pauses at the door of the playroom, and looks down into the deep darkness of the diving well. To fall is a luxury like bathing in water or flame. There is a sweetness of danger in it, although the danger is unreal. Smiling, she breathes deep, stands poised, and steps out into emptiness. The gray walls hurtle upward around her: with an effort of will she withholds the pulse of strength that would support her in midair. The floor rushes nearer, the effort mounts intolerably. At the last minute she releases it; the surge buoys her up in a brief paroxysmal joy. She come to rest, inches away from the hard stone. With her eyes dreamily closed, she rises slowly again to the top. She stretches: now she will sleep.

V

First come the good days. Dio is a man transformed, a demon of energy. He overflows with ideas and projects; he works unremittingly, accomplishes prodigies. Sector Twenty is the talk of the continent, of the world. Dio builds for permanence, but, dissatisfied, he tears down what he has built and builds again. For a season all his streets are soaring, incredibly beautiful laceworks of stone; then all the ornament vanishes and his buildings shine with classical purity: the streets are full of white light that shines from the stone. Claire waits for the cycle to turn again, but Dio's work becomes ever more massive and crude; his stone darkens. Now the streets are narrow and full of shadows; the walls frown down with heavy magnificence. He builds no more ascensor shafts; to climb in Dio's buildings, you walk up ramps or even stairs, or ride in closed elevator cars. The people murmur, but he is still a novelty; they come from all over the planet to protest, to marvel, to complain; but they still come.

Dio's figure grows heavier, more commanding: his cheeks and chin, all his features thicken; his voice becomes hearty and resonant. When he enters a public room, all heads turn: he dominates any company; where his laugh booms out, the table is in a roar.

Women hang on him by droves; drunken and triumphant, he sometimes staggers off with one while Claire watches.

But only she knows the defeat, the broken words and the tears, in the sleepless watches of the night.

There is a timeless interval when they seem to drift, without anxiety and without purpose, as if they had reached the crest of the wave. Then Dio begins to change again, swiftly and more swiftly. They are like passengers on two moving ways that have run side by side for a little distance, but now begin to diverge.

She clings to him with desperation, with a sense of vertigo. She is terrified by the massive, inexorable movement that is carrying her off: like him, she feels drawn to an unknown destination.

Suddenly the bad days are upon them. Dio is changing under her eyes. His skin grows slack and dull; his nose arches more strongly. He trains vigorously, under Benarra's instruction; when streaks of gray appear in his hair, he conceals them with pigments. But the lines are cutting themselves deeper around his mouth and at the corners of the eyes. All his bones grow knobby and thick. She cannot bear to look at his hands, they are thick-fingered, clumsy; they hold what they touch, and yet they seem to fumble.

Claire sometimes surprises herself by fits of passionate weeping. She is thin; she sleeps badly and her appetite is poor. She spends most of her time in the library, pursuing the alien thoughts that alone make it possible for her to stay in touch with Dio. One day, taking the air, she passes Katha on the street, and Katha does not recognize her.

She halts as if struck, standing by the balustrade of the little stone bridge. The building fronts are shut faces, weeping with the leaden light that falls from the ceiling. Below her, down the long straight perspective of the stair, Katha's little dark head bobs among the crowd and is lost.

The crowds are thinning; not half as many people are here this season as before. Those who come are silent and unhappy; they do not stay long. Only a few miles away, in Sector Nineteen, the air is full of streamers and pulsing with music: the light glitters, people are hurrying and laughing. Here, all colors are gray. Every surface is amorphously rounded, as if mumbled by the sea; here a baluster is missing, here a brick has fallen; here, from a ragged alcove in the wall, a deformed statue leans out to peer at her with its malevolent terra cotta face. She shudders, averting her eyes, and moves on.

A melancholy sound surges into the street, filling it brimfull. The silence throbs; then the sound comes again. It is the tolling of the great bell in Dio's latest folly, the building he calls a "cathedral." It is a vast enclosure, without beauty and without a function. No one uses it, not even Dio himself. It is an emptiness waiting to be killed. At one end, on a platform, a few candles burn. The tiled floor is always gleaming, as if freshly damp; shadows are piled high along the walls. Visitors hear their footsteps echo sharply as they enter; they turn uneasily and leave again. At intervals, for no good reason, the great bell tolls.

Suddenly Claire is thinking of the Bay of Napol, and the white gulls wheeling in the sky: the freshness, the tang of ozone, and the burning clear light.

As she turns away, on the landing below she sees two slender figures, hand in hand: a boy and a girl, both with shocks of yellow hair. They stand isolated; the slowly moving crowd surrounds them with a changing ring of faces. A memory stirs: Claire recalls the other afternoon, the street, so different then, and the two small yellow-haired children. Now they are almost grown; in a few more years they will look like anyone else.

A pang strikes at Claire's heart. She thinks, *If we could have a child . . . .*

She looks upward in a kind of incredulous wonder that there should be so much sorrow in the world. Where has it all come from? How could she have lived for so many decades without knowing of it?

The leaden light flickers slowly and ceaselessly along the blank stone ceiling overhead.

Dio is in his studio, tiny as an ant in the distance, where he swings beside the shoulder of the gigantic, half-carved figure. The echo of his hammer drifts down to Claire and Benarra at the doorway.

The figure is female, seated; that is all they can distinguish as yet. The blind head broods, turned downward; there is something malign in the shapeless hunch of the back and the thick, half-defined arms. A cloud of stone dust drifts free around the tiny shape of Dio; the bitter smell of it is in the air; the white dust coats everything.

"Dio," says Claire into the annunciator. The chatter of the distant hammer goes on. "Dio."

After a moment the hammer stops. The screen flicks on and Dio's white-masked face looks out at them. Only the dark eyes have life; they are hot and impatient. Hair, brows and beard are whitened; even the skin glitters white, as if the sculptor had turned to stone.

"Yes, what is it?"

"Dio—let's go away for a few weeks. I have such a longing to see Napol again. You know, it's been years."

"You go," says the face. In the distance, they see the small black figure hanging with its back turned to them, unmoving beside the gigantic shoulder. "I have too much to do."

"The rest would be good for you," Benarra puts in. "I advise it, Dio."

"I have too much to do," the face repeats curtly. The image blinks out; the chatter of the distant hammer begins again. The black figure blurs in a new cloud of dust.

Benarra shakes his head. "No use." They turn and walk out across the balcony, overlooking the dark reception hall. Benarra says, "I didn't want to tell you this just yet. The Planners are going to ask Dio to resign his post this year."

"I've been afraid of it," says Claire after a moment. "Have you told them how it will make him feel?"

"They say the Sector will become an Avoided Place. They're right; people already are beginning to have a feeling about it. In another few seasons they would stop coming at all."

Her hands are clasping each other restlessly. "Couldn't they give it to him, for a Project, or a museum, perhaps—?" She stops; Benarra is shaking his head.

"He's got this to go through," he says. "I've seen it coming."

"I know." Her voice is flat, defeated. "I'll help him . . . all I can."

"That's just what I don't want you to do," Benarra says.

She turns, startled; he is standing erect and somber against the balcony rail, with the gloomy gulf of the hall below. He says, "Claire, you're holding him back. He dyes his hair for you, but he has only to look at himself when he has been working in the studio, to realize what he actually looks like. He despises himself . . . he'll end hating you. You've got to go away now, and let him do what he has to."

For a moment she cannot speak; her throat aches. "What does he have to do?" she whispers.

"He has to grow old, very fast. He's put it off as long as he can." Benarra turns, looking out over the deserted hall. In a corner, the old cloth drapes trail on the floor. "Go to Napol, or to Timbuk. Don't call, don't write. You can't help him now. He has to do this all by himself."

In Djuba she acquires a little ring made of iron, very old, shaped like a serpent that bites its own tail. It is a curiosity, a student's thing; no one would wear it, and besides it is too small. But the cold touch of the little thing in her palm makes her shiver, to think how old it must be. Never before has she been so aware of the funnel-shaped maw of the past. It feels precarious, to be standing over such gulfs of time.

In Winthur she takes the waters, makes a few friends. There is a lodge on the crest of Mont Blanc, new since she was last there, from which one looks across the valley of the Doire. In the clear Alpine air, the tops of the mountains are like ships, afloat in a sea of cloud. The sunlight is pure and thin, with an aching sweetness; the cries of the skiers echo up remotely.

In Cair she meets a collector who has a curious library, full of scraps and oddments that are not to be found in the common supply. He has a baroque fancy for antiquities; some of his books are actually made of paper and bound in synthetic leather, exact copies of the originals.

" 'Again, the Alfurs of Poso, in Central Celebes,' " she reads aloud, " 'tell how the first men were supplied with their requirements direct from heaven, the Creator passing down his gifts to them by means of a rope. He first tied a stone to the rope and let it down from the sky. But the men would have none of it, and asked somewhat peevishly of what use to them was a stone. The Good God then let down a banana, which, of course they gladly accepted and ate with relish. This was their undoing. "Because you have chosen the banana," said the deity, "you shall propagate and perish like the banana, and your offspring shall step into your place. . . ." ' " She closes the book slowly. "What was a banana, Alf?"

"A phallic symbol, me dear," he says, stroking his beard, with a pleasant smile.

In Prah, she is caught up briefly in a laughing horde of athletes, playing follow-my-leader: they have volplaned from Omsk to the Baltic, tobogganed down the Rose Club chute from Danz to Warsz, cycled from there to Bucur, ballooned, rocketed, leaped from precipices, run afoot all night. She accompanies them to the mountains; they stay in a hostel, singing, and in the morning they are away again, like a flock of swallows. Claire stands grave and still; the horde rushes past her, shining faces, arrows of color, laughs, shouts. "Claire, aren't you coming?" . . "Claire, what's the matter?" . . . "Claire, come with us, we're swimming to Linz!" But she does not answer; the bright throng passes into silence.

Over the roof of the world, the long cloud-packs are moving swiftly, white against the deep blue. They come from the north; the sharp wind blows among the pines, breathing of icy fiords.

Claire steps back into the empty forum of the hostel. Her movements are slow; she is weary of escaping. For half a decade she has never been in the same spot more than a few weeks. Never once has she looked into a news unit, or tried to call anyone she knows in Sector Twenty. She has even deliberately failed to register her whereabouts: to be registered is to expect a call, and expecting one is halfway to making one.

But what is the use? Wherever she goes, she carries the same darkness with her.

The phone index glows at her touch. Slowly, with unaccustomed fingers, she selects the sector, the group, and the name: Dio.

The screen pulses; there is a long wait. Then the gray face of an autosec says politely, "The registrant has removed, and left no forwarding information."

Claire's throat is dry. "How long ago did his registry stop?"

"One moment please." The blank face falls silent. "He was

last registered three years ago, in the index of November thirty."

"Try central registry," says Claire.

"No forwarding information has been registered."

"I know. Try central, anyway. Try everywhere."

"There will be a delay for checking." The blank face is silent a long time. Claire turns away, staring without interest at the living frieze of color which flows along the borders of the room. "Your attention please."

She turns. "Yes?"

"The registrant does not appear in any sector registry."

For a moment she is numb and speechless. Then, with a gesture, she abolishes the autosec, fingers the index again, the same sector, same group; the name: Benarra.

The screen lights: his remembered face looks out at her. "Claire! Where are you?"

"In Cheky. Ben, I tried to call Dio, and it said there was no registry. Is he—?"

"No. He's still alive, Claire; he's retreated. I want you to come here as soon as you can. Get a special; my club will take care of the overs, if you're short."

"No, I have surplus. All right, I'll come."

"This was made the season after you left," says Benarra. The wall screen glows: it is a stereo view of the main plaza in Level Three, the Hub section: dark, unornamented buildings, like a cliff-dwellers' canyon. The streets are deserted; no face shows at the windows.

"Changing Day," says Benarra. "Dio had formally resigned, but he still had a day to go. Watch."

In the screen, one of the tall building fronts suddenly swells and crumbles at the top. Dingy smoke spurts. Like a stack of counters, the building leans down into the street, separating as it goes into individual bricks and stones. The roar comes dimly to them as the next building erupts, and then the next.

"He did it himself," says Benarra. "He laid all the explosive charges, didn't tell anybody. The council was horrified. The integrators weren't designed to handle all that rubble—it had to be amorphized and piped away in the end. They begged Dio to stop, and finally he did. He made a bargain with them, for Level One."

"The whole level?"

"Yes. They gave it to him; he pointed out that it would not be for long. All the game areas and so on up there were due to be changed, anyhow; Dio's successor merely canceled them out of the integrator."

She still does not understand. "Leaving nothing but the bare earth?"

"He wanted it bare. He got some seeds from collectors, and planted them. I've been up frequently. He actually grows cereal grain up there, and grinds it into bread."

In the screen, the canyon of the street has become a lake of dust. Benarra touches the controls, the screen blinks to another scene.

The sky is a deep luminous blue; the level land is bare. A single small building stands up blocky and stiff; behind it there are a few trees, and the evening light glimmers on fields scored in parallel rows. A dark figure is standing motionless beside the house; at first Claire does not recognize it as human. Then it moves, turns its head. She whispers, "Is that Dio?"

"Yes."

She cannot repress a moan of sorrow. The figure is too small for any details of face or body to be seen, but something in the proportions of it makes her think of one of Dio's grotesque statues, all stony bone, hunched, shrunken. The figure turns, moving stiffly, and walks to the hut. It enters and disappears.

She says to Benarra, "Why didn't you tell me?"

"You didn't leave any word; I couldn't reach you."

"I know, but you should have told me. I didn't know. . . ."

"Claire, what do you feel for him now? Love?"

"I don't know. A great pity, I think. But maybe there is love mixed up in it too. I pity him because I once loved him. But I think that much pity is love, isn't it, Ben?"

"Not the kind of love you and I used to know anything about," says Benarra, with his eyes on the screen.

He was waiting for her when she emerged from the kiosk. He had a face like nothing human. It was like a turtle's face, or a lizard's: horny and earth-colored, with bright eyes peering under the shelf of brow. His cheeks sank in; his nose jutted, and the bony shape of the teeth bulged behind the lips. His hair was white and fine, like thistledown in the sun.

They were like strangers together, or like visitors from different planets. He showed her his grain fields, his kitchen garden, his stand of young fruit trees. In the branches, birds were fluttering and chirping. Dio was dressed in a robe of coarse weave that hung awkwardly from his bony shoulders. He had made it himself, he told her; he had also made the pottery jug from which he poured her a clear tart wine, pressed from his own grapes. The interior of the hut was clean and bare. "Of course, I get food supplements from Ben, and a few things like needles, thread. Can't do everything, but on the whole, I haven't done too badly." His voice was abstracted; he seemed only half aware of her presence.

They sat side by side on the wooden bench outside the hut. The afternoon sunlight lay pleasantly on the flagstones; a little animation came to his withered face, and for the first time she was able to see the shape of Dio's features there.

"I don't say I'm not bitter. You remember what I was and you see what I am now." His eyes stared broodingly; his lips worked. "I sometimes think, why did it have to be me? The rest of you are going on, like children at a party, and I'll be gone. But, Claire, I've discovered something. I don't quite know if I can tell you about it."

He paused, looking out across the fields. "There's an attraction in it, a beauty. That sounds impossible, but it's true. Beauty in the ugliness. It's symmetrical, it has its rhythm. The sun rises, the sun sets. Living up here, you feel that a little more. Perhaps that's why we went below."

He turned to look at her. "No, I can't make you understand. I don't want you to think, either, that I've surrendered to it. I feel it coming sometimes, Claire, in the middle of the night. Something coming up over the horizon. Something—" He gestured. "A feeling. Something very huge and cold. Very cold. And I sit up in my bed, shouting, 'I'm not ready yet!' No. I don't want to go. Perhaps if I had grown up getting used to the idea, it would be easier now. It's a big change to make in your thinking. I tried—all this—and the sculpture, you remember—but I can't quite do it. And yet—now, this is the curious thing. I wouldn't go back, if I could. That sounds funny. Here I am, going to die, and I wouldn't go

back. You see, I want to be myself; yes, I want to go on
being myself. Those other men were not me, only someone
on the way to be me."

They walked back together to the kiosk. At the doorway,
she turned for a last glimpse. He was standing, bent and
sturdy, white-haired in his rags, against a long sweep of
violet sky. The late light glistened grayly on the fields; far
behind, in the grove of trees the birds' voices were stilled.
There was a single star in the east.

To leave him, she realized suddenly, would be intolerable.
She stepped out, embraced him: his body was shockingly
thin and fragile in her arms. "Dio, we mustn't be apart now.
Let me come and stay in your hut; let's be together."

Gently he disengaged her arms and stepped away. His eyes
gleamed in the twilight. "No, no," he said. "It wouldn't do,
Claire. Dear, I love you for it, but you see . . . you see,
you're a goddess. An immortal goddess—and I'm a man."

She saw his lips work, as if he were about to speak again,
and she waited, but he only turned, without a word or gesture, and began walking away across the empty earth: a dark
spindling figure, garments flapping gently in the breeze that
spilled across the earth. The last light glowed dimly in his
white hair. Now he was only a dot in the middle distance.
Claire stepped back into the kiosk, and the door closed.

VI

For a long time she cannot persuade herself that he is gone.
She has seen the body, stretched in a box like someone turned
to painted wax: it is not Dio, Dio is somewhere else.

She catches herself thinking, *When Dio comes back . . .*
as if he had only gone away, around to the other side of the
world. But she knows there is a mound of earth over Sector
Twenty, with a tall polished stone over the spot where Dio's
body lies in the ground. She can repeat by rote the words
carved there:

> Weak and narrow are the powers implanted in
> the limbs of man; many the woes that fall on them and
> blunt the edges of thought; short is the measure of the
> life in death through which they toil. Then are they

borne away; like smoke they vanish into air; and what
they dream they know is but the little that each hath
stumbled upon in wandering about the world. Yet boast
they all that they have learned the whole. Vain fools!
For what that is, no eye hath seen, no ear hath heard,
nor can it be conceived by the mind of man.

—*Empedocles (5th cent. B. C.)*

One day she closes up the apartment; let the Planner, Dio's
successor, make of it whatever he likes. She leaves behind all
her notes, her student's equipment, useless now. She goes to
a public inn and that afternoon the new fashions are brought
to her: robes in flame silk and in cold metallic mesh; new perfumes, new jewelry. There is new music in the memory units,
and she dances to it tentatively, head cocked to listen, living
into the rhythm. Already it is like a long-delayed spring;
dark withered things are drifting away into the past, and the
present is fresh and lovely.

She tries to call a few old friends. Katha is in Centram,
Ebert in the South; Piet and Tanno are not registered at all.
It doesn't matter; in the plaza of the inn, before the day is
out, she makes a dozen new friends. The group, pleased with
itself, grows by accretion; the resulting party wanders from
the plaza to the Vermilion Club gardens, to one member's
rooms and then another's, and finally back to Claire's own
apartment.

Leaving the circle toward midnight, she roams the apartment alone, eased by comradeship, content to hear the singing blur and fade behind her. In the playroom, she stands
idly looking down into the deep darkness of the diving well.
How luxurious, she thinks, to fall and fall, and never reach
the bottom . . . .

But the bottom is always there, of course, or it would not
be a diving well. A paradox: the well must be a shaft without
an exit at the bottom; it's the sense of danger, the imagined
smashing impact, that gives it its thrill. And yet there is no
danger of injury: levitation and the survival instinct will always prevent it.

"We have such a tidy world. . . ."

Things pass away; people endure.

Then where is Piet, the cottony haired man, with his

laughter and his wild jokes? Hiding, somewhere around the other side of the world, perhaps; forgetting to register. It often happens; no one thinks about it. But then, her own mind asks coldly, where is the woman named Marla, who used to hold you on her knee when you were small? Where is Hendry, your own father, whom you last saw . . . when? Five hundred, six hundred years ago, that time in Rio. Where do people go when they disappear . . . the people no one talks about?

The singing drifts up to her along the dark hallway. Claire is staring transfixed down into the shadows of the well. She thinks of Dio, looking out at the gathering darkness: "I feel it coming sometimes, up over the horizon. Something very huge, and cold."

The darkness shapes itself in her imagination into a gray face, beautiful and terrible. The smiling lips whisper, for her ears alone, *Some day.*

EASTWARD HO!

William Tenn

It's an unclosely guarded secret among science fiction writers that one good method for generating story ideas is to take some very familiar situation, turn it upside down, and see what emerges. That's what William Tenn has done, most literally, in this tale of a North America in which the Indians control almost everything and the whites are a harried, battered minority clinging with difficulty to an ever-shrinking domain. And because the elegantly convoluted mind of William Tenn was at work, the result is no mere formula job, but a lovely, delectable parable of inversions.

The New Jersey turnpike had been hard on the horses. South of New Brunswick the potholes had been so deep, the scattered boulders so plentiful, that the two men had been forced to move at a slow trot, to avoid crippling their three precious animals. And, of course, this far south, farms were non-existent: they had been able to eat nothing but the dried provisions in the saddlebags, and last night they had slept in a roadside service station, suspending their hammocks between the tilted, rusty gas pumps.

But it was still the best, the most direct route, Jerry Franklin knew. The turnpike was a government road: its rubble was cleared semiannually. They had made excellent time and come through without even developing a limp in the pack horse. As they swung out on the last lap, past the riven tree stump with the words TRENTON EXIT carved on its side, Jerry relaxed a bit. His father, his father's colleagues, would be proud of him. And he was proud of himself.

But the next moment, he was alert again. He roweled his horse, moved up alongside his companion, a young man of his own age.

"Protocol," he reminded. "I'm the leader here. You know better than to ride ahead of me this close to Trenton."

He hated to pull rank. But facts were facts, and if a subordinate got above himself he was asking to be set down. After all, he was the son—and the oldest son, at that—of the Senator from Idaho; Sam Rutherford's father was a mere Undersecretary of State and Sam's mother's family was pure post office clerk all the way back.

Sam nodded apologetically and reined his horse back the proper couple of feet. "Thought I saw something odd," he explained. "Looked like an advance party on the side of the road—and I could have sworn they were wearing buffalo robes."

"Seminole don't wear buffalo robes, Sammy. Don't you remember your sophomore political science?"

"I never had any political science, Mr. Franklin: I was an engineering major. Digging around in ruins has always been my dish. But, from the little I know, I didn't *think* buffalo robes went with the Seminole. That's why I was—"

"Concentrate on the pack horse," Jerry advised. "Negotiations are my job."

As he said this, he was unable to refrain from touching the pouch upon his breast with rippling fingertips. Inside it was his commission, carefully typed on one of the last precious sheets of official government stationery (and it was not one whit less official because the reverse side had been used years ago as a scribbled interoffice memo), and signed by the President himself. In ink!

The existence of such documents was important to a man in later life. He would have to hand it over, in all probability, during the conferences, but the commission to which it attested would be on file in the capitol up north. And, when his father died, and he took over one of the two hallowed Idaho seats, it would give him enough stature to make an attempt at membership on the Appropriations Committee. Or, for that matter, why not go the whole hog—the Rules Committee itself? No Senator Franklin had ever been a member of the Rules Committee. . . .

The two envoys knew they were on the outskirts of Trenton when they passed the first gangs of Jerseyites working to clear the road. Frightened faces glanced at them briefly, and quickly bent again to work. The gangs were working without any visible supervision. Evidently the Seminole felt that simple instructions were sufficient.

But as they rode into the blocks of neat ruins that was the city proper and still came across nobody more important than white men, another explanation began to occur to Jerry Franklin. This all had the look of a town still at war, but where were the combatants? Almost certainly on the other side of Trenton, defending the Delaware River—that was the direction from which the new rulers of Trenton might fear attack—not from the north where there was only the United States of America.

But if that were so, who in the world could they be defending against? Across the Delaware to the south there was nothing but more Seminole. Was it possible—was it possible that the Seminole had at last fallen to fighting among themselves?

Or was it possible that Sam Rutherford had been right? Fantastic. Buffalo robes in Trenton! There should be no buffalo robes closer than a hundred miles westward, in Harrisburg.

But when they turned onto State Street, Jerry bit his lip in chagrin. Sam had seen correctly, which made him one up.

Scattered over the wide lawn of the gutted state capitol were dozens of wigwams. And the tall, dark men who sat impassively, or strode proudly among the wigwams, all wore buffalo robes. There was no need even to associate the paint on their faces with a remembered lecture in political science: these were Sioux.

So the information that had come drifting up to the government about the identity of the invader was totally inaccurate—as usual. Well, you couldn't expect communication miracles over this long a distance. But that inaccuracy made things difficult. It might invalidate his commission for one thing: his commission was addressed directly to Osceola VII,

Ruler of All the Seminoles. And if Sam Rutherford thought this gave him a right to preen himself—

He looked back dangerously. No, Sam would give no trouble. Sam knew better than to dare an I-told-you-so. At his leader's look, the son of the Undersecretary of State dropped his eyes groundwards to immediate humility.

Satisfied, Jerry searched his memory for relevant data on recent political relationships with the Sioux. He couldn't recall much—just the provisions of the last two or three treaties. It would have to do.

He drew up before an important-looking warrior and carefully dismounted. You might get away with talking to a Seminole while mounted, but not the Sioux. The Sioux were very tender on matters of protocol with white men.

"We come in peace," he said to the warrior standing as impassively straight as the spear he held, as stiff and hard as the rifle on his back. "We come with a message of importance and many gifts to your chief. We come from New York, the home of our chief." He thought a moment, then added: "You know, the Great White Father?"

Immediately, he was sorry for the addition. The warrior chuckled briefly; his eyes lit up with a lightning-stroke of mirth. Then his face was expressionless again, and serenely dignified as befitted a man who had counted coup many times.

"Yes," he said. "I have heard of him. Who has not heard of the wealth and power and far dominions of the Great White Father? Come. I will take you to our chief. Walk behind me, white man."

Jerry motioned Sam Rutherford to wait.

At the entrance to a large, expensively decorated tent, the Indian stood aside and casually indicated that Jerry should enter.

It was dim inside, but the illumination was rich enough to take Jerry's breath away. Oil lamps! Three of them! These people lived well.

A century ago, before the whole world had gone smash in the last big war, his people had owned plenty of oil lamps themselves. Better than oil lamps, perhaps, if one could believe the stories the engineers told around the evening fires.

Such stories were pleasant to hear, but they were glories of the distant past. Like the stories of overflowing granaries and chock-full supermarkets, they made you proud of the history of your people, but they did nothing for you now. They made your mouth water, but they didn't feed you.

The Indians whose tribal organization had been the first to adjust to the new conditions, in the all-important present, the Indians had the granaries, the Indians had the oil lamps. And the Indians . . . .

There were two nervous white men serving food to the group squatting on the floor. An old man, the chief, with a carved, chunky body. Three warriors, one of them surprisingly young for council. And a middle-aged Negro, wearing the same bound-on rags as Franklin, except that they looked a little newer, a little cleaner.

Jerry bowed low before the chief, spreading his arms apart palms down.

"I come from New York, from our chief," he mumbled. In spite of himself, he was more than a little frightened. He wished he knew their names so that he could relate them to specific events. Although he knew what their names would be like—approximately. The Sioux, the Seminole, all the Indian tribes renaissant in power and number, all bore names garlanded with anachronism. That queer mixture of several levels of the past, overlaid always with the cocky, expanding present. Like the rifles *and* the spears, one for the reality of fighting, the other for the symbol that was more important than reality. Like the use of wigwams on campaign, when, according to the rumors that drifted smokily across country, their slave artisans could now build the meanest Indian noble a damp-free, draftproof dwelling such as the President of the United States, lying on his special straw pallet, did not dream about. Like painted-spattered faces peering through newly reinvented, crude microscopes. What had microscopes been like? Jerry tried to remember the Engineering Survey Course he'd taken in his freshman year—and drew a blank. All the same, the Indians were so queer, *and* so awesome. Sometimes you thought that destiny had meant them to be conquerors, with a conqueror's careless inconsistency. Sometimes . . . .

He noticed that they were waiting for him to continue.

"From our chief," he repeated hurriedly. "I come with a message of importance and many gifts."

"Eat with us," the old man said. "Then you will give us your gifts and your message."

Gratefully, Jerry squatted on the ground a short distance from them. He was hungry, and among the fruit in the bowls he had seen something that must be an orange. He had heard so many arguments about what oranges tasted like!

After a while, the old man said, "I am Chief Three Hydrogen Bombs. This"—pointing to the young man—"is my son, Makes Much Radiation. And this"—pointing to the middle-aged Negro—"is a sort of compatriot of yours."

At Jerry's questioning look, and the chief's raised finger of permission, the Negro explained. "Sylvester Thomas. Ambassador to the Sioux from the Confederate States of America."

"The Confederacy? She's still alive? We heard ten years ago—"

"The Confederacy is very much alive, sir. The Western Confederacy that is, with its capital at Jackson, Mississippi. The Eastern Confederacy, the one centered at Richmond, Virginia, did go down under the Seminole. We have been more fortunate. The Arapahoe, the Cheyenne, and"—with a nod to the chief—"especially the Sioux, if I may say so, sir, have been very kind to us. They allow us to live in peace, so long as we till the soil quietly and pay our tithes."

"Then would you know, Mr. Thomas—" Jerry began eagerly. "That is . . . the Lone Star Republic—Texas— Is it possible that Texas, too . . . ?"

Mr. Thomas looked at the door of the wigwam unhappily. "Alas, my good sir, the Republic of the Lone Star Flag fell before the Kiowa and the Comanche long years ago when I was still a small boy. I don't remember the exact date, but I do know it was before even the last of California was annexed by the Apache and the Navajo, and well before the nation of the Mormons under the august leadership of—"

Makes Much Radiation shifted his shoulders back and forth and flexed his arm muscles. "All this talk," he growled. "Paleface talk. Makes me tired."

"Mr. Thomas is not a paleface," his father told him sharply. "Show respect! He's our guest and an accredited ambassador—you're not to use a word like paleface in his presence!"

One of the other, older warriors near the child spoke up. "In the old days, in the days of the heroes, a boy of Makes Much Radiation's age would not dare raise his voice in council before his father. Certainly not to say the things he just has. I cite as reference, for those interested, Robert Lowie's definitive volume, *The Crow Indians,* and Lesser's fine piece of anthropological insight, *Three Types of Siouan Kinship.* Now, whereas we have not yet been able to reconstruct a Siouan kinship pattern on the classic model described by Lesser, we have developed a working arrangement that—"

"The trouble with you, Bright Book Jacket," the warrior on his left broke in, "is that you're too much of a classicist. You're always trying to live in the Golden Age instead of the present, and a Golden Age that really has little to do with the Sioux. Oh, I'll admit that we're as much Dakotan as the Crow, from the linguist's point of view at any rate, and that, superficially, what applies to the Crow should apply to us. But what happens when we quote Lowie in so many words and try to bring his precepts into daily life?"

"Enough," the chief announced. "Enough, Hangs A Tale. And you, too, Bright Book Jacket—enough, enough! These are private tribal matters. Though they do serve to remind us that the paleface was once great before he became sick and corrupt and frightened. These men whose holy books teach us the lost art of living like Sioux, men like Lesser, men like Robert H. Lowie, were not these men palefaces? And in memory of them should we not show tolerance?"

"A-ah!" said Makes Much Radiation impatiently. "As far as I'm concerned, the only good palefaces are dead. And that's that." He thought a bit. "Except their women. Paleface women are fun when you're a long way from home and feel like raising a little hell."

Chief Three Hydrogen Bombs glared his son into silence. Then he turned to Jerry Franklin. "Your message and your gifts. First your message."

"No, Chief," Bright Book Jacket told him respectfully but definitely. "First the gifts. *Then* the message. That's the way it was done."

"I'll have to get them. Be right back." Jerry walked out of the tent backwards and ran to where Sam Rutherford had tethered the horses. "The presents," he said urgently. "The presents for the chief."

The two of them tore at the pack straps. With his arms loaded, Jerry returned through the warriors who had assembled to watch their activity with quiet arrogance. He entered the tent, set the gifts on the ground and bowed low again.

"Bright beads for the chief," he said, handing over two star sapphires and a large white diamond, the best that the engineers had evacuated from the ruins of New York in the past ten years.

"Cloth for the chief," he said, handing over a bolt of linen and a bolt of wool, spun and loomed in New Hampshire expecially for this occasion and painfully, expensively carted to New York.

"Pretty toys for the chief," he said, handing over a large only slightly rusty alarm clock and a precious typewriter, both of them put in operating order by batteries of engineers and artisans working in tandem (the engineers interpreting the brittle old documents to the artisans) for two and a half months.

"Weapons for the chief," he said, handing over a beautifully decorated cavalry saber, the prized hereditary possession of the Chief of Staff of the United States Air Force, who had protested its requisitioning most bitterly ("Damn it all, Mr. President, do you expect me to fight these Indians with my bare hands?" "No, I don't, Johnny, but I'm sure you can pick up one just as good from one of your eager junior officers").

Three Hydrogen Bombs examined the gifts, particularly the typewriter, with some interest. Then he solemnly distributed them among the members of his council, keeping only the typewriter and one of the sapphires for himself. The sword he gave to his son.

Makes Much Radiation tapped the steel with his fingernail. "Not so much," he stated. "Not-*so-much*. Mr. Thomas came up with better stuff than this from the Confederate States of America for my sister's puberty ceremony." He tossed the saber negligently to the ground. "But what can you expect from a bunch of lazy, good-for-nothing whiteskin stinkards?"

When he heard the last word, Jerry Franklin went rigid. That meant he'd have to fight Makes Much Radiation—and the prospect scared him right down to the wet hairs on his legs. The alternative was losing face completely among the Sioux.

"Stinkard" was a term from the Natchez system and was applied these days indiscriminately to all white men bound to field or factory under their aristocratic Indian overlords. A "stinkard" was something lower than a serf, whose one value was that his toil gave his masters the leisure to engage in the activities of full manhood: hunting, fighting, thinking.

If you let someone call you a stinkard and didn't kill him, why, then you *were* a stinkard—and that was all there was to it.

"I am an accredited representative of the United States of America," Jerry said slowly and distinctly, "and the oldest son of the Senator from Idaho. When my father dies, I will sit in the Senate in his place. I am a free-born man, high in the councils of my nation, and anyone who calls me a stinkard is a rotten, no-good, foul-mouthed liar!"

There—it was done. He waited as Makes Much Radiation rose to his feet. He noted with dismay the well-fed, well-muscled sleekness of the young warrior. He wouldn't have a chance against him. Not in hand-to-hand combat—which was the way it would be.

Makes Much Radiation picked up the sword and pointed it at Jerry Franklin. "I could chop you in half right now like a fat onion," he observed. "Or I could go into a ring with you knife to knife and cut your belly open. I've fought and killed Seminole, I've fought Apache, I've even fought and killed Comanche. But I've never dirtied my hands with paleface blood, and I don't intend to start now. I leave such simple butchery to the overseers of our estates. Father, I'll be outside until the lodge is clean again." Then he threw the sword ringingly at Jerry's feet and walked out.

Just before he left, he stopped, and remarked over his shoulder: "The oldest son of the Senator from Idaho! Idaho has been part of the estates of my mother's family for the past forty-five years! When will these romantic children stop playing games and start living in the world as it is now?"

"My son," the old chief murmured. "Younger generation. A bit wild. Highly intolerant. But he means well. Really does. Means well."

He signaled to the white serfs who brought over a large chest covered with great splashes of color.

While the chief rummaged in the chest, Jerry Franklin relaxed inch by inch. It was almost too good to be true: he wouldn't have to fight Makes Much Radiation, and he hadn't lost face. All things considered, the whole business had turned out very well indeed.

And as for that last comment—well, why expect an Indian to understand about things like tradition and the glory that could reside forever in a symbol? When his father stood up under the cracked roof of Madison Square Garden and roared across to the Vice-President of the United States: "The people of the sovereign state of Idaho will never and can never in all conscience consent to a tax on potatoes. From time immemorial, potatoes have been associated with Idaho, potatoes have been the pride of Idaho. The people of Boise say *no* to a tax on potatoes, the people of Pocatello say *no* to a tax on potatoes, the very rolling farmlands of the Gem of the Mountain say *no, never*, a thousand times *no*, to a tax on potatoes!"—when his father spoke like that, he *was* speaking for the people of Boise and Pocatello. Not the crushed Boise or desolate Pocatello of today, true, but the magnificent cities as they had been of yore . . . and the rich farms on either side of the Snake River. . . . And Sun Valley, Moscow, Idaho Falls, American Falls, Weiser, Grangeville, Twin Falls. . . .

"We did not expect you, so we have not many gifts to offer in return," Three Hydrogen Bombs was explaining. "However, there is this one small thing. For you."

Jerry gasped as he took it. It was a pistol, a real, brand-new pistol! And a small box of cartridges. Made in one of the Sioux slave workshops of the Middle West that he had heard about. But to hold it in his hand, and to know that it belonged to him!

It was a Crazy Horse forty-five, and, according to all reports, far superior to the Apache weapon that had so long dominated the West, the Geronimo thirty-two. This was a weapon a General of the Armies, a President of the United States, might never hope to own—and it was his!

"I don't know how— Really, I—I—"

"That's all right," the chief told him genially. "Really it is.

My son would not approve of giving firearms to palefaces, but I feel that palefaces are like other people—it's the individual that counts. You look like a responsible man for a paleface: I'm sure you'll use the pistol wisely. Now your message."

Jerry collected his faculties and opened the pouch that hung from his neck. Reverently, he extracted the precious document and presented it to the chief.

Three Hydrogen Bombs read it quickly and passed it to his warriors. The last one to get it, Bright Book Jacket, wadded it up into a ball and tossed it back at the white man.

"Bad penmanship," he said. "And 'receive' is spelled three different ways. The rule is: '*i* before *e*, except after *c*'. But what does it have to do with us? It's addressed to the Seminole chief, Osceola VII, requesting him to order his warriors back to the southern bank of the Delaware River, or to return the hostage given him by the Government of the United States as an earnest of good will and peaceful intentions. We're no Seminole: why show it to us?"

As Jerry Franklin smoothed out the wrinkles in the paper with painful care and replaced the document in his pouch, the confederate ambassador, Sylvester Thomas, spoke up. "I think I might explain," he suggested, glancing inquiringly from face to face. "If you gentlemen don't mind . . . ? It is obvious that the United States Government has heard that an Indian tribe finally crossed the Delaware at this point, and assumed it was the Seminole. The last movement of the Seminole, you will recall, was to Philadelphia, forcing the evacuation of the capital once more and its transfer to New York City. It was a natural mistake: the communications of the American States, whether Confederate or United"—a small, coughing, diplomatic laugh here—"have not been as good as might have been expected in recent years. It is quite evident that neither this young man nor the government he represents so ably and so well, had any idea that the Sioux had decided to steal a march on his majesty, Osceola VII, and cross the Delaware at Lambertville."

"That's right," Jerry broke in eagerly. "That's exactly right. And now, as the accredited emissary of the President of the United States, it is my duty formally to request that the Sioux nation honor the treaty of eleven years ago as well as the treaty of fifteen—I *think* it was fifteen—years ago, and retire once more behind the banks of the Susquehanna River. I must remind you that when we retired from Pittsburgh, Altoona, and Johnstown, you swore that the Sioux would take no more land from us and would protect us in the little we had left. I am certain that the Sioux want to be known as a nation that keeps its promises."

Three Hydrogen Bombs glanced questioningly at the faces of Bright Book Jacket and Hangs A Tale. Then he leaned forward and placed his elbows on his crossed legs. "You speak well, young man," he commented. "You are a credit to your chief. . . . Now, then. Of course the Sioux want to be known as a nation that honors its treaties and keeps its promises. And so forth and so forth. But we have an expanding population. You don't have an expanding population. We need more land. You don't use most of the land you have. Should we sit by and see the land go to waste—worse yet, should we see it acquired by the Seminole who already rule a domain stretching from Philadelphia to Key West? Be reasonable. You can retire—to other places. You have most of New England left and a large part of New York State. Surely you can afford to give up New Jersey."

In spite of himself, in spite of his ambassadorial position, Jerry Franklin began yelling. All of a sudden it was too much. It was one thing to shrug your shoulders unhappily back home in the blunted ruins of New York, but here on the spot where the process was actually taking place—no, it was too much.

"What else can we afford to give up? Where else can we retire to? There's nothing left of the United States of America but a handful of square miles, and still we're supposed to move back! In the time of my forefathers, we were a great nation, we stretched from ocean to ocean, so say the legends of my people, and now we are huddled in a miserable corner of our land, starving, filthy, sick, dying, and ashamed. In the North, we are oppressed by the Ojibway and the Cree, we are pushed southward relentlessly by the Montaignais; in the South, the Seminole climb up our land yard by yard; and in the West, the Sioux take a piece more of New Jersey, and the Cheyenne come up and nibble yet another slice out of Elmira and Buffalo. When will it stop—where are we to go?"

The old man shifted uncomfortably at the agony in his voice. "It *is* hard; mind you, I don't deny that it *is* hard. But facts are facts, and weaker peoples always go to the wall. . . Now, as to the rest of your mission. If we don't retire as you request, you're supposed to ask for the return of your hostage. Sounds reasonable to me. You ought to get something out of it. However, I can't for the life of me remember a hostage. Do we have a hostage from you people?"

His head hanging, his body exhausted, Jerry muttered in misery, "Yes. All the Indian nations on our border have hostages. As earnests of our good will and peaceful intentions."

Bright Book Jacket snapped his fingers. "That girl. Sarah Cameron—Canton—what's-her-name."

Jerry looked up. "Calvin?" he asked. "Could it be *Calvin?* Sarah Calvin? The daughter of the Chief Justice of the United States Supreme Court?"

"Sarah Calvin. That's the one. Been with us for five, six years. You remember, Chief? The girl your son's been playing around with?"

Three Hydrogen Bombs looked amazed. "Is *she* the hostage? I thought she was some paleface female he had imported from his plantations in southern Ohio. Well, well, well. Makes Much Radiation is just a chip off the old block, no doubt about it." He became suddenly serious. "But that girl will never go back. She rather goes for Indian loving. Goes for it all the way. And she has the idea that my son will eventually marry her. Or some such."

He looked Jerry Franklin over. "Tell you what, my boy. Why don't you wait outside while we talk this over? And take the saber. Take it back with you. My son doesn't seem to want it."

Jerry wearily picked up the saber and trudged out of the wigwam.

Dully, uninterestedly, he noticed the band of Sioux warriors around Sam Rutherford and his horses. Then the group parted for a moment, and he saw Sam with a bottle in his hand. Tequila! The damned fool had let the Indians give him tequila—he was drunk as a pig.

Didn't he know that white men couldn't drink, didn't dare drink? With every inch of their unthreatened arable land under cultivation for foodstuffs, they were all still on the edge of starvation. There was absolutely no room in their economy for such luxuries as intoxicating beverages—and no white man in the usual course of a lifetime got close to so much as a glassful of the stuff. Give him a whole bottle of tequila and he was a stinking mess.

As Sam was now. He staggered back and forth in dipping semicircles, holding the bottle by its neck and waving it idiotically. The Sioux chuckled, dug each other in the ribs and pointed. Sam vomited loosely down the rags upon his chest and belly, tried to take one more drink, and fell over backwards. The bottle continued to pour over his face until it was empty. He was snoring loudly. The Sioux shook their heads, made grimaces of distaste, and walked away.

Jerry looked on and nursed the pain in his heart. Where could they go? What could they do? And what difference did it make? Might as well be as drunk as Sammy there. At least you wouldn't be able to feel.

He looked at the saber in one hand, the bright new pistol in the other. Logically, he should throw them away. Wasn't it ridiculous when you came right down to it, wasn't it pathetic—a white man carrying weapons?

Sylvester Thomas came out of the tent. "Get your horses ready, my dear sir," he whispered. "Be prepared to ride as soon as I come back. Hurry!"

The young man slouched over to the horses and followed instructions—might as well do that as anything else. Ride where? Do what?

He lifted Sam Rutherford up and tied him upon his horse. Go back home? Back to the great, the powerful, the respected, capital of what had once been the United States of America?

Thomas came back with a bound-and-gagged girl in his grasp. She wriggled madly. Her eyes crackled with anger and rebellion. She kept trying to kick the Confederate Ambassador.

She wore the rich robes of an Indian princess. Her hair was braided in the style currently fashionable among Sioux women. And her face had been stained carefully with some darkish dye.

Sarah Calvin. The daughter of the Chief Justice. They tied her to the pack horse.

"Chief Three Hydrogen Bombs," the Negro explained. "He

feels his son plays around too much with paleface females. He wants this one out of the way. The boy has to settle down, prepare for the responsibilities of chieftainship. This may help. And listen, the old man likes you. He told me to tell you something."

"I'm grateful. I'm grateful for every favor, no matter how small, how humiliating."

Sylvester Thomas shook his head decisively. "Don't be bitter, young sir. If you want to go on living you have to be alert. And you can't be alert and bitter at the same time. . . . The chief wants you to know there's no point in your going home. He couldn't say it openly in council, but the reason the Sioux moved in on Trenton has nothing to do with the Seminole on the other side. It has to do with the Ojibway-Cree-Montaignais situation in the North. They've decided to take over the eastern seaboard—that includes what's left of your country. By this time, they're probably in Yonkers or the Bronx, somewhere inside New York City. In a matter of hours, your government will no longer be in existence. The Chief had advance word of this and felt it necessary for the Sioux to establish some sort of bridgehead on the coast before matters were permanently stabilized. By occupying New Jersey he is preventing an Ojibway-Seminole junction. But he likes you, as I said, and wants you warned against going home."

"Fine. But where *do* I go? Up a rain cloud? Down a well?"

"No," Thomas admitted without smiling. He hoisted Jerry up on his horse. "You might come back with me to the Confederacy—" He paused, and when Jerry's sullen expression did not change, he went on, "Well, then, may I suggest —and mind you, this is my advice, not the chief's—head straight out to Asbury Park. It's not far away—you can make it in reasonable time if you ride hard. According to reports I've overheard, there should be units of the United States Navy there, the Tenth Fleet, to be exact."

"Tell me," Jerry asked, bending down. "Have you heard any other news? Anything about the rest of the world? How has it been with those people—the Russkies, the Sovietskis, whatever they were called—the ones the United States had so much to do with years ago?"

"According to several of the chief's councilors, the Soviet Russians were having a good deal of difficulty with people called Tatars. I *think* they were called Tatars. But, my good sir, you should be on your way."

Jerry leaned down farther and grasped his hand. "Thanks," he said. "You've gone to a lot of trouble for me. I'm grateful."

"That's quite all right," said Mr. Thomas earnestly. "After all, by the rocket's red glare, and all that. We were a single nation once."

Jerry moved off, leading the other two horses. He set a fast pace, exercising the minimum of caution made necessary by the condition of the road. By the time they reached Route 33, Sam Rutherford, though not altogether sober or well, was able to sit in his saddle. They could then untie Sarah Calvin and ride with her between them.

She cursed and wept. "Filthy paleface! Foul, ugly, stinking whiteskins! I'm an Indian, can't you see I'm an Indian? My skin isn't white—it's brown, brown!"

They kept riding.

Asbury Park was a dismal clatter of rags and confusion and refugees. There were refugees from the north, from Perth Amboy, from as far as Newark. There were refugees from Princeton in the west, flying before the Sioux invasion. And from the south, from Atlantic City—even, unbelievably, from distant Camden—were still other refugees, with stories of a sudden Seminole attack, an attempt to flank the armies of Three Hydrogen Bombs.

The three horses were stared at enviously, even in their lathered, exhausted condition. They represented food to the hungry, the fastest transportation possible to the fearful. Jerry found the saber very useful. And the pistol was even better— it had only to be exhibited. Few of these people had ever seen a pistol in action: they had a mighty, superstitious fear of firearms. . . .

With this fact discovered, Jerry kept the pistol out nakedly in his right hand when he walked into the United States Naval Depot on the beach at Asbury Park. Sam Rutherford was at his side; Sarah Calvin walked sobbing behind.

He announced their family backgrounds to Admiral Milton Chester. The son of the Undersecretary of State. The daughter of the Chief Justice of the Supreme Court. The oldest son of the Senator from Idaho. "And now. Do you recognize the authority of this document?"

Admiral Chester read the wrinkled commission slowly, spelling out the harder words to himself. He twisted his head respectfully when he had finished, looking first at the seal of the United States on the paper before him, and then at the glittering pistol in Jerry's hand.

"Yes," he said at last. "I recognize its authority. Is that a real pistol?"

Jerry nodded. "A Crazy Horse forty-five. The latest. *How* do you recognize its authority?"

The admiral spread his hands. "Everything is confused out here. The latest word I've received is that there are Ojibway warriors in Manhattan—that there is no longer any United States Government. And yet this"—he bent over the document once more—"this is a commission by the President himself, appointing you full plenipotentiary. To the Seminole, of course. But full plenipotentiary. The last official appointment, to the best of my knowledge, of the President of the United States of America."

He reached forward and touched the pistol in Jerry Franklin's hand curiously and inquiringly. He nodded to himself, as if he'd come to a decision. He stood up, and saluted with a flourish.

"I hereby recognize you as the last legal authority of the United States Government. And I place my fleet at your disposal."

"Good." Jerry stuck the pistol in his belt. He pointed with the saber. "Do you have enough food and water for a long voyage?"

"No, sir," Admiral Chester said. "But that can be arranged in a few hours at most. May I escort you aboard, sir?"

He gestured proudly down the beach and past the surf to where the three, forty-five foot, gaff-rigged schooners rode at anchor. "The United States Tenth Fleet, sir. Awaiting your orders."

Hours later when the three vessels were standing out to sea, the admiral came to the cramped main cabin where Jerry Franklin was resting. Sam Rutherford and Sarah Calvin were asleep in the bunks above.

"And the orders, sir . . .?"

Jerry Franklin walked out on the narrow deck, looked up at the taut, patched sails. "Sail east."

"East, sir? *Due* east?"

"Due east all the way. To the fabled lands of Europe. To a place where a white man can stand at last on his own two legs. Where he need not fear persecution. Where he need not fear slavery. Sail east, Admiral, until we discover a new and hopeful world—a world of freedom!"

JUDAS DANCED

Brian M. Aldiss

The general reading public of Great Britain knows Brian Aldiss as the author of that best-selling hymn to the joys of autoeroticism, **The Hand-Reared Boy,** and its equally popular sequels, of which several evidently exist. A more select audience regards him as one of the half-dozen or so writers who by approaching the themes of science fiction with serious artistry helped transform a genre of commercial action fiction into a vital and exciting realm of literature. The present story, dating from 1958, shows the extent of Aldiss' technical virtuosity and narrative energy at the outset of his formidable career.

It was not a fair trial.

You understand I was not inclined to listen properly, but it was not a fair trial. It had a mistrustful and furtive haste about it. Judge, counsel and jury all took care to be as brief and explicit as possible. I said nothing, but I knew why: everyone wanted to get back to the dances.

So it was not very long before the judge stood up and pronounced sentence:

"Alexander Abel Crowe, this court finds you guilty of murdering Parowen Scryban for the second time."

I could have laughed out loud. I nearly did.

He went on: "You are therefore condemned to suffer

death by strangulation for the second time, which sentence
will be carried out within the next week."

Around the court ran a murmur of excitement.

In a way, even I felt satisfied. It had been an unusual case:
few are the people who care to risk facing death a second
time; the first time you die makes the prospect worse, not
better. For just a minute, the court was still; then it cleared
with almost indecent haste. In a little while, only I was left
there.

I, Alex Abel Crowe—or approximately he—came carefully
down out of the prisoner's box and limped the length of the
dusty room to the door. As I went, I looked at my hands.
They weren't trembling.

Nobody bothered to keep a check on me. They knew they
could pick me up whenever they were ready to execute sentence. I was unmistakable, and I had nowhere to go. I was
the man with the clubfoot who could not dance; nobody
could mistake me for anyone else. Only I could do that.

Outside in the dark sunlight, that wonderful woman stood
waiting for me with her husband, waiting on the court steps.
The sight of her began to bring back life and hurt to my
veins. I raised my hand to her as my custom was.

"We've come to take you home, Alex," Husband said,
stepping towards me.

"I haven't got a home," I said, addressing her.

"I mean *our* home," he informed me.

"Elucidation accepted," I said. "Take me away, take me
away, take me away, Charlemagne. And let me sleep."

"You need sleep after all you have been through," he said.
Why, he sounded nearly sympathetic.

Sometimes I called him Charlemagne, sometimes just
Charley. Or Cheeps, or Jags, or Jaggers, or anything, as the
mood took me. He seemed to forgive me. Perhaps he even
liked it—I don't know. Personal magnetism takes you a long
way; it has taken me so far I don't even have to remember
names.

They stopped a passing taxi and we all climbed in. It was
a tumbrel, they tell me. You know, French? Circa seventeen-
eighty-something. Husband sat one side, Wife the other,

each holding one of my arms, as if they thought I might get violent. I let them do it, although the idea amused me.

"Hallo, friends!" I said ironically. Sometimes I called them "parents," or "disciples," or sometimes "patients." Anything.

The wonderful woman was crying slightly.

"Look at her!" I said to Husband. "She's lovely when she cries, that I swear. I could have married her, you know, if I had not been dedicated. Tell him, you wonderful creature, tell him how I turned you down!"

Through her sobbing, she said, "Alex said he had more important things to do than sex."

"So you've got me to thank for Perdita!" I told him. "It was a big sacrifice, but I'm happy to see you happy." Often now I called her Perdita. It seemed to fit her. He laughed at what I had said, and then we were all laughing. Yes, it was good to be alive; I knew I made them feel good to be alive. They were loyal. I had to give them something—I had no gold and silver.

The tumbrel stopped outside Charley's place—the Husband residence, I'd better say. Oh, the things I've called that place! Someone should have recorded them all. It was one of those inverted beehive houses: just room for a door and an elevator on the ground floor, but the fifth floor could hold a ballroom. Topply, topply. Up we went to the fifth. There was no sixth floor; had there been, I should have gone up there, the way I felt. I asked for it anyhow, just to see the wonderful woman brighten up. She liked me to joke, even when I wasn't in a joking mood. I could tell she still loved me so much it hurt her.

"Now for a miracle, ye pampered jades," I said, stepping forth, clumping into the living room.

I seized an empty vase from a low shelf and spat into it. Ah, the old cunning was still there! It filled at once with wine, sweet and bloody-looking. I sipped and found it good.

"Go on and taste it, Perdy!" I told her.

Wonderful w. turned her head sadly away. She would not touch that vase. I could have eaten every single strand of hair on her head, but she seemed unable to see the wine. I really believe she could not see that wine.

"Please don't go through all that again, Alex," she implored me wearily. Little faith, you see—the old, old story. (Remind me to tell you a new one I heard the other day.) I put my behind on one chair and my bad foot on another and sulked.

They came and stood by me . . . not too close.

"Come nearer," I coaxed, looking up under my eyebrows and pretending to growl at them. "I won't hurt you. I only murder Parowen Scryban, remember?"

"We've got to talk to you about that," Husband said desperately. I thought he looked as if he had aged.

"I think you look as if you have aged, Perdita," I said. Often I called him Perdita, too; why, man, they sometimes looked so worried you couldn't tell them apart.

"I cannot live forever, Alex," he replied. "Now try and concentrate about this killing, will you?"

I waved a hand and tried to belch. At times I can belch like a sinking ship.

"We do all we can to help you, Alex," he said. I heard him although my eyes were shut; can *you* do that? "But we can only keep you out of trouble if you co-operate. It's the dancing that does it; nothing else betrays you like dancing. You've got to promise you'll stay away from it. In fact, we want you to promise that you'll let us restrain you. To keep you away from the dancing. Something about that dancing . . ."

He was going on and on, and I could still hear him. But other things were happening. That word "dancing" got in the way of all his other words. It started a sort of flutter under my eyelids. I crept my hand out and took the wonderful woman's hand, so soft and lovely, and listened to that word "dancing" dancing. It brought its own rhythm, bouncing about like an eyeball inside my head. The rhythm grew louder. He was shouting.

I sat up suddenly, opening my eyes.

W. woman was on the floor, very pale.

"You squeezed too hard," she whispered.

I could see that her little hand was the only red thing she had.

"I'm sorry," I said. "I really wonder you two don't throw me out for good!" I couldn't help it, I just started laughing.

I like laughing. I can laugh even when nothing's funny. Even when I saw their faces, I still kept laughing like mad.

"Stop it!" Husband said. For a moment he looked as if he would have hit me. But I was laughing so much I did not recognize him. It must have done them good to see me enjoying myself; they both needed a fillip, I could tell.

"If you stop laughing, I'll take you down to the club," he said, greasily bribing.

I stopped. I always know when to stop. With all humility, it is a great natural gift.

"The club's the place for me," I said. "I've already got a clubfoot—I'm halfway there!"

I stood up.

"Lead on, my loyal supporters, my liege lords," I ordered.

"You and I will go alone, Alex," Husband said. "The wonderful woman will stay here. She really ought to go to bed."

"What's in it for her?" I joked. Then I followed him to the elevator. He knows I don't like staying in any one place for long.

When I got to the club, I knew, I would want to be somewhere else. That's the worst of having a mission: it makes you terribly restless. Sometimes I am so restless I could die. Ordinary people just don't know what the word means. I could have married her if I had been ordinary. They call it destiny.

But the club was good.

We walked there. I limped there. I made sure I limped badly.

The club had a timescreen. That, I must admit, was my only interest in the club. I don't care for women. Or men. Not living women or men. I only enjoy them when they are back in time.

This night—I nearly said "this particular night," but there was nothing particularly particular about it—the timescreen had only been turned roughly three centuries back into the past. At least, I guessed it was twenty-first-century stuff by the women's dresses and a shot of a power station. A large crowd of people was looking in as Perdita Caesar and I entered, so I started to pretend he had never seen one of the wall-screens before.

"The tele-eyes which are projected back over history consume a fabulous amount of power every second," I told him loudly in a voice which suggested I had swallowed a poker. "It makes them very expensive. It means private citizens cannot afford screens and tele-eyes, just as once they could not afford their own private motion pictures. This club is fortunately very rich. Its members sleep in gold leaf at night."

Several people were glancing around at me already. Caesar was shaking his head and rolling his eyes.

"The tele-eyes cannot get a picture further than twenty-seven centuries back," I told him, "owing to the limitations of science. Science, as you know, is a system for taking away with one hand while giving with the other."

He could not answer cleverly. I went on: "It has also proved impossible, due to the aforesaid limitations, to send human beings further back in time than one week. And that costs so much that only governments can do it. As you may have heard, nothing can be sent ahead into time—there's no future in it!"

I had to laugh at that. It was funny, and quite spontaneous.

Many people were calling out to me, and Caesar Borgia was dragging at my arm, trying to make me be quiet.

"I wouldn't spoil anyone's fun!" I shouted. "You people get on with your watching; I'll get on with my speech."

But I did not want to talk to a lot of feather-bedders like them. So I sat down without saying another word, Boy Borgia collapsing beside me with a sigh of relief. Suddenly I felt very, very sad. Life just is not what is was; once upon a time, I could have married this husband's wife.

"Physically, you can go back one week," I whispered, "optically, twenty-seven centuries. It's very sad."

It was very sad. The people on the screen were also sad. They lived in the Entertainment Era, and appeared to be getting little pleasure from it. I tried to weep for them but failed because at the moment they seemed just animated history. I saw them as period pieces, stuck there a couple of generations before reading and writing had died out altogether and the fetters of literacy fell forever from the world. Little any of them cared for the patterns of history.

"I've had an idea I want to tell you about, Cheezer," I said. It was a good idea.

"Can't it wait?" he asked. "I'd like to see this scan. It's all about the European Allegiance."

"I must tell you before I forget."

"Come on," he said resignedly, getting up.

"You are too loyal to me," I complained. "You spoil me. I'll speak to St. Peter about it."

As meek as you like, I followed him into an anteroom. He drew himself a drink from an automatic man in one corner. He was trembling. I did not tremble, although at the back of my mind lurked many things to tremble about.

"Go on then, say whatever in hell you want to say," he told me, shading his eyes with his hand. I have seen him use that trick before; he did it after I killed Parowen Scryban the first time, I remember. There's nothing wrong with my memory, except in patches.

"I had this idea," I said, trying to recall it. "This idea—oh, yes. History. I got the idea looking at those twenty-first-century people. Mythology is the key to everything, isn't it? I mean, a man builds his life on a set of myths, doesn't he? Well, in our world, the so-called Western World, those accepted myths were religious until about mid-nineteenth century. By then, a majority of Europeans were literate, or within reach of it, and for a couple of centuries the myths became literary ones: tragedy was no longer the difference between grace and nature, but between art and reality."

Julius had dropped his hand. He was interested. I could see he wondered what was coming next. I hardly knew myself.

"Then mechanical aids—television, computers, scanners of every type—abolished literacy," I said. "Into the vacuum came the timescreens. Our mythologies are now historical: tragedy has become simply a failure to see the future."

I beamed at him and bowed, not letting him know I was beyond tragedy. He just sat there. He said nothing. Sometimes such terrible boredom descends on me that I can hardly fight against it.

"Is my reasoning sound?" I asked. (Two women looked into the room, saw me, and left again hurriedly. They must have sensed I did not want them, otherwise they would have come to me; I am young and handsome—I am not thirty-three yet.)

"You could always reason well," Marcus Aurelius Marconi said, "but it just never leads anywhere. God, I'm so tired."

"This bit of reasoning leads somewhere. I beg you to believe it, Holy Roman," I said, flopping on my knees before him. "It's the state philosophy I've really been telling you about. That's why, although they keep the death penalty for serious crimes—like murdering a bastard called Parowen Scryban—they go back in time the next day and call off the execution. They believe you should die for your crime, you see? But more deeply they believe every man should face his true future. They've—we've all seen too many premature deaths on the timescreens. Romans, Normans, Celts, Goths, English, Israelis. Every race. Individuals—all dying too soon, failing to fulfil—"

Oh, I admit it, I was crying on his knees by then, although bravely disguising it by barking like a dog: a Great Dane. Hamlet. Not in our stars but in our selves. (I've watched W.S. write that bit.)

I was crying at last to think the police would come without fail within the next week to snuff me out, and then resurrect me again, according to my sentence. I was remembering what it was like last time. They took so long about it.

They took so long. Though I struggled, I could not move; those police know how to hold a man. My windpipe was blocked, as sentence of court demanded.

And then, it seemed, the boxes sailed in. Starting with small ones, they grew bigger. They were black boxes, all of them. Faster they came, and faster, inside me and out. I'm telling you how it felt, my God! And they blocked the whole, whole universe, black and red. With my lungs really crammed tight with boxes, out of the world I went. Dead!

Into limbo I went.

I don't say nothing happened, but I could not grasp what was happening there, and I was unable to participate. Then I was alive again.

It was abruptly the day before the strangulation once more, and the government agent had come back in time and rescued me, so that from one point of view I was not strangled. *But* I still remembered it happening, and the boxes, and limbo. Don't talk to me about paradoxes. The government expended several billion megavolts sending that man back for me, and those megavolts account for all paradoxes. I was dead and then alive again.

Now I had to undergo it all once more. No wonder there was little crime nowadays; the threat of that horrible experience held many a likely criminal back. But I *had* to kill Parowen Scryban; just so long as they went back and resurrected him after I had finished with him, I had to go and do it again. Call it a moral obligation. No one understands. It is as if I were living in a world of my own.

"Get up, get up! You're biting my ankles."

Where had I heard that voice before? At last I could no longer ignore it. Whenever I try to think, voices interrupt. I stopped chewing whatever I was chewing, unblocked my eyes, and sat up. This was just a room; I had been in rooms before. A man was standing over me; I did not recognize him. He was just a man.

"You look as if you have aged," I told him.

"I can't live forever, thank God," he said. "Now get up and let's get you home. You're going to bed."

"What home?" I asked. "What bed? Who in the gentle name of anyone may you be?"

"Just call me Adam," he said sickly.

I recognized him then and went with him. We had been in some sort of a club; he never told my why. I still don't know why we went to that club.

The house he took me to was shaped like a beehive upside down, and I walked there like a drunk. A clubfooted drunk.

This wonderful stranger took me up in an elevator to a soft bed. He undressed me and put me in that soft bed as gently as if I had been his son. I am really impressed by the kindness strangers show me; personal magnetism, I suppose.

For as long as I could after he had left me, I lay in the bed in the inverted beehive. Then the darkness grew thick and sticky, and I could imagine all the fat, furry bodies, chitinously winged, of the bees on the ceiling. A minute more and I should fall headfirst into them. Stubbornly, I fought to sweat it out, but a man can stand only so much.

On hands and knees I crawled out of bed and out of the

room. Quickly, softly, I clicked the door shut behind me; not a bee escaped.

People were talking in a lighted room along the corridor. I crawled to the doorway, looking and listening. The wonderful stranger talked to the wonderful woman; she was in night attire, with a hand bandaged.

She was saying: "You will have to see the authorities in the morning and petition them."

He was saying: "It'll do no good. I can't get the law changed. You know that. It's hopeless."

I merely listened.

Sinking onto the bed, he buried his face in his hands, finally looking up to say: "The law insists on personal responsibility. We've got to take care of Alex. It's a reflection of the time we live in; because of the timescreens, we've got—whether we like it or not—historical perspectives. We can see that the whole folly of the past was due to failures in individual liability. Our laws are naturally framed to correct that, which they do; it just happens to be tough on us."

He sighed and said, "The sad thing is, even Alex realizes that. He talked quite sensibly to me at the club about not evading the future."

"It hurts me most when he talks sensibly," the wonderful double-you said. "It makes you realize he is still capable of suffering."

He took her bandaged hand, almost as if they had a pain they hoped to alleviate by sharing it between them.

"I'll go and see the authorities in the morning," he promised, "and ask them to let the execution be final—no reprieve afterwards."

Even that did not seem to satisfy her.

Perhaps, like me, she could not tell what either of them was talking about. She shook her head miserably from side to side.

"If only it hadn't been for his clubfoot," she said. "If only it hadn't been for that, he could have danced the sickness out of himself."

Her face was growing more and more twisted.

It was enough. More.

"Laugh and grow fat," I suggested. I croaked because my throat was dry. My glands are always like bullets. It reminded me of a frog, so I hopped spontaneously into the room. They did not move; I sat on the bed with them.

"All together again," I said.

They did not move.

"Go back to bed, Alex," she of the wonderfulness said in a low voice.

They were looking at me; goodness knows what they wanted me to say or do. I stayed where I was. A little green clock on a green shelf said nine o'clock.

"Oh, holy heavens!" the double-you said. "What does the future hold?"

"Double chins for you, double-yous for me," I joked. That green clock said a minute past nine. I felt as if its little hand were slowly, slowly disemboweling me.

If I waited long enough, I knew I should think of something. They talked to me while I thought and waited; what good they imagined they were doing is beyond me, but I would not harm them. They mean well. They're the best people in the world. That doesn't mean to say I have to listen to them.

The thought about the clock arrived. Divine revelation.

"The dancing will be on now," I said, standing up like a jackknife.

"No!" Husband said.

"No!" Perdita said.

"You look as if you have aged," I told them. That is my favorite line in all speech.

I ran out of the room, slamming the door behind me, ran step-club-step-club down the passage, and hurled myself into the elevator. With infinitesimal delay, I chose the right button and sank to ground level. There, I wedged the lattice door open with a chair; that put the elevator out of action.

People in the street took no notice of me. The fools just did not realize who I was. Nobody spoke to me as I hurried along, so of course I replied in kind.

Thus I came to the dance area.

Every community has its dance area. Think of all that drama, gladiatorial contests, reading, and sport have ever meant in the past; now they are all merged into dance, inevitable, for only by dance—our kind of dance—can history be interpreted. And interpretation of history is our being, because through the timescreens we see that history is life. It lives around us, so we dance it. Unless we have clubfeet.

Many dances were in progress among the thirty permanent sets. The sets were only casually separated from each other, so that spectators or dancers, going from one to another, might get the sense of everything happening at once, which is the sense the timescreens give you.

That is what I savagely love about history. It is not past; it is always going on. Cleopatra lies forever in the sweaty arms of Anthony. Socrates continually gulps his hemlock down. You just have to be watching the right screen or the right dance.

Most of the dancers were amateurs—although the term means little where everyone dances out his role whenever possible. I stood among a crowd, watching. The bright movements have a dizzying effect; they excite me. To one side of me, Marco Polo sweeps exultantly through Cathay to Kubla Khan. Ahead, four children, who represent the satellites of Jupiter, glide out to meet the somber figure of Galileo Galilei. To the other side, the Persian poet Firdausi leaves for exile in Baghdad. Farther still, I catch a glimpse of Heyerdahl turning toward the tide.

And if I cross my eyes, raft, telescope, pagoda, palm, all mingle. That is meaning! If I could only dance it!

I cannot stay still. Here is my restlessness again, my only companion. I move, eyes unfocused. I pass around the sets or across them, mingling stiff-legged among the dancers. Something compels me, something I cannot remember. Now I cannot even remember who I am. I've gone beyond mere identity.

Everywhere the dancing is faster, matching my heart. I would not harm anyone, except one person who harmed me eternally. It is he I must find. Why do they dance so fast? The movements drive me like whips.

Now I run into a mirror. It stands on a crowded set. I fight with the creature imprisoned in it, thinking it real. Then I understand that it is only a mirror. Shaking my head, I clear the blood from behind my eyes and regard myself. Yes, that is unmistakably me. And I remember who I am meant to be.

I first found who I was meant to be as a child, when I saw one of the greatest dramas of all. There it was, captured by the timescreens! The soldiers and centurions came, and a bragging multitude. The sky grew dark as they banged three crosses into the ground. And when I saw the Man they nailed upon the central cross, I knew I had His face.

Here it is now, that same sublime face, looking at me in pity and pain out of the glass. Nobody believes me; I no longer tell them who I think I am. But one thing I know I have to do. I have to do *it*.

So now I run again clump-trot-clump-trot, knowing just what to look for. All these great sets, pillars and panels of concrete and plastic, I run around them all, looking.

And here it is. Professionals dance out this drama, my drama, so difficult and intricate and sad. Pilate in dove-gray, Mary Magdalene moves in green. Hosts of dancers fringe them, representing the crowd who did not care. I care! My eyes burn among them, seeking. Then I have the man I want.

He is just leaving the set to rest out of sight until the cue for his last dance. I follow him, keeping behind cover like a crab in a thicket.

Yes! He looks just like me! He is my living image, and consequently bears That face. Yet it is now overlaid with make-up, pink and solid, so that when he comes out of the bright lights he looks like a corpse.

I am near enough to see the thick muck on his skin, with its runnels and wrinkles caused by sweat and movement. Underneath it all, the true face is clear enough to me, although the make-up plastered on it represents Judas.

To have That face and to play Judas! It is the most terrible of all wickedness. But this is Parowen Scryban, whom I have twice murdered for this very blasphemy. It is some consolation to know that although the government slipped back in time and saved him afterwards, he must still remember those good deaths. Now I must kill him again.

As he turns into a restroom, I have him. Ah, my fingers slip into that slippery pink stuff; but underneath, the skin is firm. He is small, slender, tired with the strain of dancing. He falls forward with me on his back.

I kill him now, although in a few hours they will come

back and rescue him and it will all not have happened. Never mind the shouting: squeeze. Squeeze, dear God!

When blows fall on my head from behind, it makes no difference. Scryban should be dead by now, the traitor. I roll off him and let many hands tie me into a strait jacket.

Many lights are in my eyes. Many voices are talking. I just lie there, thinking I recognize two of the voices, one a man's, one a woman's.

The man says: "Yes, Inspector, I *know* that under law parents are responsible for their own children. We look after Alex as far as we can, but he's mad. He's a throwback! I— God, Inspector, I *hate* the creature."

"You mustn't say that!" the woman cries. "Whatever he does, he's our son."

They sound too shrill to be true. I cannot think what they make such a fuss about. So I open my eyes and look at them. She is a wonderful woman but I recognize neither her nor the man; they just do not interest me. Scryban I do recognize.

He is standing rubbing his throat. He is a mess with his two faces all mixed in together like a Picasso. Because he is breathing, I know they have come back and saved him again. No matter; he will remember.

The man they call Inspector (and who, I ask, would want a name like that?) goes over to speak to Scryban.

"Your father tells me you are actually this madman's brother," he says to Scryban. Judas hangs his head, though he continues to massage his neck.

"Yes," he says. He is as quiet as the woman was shrill; strange how folks vary. "Alex and I are twin brothers. I changed my name years ago—the publicity, you know . . . harmful to my professional career . . ."

How terribly tired and bored I feel.

Who is whose brother, I ask myself, who mothers whom? I'm lucky; I own no relations. These people look like sad company. The saddest in the universe.

"I think you all look as if you have aged!" I shout suddenly.

That makes the Inspector come and stand over me, which I dislike. He has knees halfway up his legs. I manage to re-

semble one of the tritons on one of Benvenuto Cellini's salt-
cellars, and so he turns away at last to speak to Husband.

"All right," he says. "I can see this is just one of those
things nobody can be responsible for. I'll arrange for the
reprieve to be countermanded. This time, when the devil is
dead he stays dead."

Husband embraces Scryban. Wonderful woman begins to
cry. Traitors all! I start to laugh, making it so harsh and loud
and horrible it frightens even me.

What none of them understands is this: on the third time
I shall rise again.

ANGEL'S EGG

Edgar Pangborn

Edgar Pangborn is a quiet, retiring man of middle years who lives in rural New York State and, all too infrequently, offers the world some glowing, magical work of fiction. The rich and tender story you are about to read marked his debut as an author of science fiction in 1951. It was followed by several novels, including the lovely **A Mirror for Observers** and the rollicking picaresque **Davy.** After a prolonged absence from science fiction, Pangborn is producing some new stories: cause to rejoice.

LETTER OF RECORD, BLAINE TO MC CARRAN, DATED AUGUST 10, 1951.

Mr. Cleveland McCarran
Federal Bureau of Investigation
Washington, D.C.

Dear Sir:

In compliance with your request I enclose herewith a transcript of the pertinent sections of the journal of Dr. David Bannerman, deceased. The original document is being held at this office until proper disposition can be determined.

Our investigation has shown no connection between Dr. Bannerman and any organization, subversive or otherwise. So

far as we can learn, he was exactly what he seemed, an in-
offensive summer resident, retired, with a small independent
income—a recluse to some extent, but well spoken of by
local tradesmen and other neighbors. A connection between
Dr. Bannerman and the type of activity that concerns your
department would seem most unlikely.

The following information is summarized from the earlier
parts of Dr. Bannerman's journal, and tallies with the results
of our own limited inquiry. He was born in 1898 at Spring-
field, Massachusetts, attended public school there, and was
graduated from Harvard College in 1922, his studies having
been interrupted by two years' military service. He was
wounded in action in Argonne, receiving a spinal injury. He
earned a doctorate in biology in 1926. Delayed aftereffects of
his war injury necessitated hospitalization, 1927-28. From
1929 to 1948 he taught elementary sciences in a private school
in Boston. He published two textbooks in introductory biology,
1929 and 1937. In 1948 he retired from teaching: a pension
and a modest income from textbook royalties evidently
made this possible. Aside from the spinal deformity, which
caused him to walk with a stoop, his health is said to have
been fair. Autopsy findings suggested that the spinal condition
must have given him considerable pain; he is not known to
have mentioned this to anyone, not even to his physician, Dr.
Lester Morse. There is no evidence whatever of drug addiction or alcoholism.

At one point early in his journal Dr. Bannerman describes
himself as "a naturalist of the puttering type—I would rather
sit on a log than write monographs: it pays off better." Dr.
Morse, and others who knew Dr. Bannerman personally, tell
me that this conveys a hint of his personality.

I am not qualified to comment on the material of this
journal, except to say I have no evidence to support (or to
contradict) Dr. Bannerman's statements. The journal has been
studied only by my immediate superiors, by Dr. Morse, and
by myself. I take it for granted you will hold the matter in
strictest confidence.

With the journal I am also enclosing a statement by Dr.
Morse, written at my request for our records and for your
information. You will note that he says, with some quali-
fications, that "death was not inconsistent with an embolism."

He has signed a death certificate on that basis. You will recall from my letter of August 5 that it was Dr. Morse who discovered Dr. Bannerman's body. Because he was a close personal friend of the deceased, Dr. Morse did not feel able to perform the autopsy himself. It was done by a Dr. Stephen Clyde of this city, and was virtually negative as regards cause of death, neither confirming nor contradicting Dr. Morse's original tentative diagnosis. If you wish to read the autopsy report in full I shall be glad to forward a copy.

Dr. Morse tells me that so far as he knows Dr. Bannerman had no near relatives. He never married. For the last twelve summers he occupied a small cottage on a back road about twenty-five miles from this city, and had few visitors. The neighbor, Steele, mentioned in the journal is a farmer, age 68, of good character, who tells me he "never got really acquainted with Dr. Bannerman."

At this office we feel that unless new information comes to light, further active investigation is hardly justified.

> Respectfully yours,
> Garrison Blaine
> Capt., State Police
> Augusta, Me.

Encl: Extract from Journal of David Bannerman, dec'd.
      Statement by Lester Morse, M.D.

LIBRARIAN'S NOTE: The following document, originally attached as an unofficial "rider" to the foregoing letter, was donated to this institution in 1994 through the courtesy of Mrs. Helen McCarran, widow of the martyred first President of the World Federation. Other personal and state papers of President McCarran, many of them dating from the early period when he was employed by the FBI, are accessible to public view at the Institute of World History, Copenhagen.

PERSONAL NOTE, BLAINE TO MC CARRAN, DATED AUGUST 10, 1951

Dear Cleve:
    Guess I didn't make it clear in my other letter that that

bastard Clyde was responsible for my having to drag you into this. He is something to handle with tongs. Happened thusly— When he came in to heave the autopsy report at me, he was already having pups just because it was so completely negative (he does have certain types of honesty), and he caught sight of a page or two of the journal on my desk. Doc Morse was with me at the time. I fear we both got upstage with him (Clyde has that effect, and we were both in a State of Mind anyway), so right away the old drip thinks he smells something subversive. Belongs to the atomize-'em-NOW-WOW-WOW school of thought—nuf sed? He went into a grand whuff-whuff about referring to Higher Authority, and I knew that meant your hive, so I wanted to get ahead of the letter I knew he'd write. I suppose his literary effort couldn't be just sort of quietly transferred to File 13, otherwise known as the Appropriate Receptacle?

He can say what he likes about my character, if any, but even I never supposed he'd take a sideswipe at his professional colleague. Doc Morse is the best of the best and would not dream of suppressing any evidence important to us, as you say Clyde's letter hints. What Doc did do was to tell Clyde, pleasantly, in the privacy of my office, to go take a flying this-and-that at the moon. I only wish I'd thought of the expression myself. So Clyde rushes off to tell teacher. See what I mean about the tongs? However (knock on wood) I don't think Clyde saw enough of the journal to get any notion of what it's all about.

As for that journal, damn it, Cleve, I don't know. If you have any ideas I want them, of course. I'm afraid I believe in angels, myself. But when I think of the effect on local opinion if the story ever gets out—brother! Here was this old Bannerman living alone with a female angel and they wuzn't even common-law married. Aw, gee. . . . And the flood of phone calls from other crackpots anxious to explain it all to me. Experts in the care and feeding of angels. Methods of angel-proofing. Angels right outside the window a minute ago. Make Angels a Profitable Enterprise in Your Spare Time! ! !

When do I see you? You said you might have a week clear in October. If we could get together maybe we could make sense where there is none. I hear the cider promises to be good this year. Try and make it. My best to Ginny and the other young fry, and Helen of course.

Respeckfully yourn,
Garry

P.S. If you do see any angels down your way, and they aren't willing to wait for a Republican Administration, by all means have them investigated by the Senate—then we'll *know* we're all nuts.

G.

EXTRACT FROM JOURNAL OF DAVID BANNERMAN, JUNE 1-JULY 29, 1951

June 1

It must have been at least three weeks ago when we had that flying saucer flurry. Observers the other side of Katahdin saw it come down this side; observers this side saw it come down the other. Size anywhere from six inches to sixty feet in diameter (or was it cigar-shaped?) and speed whatever you please. Seem to recall that witnesses agreed on a rosy-pink light. There was the inevitable gobbledegookery of official explanation designed to leave everyone impressed, soothed, and disappointed. I paid scant attention to the excitement and less to the explanations—naturally, I thought it was just a flying saucer. But now Camilla has hatched out an angel.

It would have to be Camilla. Perhaps I haven't mentioned my hens enough. In the last day or two it has dawned on me that this journal may be of importance to other eyes than mine, not merely a lonely man's plaything to blunt the edge of mortality: an angel in the house makes a difference. I had better show consideration for possible readers.

I have eight hens, all yearlings except Camilla: this is her third spring. I boarded her two winters at my neighbor Steele's farm when I closed this shack and shuffled my chilly bones off to Florida, because even as a pullet she had a manner which overbore me. I could never have eaten Camilla: if she had looked at the ax with that same expression of rancid disapproval (and she would), I should have felt I was be-

heading a favorite aunt. Her only concession to sentiment is
the annual rush of maternity to the brain—normal, for a
case-hardened White Plymouth Rock.

This year she stole a nest successfully in a tangle of blackberry. By the time I located it, I estimated I was about two
weeks too late. I had to outwit her by watching from a window—she is far too acute to be openly trailed from feeding
ground to nest. When I had bled and pruned my way to her
hideout she was sitting on nine eggs and hating my guts.
They could not be fertile, since I keep no rooster, and I was
about to rob her when I saw the ninth egg was nothing of
hers. It was a deep blue and transparent, with flecks of inner
light that made me think of the first stars in a clear evening.
It was the same size as Camilla's own. There was an embryo,
but I could make nothing of it. I returned the egg to
Camilla's bare and fevered breastbone and went back to the
house for a long, cool drink.

That was ten days ago. I know I ought to have kept a
record; I examined the blue egg every day, watching how
some nameless life grew within it. The angel has been out of
the shell three days now. This is the first time I have felt
equal to facing pen and ink.

I have been experiencing a sort of mental lassitude unfamiliar to me. Wrong word: not so much lassitude as a
preoccupation, with no sure clue to what it is that preoccupies
me. By reputation I am a scientist of sorts. Right now I
have no impulse to look for data; I want to sit quiet and let
truth come to a relaxed mind if it will. Could be merely a
part of growing older, but I doubt that. The broken pieces
of the wonderful blue shell are on my desk. I have been peering at them—into them—for the last ten minutes or more.
Can't call it study: my thought wanders into their blue,
learning nothing I can retain in words. It does not convey
much to say I have gone into a vision of open sky—and
of peace, if such a thing there be.

The angel chipped the shell deftly in two parts. This was
evidently done with the aid of small horny outgrowths on
her elbows; these growths were sloughed off on the second
day. I wish I had seen her break the shell, but when I
visited the blackberry tangle three days ago she was already

out. She poked her exquisite head through Camilla's neck feathers, smiled sleepily, and snuggled back into darkness to finish drying off. So what could I do, more than save the broken shell and wriggle my clumsy self out of there? I had removed Camilla's own eggs the day before—Camilla was only moderately annoyed. I was nervous about disposing of them, even though they were obviously Camilla's, but no harm was done. I cracked each one to be sure. Very frankly rotten eggs and nothing more.

In the evening of that day I thought of rats and weasels, as I should have done earlier. I prepared a box in the kitchen and brought the two in, the angel quiet in my closed hand. They are there now. I think they are comfortable.

Three days after hatching, the angel is the length of my forefinger, say three inches tall, with about the relative proportions of a six-year-old girl. Except for head, hands, and probably the soles of her feet, she is clothed in down the color of ivory; what can be seen of her skin is a glowing pink—I do mean glowing, like the inside of certain sea shells. Just above the small of her back are two stubs which I take to be infantile wings. They do not suggest an extra pair of specialized forelimbs. I think they are wholly differentiated organs; perhaps they will be like the wings on an insect. Somehow, I never thought of angels buzzing. Maybe she won't. I know very little about angels. At present the stubs are covered with some dull tissue, no doubt a protective sheath to be discarded when the membranes (if they are membranes) are ready to grow. Between the stubs is a not very prominent ridge—special musculature, I suppose. Otherwise her shape is quite human, even to a pair of minuscule mammalian buttons just visible under the down; how that can make sense in an egg-laying organism is beyond my comprehension. (Just for the record, so is a Corot landscape; so is Schubert's *Unfinished;* so is the flight of a hummingbird, or the other-world of frost on a window pane.) The down on her head has grown visibly in three days and is of different quality from the body down—later it may resemble human hair, as a diamond resembles a chunk of granite. . . .

A curious thing has happened. I went to Camilla's box

after writing that. Judy* was already lying in front of it, unexcited. The angel's head was out from under the feathers, and I thought—with more verbal distinctness than such thoughts commonly take, "So here I am, a naturalist of middle years and cold sober, observing a three-inch oviparous mammal with down and wings." The thing is—she giggled. Now, it might have been only amusement at my appearance, which to her must be enormously gross and comic. But another thought formed unspoken: "I am no longer lonely." And her face (hardly bigger than a dime) immediately changed from laughter to a brooding and friendly thoughtfulness.

Judy and Camilla are old friends. Judy seems untroubled by the angel. I have no worries about leaving them alone together. I must sleep.

June 3

I made no entry last night. The angel was talking to me, and when that was finished I drowsed off immediately on a cot that I have moved into the kitchen so as to be near them.

I had never been strongly impressed by the evidence for extrasensory perception. It is fortunate my mind was able to accept the novelty, since to the angel it is clearly a matter of course. Her tiny mouth is most expressive but moves only for that reason and for eating—not for speech. Probably she could speak to her own kind if she wished, but I dare say the sound would be outside the range of my hearing as well as my understanding.

Last night after I brought the cot in and was about to finish my puttering bachelor supper, she climbed to the edge of the box and pointed, first at herself and then at the top of the kitchen table. Afraid to let my vast hand take hold of her, I held it out flat and she sat in my palm. Camilla was inclined to fuss, but the angel looked over her shoulder and Camilla subsided, watchful but no longer alarmed.

The table top is porcelain, and the angel shivered. I folded a towel and spread a silk handkerchief on top of that; the angel sat on this arrangement with apparent comfort,

* Dr. Bannerman's dog, mentioned often earlier in the journal. A nine-year-old English setter. According to an entry of May 15, 1951, she was then beginning to go blind.   —BLAINE.

near my face. I was not even bewildered. Possibly she had already instructed me to blank out my mind. At any rate, I did so, without conscious effort to that end.

She reached me first with visual imagery. How can I make it plain that this had nothing in common with my sleeping dreams? There was no weight of symbolism from my littered past; no discoverable connection with any of yesterday's commonplace; indeed, no actual involvement of my personality at all. I saw. I was moving vision, though without eyes or other flesh. And while my mind saw, it also knew where my flesh was, slumped at the kitchen table. If anyone had entered the kitchen, if there had been a noise of alarm out in the henhouse, I should have known it.

There was a valley such as I have not seen (and never will) on Earth. I have seen many beautiful places on this planet—some of them were even tranquil. Once I took a slow steamer to New Zealand and had the Pacific as a plaything for many days. I can hardly say how I knew this was not Earth. The grass of the valley was an earthly green; a river below me was a blue-and-silver thread under familiar-seeming sunlight; there were trees much like pine and maple, and maybe that is what they were. But it was not Earth. I was aware of mountains heaped to strange heights on either side of the valley—snow, rose, amber, gold. Perhaps the amber tint was unlike any mountain color I have noticed in this world at midday.

Or I may have known it was not Earth simply because her mind—dwelling within some unimaginable brain smaller than the tip of my little finger—told me so.

I watched two inhabitants of that world come flying, to rest in the field of sunny grass where my bodiless vision had brought me. Adult forms, such as my angel would surely be when she had her growth, except that both of these were male and one of them was dark-skinned. The latter was also old, with a thousand-wrinkled face, knowing and full of tranquility; the other was flushed and lively with youth; both were beautiful. The down of the brown-skinned old one was reddish-tawny; the other's was ivory with hints of orange. Their wings were true membranes, with more variety of subtle iridescence than I have seen even in the wings of a dragonfly; I could not say that any color was dominant, for each motion brought a ripple of change. These two sat at their ease on the grass. I realized that they were talking to each other, though their lips did not move in speech more than once or twice. They would nod, smile, now and then illustrate something with twinkling hands.

A huge rabbit lolloped past them. I knew (thanks to my own angel's efforts, I suppose) that this animal was of the same size of our common wild ones. Later, a blue-green snake three times the size of the angels came flowing through the grass; the old one reached out to stroke its head carelessly, and I think he did it without interrupting whatever he was saying.

Another creature came, in leisured leaps. He was monstrous, yet I felt no alarm in the angels or in myself. Imagine a being built somewhat like a kangaroo up to the head, about eight feet tall, and katydid-green. Really, the thick balancing tail and enormous legs were the only kangaroo-like features about him: the body above the massive thighs was not dwarfed but thick and square; the arms and hands were quite humanoid: the head was round, manlike except for its face—there was only a single nostril and his mouth was set in the vertical; the eyes were large and mild. I received an impression of high intelligence and natural gentleness. In one of his manlike hands two tools so familiar and ordinary that I knew my body by the kitchen table had laughed in startled recognition. But, after all, a garden spade and rake are basic. Once invented—I expect we did it ourselves in the Neolithic Age—there is little reason why they should change much down the millennia.

This farmer halted by the angels, and the three conversed a while. The big head nodded agreeably. I believe the young angel made a joke; certainly the convulsions in the huge green face made me think of laughter. Then this amiable monster turned up the grass in a patch a few yards square, broke the sod and raked the surface smooth, just as any competent gardener might do—except that he moved with the relaxed smoothness of a being whose strength far exceeds the requirements of his task. . . .

I was back in my kitchen with everyday eyes. My angel was exploring the table. I had a loaf of bread there and a dish of strawberries and cream. She was trying a bread crumb; seemed to like it fairly well. I offered the strawberries; she broke off one of the seeds and nibbled it but didn't care so much for the pulp. I held up the great spoon with sugary cream; she steadied it with both hands to try some. I think she liked it. It had been most stupid of me not to realize that she would be hungry. I brought wine from the cupboard; she watched inquiringly, so I put a couple of drops on the handle of a spoon. This really pleased her: she chuckled and patted her tiny stomach, though I'm afraid it wasn't awfully good sherry. I brought some crumbs of cake, but she indicated that she was full, came close to my face, and motioned me to lower my head.

She reached towards me until she could press both hands against my forehead—I felt it only enough to know her hands were there—and she stood so a long time, trying to tell me something.

It was difficult. Pictures come through with relative ease, but now she was transmitting an abstraction of a complex kind: my clumsy brain really suffered in the effort to receive. Something did come across. I have only the crudest way of passing it on. Imagine an equilateral triangle; place the following words one at each corner—"recruiting," "collecting," "saving." The meaning she wanted to convey ought to be near the center of the triangle.

I had also the sense that her message provided a partial explanation of her errand in this lovable and damnable world.

She looked weary when she stood away from me. I put out my palm and she climbed into it, to be carried back to the nest.

She did not talk to me tonight, nor eat, but she gave a reason, coming out from Camilla's feathers long enough to turn her back and show me the wing stubs. The protective sheaths have dropped off; the wings are rapidly growing. They are probably damp and weak. She was quite tired and went back into the warm darkness almost at once.

Camilla must be exhausted, too. I don't think she has been off the nest more than twice since I brought them into the house.

June 4

Today she can fly.
I learned it in the afternoon, when I was fiddling about in

the garden and Judy was loafing in the sunshine she loves. Something apart from sight and sound called me to hurry back to the house. I saw my angel through the screen door before I opened it. One of her feet had caught in a hideous loop of loose wire at a break in the mesh. Her first tug of alarm must have tightened the loop so that her hands were not strong enough to force it open.

Fortunately I was able to cut the wire with a pair of shears before I lost my head; then she could free her foot without injury. Camilla had been frantic, rushing around fluffed up, but—here's an odd thing—perfectly silent. None of the recognized chicken noises of dismay: if an ordinary chick had been in trouble she would have raised the roof.

The angel flew to me and hovered, pressing her hands on my forehead. The message was clear at once: "No harm done." She flew down to tell Camilla the same thing.

Yes, in the same way. I saw Camilla standing near my feet with her neck out and head low, and the angel put a hand on either side of her scraggy comb. Camilla relaxed, clucked in the normal way, and spread her wings for a shelter. The angel went under it, but only to oblige Camilla, I think—at least, she stuck her head through the wing feathers and winked.

She must have seen something else, then, for she came out and flew back to me and touched a finger to my cheek, looked at the finger, saw it was wet, put it in her mouth, made a face and laughed at me.

We went outdoors into the sun (Camilla, too), and the angel gave me an exhibition of what flying ought to be. Not even Schubert can speak of joy as her first free flying did. At one moment she would be hanging in front of my eyes, radiant and delighted; the next instant she would be a dot of color against a cloud. Try to imagine something that would make a hummingbird seem a bit dull and sluggish.

They do hum. Softer than a hummingbird, louder than a dragonfly.

Something like the sound of hawk-moths—*Heinmaris thisbe,* for instance: the one I used to call Hummingbird Moth when I was a child.

I was frightened, naturally. Frightened first at what might happen to her, but that was unnecessary; I don't think she would be in danger from any savage animal except possibly Man. I saw a Cooper's hawk slant down the visible ray toward the swirl of color where she was dancing by herself; presently she was drawing iridescent rings around him; then, while he soared in smaller circles, I could not see her, but (maybe she felt my fright) she was again in front of me, pressing my forehead in the now familiar way. I knew she was amused and caught the idea that the hawk was a "lazy character." Not quite the way I'd describe *Accipiter Cooperi*, but it's all in the point of view. I believe she had been riding his back, no doubt with her speaking hands on his terrible head.

And later I was frightened by the thought that she might not want to return to me. Can I compete with sunlight and open sky? The passage of that terror through me brought her back swiftly, and her hands said with great clarity: "Don't ever be afraid of anything—it isn't necessary for you"

Once this afternoon I was saddened by the realization that old Judy can take little part in what goes on now. I can well remember Judy running like the wind. The angel must have heard this thought in me, for she stood a long time beside Judy's drowsy head, while Judy's tail thumped cheerfully on the warm grass. . . .

In the evening the angel made a heavy meal on two or three cake crumbs and another drop of sherry, and we had what was almost a sustained conversation. I will write it in that form this time, rather than grope for anything more exact. I asked her, "How far away is your home?"

"My home is here."

"Thank God!—but I meant, the place your people came from."

"Ten light-years."

"The images you showed me—that quiet valley—that is ten light-years away?"

"Yes. But that was my father talking to you, through me. He was grown when the journey began. He is two hundred and forty years old—our years, thirty-two days longer than yours."

Mainly I was conscious of a flood of relief: I had feared, on the basis of terrestrial biology, that her explosively rapid growth after hatching must foretell a brief life. But it's all right—she can outlive me, and by a few hundred years, at that. "Your father is here now, on this planet—shall I see him?"

She took her hands away—listening, I believe. The answer was: "No. He is sorry. He is ill and cannot live long. I am to see him in a few days, when I fly a little better. He taught me for twenty years after I was born."

"I don't understand. I thought—"

"Later, friend. My father is grateful for your kindness to me."

I don't know what I thought about that. I felt no faintest trace of condescension in the message. "And he was showing me things he had seen with his own eyes, ten light-years away?"

"Yes." Then she wanted me to rest a while; I am sure she knows what a huge effort it is for my primitive brain to function in this way. But before she ended the conversation by humming down to her nest she gave me this, and I received it with such clarity that I cannot be mistaken: "He says that only fifty million years ago it was a jungle there, just as Terra is now."

June 8

When I woke four days ago the angel was having breakfast, and little Camilla was dead. The angel watched me rub sleep out of my eyes, watched me discover Camilla, and then flew to me. I received this: "Does it make you unhappy?"

"I don't know exactly." You can get fond of a hen, especially a cantankerous and homely old one whose personality has a lot in common with your own.

"She was old. She wanted a flock of chicks, and I couldn't stay with her. So I—" Something obscure here: probably my mind was trying too hard to grasp it—" . . . so I saved her life." I could make nothing else out of it. She said "saved."

Camilla's death looked natural, except that I should have expected the death contractions to muss the straw, and that hadn't happened. Maybe the angel had arranged the old lady's body for decorum, though I don't see how her muscular strength would have been equal to it—Camilla weighed at least seven pounds.

As I was burying her at the edge of the garden and the

angel was humming over my head, I recalled a thing which, when it happened, I had dismissed as a dream. Merely a moonlight image of the angel standing in the nest box with her hands on Camilla's head, then pressing her mouth gently on Camilla's throat, just before the hen's head sank down out of my line of vision. Probably I actually waked and saw it happen. I am somehow unconcerned—even, as I think more about it, pleased. . . .

After the burial the angel's hands said, "Sit on the grass and we'll talk. . . . Question me. I'll tell you what I can. My father asks you to write it down."

So that is what we have been doing for the last four days, I have been going to school, a slow but willing pupil. Rather than enter anything in this journal (for in the evenings I was exhausted), I made notes as best I could. The angel has gone now to see her father and will not return until morning. I shall try to make a readable version of my notes.

Since she had invited questions, I began with something which had been bothering me, as a would-be naturalist, exceedingly. I couldn't see how creatures no larger than the adults I had observed could lay eggs as large as Camilla's. Nor could I understand why, if they were hatched in an almost adult condition and able to eat a varied diet, she had any use for that ridiculous, lovely, and apparently functional pair of breasts. When the angel grasped my difficulty she exploded with laughter—her kind, which buzzed her all over the garden and caused her to fluff my hair on the wing and pinch my ear lobe. She lit on a rhubarb leaf and gave a delectably naughty representation of herself as a hen laying an egg, including the cackle. She got me to bumbling helplessly—my kind of laughter—and it was some time before we could quiet down. Then she did her best to explain.

They are true mammals, and the young—not more than two or at most three in a lifetime averaging two hundred and fifty years—are delivered in very much the human way. The baby is nursed—human fashion—until his brain begins to respond a little to their unspoken language; that takes three to four weeks. Then he is placed in an altogether different medium. She could not describe that clearly, because there was very little in my educational storehouse to help me grasp it. It is some gaseous medium that arrests bodily growth for an almost indefinite period, while mental growth continues. It took them, she says, about seven thousand years to perfect this technique after they first hit on the idea: they are never in a hurry. The infant remains under this delicate and precise control for anywhere from fifteen to thirty years, the period depending not only on his mental vigor but also on the type of lifework he tentatively elects as soon as his brain is knowing enough to make a choice. During this period his mind is guided with unwavering patience by teachers who—

It seems those teachers know their business. This was peculiarly difficult for me to assimilate, although the fact came through clearly enough. In their world, the profession of teacher is more highly honored than any other—can such a thing be possible?—and so difficult to enter that only the strongest minds dare attempt it. (I had to rest a while after absorbing that.) An aspirant must spend fifty years (not including the period of infantile education) in merely getting ready to begin, and the acquisition of factual knowledge, while not understressed, takes only a small portion of those fifty years. Then—if he's good enough—he can take a small part in the elementary instruction of a few babies, and if he does well on that basis for another thirty or forty years, he is considered a fair beginner. . . . Once upon a time I lurched around stuffy classrooms trying to insert a few predigested facts (I wonder how many of them *were* facts?) into the minds of bored and preoccupied adolescents, some of whom may have liked me moderately well. I was even able to shake hands and be nice while their terribly well-meaning parents explained to me how they ought to be educated. So much of our human effort goes down the drain of futility, I sometimes wonder how we ever got as far as the Bronze Age. Somehow we did, though, and a short way beyond.

After that preliminary stage of an angel's education is finished, the baby is transferred to more ordinary surroundings, and his bodily growth completes itself in a very short time. Wings grow abruptly (as I have seen), and he reaches a maximum height of six inches (our measure). Only then does he enter on that lifetime of two hundred and fifty years, for not until then does his body begin to age. My angel has been a living personality for many years but will not celebrate her first birthday for almost a year. I like to think of that.

At about the same time that they learned the principles of interplanetary travel (approximately twelve million years ago) these people also learned how, by use of a slightly different method, growth could be arrested at any point short of full maturity. At first the knowledge served no purpose except in the control of illnesses which still occasionally struck them at that time. But when the long periods of time required for space travel were considered, the advantages became obvious.

So it happens that my angel was born ten light-years away. She was trained by her father and many others in the wisdom of seventy million years (that, she tells me, is the approximate sum of their *recorded* history), and then she was safely sealed and cherished in what my superamoebic brain regarded as a blue egg. Education did not proceed at that time; her mind went to sleep with the rest of her. When Camilla's temperature made her wake and grow again, she remembered what to do with the little horny bumps provided for her elbows. And came out—into this planet, God help her.

I wondered why her father should have chosen any combination so unreliable as an old hen and a human being. Surely he must have had plenty of excellent ways to bring the shell to the right temperature. Her answer should have satisfied me immensely, but I am still compelled to wonder about it. "Camilla was a nice hen, and my father studied your mind while you were asleep. It was a bad landing, and much was broken—no such landing was ever made before after so long a journey: forty years. Only four other grownups could come with my father. Three of them died en route and he is very ill. And there were nine other children to care for."

Yes, I knew she'd said that an angel thought I was good enough to be trusted with his daughter. If it upsets me, all I need do is look at her and then in the mirror. As for the explanation, I can only conclude there must be more that I am not ready to understand. I was worried about those nine others, but she assured me they were all well, and I sensed that I ought not to ask more about them at present. . . .

Their planet, she says, is closely similar to this. A trifle larger, moving in a somewhat longer orbit around a sun like ours. Two gleaming moons, smaller than ours—their orbits are such that two-moon nights come rarely. They are magic, and she will ask her father to show me one, if he can. Their year is thirty-two days longer than ours; because of a slower rotation, their day has twenty-six of our hours. Their atmosphere is mainly nitrogen and oxygen in the proportions familiar to us; slightly richer in some of the rare gases. The climate is now what we should call tropical and subtropical, but they have known glacial rigors like those in our world's past. There are only two great continental land masses, and many thousands of large islands.

Their total population is only five billion. . . .

Most of the forms of life we know have parallels there—some quite exact parallels: rabbits, deer, mice, cats. The cats have been bred to an even higher intelligence than they possess on our Earth; it is possible, she says, to have a good deal of intellectual intercourse with their cats, who learned several million years ago that when they kill, it must be done with lightning precision and without torture. The cats had some difficulty grasping the possibility of pain in other organisms, but once that educational hurdle was passed, development was easy. Nowadays many of the cats are popular storytellers; about forty million years ago they were still occasionally needed as a special police force, and served the angels with real heroism.

It seems my angel wants to become a student of animal life here on Earth. I, a teacher!—but bless her heart for the notion, anyhow. We sat and traded animals for a couple of hours last night. I found it restful, after the mental struggle to grasp more difficult matters. Judy was something new to her. They have several luscious monsters on that planet but, in her view, so have we. She told me of a blue sea snake fifty feet long (relatively harmless) that bellows cow-like and comes into the tidal marshes to lay black eggs; so I gave her a whale. She offered a bat-winged, day-flying ball of mammalian fluff as big as my head and weighing under an ounce; I matched her with a marmoset. She tried me with a small-sized pink brontosaur (very rare), but I was ready with the duck-billed platypus, and that caused us to exchange some pretty smart remarks about mammalian eggs; she bounced. All trivial in a way; also, the happiest evening in my fifty-three tangled years of life.

She was a trifle hesitant to explain these kangaroo-like people, until she was sure I really wanted to know. It seems they are about the nearest parallel to human life on that planet; not a near parallel, of course, as she was careful to explain. Agreeable and always friendly souls (though they weren't always so, I'm sure) and of a somewhat more alert intelligence than we possess. Manual workers, mainly, because they prefer it nowadays, but some of them are excellent mathematicians. The first practical spaceship was invented by a group of them, with some assistance. . . .

Names offer difficulties. Because of the nature of the angelic language, they have scant use for them except for the purpose of written record, and writing naturally plays little part in their daily lives—no occasion to write a letter when a thousand miles is no obstacle to the speech of your mind. An angel's formal name is about as important to him as, say, my Social Security number is to me. She has not told me hers, because the phonetics on which their written language is based have no parallel in my mind. As we would speak a friend's name, an angel will project the friend's image to his friend's receiving mind. More pleasant and more intimate, I think—although it was a shock to me at first to glimpse my own ugly mug in my mind's eye. Stories are occasionally written, if there is something in them that should be preserved precisely as it was in the first telling; but in their world the true storyteller has a more important place than the printer—he offers one of the best of their quieter pleasures: a good one can hold his audience for a week and never tire them.

"What is this 'angel' in your mind when you think of me?"

"A being men have imagined for centuries, when they thought of themselves as they might like to be and not as they are."

I did not try too painfully hard to learn much about the principles of space travel. The most my brain could take in of her explanation was something like: "Rocket—then phototropism." Now, that makes scant sense. So far as I know, phototropism—movement toward light—is an organic phenomenon. One thinks of it as a response of protoplasm, in some plants and animal organisms (most of them simple), to the stimulus of light; certainly not as a force capable of moving inorganic matter. I think that whatever may be the principle she was describing, this word "phototropism" was merely the nearest thing to it in my reservior of language. Not even the angels can create understanding out of blank ignorance. At least I have learned not to set neat limits to the possible.

(There was a time when I did, though. I can see myself, not so many years back, like a homunculus squatting at the foot of Mt. McKinley, throwing together two handfuls of mud and shouting, "Look at the big mountain *I* made!")

And if I did know the physical principles which brought them here, and could write them in terms accessible to technicians resembling myself, I would not do it.

Here is a thing I am afraid no reader of this journal will believe: These people, as I have written, learned their method of space travel some twelve million years ago. But this is the first time they have ever used it to convey them to another planet. The heavens are rich in worlds, she tells me; on many of them there is life, often on very primitive levels. No external force prevented her people from going forth, colonizing, conquering, as far as they pleased. They could have populated a Galaxy. They did not, and for this reason: they believed they were not ready. More precisely: *Not good enough.*

Only some fifty million years ago, by her account, did they learn (as we may learn eventually) that intelligence without goodness is worse than high explosive in the hands of a baboon. For beings advanced beyond the level of Pithecanthropus, intelligence is a cheap commodity—not too hard to develop, hellishly easy to use for unconsidered ends. Whereas goodness is not to be achieved without unending effort of the hardest kind, within the self, whether the self be man or angel.

It is clear even to me that the conquest of evil is only one step, not the most important. For goodness, so she tried to tell me, is an altogether positive quality; the part of living nature that swarms with such monstrosities as cruelty, meanness, bitterness, greed, is not to be filled by a vacuum when these horrors are eliminated. When you clear away a poisonous gas, you try to fill the whole room with clean air. Kindness, for only one example: one who can define kindness only as the absence of cruelty has surely not begun to understand the nature of either.

They do not aim at perfection, these angels: only at the attainable. . . . That time fifty million years ago was evidently one of great suffering and confusion. War and all its attendant plagues. They passed through many centuries while advances in technology merely worsened their condition and increased the peril of self-annihilation. They came through that, in time. War was at length so far outgrown that its recurrence was impossible, and the development of wholly rational beings could begin. Then they were ready to start growing up, through millennia of self-searching, self-discipline, seeking to derive the simple from the complex, discovering how to use knowledge and not be used by it. Even then, of course, they slipped back often enough. There were what she refers to as "eras of fatigue." In their dimmer past, they had had many dark ages, lost civilizations, hopeful beginnings ending in dust. Earlier still, they had come out of the slime, as we did.

But their period of deepest uncertainty and sternest self-appraisal did not come until twelve million years ago, when they knew a Universe could be theirs for the taking and knew they were not yet good enough.

They are in no more hurry than the stars. She tried to convey something tentatively, at this point, which was really beyond both of us. It had to do with time (not as I understand time) being perhaps the most essential attribute of God (not as I was ever able to understand that word). Seeing my mental exhaustion, she gave up the effort and later told me that the conception was extremely difficult for her, too—not only, I gathered, because of her youth and relative ignorance. There was also a hint that her father might not have wished her to bring my brain up to a hurdle like that one. . . .

Of course, they explored. Their little spaceships were roaming the ether before there was anything like Man on this earth—roaming and listening, observing, recording; never entering nor taking part in the life of any home but their own. For five million years they even forbade themselves to go beyond their own Solar System, though it would have been easy to do so. And in the following seven million years, although they traveled to incredible distances, the same stern restraint was in force. It was altogether unrelated to what we should call fear—that, I think, is as extinct in them as hate. There was so much to do at home!—I wish I could imagine it. They mapped the heavens and played in their own sunlight.

Naturally, I cannot tell you what goodness is. I know only, moderately well, what it seems to mean to us human beings. It appears that the best of us can, with enormous difficulty, achieve a manner of life in which goodness is reasonably dominant, by a not too precarious balance, for the greater part of the time. Often, wise men have indicated they hope for nothing better than that in our present condition. We are, in other words, a fraction alive; the rest is in the dark. Dante was a bitter masochist, Beethoven a frantic and miserable snob, Shakespeare wrote potboilers. And Christ said, "My Father, if it be possible, let this cup pass from me."

But give us fifty million years—I am no pessimist. After all, I've watched one-celled organisms on the slide and listened to Brahms' Fourth. Night before last I said to the angel, "In spite of everything, you and I are kindred."

She granted me agreement.

June 9

She was lying on my pillow this morning so that I could see her when I waked.

Her father has died, and she was with him when it happened. There was again that thought-impression that I could interpret only to mean that his life had been "saved." I was still sleep-bound when my mind asked, "What will you do?"

"Stay with you, if you wish it, for the rest of your life." Now, the last part of the message was clouded, but I am familiar with that—it seems to mean there is some further element that eludes me. I could not be mistaken about the part I did receive. It gives me amazing speculations. After all, I am only fifty-three; I might live for another thirty or forty years. . . .

She was preoccupied this morning, but whatever she felt

about her father's death that might be paralleled by sadness in a human being was hidden from me. She did say her father was sorry he had not been able to show me a two-moon night.

One adult, then, remains in this world. Except to say that he is two hundred years old and full of knowledge, and that he endured the long journey without serious ill effects, she has told me little about him. And there are ten children, including herself.

Something was sparkling at her throat. When she was aware of my interest in it she took it off, and I fetched a magnifying glass. A necklace; under the glass, much like our finest human workmanship, if your imagination can reduce it to the proper scale. The stones appeared similar to the jewels we know: diamonds, sapphires, rubies, emeralds, the diamonds snapping out every color under heaven; but there were two or three very dark-purple stones unlike anything I know—not amethysts, I am sure. The necklace was strung on something more slender than cobweb, and the design of the joining clasp was too delicate for my glass to help me. The necklace had been her mother's, she told me; as she put it back around her throat I thought I saw the same shy pride that any human girl might feel in displaying a new pretty.

She wanted to show me other things she had brought, and flew to the table where she had left a sort of satchel an inch and a half long—quite a load for her to fly with, but the translucent substance is so light that when she rested the satchel on my finger I scarcely felt it. She arranged a few articles happily for my inspection, and I put the glass to work again. One was a jeweled comb; she ran it through the down on her chest and legs to show me its use. There was a set of tools too small for the glass to interpret; I learned later they were a sewing kit. A book, and some writing instrument much like a metal pencil: imagine a book and pencil that could be used comfortably by hands hardly bigger than the paws of a mouse—that is the best I can do. The book, I understand, is a blank record for her use as needed.

And finally, when I was fully awake and dressed and we had finished breakfast, she reached in the bottom of the satchel for a parcel (heavy for her) and made me understand it was a gift for me. "My father made it for you, but I put in the stone myself, last night." She unwrapped it. A ring, precisely the size for my little finger.

I broke down, rather. She understood that, and sat on my shoulder petting my ear lobe till I had command of myself.

I have no idea what the jewel is. It shifts with the light from purple to jade-green to amber. The metal resembles platinum in appearance except for a tinge of rose at certain angles of light. . . . When I stare into the stone, I think I see—never mind that now. I am not ready to write it down, and perhaps never will be; anyway, I must be sure.

We improved our housekeeping later in the morning. I showed her over the house. It isn't much—Cape Codder, two rooms up and two down. Every corner interested her, and when she found a shoe box in the bedroom closet, she asked for it. At her direction, I have arranged it on a chest near my bed and near the window, which will be always open; she says the mosquitoes will not bother me, and I don't doubt her. I unearthed a white silk scarf for the bottom of the box; after asking my permission (as if I could want to refuse her anything!) she got her sewing kit and snipped off a piece of the scarf several inches square, folded it on itself several times, and sewed it into a narrow pillow an inch long. So now she had a proper bed and a room of her own. I wish I had something less coarse than silk, but she insists it's nice.

We have not talked very much today. In the afternoon she flew out for an hour's play in the cloud country; when she returned she let me know that she needed a long sleep. She is still sleeping, I think; I am writing this downstairs, fearing the light might disturb her.

Is it possible I can have thirty or forty years in her company? I wonder how teachable my mind still is. I seem to be able to assimilate new facts as well as I ever could; this ungainly carcass should be durable, with reasonable care. Of course, facts without a synthetic imagination are no better than scattered bricks; but perhaps my imagination—

I don't know.

Judy wants out. I shall turn in when she comes back. I wonder if poor Judy's life could be—the word is certainly "saved." I must ask.

Last night when I stopped writing I did go to bed but I was restless, refusing sleep. At some time in the small hours —there was light from a single room—she flew over to me. The tensions dissolved like an illness, and my mind was able to respond with a certain calm.

I made plain (what I am sure she already knew) that I would never willingly part company with her, and then she gave me to understand that there are two alternatives for the remainder of my life. The choice, she says, is altogether mine, and I must take time to be sure of my decision.

I can live out my natural span, whatever it proves to be, and she will not leave me for long at any time. She will be there to counsel, teach, help me in anything good I care to undertake. She says she would enjoy this; for some reason she is, as we'd say in our language, fond of me. We'd have fun.

Lord, the books I could write! I fumble for words now, in the usual human way: whatever I put on paper is a miserable fraction of the potential; the words themselves are rarely the right ones. But under her guidance—

I could take a fair part in shaking the world. With words alone. I could preach to my own people. Before long, I would be heard.

I could study and explore. What small nibblings we have made at the sum of available knowledge! Suppose I brought in one leaf from outdoors, or one common little bug—in a few hours of studying it with her I'd know more of my own specialty than a flood of the best textbooks could tell me.

She has also let me know that when she and those who came with her have learned a little more about the human picture, it should be possible to improve my health greatly, and probably my life expectancy. I don't imagine my back could ever straighten, but she thinks the pain might be cleared away, possibly without drugs. I could have a clearer mind, in a body that would neither fail nor torment me.

Then there is the other alternative.

It seems they have developed a technique by means of which any unresisting living subject whose brain is capable of memory at all can experience a total recall. It is a by-product, I understand, of their silent speech, and a very recent one. They have practiced it for only a few thousand years, and since their own understanding of the phenomenon is very incomplete, they classify it among their experimental techniques. In a general way, it may somewhat resemble that reliving of the past that psychoanalysis can sometimes bring about in a limited way for therapeutic purposes; but you must imagine that sort of thing tremendously magnified and clarified, capable of including every detail that has ever registered on the subject's brain; and the end result is very different. The purpose is not therapeutic, as we would understand it: quite the opposite. The end result is death. Whatever is recalled by this process is transmitted to the receiving mind, which can retain it and record any or all of it if such a record is desired; but to the subject who recalls it, it is a flowing away, without return. Thus it is not a true "remembering" but a giving. The mind is swept clear, naked of all its past, and, along with memory, life withdraws also. Very quietly. At the end, I suppose it must be like standing without resistance in the engulfment of a flood time, until finally the waters close over.

That, it seems, is how Camilla's life was "saved." Now, when I finally grasped that, I laughed, and the angel of course caught my joke. I was thinking about my neighbor Steele, who boarded the old lady for me in his henhouse for a couple of winters. Somewhere safe in the angelic records there must be a hen's-eye image of the patch in the seat of Steele's pants. Well—good. And, naturally, Camilla's view of me, too: not too unkind, I hope—she couldn't help the expression on her rigid little face, and I don't believe it ever meant anything.

At the other end of the scale is the saved life of my angel's father. Recall can be a long process, she says, depending on the intricacy and richness of the mind recalling; and in all but the last stages it can be halted at will. Her father's recall was begun when they were still far out in space and he knew that he could not long survive the journey. When that journey ended, the recall had progressed so far that very little actual memory remained to him of his life on that other planet. He had what must be called a "deductive memory"; from the material of the years not yet given away, he could reconstruct what must have been; and I assume the other adult who survived the passage must have been able to shelter him from errors that loss of memory might involve. This, I infer, is why he could not show me a two-moon night. I forgot to ask her whether the images he did send me were from actual or deductive memory. Deductive, I think, for there was a certain dimness about them not present when my angel gives me a picture of something seen with her own eyes.

Jade-green eyes, by the way—were you wondering?

In the same fashion, my own life could be saved. Every aspect of existence that I even touched, that ever touched me, could be transmitted to some perfect record. The nature of the written record is beyond me, but I have no doubt of its relative perfection. Nothing important, good or bad, would be lost. And they need a knowledge of humanity, if they are to carry out whatever it is they have in mind.

It would be difficult, she tells me, and sometimes painful. Most of the effort would be hers, but some of it would have to be mine. In her period of infantile education, she elected what we should call zoology as her lifework; for that reason she was given intensive theoretical training in this technique. Right now, I guess she knows more than anyone else on this planet not only about what makes a hen tick but about how it feels to be a hen. Though a beginner, she is in all essentials already an expert. She can help me, she thinks (if I choose this alternative)—at any rate, ease me over the toughest spots, soothe away resistance, keep my courage from too much flagging.

For it seems that this process of recall is painful to an advanced intellect (she, without condescension, calls us very advanced) because, while all pretense and self-delusion are stripped away, there remains conscience, still functioning by whatever standards of good and bad the individual has developed in his lifetime. Our present knowledge of our own motives is such a pathetically small beginning!— hardly stronger than an infant's first effort to focus his eyes. I am merely wondering how much of my life (if I choose this way) will seem to me altogether hideous. Certainly plenty of the "good deeds" that I still cherish in memory like so many well-behaved cherubs will turn up with the leering aspect of greed or petty vanity or worse.

Not that I am a bad man, in any reasonable sense of the

term; not a bit of it. I respect myself; no occasion to grovel and beat my chest; I'm not ashamed to stand comparison with any other fair sample of the species. But there you are: I *am* human, and under the aspect of eternity so far, plus this afternoon's newspaper, that is a rather serious thing.

Without real knowledge, I think of this total recall as something like a passage down a corridor of myriad images —now dark, now brilliant; now pleasant, now horrible— guided by no certainty except an awareness of the open blind door at the end of it. It could have its pleasing moments and its consolations. I don't see how it could ever approximate the delight and satisfaction of living a few more years in this world with the angel lighting on my shoulder when she wishes, and talking to me.

I had to ask her of how great value such a record would be to them. Very great. Obvious enough—they can be of little use to us, by their standards, until they understand us; and they came here to be of use to us as well as to themselves. And understanding us, to them, means knowing us inside out with a completeness such as our most dedicated and laborious scholars could never imagine. I remember those twelve million years: they will not touch us until they are certain no harm will come of it. On our tortured planet, however, there is a time factor. They know that well enough, of course. . . . Recall cannot begin unless the subject is willing or unresisting; to them, that has to mean willing, for any being with intellect enough to make a considered choice. Now, I wonder how many they could find who would be honestly willing to make that uneasy journey into death, for no reward except an assurance that they were serving their own kind and the angels?

More to the point, I wonder if I would be able to achieve such willingness myself, even with her help?

When this had been explained to me, she urged me again to make no hasty decision. And she pointed out to me what my thoughts were already groping at—why not both alternatives, within a reasonable limit of time? Why couldn't I have ten or fifteen years or more with her and then undertake the total recall—perhaps not until my physical powers had started toward senility? I thought that over.

This morning I had almost decided to choose that most

welcome and comforting solution. Then the mailman brought my daily paper. Not that I needed any such reminder.

In the afternoon I asked her if she knew whether, in the present state of human technology, it would be possible for our folly to actually destroy this planet. She did not know, for certain. Three of the other children have gone away to different parts of the world, to learn what they can about that. But she had to tell me that such a thing has happened before, elsewhere in the heavens. I guess I won't write a letter to the papers advancing an explanation for the occasional appearance of a nova among the stars. Doubtless others have hit on the same hypothesis without the aid of angels.

And that is not all I must consider. I could die by accident or sudden disease before I had begun to give my life.

Only now, at this very late moment, rubbing my sweaty forehead and gazing into the lights of that wonderful ring, have I been able to put together some obvious facts in the required synthesis.

I don't know, of course, what forms their assistance to us will take. I suspect human beings won't see or hear much of the angels for a long time to come. Now and then disastrous decisions may be altered, and those who believe themselves wholly responsible won't quite know why their minds worked that way. Here and there, maybe an influential mind will be rather strangely nudged into a better course. Something like that. There may be sudden new discoveries and inventions of kinds that will tend to neutralize the menace of our nastiest playthings. But whatever the angels decide to do, the record and analysis of my not too atypical life will be an aid: it could even be the small weight deciding the balance between triumph and failure. That is fact one.

Two: my angel and her brothers and sisters, for all their amazing level of advancement, are of perishable protoplasm, even as I am. Therefore, if this ball of earth becomes a ball of flame, they also will be destroyed. Even if they have the means to use their spaceship again or to build another, it might easily happen that they would not learn their danger in time to escape. And for all I know, this could be tomorrow. Or tonight.

So there can no longer be any doubt as to my choice, and I will tell her when she wakes.

Tonight* there is no recall—I am to rest a while. I see it
is almost a month since I last wrote in this journal. My total
recall began three weeks ago, and I have already been able to
give away the first twenty-eight years of my life.

Since I no longer require normal sleep, the recall begins at
night, as soon as the lights begin to go out over there in the
village and there is little danger of interruption. Daytimes, I
putter about in my usual fashion. I have sold Steele my hens,
and Judy's life was saved a week ago; that practically winds
up my affairs, except that I want to write a codicil to my will. I
might as well do that now, right here in this journal, instead
of bothering my lawyer. It should be legal.

> TO WHOM IT MAY CONCERN: I hereby be-
> queath to my friend Lester Morse, M.D., of Au-
> gusta, Maine, the ring which will be found at my
> death on the fifth finger of my left hand; and I
> would urge Dr. Morse to retain this ring in his pri-
> vate possession at all times, and to make provision
> for its disposal, in the event of his own death, to
> some person in whose character he places the ut-
> most faith.
>
> (Signed) David Bannerman†

Tonight she has gone away for a while, and I am to
rest and do as I please until she returns. I shall spend the
time filling in some blanks in this record, but I am afraid
it will be a spotty job, unsatisfactory to any readers who
are subject to the blessed old itch for facts. Mainly because
there is so much I no longer care about. It is troublesome
to try to decide what things would be considered important
by interested strangers.

Except for the lack of any desire for sleep, and a bodily

---

* At this point Dr. Bannerman's handwriting alters curiously.
From here on he used a soft pencil instead of a pen, and the
script shows signs of haste. In spite of this, however, it is actually
much clearer, steadier, and easier to read than the earlier
entries in his normal hand.   —BLAINE.

† In spite of superficial changes in the handwriting, this signature
has been certified genuine by an expert graphologist.—BLAINE.

weariness that is not at all unpleasant, I notice no physical effects thus far. I have no faintest recollection of anything that happened earlier than my twenty-eighth birthday. My deductive memory seems rather efficient, and I am sure I could reconstruct most of the story if it were worth the bother: this afternoon I grubbed around among some old letters of that period, but they weren't very interesting. My knowledge of English is unaffected; I can still read scientific German and some French, because I had occasion to use those languages fairly often after I was twenty-eight. The scraps of Latin dating from high school are quite gone. So are algebra and all but the simplest propositions of high-school geometry: I never needed 'em. I can remember thinking of my mother after twenty-eight, but do not know whether the image this provides really resembles her; my father died when I was thirty-one, so I remember him as a sick old man. I believe I had a younger brother, but he must have died in childhood.*

Judy's passing was tranquil—pleasant for her, I think. It took the better part of a day. We went out to an abandoned field I know, and she lay in the sunshine with the angel sitting by her, while I dug a grave and then rambled off after wild raspberries. Toward evening the angel came and told me it was finished. And most interesting, she said. I don't see how there can have been anything distressing about it for Judy; after all, what hurts us worst is to have our favorite self-deceptions stripped away.

As the angel has explained it to me, her people, their oats, those kangaroo-folk, Man, and just possibly the cats on our planet (she hasn't met them yet) are the only animals she knows who are introspective enough to develop self-delusion and related pretenses. I suggested she might find something of the sort, at least in rudimentary form, among some of the other primates. She was immensely interested and wanted to learn everything I could tell her about monkeys and apes. It seems that long ago on the other planet there used to be clumsy, winged creatures resembling the angels to about the degree that the large anthropoids resemble

* Dr. Bannerman's mother died in 1918 of influenza. His brother (three years older, not younger) died of pneumonia, 1906.
                                                        —BLAINE.

us. They became extinct some forty million years ago, in spite of enlightened efforts to keep their kind alive. Their birth rate became insufficient for replacement, as if some necessary spark had simply flickered out; almost as if nature, or whatever name you prefer for the unknown, had with gentle finality written them off. . . .

I have not found the recall painful, at least not in retrospect. There must have been sharp moments, mercifully forgotten, along with their causes, as if the process had gone on under anesthesia. Certainly there were plenty of incidents in my first twenty-eight years that I should not care to offer to the understanding of any but the angels. Quite often I must have been mean, selfish, base in any number of ways, if only to judge by the record since twenty-eight. Those old letters touch on a few of these things. To me, they now matter only as material for a record which is safely out of my hands.

However, to any persons I may have harmed, I wish to say this: you were hurt by aspects of my humanity which may not, in a few million years, be quite so common among us all. Against these darker elements I struggled, in my human fashion, as you do yourselves. The effort is not wasted.

It was a week after I told the angel my decision before she was prepared to start the recall. During that week she searched my present mind more closely than I should have imagined was possible: she had to be sure. During that week of hard questions I dare say she learned more about my kind than has ever gone on record even in a physician's office; I hope she did. To any psychiatrist who might question that, I offer a naturalist's suggestion: it is easy to imagine, after some laborious time, that we have noticed everything a given patch of ground can show us; but alter the viewpoint only a little—dig down a foot with a spade, say, or climb a tree branch and look downward—it's a whole new world.

When the angel was not exploring me in this fashion, she took pains to make me glimpse the satisfactions and million rewarding experiences I might have if I chose the other way. I see how necessary that was; at the time it seemed almost cruel. She had to do it, for my own sake, and I am glad that

I was somehow able to stand fast to my original choice. So was she, in the end; she has even said she loves me for it. What that troubling word means to her is not within my mind: I am satisfied to take it in the human sense.

Some evening during that week—I think it was June 12—Lester dropped around for sherry and chess. Hadn't seen him in quite a while, and haven't since. There is a moderate polio scare this summer, and it keeps him on the jump. The angel retired behind some books on an upper shelf—I'm afraid it was dusty—and had fun with our chess. She had a fair view of your bald spot, Lester; later she remarked that she liked your looks, and can't you do something about that weight? She suggested an odd expedient, which I believe has occurred to your medical self from time to time—eating less.

Maybe she shouldn't have done what she did with those chess games. Nothing more than my usual blundering happened until after my first ten moves; by that time I suppose she had absorbed the principles and she took over, slightly. I was not fully aware of it until I saw Lester looking like a boiled duck: I had imagined my astonishing moves were the result of my own damn cleverness.

Seriously, Lester, think back to that evening. You've played in stiff amateur tournaments; you know your own abilities and you know mine. Ask yourself whether I could have done anything like that without help. I tell you again, I didn't study the game in the interval when you weren't there. I've never had a chess book in the library, and if I had, no amount of study would take me into your class. Haven't that sort of mentality—just your humble sparring partner, and I've enjoyed it on that basis, as you might enjoy watching a prima-donna surgeon pull off some miracle you wouldn't dream of attempting yourself. Even if your game had been way below par that evening (I don't think it was), I could never have pinned your ears back three times running, without help. That evening you were a long way out of *your* class, that's all.

I couldn't tell you anything about it at the time—she was clear on that point—so I could only bumble and preen myself and leave you mystified. But she wants me to write anything I choose in this journal, and somehow, Lester, I think you may find the next few decades pretty interesting. You're still young—some ten years younger than I. I think you'll see many things that I do wish I myself might see come to pass—or I would so wish if I were not convinced that my choice was the right one.

Most of those new events will not be spectacular, I'd guess. Many of the turns to a better way will hardly be recognized at the time for what they are, by you or anyone else. Obviously, our nature being what it is, we shall not jump into heaven overnight. To hope for that would be as absurd as it is to imagine that any formula, ideology, theory of social pattern, can bring us into Utopia. As I see it, Lester—and I think your consulting room would have told you the same even if your own intuition were not enough—there is only one battle of importance: Armageddon. And Armageddon field is within each self, world without end.

At the moment I believe I am the happiest man who ever lived.

July 20

All but the last ten years now given away. The physical fatigue (still pleasant) is quite overwhelming. I am not troubled by the weeds in my garden patch—merely a different sort of flowers where I had planned something else. An hour ago she brought me the seed of a blown dandelion, to show me how lovely it was—I don't suppose I had ever noticed. I hope whoever takes over this place will bring it back to farming: they say the ten acres below the house used to be good potato land—nice early ground.

It is delightful to sit in the sun, as if I were old.

After thumbing over earlier entries in this journal, I see I have often felt quite bitter toward my own kind. I deduce that I must have been a lonely man—much of the loneliness self-imposed. A great part of my bitterness must have been no more than one ugly by-product of a life spent too much apart. Some of it doubtless came from objective causes, yet I don't believe I ever had more cause than any moderately intelligent man who would like to see his world a pleasanter place than it ever has been. My angel tells me that the pain in my back is due to an injury received in some early stage of the world war that still goes on. That could have soured me, perhaps. It's all right—it's all in the record.

She is racing with a hummingbird—holding back, I think, to give the ball of green fluff a break.

Another note for you, Lester. I have already indicated that my ring is to be yours. I don't want to tell you what I have discovered of its properties, for fear it might not give you the same pleasure and interest that it has given me. Of course, like any spot of shifting light and color, it is an aid to self-hypnosis. It is much, much more than that, but—find out for yourself, at some time when you are a little protected from everyday distractions. I know it can't harm you, because I know its source.

By the way, I wish you would convey to my publishers my request that they either discontinue manufacture of my *Introductory Biology* or else bring out a new edition revised in accordance with some notes you will find in the top left drawer of my library desk. I glanced through that book after my angel assured me that I wrote it, and I was amazed. However, I'm afraid my notes are messy (I call them mine by a poetic license), and they may be too advanced for the present day—though the revision is mainly a matter of leaving out certain generalities that ain't so. Use your best judgment: it's a very minor textbook, and the thing isn't too important. A last wriggle of my personal vanity.

July 27

I have seen a two-moon night.

It was given to me by that other grownup, at the end of a wonderful visit, when he and six of those nine other children came to see me. It was last night, I think—yes, must have been. First there was a murmur of wings above the house; my angel flew in, laughing; then they were here, all about me. Full of gaiety and colored fire, showing off in every way they knew would please me. Each one had something graceful and friendly to say to me. One brought me a moving image of the St. Lawrence seen at morning from half a mile up—clouds—eagles; now, how could he know that would delight me so much? And each one thanked me for what I had done.

But it's been so easy!

And at the end the old one—his skin is quite brown, and his down is white and gray—gave the remembered image of a two-moon night. He saw it some sixty years ago.

I have not even considered making an effort to describe it—my fingers will not hold this pencil much longer tonight. Oh—soaring buildings of white and amber, untroubled countryside, silver on curling rivers, a glimpse of open sea; a moon rising in clarity, another setting in a wreath of cloud, between them a wide wandering of unfamiliar stars; and here and there the angels, worthy after fifty million years to live in such a night. No, I cannot describe anything like that. But, you human kindred of mine, I can do something better. I can tell you that this two-moon night, glorious as it was, was no more beautiful than a night under a single moon on this ancient and familiar Earth might be—if you will imagine that the rubbish of human evil has been cleared away and that our own people have started at last on the greatest of all explorations.

July 29

Nothing now remains to give away but the memory of the time that has passed since the angel came. I am to rest as long as I wish, write whatever I want to. Then I shall get myself over to the bed and lie down as if for sleep. She tells me that I can keep my eyes open: she will close them for me when I no longer see her.

I remain convinced that our human case is hopeful. I feel sure that in only a few thousand years we may be able to perform some of the simpler preparatory tasks, such as casting out evil and loving our neighbors. And if that should prove to be so, who can doubt that in another fifty million years we might well be only a little lower than the angels?

LIBRARIAN'S NOTE: As is generally known, the original of the Bannerman Journal is said to have been in the possession of Dr. Lester Morse at the time of the latter's disappearance in 1964, and that disapppearance has remained an unsolved mystery to the present day. McCarran is known to have visited Captain Garrison Blaine in October, 1951, but no record remains of that visit. Captain Blaine appears to have been a bachelor who lived alone. He was killed in line of duty, December, 1951. McCarran is believed not to have written about nor discussed the Bannerman affair with anyone else. It is almost certain that he himself removed the extract and related papers from the files (unofficially, it would seem!) when he severed his connection with the FBI in 1957; at any rate, they were found among his effects after his assassination and were released to the public, considerably later, by Mrs. McCarran.

The following memorandum was originally attached to the extract from the Bannerman Journal; it carries the McCarran initialing.

Aug. 11, 1951

The original letter of complaint written by Stephen Clyde, M.D., and mentioned in the accompanying letter of Captain Blaine, has unfortunately been lost, owing perhaps to an error in filing.

Personnel presumed responsible have been instructed not to allow such error to be repeated except if, as, and/or when necessary.

C. McC.

On the margin of this memorandum there was a penciled notation, later erased. The imprint is sufficient to show the unmistakable McCarran script. The notation read in part as follows: *Far be it from a McC. to lose his job except if, as, and/or*—the rest is undecipherable, except for a terminal word which is regrettably unparliamentary.

STATEMENT BY LESTER MORSE, M.D., DATED AUGUST 9, 1951

On the afternoon of July 30, 1951, acting on what I am obliged to describe as an unexpected impulse, I drove out to the country for the purpose of calling on my friend Dr. David Bannerman. I had not seen him nor had word from him since the evening of June 12 of this year.

I entered, as was my custom, without knocking. After calling to him and hearing no response, I went upstairs to his bedroom and found him dead. From superficial indications I judged that death must have taken place during the previous night. He was lying on his bed on his left side, comfortably disposed as if for sleep but fully dressed, with a fresh shirt and clean summer slacks. His eyes and mouth were closed, and there was no trace of the disorder to be expected at even the easiest natural death. Because of these signs I assumed, as soon as I had determined the absence of breath and heartbeat and noted the chill of the body, that some neighbor must have found him already, performed these simple rites out of respect for him, and probably notified a local physician or other responsible person. I therefore waited (Dr. Bannerman had no telephone), expecting that someone would soon call.

Dr. Bannerman's journal was on a table near his bed, open to that page on which he has written a codicil to his will. I read that part. Later, while I was waiting for others to come, I read the remainder of the journal, as I believe he wished me to do. The ring he mentions was on the fifth finger of his left hand, and it is now in my possession. When writing that codicil Dr. Bannerman must have overlooked or forgotten the fact that in his formal will, written some months earlier, he had appointed me executor. If there are legal technicalities involved, I shall be pleased to cooperate fully with the proper authorities.

The ring, however, will remain in my keeping, since that was Dr. Bannerman's expressed wish, and I am not prepared to offer it for examination or discussion under any circumstances.

The notes for a revision of one of his textbooks were in his desk, as noted in the journal. They are by no means "messy"; nor are they particularly revolutionary except insofar as he wished to rephrase, as theory or hypothesis, certain statements that I would have supposed could be regarded as axiomatic. This is not my field, and I am not competent to judge. I shall take up the matter with his publishers at the earliest opportunity.*

So far as I can determine, and bearing in mind the results of the autopsy performed by Stephen Clyde, M.D., the death of Dr. David Bannerman was not inconsistent with the presence of an embolism of some type not distinguishable

---

* LIBRARIAN'S NOTE: But it seems he never did. No new edition of *Introductory Biology* was ever brought out, and the textbook has been out of print since 1952.

post mortem. I have so stated on the certificate of death. It would seem to be not in the public interest to leave such questions in doubt. I am compelled to add one other item of medical opinion for what it may be worth:

I am not a psychiatrist, but, owing to the demands of general practice, I have found it advisable to keep as up to date as possible with current findings and opinion in this branch of medicine. Dr. Bannerman possessed, in my opinion, emotional and intellectual stability to a better degree than anyone else of comparable intelligence in the entire field of my acquaintance, personal and professional. If it is suggested that he was suffering from a hallucinatory psychosis, I can only say that it must have been of a type quite outside my experience and not described, so far as I know, anywhere in the literature of psychopathology.

Dr. Bannerman's house, on the afternoon of July 30, was in good order. Near the open, unscreened window of his bedroom there was a coverless shoe box with a folded silk scarf in the bottom. I found no pillow such as Dr. Bannerman describes in the journal, but observed that a small section had been cut from the scarf. In this box, and near it, there was a peculiar fragrance, faint, aromatic, and very sweet, such as I have never encountered before and therefore cannot describe.

It may or may not have any bearing on the case that, while I remained in this house that afternoon, I felt no sense of grief or personal loss, although Dr. Bannerman had been a loved and honored friend for a number of years. I merely had, and have, a conviction that after the completion of some very great undertaking, he had found peace.

IN HIS IMAGE

Terry Carr

Until 1971 Terry Carr was best known as the creative and venturesome editor who helped some of the finest science-fiction novels of recent years reach print—among them Ursula LeGuin's **The Left Hand of Darkness**, Joanna Russ's **And Chaos Died**, and R.A. Lafferty's **Fourth Mansions**. Now a freelance based in the San Francisco area, Carr continues to edit—the **Universe** series of anthologies for Random House and an annual compilation of the year's best s-f for Ballantine—but he has also resumed his own writing career after too long a hiatus. This crisp, moving little story is a good sample of his current output.

I am quite beautiful, truthfully, built in the image of man though of course I am not an exact copy. But I have two arms and two legs, each articulated once at elbows and knees and each having either hands or feet.

I have a head also, which contains my sensory organs for sight, sound and radio; unlike humans, however, my logic processes are housed outside my head, mostly in my torso, thought I also have a radio link with the public computer. Good for calculations of all kinds, nearly instantaneous when I might take seconds, minutes. I never have to guess about chances; pubcomp calculates them for me.

Pubcomp says it is 98 to 3 that there is a human being alive in the city.

That is the easy calculation: "a human being." But when we begin to speak of *the* human being, calculations become less sure. Pubcomp says it is .009% possible the human is in my city sector, and that is one of the highest probabilities, so I am searching diligently.

The other cities report no humans since two years four months plus past, so our human must be the last. (Correction: with all factors calculated, there is .0000000012 chance of another human on Earth. But that includes such hypotheses as human mutations to enable them to extract oxygen from oxides of sulfur or nitrogen. I ignore this hypothesis and others like it.)

I have quartered my sector, and I have eliminated three of these areas. What is left is not large: there are many of us in the city, having moved here from other cities as they became empty of humans, so each of us has a sector that is small to begin with.

(Few of the others are as beautiful as I. Most were built as street sweepers or industrial workers, not as wide-purpose wardens such as I. The older types—pubcomp designates them "classics"—have been redesigned and retooled for perception, and they search too. But they are not beautiful, and I hope that when the human is found it will be by me or at least someone as beautiful. Would the human want to be rescued by a sanitation burner?)

The area I have left to search consists of one street three blocks long. Most of the buildings are low, five stories or less, but one extends to the dome. There used to be luxury living quarters there, but of course we haven't been able to keep them up; the classics that used to service them were repurposed as wardens like the rest of us. Why upkeep living quarters when there are no humans to live in them?

Still, I am thinking about that building. I believe I understand humans better than others of us do; I think about them a great deal. I try to think like a man. I am looking at that building now, thinking like a man, and it appeals to me. I think I like heights.

I am going in. The lobby's carpet is dark from oxidation, and I note that the air circulation no longer works. Will that matter to a human? No—why should he care whether unbreathable air is regularly replaced by other unbreathable air?

One bank of elevators registers non-function, but the other is in working order. Is there any way of knowing if these have been used recently? Pubcomp says no data. Doors open smoothly before me, thought there is a slight rasping of metal on metal. No serious malfunction; the elevators are safe to ride.

I step inside one of them and look at the bank of buttons; the numbers go up only to 25. I punch 25, but nothing happens. I press the button again, and then press 24, 23, 18, 2. The elevator is motionless.

Pubcomp says the buttons are operable by human body-heat. I feed current through one of my metal fingers till it is 70°, and again I touch the 25 button. It lights up, the doors close, the elevator begins to rise.

I look around the elevator cubicle. Some of the lights in the ceiling have gone out; plastic handrails are corroded from exposure to the air. The rug is darkened, like that in the building's lobby, but in the uneven light I see markings that look like footprints.

I bend to look closely. They are footprints—*shoe* prints.

Was it my human? How old are these prints? I compare them to the marks made by my own feet, and see little difference. My prints are more deeply imbedded because of my greater weight. There is another difference: the human's prints are linked by dragmarks. Is he weak, sick? (Of course he is; it is a wonder he remains alive at all.) The prints move back from the panel of buttons, uneven prints (staggering?), and I believe he fell against the plastic handrail to hold himself up. (78% chance.)

The elevator stops, the doors open. I exit, looking for the elevators going to floor 50. There they are, to the right. On this floor's elevator lobby is a barber shop whose striped pole still revolves, a Bew-tee Parlour with lettering flaked and peeling from the window, a candy and gum machine: the glass of its front has been smashed.

I look for shoe prints leading from the elevator I have just left to the elevators leading higher. But there are no shoe prints, no marks at all on the carpet.

I pause, studying the question. The carpet is a richer red than those I saw in the elevator or the lobby downstairs. I look again at the glass front of the Bew-tee Parlour, the barbershop: the glass is almost clear, untainted by the air here.

The building was totally air-conditioned, says pubcomp. But that system has broken down, as I have already discovered. Conclusion: since the breakdown, no air has been pumped in from outside; the air here is twenty, forty, fifty years old.

If I were a man, if I breathed, the air would smell "musty," "stale." But it would be far more breathable than the air outside.

I am sure now that my human is here, in this building. But with no shoe prints to guide me, how shall I find him?

I think like a man again. I believe he has continued to go up in the elevators. Probably to the top, to the dome itself. Humans are drawn to heights; that is what makes them human.

I follow my human upward. I step into the next elevator, heat a finger, press 50. The doors close, the elevator and I rise.

I exit at 50. Here there are ice machines, a gum-ball dispenser, a shoeshine machine, the entrance to a gymnasium. The globe of the gum-ball dispenser has long since been smashed and emptied; plastic shards are scattered on the carpet. The ice machine still works, though its interior is frozen solid. The shoe-shine machine has been recently used.

I look at the machine, at a spray of crusted shoe polish that was thrown out onto the carpet from the buffers and rollers as they turned for the first time in decades. I touch a roller with a finger and dry but not powdery polish comes off onto my metal. I send current to the finger and the brown coating blackens and drops away.

I look around the lobby of this floor. There are between five and eight apartments on each floor of this building; my human could be in any of them. Odds 657 to 1 against any individual apartment (first 24 floors eliminated).

I do not believe he is in any of the apartments here. I believe he has gone on upward.

I enter the next elevator, go to 75. A self-service supermart is here, its doors wide open, its shelves long empty. I hardly pause; I go on to floor 100. The Century Note night-club stands dark and empty; someone has scratched out "Century" and written above it "Helluva." I go to the next elevator, to floor 120.

There are no shops or services on this floor except for another ice machine; the floor is occupied only by apart-ments. I enter the last elevator, press 130 and am taken to the top floor of the building.

Here is the Top o' the World Bar & Lounge, very famous. The view was spectacular when the air was clear. In latter years its tourist business declined, but the residents of the building continued to come up here. They were humans; they were drawn to height, even if only metaphorical, with a view of grayness outside and below.

Metal stairs at the end of a corridor lead up to the city dome, where there is an exit to the empty outside. That is where my human will be, and I hurry upward, worried now when I think of human lungs trying to breathe the air of the sky. How much worse is it than the air inside the dome? (Only 27% more pollutants, says pubcomb, 6% of them toxic. Not as bad as I feared, but I hurry anyway.)

The port is round; I press the button that slides it back into the dome, and I step outside.

There is no one here. I stand outside a bubble atop the huge dome of the city, and it is empty. Did my human step out here, try to breathe the air, collapse and slide down onto the dome proper? I search the metal expanse of the dome on all sides of the bubble, but there is no sign of any human figure. I was wrong; he did not come up here after all.

(What was the probability to begin with?—I never thought to consider it. 2.1%, says pubcomp. I would feel like a fool, but pubcomp does not think like a human. I believe the chance was greater.)

There is nothing up here. The sky of early afternoon is red shading into brown. The moon, swollen with proximity to Earth, dominates the horizon, clearly visible in the dark day sky. Its color appears yellow seen through Earth's waste-laden air; its mares and mountains are indistinct.

Once men walked on that world—over three hundred years ago. On the planet Mars, also. The exhaust of their rockets is still carried in the air.

Closer to the city, mountain sculptures stretch for the sky. They are not real mountains; this is a desert area. They are constructed of metal and plastic and they angle into the sky purely for the sake of beauty. Men built them. Most have turned dark from chemical reactions with the air, but there is still one that retains its original bright colors.

I stare at them all, the bright and dark ones alike. Men built them for beauty alone, those huge jagged cliffs and colors. I have never seen them before, only televised images in my head. I think if I were a human I would be moved; as it is, I stare and wonder. Are they still beautiful, even marked by the corrosion of time? I think so, but would a man think so?

I must find my human; he can tell me. I turn and go back down the ramp, closing the port behind me.

Standing in the lobby of floor 130, I recalculate plans. Odds 657 to 1 against his being in any individual apartment of this building; chances much greater that he is near the top of the building. I shall continue to think this way.

I hear a noise.

Instantly I am analyzing and triangulating the sound. It was something falling in the Top o' the World Bar & Lounge. It could have been anything: a piece of a table falling away, plastic from the ceiling, anything. Never mind; I feel a certainty.

I enter the Top o' the World. There is darkness to my right: a coat room. The lounge itself is dim, many of the lights no longer working, some actually smashed. There is a long bar to my left, and there all the lights are on.

There is another noise, and it is from the bar. From behind the bar. A scuffling noise, fabric on fabric. Clothing on carpet. My human is hiding behind the bar.

I walk around the open end of the bar and look inside. He is there, lying on the floor.

He looks at me coldly for seconds. His face is gray, traced with scarlet veins. He is breathing shallowly.

He draws a full breath, and the sound of air passing into

his lungs is thin. I don't believe there should be any noticeable sound.

"I broke my fucking ankle," he says.

I see this is true. He has it drawn up to where he can cradle it in his hands. His shoe lies beside him.

"Bastard hurts," he says. "It's killing me, God damn it."

I move to him and bend down, but I do not touch him. "I am not a medical crewman," I say. "But I am sending for help." Simultaneously I have been radioing our position.

"Fuck you," he says. "Fuck your medicine, fuck your help. Inject me with high octane and let me alone." He raises the bottle he has in his hand and drinks; then he chokes, and begins to cough. He does it wearily, with no surprise. When the spasm passes he drinks again.

"It was my function to find you," I explain. "Others will help. They can stop the pain of your ankle."

He drags himself back to lean against a glass cabinet, wincing. Without looking at me he says, "Can openers."

"Excuse me?"

"Fucking lawn mowers," he says. He coughs again.

Six minutes till the medical crew will arrive, says pubcomp.

"I have nothing to do with lawns," I say to the human. "I am a warden."

"You're a drawbridge," he mutters. "You're a fucking drawbridge. No no, you're a stapler. Stapler." He laughs, wheezes, coughs. The spasms cause him to move his foot, and he groans in pain.

I watch. There is nothing I can do for him. Five minutes thirty-seven seconds to go.

He leans back against the glass cabinet and breathes carefully, getting it under control.

"You can't help me," he says. He is still not looking at me. "Fucking stapler could help as much. Staple my foot. Staple my chest. Staple my fucking head."

"That would not help you," I say. We are not talking about the same thing, however; I know it, but he is giving me no clue to what he is really trying to say.

He does look up at me now. "Christ. You're a vacuum cleaner."

"I was never tooled for maintenance," I tell him. He is drinking again. He must be very drunk.

"You're all vacuum cleaners," he says. "Vacuum cleaners. . . . Tanks. Bazookas. Fucking riveting guns. Garbage trucks. Walking typewriters." He drinks till the bottle is empty. Coughing but not paying attention to it he swings the empty bottle against a glass cabinet next to him; the glass smashes and he reaches in to take a bottle of clear liquor. He begins to drink it, grimacing. His face, which was gray earlier, is nearly blue now.

Four minutes seven seconds more.

"I admire humans," I say. "We all do. We try to help you."

"Fuck you. I'd rather have a dog." He breathes, breathes again. "Jesus Christ, I've got a city full of putt-putts that want to take care of me."

"We truthfully do want to take care of you," I say. "We can heal your ankle. We can give you an oxygen-rich environment."

"I know, I know," he says wearily. He drinks.

He stares dully at me. He coughs once, then doubles over and begins to vomit. It splashes against the glass and imitation walnut side of the bar. He breathes in gasps, coughs, chokes, vomits again. There is no expression on his face.

It does not take long till he stops. He leans back weakly, getting his breath. Three minutes eighteen seconds more.

Finally he says, "You admire humans, do you? You admire puke and everything?"

I say, "Whatever humans do is necessary to being human." Was that the right answer? It is true.

"Oh shit, you're a can opener. Quick, divide 3,468 by 2,125."

Pubcomp answers and I say, "1.06032. Exactly."

"Christ," he says. "Do you care about that?"

"Only because you wanted to know."

"I didn't. I thought it might be funny to see you answer. You *are* like a dog. Do you shit on the grass?" He drinks.

"No. Did you really want me to answer that?"

"Jesus it stinks here. Pick me up and move me somewhere else."

I bend to do this.

"Gently, God damn you! Fucking foot. . . ."

I am as gentle as possible as I move him around to the

outside of the bar. When I put him down he is saying, "Shit shit shit shit shit shit," quietly but intensely.

One minute fifty-four seconds.

He settles himself, wincing. "Bend your head down," he says.

I do as he says. He pats the top of my head, then begins to chuckle. He stops when it threatens to become a cough. He gets his breath and says, "Would you like me to scratch you behind the antenna?"

"Excuse me?"

"Forget it." He drinks. " 'We honestly want to take care of you,' " he says, trying to imitate the comparatively flat quality of my voice. "Why?"

"We admire you. You made us. Humanity is a great race."

"Oh shit, who told you so? Humans." He closes his eyes and I see he is resisting another coughing fit. "We made garbage trucks too. Made bombs and dum-dum bullets and puke gas. Killed each other, put a lot of shit in the air, killed ourselves. You looked at the air lately? Shit, even the domes didn't help."

"We can give you enough oxygen to breathe."

"Swell," he says. "While you're at it, cure my emphysema."

"No, we cannot do that," I say. Does he really have emphysema, or is he taunting me?

"Then fuck you," he says, and slumps back against the bar. "Staple my head," he says vaguely. He lifts the bottle, judges how much is left in it, drinks three, four, five, six swallows. He almost chokes. "Fuck you, fuck you. Go mow a lawn."

The medical crew arrives. There are five of them. They surround him, because we have had some humans try to fight us.

"His left ankle is broken," I say. "Be very careful."

"We know about pain," says the head of the crew.

"Like hell you do," the human says. Two of the crew lift him gently and put him on a rolling stretcher. One wipes vomit from his clothing.

As they start to wheel him out he looks back to me and says urgently, "Hey, stapler, quick, gimme two bottles. Bourbon, scotch, anything."

The crewmen make no objection, so I do as he says. He takes one in each hand and smiles weakly. "Good boy, Spot."

They wheel him out. I tell the head of the crew that he may have emphysema. He acknowledges the information and leaves.

I am alone in the Top o' the World Bar & Lounge. I think about the human for minutes after they have gone down in the elevator. Does he know he is the last? Does he hate us, the machines? Does he hate his own kind? Does he hate himself?

Pubcomp says insufficient data. But I have opinions.

I leave the Top o' the World and go to the stairs leading up to the outside of the city dome. Near the foot of the stairs are discarded parts from the mechanism of the port; I pick up several and take them with me as I climb.

I pause at the top of the stairs to look at the mountain sculptures. They are many miles away and I will not be able to reach them before tomorrow. But I believe I can climb them. In places they are probably unsafe for my weight, but I believe I can judge this. I believe I can climb all the way to the top of one of them. That one, the one that retains its colors.

I am going to make a marker from the parts I picked up below, and I will fasten it at the top.

I ask pubcomp to plot a route for me down the maintenance stairs and ramps so that I can reach the desert, and pubcomp provides the information.

Pubcomp adds that there is insufficient data to calculate my chance of reaching the top of the mountain sculpture I have chosen. I find that I am pleased.

ALL PIECES OF A RIVER SHORE

R. A. Lafferty

It has justly been said of Lafferty that he writes like a stoned Mark Twain. Indeed he works within the great nineteenth-century American tradition of romantic exaggeration and robust whackiness, and the hearty exuberance of his work identifies him plainly as the literary descendant of the man who created Huck Finn and the Connecticut Yankee. But Lafferty's sensibility is very much of the twentieth century (or the twenty-first, or the twenty-fifth) as well as of the nineteenth; the tricks he plays with time and space are his own, beyond doubt his own, and never were conceived before he came along. He chooses to cast his stories in the mode of science fiction, to our great gain; but one of these days the larger literary world will discover him, and he'll soar like a rocket out of our little ghetto.

It had been a very long and ragged and incredibly interlocked and detailed river shore. Then a funny thing had happened to it. It had been broken up, sliced up into pieces. Some of the pieces had been folded and compressed into bales. Some of them had been rolled up on rollers. Some of them had been cut into still smaller pieces and used for ornaments and as Indian medicine. Rolled and baled pieces of the shore came to rest in barns and old warehouses, in attics, in caves. Some were buried in the ground.

And yet the river itself still exists physically, as do its shores, and you may go and examine them. But the shore you will see along the river now is not quite the same as that old shore that was broken up and baled into bales and rolled onto rollers, not quite the same as the pieces you will find in attics and caves.

His name was Leo Nation and he was known as a rich Indian. But such wealth as he had now was in his collections, for he was an examining and acquiring man. He had cattle, he had wheat, he had a little oil, and he spent everything that came in. Had he had more income he would have collected even more.

He collected old pistols, old ball shot, grindstones, early windmills, walking-horse threshing machines, flax combs, Contestoga wagons, brass-bound barrels, buffalo robes, Mexican saddles, slick horn saddles, anvils, Argand lamps, rush holders, hay-burning stoves, hackamores, branding irons, chuck wagons, longhorn horns, beaded serapes, Mexican and Indian leather work, buckskins, beads, feathers, squirrel-tail anklets, arrowheads, deerskin shirts, locomotives, street-cars, mill wheels, keelboats, buggies, ox yokes, old parlor organs, blood-and-thunder novels, old circus posters, harness bells, Mexican oxcarts, wooden cigar-store Indians, cable-twist tobacco a hundred years old and mighty strong, cus-pidors (four hundred of them), Ferris wheels, carnival wagons, carnival props of various sorts, carnival proclama-tions painted big on canvas. Now he was going to collect something else. He was talking about it to one of his friends, Charles Longbank who knew everything.

"Charley," he said, "do you know anything about 'The Longest Pictures in the World' which used to be shown by carnivals and in hippodromes?"

"Yes, I know a little about them, Leo. They are an in-teresting bit of Americana: a bit of nineteenth-century back country mania. They were supposed to be pictures of the Mississippi River shore. They were advertised as one mile long, five miles long, nine miles long. One of them, I be-lieve, was actually over a hundred yards long. They were badly painted on bad canvas, crude trees and mudbank and water ripples, simplistic figures and all as repetitious as wallpaper. A strong-armed man with a big brush and plenty of barn paint of three colors could have painted quite a few yards of such in one day. Yet they are truly Americana. Are you going to collect them, Leo?"

"Yes. But the real ones aren't like you say."

"Leo, I saw one. There is nothing to them but very large crude painting."

"I have twenty that are like you say, Charley. I have three that are very different. Here's an old carnival poster that mentions one."

Leo Nation talked eloquently with his hands while he also talked with his mouth, and now he spread out an old browned poster with loving hands:

"The Arkansas Traveler, World's Finest Carnival, Eight Wagons, Wheel, Beasts, Dancing Girls, Baffling Acts, Monsters, Games of Chance. And Featuring the World's Longest Picture, Four Miles of Exquisite Painting. This is from the Original Panorama; it is Not a Cheap-Jack imitation."

"So you see, Charley, there was a distinction: there were the original pieces, and there were the crude imitations."

"Possibly some were done a little better than others, Leo; they could hardly have been done worse. Certainly, collect them if you want to. You've collected lots of less interesting things."

"Charley, I have a section of that panoramic picture that once belonged to the Arkansas Traveler Carnival. I'll show it to you. Here's another poster:

"King Carnival, The King of them All. Fourteen Wagons. Ten Thousand Wonders. See the Rubber Man. See the Fire Divers. See the Longest Picture in the World, see Elephants on the Mississippi River. This is a Genuine Shore Depictment, not the Botches that Others show."

"You say that you have twenty of the ordinary pictures, Leo, and three that are different?"

"Yes I have, Charley. I hope to get more of the genuine. I hope to get the whole river."

"Let's go look at one, Leo, and see what the difference is."

They went out to one of the hay barns. Leo Nation kept his collections in a row of hay barns. "What would I do?" he had asked once, "call in a carpenter and tell him to build me a museum? He'd say, 'Leo, I can't build a museum without plans and stuff. Get me some plans.' And where would I get plans? So I always tell him to build me another hay barn one hundred feet by sixty feet and fifty feet high. Then I always put in four or five decks myself and floor them, and leave open vaults for the tall stuff. Besides, I believe a hay barn won't cost as much as a museum."

"This will be a big field, Charley," Leo Nation said now as they came to one of the hay-barn museums. "It will take all your science in every field to figure it out. Of the three genuine ones I have, each is about a hundred and eighty yards long. I believe this is about the standard length, though some may be multiples of these. They passed for paintings in the years of their display, Charley, *but they are not paintings.*"

"What are they then, Leo?"

"I hire you to figure this out. You are the man who knows everything."

Well, there were two barrel reels there, each the height of a man, and several more were set further back.

"The old turning mechanism is likely worth a lot more than the picture," Charles Longbank told Leo Nation. "This was turned by a mule on a treadmill, or by a mule taking a mill pole round and round. It might even be eighteenth century."

"Yeah, but I use an electric motor on it," Leo said. "The only mule I have left is a personal friend of mine. I'd no more make him turn that than he'd make me if I was the mule. I line it up like I think it was, Charley, the full reel north and the empty one south. Then we run it. So we travel, we scan, from south to north, going upstream as we face west."

"It's funny canvas and funny paint, much better than the one I saw," said Charles Longbank, "and it doesn't seem worn at all by the years."

"It isn't either one, canvas or paint," said Ginger Nation, Leo's wife, as she appeared from somewhere. "It is picture."

Leo Nation started the reeling and ran it. It was the wooded bank of a river. It was a gravel and limestone bank with mud overlay and the mud undercut a little. And it was thick timber to the very edge of the shore.

"It is certainly well done," Charles Longbank admitted. "From the one I saw and from what I had read about these, I wasn't prepared for this." The rolling picture was certainly not repetitious, but one had the feeling that the riverbank itself might have been a little so, to lesser eyes than those of the picture.

"It is a virgin forest, mostly deciduous," said Charles Longbank, "and I do not believe that there is any such temperate forest on any large river in the world today. It would have been logged out. I do not believe that there were many such stretches even in the nineteenth century. Yet I have the feeling that it is a faithful copy of something, and not imaginary."

The rolling shores: cottonwood trees, slash pine, sycamore, slippery elm, hackberry, pine again.

"When I get very many of the pictures, Charley, you will put them on film and analyze them or have some kind of computer do it. You will be able to tell from the sun's angle what order the pictures should have been in, and how big are the gaps between."

"No, Leo, they would all have to reflect the same hour of the same day to do that."

"But it *was* all the same hour of the same day," Ginger Nation cut in. "How would you take one picture at two hours of two days?"

"She's right, Charley," Leo Nation said. "All the pictures of the genuine sort are pieces of one original authentic picture. I've known that all along."

Rolling shore of pine, laurel oak, butternut, persimmon, pine again.

"It is a striking reproduction, whatever it is," Charles Longbank said, "but I'm afraid that after a while even this would become as monotonous as repeating wallpaper."

"Hah," said Leo. "For a smart man you have dumb eyes, Charley. Every tree is different, every leaf is different. All the trees are in young leaf too. It's about a last-week-of-March picture. What it hangs on, though, is what part of the river it is. It might be a third-week-in-March picture, or a first-week-in-April. The birds, old Charley who know everything, why don't we pick up more birds in this section? And what birds are those there?"

"Passenger pigeons, Leo, and they've been gone for quite a few decades. Why don't we see more birds there? I've a humorous answer to that, but it implies that this thing is early and authentic. We don't see more birds because they are

too well camouflaged. North America is today a bird
watchers' paradise because very many of its bright birds are
later European intrusions that have replaced native varieties.
They have not yet adjusted to the native backgrounds, so they
stand out against them visually. Really, Leo, that is a fact. A
bird can't adapt in a short four or five hundred years. And
there are birds, birds, birds in that, Leo, if you look sharp
enough."

"I look sharp to begin with, Charley; I just wanted you to
look sharp."

"This rolling ribbon of canvas or whatever is about six feet
high, Leo, and I believe the scale is about one to ten, going
by the height of mature trees and other things."

"Yeah, I think so, Charley. I believe there's about a mile
of river shore in each of my good pictures. There's things
about these pictures though, Charley, that I'm almost afraid
to tell you. I've never been quite sure of your nerves. But
you'll see them for yourself when you come to examine the
pictures closely."

"Tell me the things now, Leo, so I'll know what to look for."

"It's all there, Charley, every leaf, every knob of bark,
every spread of moss. I've put parts of it under a microscope,
ten power, fifty power, four hundred power. There's detail
there that you couldn't see with your bare eyes if you had
your nose right in the middle of it. You can even see cells of
leaf and moss. You put a regular painting under that magnification and all you see is details of pigment, and canyons
and mountains of brush strokes. Charley, you can't find a
brush stroke in that whole picture! Not in any of the real
ones."

It was rather pleasant to travel up that river at the lei-
surely equivalent rate of maybe four miles an hour, figuring a
one to ten ratio. Actually the picture rolled past them at
about half a mile an hour. Rolling bank and rolling trees,
pin oak, American elm, pine, black willow, shining willow.

"How come there is shining willow, Charley, and no white
willow, you tell me that?" Leo asked.

"If this *is* the Mississippi, Leo, and if it is authentic, then
this must be a far northern sector of it."

"Naw. It's Arkansas, Charley. I can tell Arkansas any-where. How come there was shining willow in Arkansas?"

"If that is Arkansas, and if the picture is authentic, it was colder then."

"Why aren't there any white willow?"

"The white willow is a European introduction, though a very early one, and it spread rapidly. There are things in this picture that check *too* well. The three good pictures that you have, are they pretty much alike?"

"Yeah, but not quite the same stretch of the river. The sun's angle is a little different in each of them, and the sod and the low plants are a little different."

"You think you will be able to get more of the pictures?"

"Yeah. I think more than a thousand miles of river was in the picture. I think I get more than a thousand sections if I know where to look."

"Probably most have been destroyed long ago, Leo, if there ever were more than the dozen or so that were adver-tised by the carnivals. And probably there were duplications in that dozen or so. Carnivals changed their features often, and your three pictures may be all that there ever were. Each could have been exhibited by several carnivals and in several hippodromes at different times."

"Nah, there were more, Charley. I don't have the one with the elephants in it yet. I think there are more than a thousand of them somewhere. I advertise for them (for originals, not the cheap-jack imitations), and I will begin to get answers."

"How many there were, there still are," said Ginger Na-tion. "They will not destroy. One of ours has the reel burned by fire, but the picture did not burn. And they won't burn."

"You might spend a lot of money on a lot of old canvas, Leo," said Charles Longbank. "But I will analyze them for you: now, or when you think you have enough of them for it."

"Wait till I get more, Charley," said Leo Nation. "I will make a clever advertisement. 'I take those things off your hands,' I will say, and I believe that people will be glad to get rid of the old things that won't burn and won't destroy, and weigh a ton each with reels. It's the real ones that won't destroy. Look at that big catfish just under the surface there,

Charley! Look at the mean eyes of that catfish! The river
wasn't as muddy then as it is now, even if it was springtime
and the water was high."

Rolling shore and trees: pine, dogwood, red cedar, bur
oak, pecan, pine again, shagbark hickory. Then the rolling
picture came to an end.

"A little over twenty minutes I timed it," said Charles
Longbank. "Yes, a yokel of the past century might have
believed that the picture was a mile long, or even five or nine
miles long."

"Nah," said Leo. "They were smarter then, Charley; they
were smarter then. Most likely that yokel would have believed that it was a little less than a furlong long, as it is. He'd
have liked it, though. And there may be pieces that are five
miles long or nine miles long. Why else would they have advertised them? I think I can hit the road and smell out where
a lot of those pictures are. And I will call in sometimes and
Ginger can tell me who have answered the advertisements.
Come here again in six months, Charley, and I will have
enough sections of the river for you to analyze. You won't get
lonesome in six months, will you, Ginger?"

"No. There will be the hay cutters, and the men from the
cattle auctions, and the oil gaugers, and Charley Longbank
here when he comes out, and the men in town and the men
in the Hill-Top Tavern. I won't get lonesome."

"She jokes, Charley," said Leo. "She doesn't really fool
around with the fellows."

"I do not joke," said Ginger. "Stay gone seven months, I
don't care."

Leo Nation did a lot of traveling for about five months.
He acquired more than fifty genuine sections of the river and
he spent quite a few thousands of dollars on them. He went
a couple of years into hock for them. It would have been
much worse had not many people given him the things and
many others sold them to him for very small amounts. But
there were certain stubborn men and women who insisted on
a good price. This is always the hazard of collecting, the
thing that takes most of the fun out of it. All these expensively acquired sections were really prime pieces and Leo
could not let himself pass them by.

How he located so many pieces is his own mystery, but Leo Nation did really have a nose for these things. He smelt them out; and all collectors of all things must have such long noses.

There was a professor man in Rolla, Missouri, who had rugged his whole house with pieces of a genuine section.

"That sure is tough stuff, Nation," the man said. "I've been using it for rugs for forty years and it isn't worn at all. See how fresh the trees still are! I had to cut it up with a chain saw, and I tell you that it's tougher than any wood in the world for all that it's nice and flexible."

"How much for all the rugs, for all the pieces of pieces that you have?" Leo asked uneasily. There seemed something wrong in using the pieces for rugs, and yet this didn't seem like a wrong man.

"Oh, I won't sell you any of my rugs, but I will give you pieces of it, since you're interested, and I'll give you the big piece I have left. I never could get anyone much interested in it. We analyzed the material out at the college. It is very sophisticated plastic material. We could reproduce it, or something very like it, but it would be impossibly expensive, and plastics two-thirds as tough are quite cheap. The funny thing, though, I can trace the history of the thing back to quite a few decades before any plastic was first manufactured in the world. There is a big puzzle there, for some man with enough curiosity to latch onto it."

"I have enough curiosity; I have already latched onto it," Leo Nation said. "That piece you have on the wall—it looks like—if I could only see it under magnification—"

"Certainly, certainly, Nation. It looks like a swarm of bees there, and it is. I've a slide prepared from a fringe of it. Come and study it. I've shown it to lots of intelligent people and they all say 'So what?' It's an attitude that I can't understand."

Leo Nation studied the magnification with delight. "Yeah," he said. "I can even see the hairs on the bees' legs. In one flaking-off piece there I can even make out the cells of a hair." He fiddled with low and high magnification for a long while. "But the bees sure are funny ones," he said. "My father told me about bees like that once and I thought he lied."

"Our present honeybees are of late European origin, Nation," the man said. "The native American bees *were* funny and inefficient from a human viewpoint. They are not quite extinct even yet, though. There are older-seeming creatures in some of the scenes."

"What are the clown animals in the pieces on your kitchen floor?" Leo asked. "Say, those clowns are big!"

"Ground sloths, Nation. They set things as pretty old. If they are a hoax, they are the grandest hoax I ever ran into. A man would have to have a pretty good imagination to give a peculiar hair form to an extinct animal—a hair form that living sloths in the tropics do not have . . . a hair form that sloths of a colder climate just possibly might have. But how many lifetimes would it have taken to paint even a square foot of this in such microscopic detail? There is no letdown anywhere, Nation; there is prodigious detail in every square centimeter of it."

"Why are the horses so small and the buffaloes so big?"

"I don't know, Nation. It would take a man with a hundred sciences to figure it out, unless a man with a hundred sciences had hoaxed it. And where was such a man two hundred and fifty years ago?"

"You trace your piece that far back?"

"Yes. And the scene itself might well be fifteen thousand years old. I tell you that this is a mystery. Yes, you can carry those scraps with you if you wish, and I'll have the bale that's the remaining big piece freighted up to your place."

There was a man in Arkansas who had a section of the picture stored in a cave. It was a tourist-attraction cave, but the river-shore picture had proved a sour attraction.

"The people all think it is some sort of movie projection I have set up in my cave here," he said. " 'Who wants to come down in a cave to see movies,' they say. 'If we want to see a river shore we will go see a river shore,' they say, 'we won't come down in a cave to see it.' Well, I thought it would be a good attraction, but it wasn't."

"How did you ever get it in here, man?" Leo Nation asked him. "That passage just isn't big enough to bring it in."

"Oh, it was already here, rock rollers and all, fifteen years ago when I broke out that little section to crawl through."

"Then it had to be here a very long time. That wall has formed since."

"Nah, not very long," the man said. "These limestone curtains form fast, what with all the moisture trickling down here. The thing could have been brought in here as recent as five hundred years ago. Sure, I'll sell it. I'll even break out a section so we can get it out. I have to make the passage big enough for people to walk in anyhow. Tourists don't like to have to crawl on their bellies in caves. I don't know why. I always liked to crawl on my belly in caves."

This was one of the most expensive sections of the picture that Nation bought. It would have been even more expensive if he had shown any interest in certain things seen through trees in one sequence of the picture. Leo's heart had come up into his mouth when he had noticed those things, and he'd had to swallow it again and maintain his wooden look. This was a section that had elephants on the Mississippi River.

The elephant (*Mammut americanum*) was really a mastodon, Leo had learned that much from Charles Longbank. Ah, but now he owned elephants; now he had one of the key pieces of the puzzle.

You find a lot of them in Mexico. Everything drifts down to Mexico when it gets a little age on it. Leo Nation was talking with a rich Mexican man who was as Indian as himself.

"No, I don't know where the Long Picture first came from," the man said, "but it did come from the North, somewhere in the region of the River itself. In the time of De Soto (a little less than five hundred years ago) there was still Indian legend of the Long Picture, which he didn't understand. Yourselves of the North, of course, are like children. Even the remembering tribes of you like the Caddos have memories no longer than five hundred years.

"We ourselves remember longer. But as to this, all that we remember is that each great family of us took a section of the Long Picture along when we came south to Mexico. That was, perhaps, eight hundred years ago that we came south as conquerors. These pictures are now like treasures to the old great Indian families, like hidden treasures, memories of one of our former homes. Others of the old families will not talk to you about them. They will even deny that they have them. I talk to you about it, I show it to you, I even give it to you because I am a dissident, a sour man, not like the others."

"The early Indian legends, Don Caetano, did they say where the Long Picture first came from or who painted it?"

"Sure. They say it was painted by a very peculiar great being, and his name (hold onto your *capelo*) was Great River Shore Picture Painter. I'm sure that will help you. About the false or cheap-jack imitations for which you seem to have contempt, don't. They are not what they seem to you, and they were not done for money. These cheap-jack imitations are of Mexican origin, just as the shining originals were born in the States. They were done for the new great families in their aping the old great families, in the hope of also sharing in ancient treasure and ancient luck. Having myself just left off aping great families of another sort, I have a bitter understanding of these imitations. Unfortunately they were done in the late age that lacked art, but the contrast would have been as great in any case: all art would seem insufficient beside that of the Great River Shore Picture Painter himself.

"The cheap-jack imitation pictures were looted by gringo soldiers of the U.S. Army during the Mexican War, as they seemed to be valued by certain Mexican families. From the looters they found their way to mid-century carnivals in the States."

"Don Caetano, do you know that the pictures segments stand up under great magnification, that there are details in them far too fine to be seen by the unaided eye?"

"I am glad you say so. I have always had this on faith but I've never had enough faith to put it to the test. Yes, we have always believed that the pictures contained depths within depths."

"Why are there Mexican wild pigs in this view, Don Caetano? It's as though this one had a peculiar Mexican slant to it."

"No. The peccary was an all-American pig, Leo. It went all the way north to the ice. But it's been replaced by the European pig everywhere but in our own wilds. You want the picture? I will have my man load it and ship it to your place."

"Ah, I would give you something for it surely—"

"No, Leo, I give it freely. You are a man that I like. Receive it, and God be with you! Ah, Leo, in parting, and since you collect strange things, I have here a box of bright things that I think you might like. I believe they are no more than worthless garnets, but are they not pretty?"

Garnets? They were not garnets. Worthless? Then why did Leo Nation's eyes dazzle and his heart come up in his throat? With trembling hands he turned the stones over and worshiped. And when Don Caetano gave them to him for the token price of one thousand dollars, his heart rejoiced.

You know what? They really were worthless garnets. But what had Leo Nation thought that they were in that fateful moment? What spell had Don Caetano put on him to make him think that they were something else?

Oh well, you win here and you lose there. And Don Caetano really did ship the treasured picture to him free.

Leo Nation came home after five months of wandering and collecting.

"I stand it without you for five months," Ginger said. "I could not have stood it for six months, I sure could not have stood it for seven. I kidded. I didn't really fool around with the fellows. I had the carpenter build another hay barn to hold all the pieces of picture you sent in. There were more than fifty of them."

Leo Nation had his friend Charles Longbank come out.

"Fifty-seven new ones, Charley," Leo said. "That makes sixty with what I had before. Sixty miles of river shore I have now, I think. Analyze them, Charley. Get the data out of them somehow and feed it to your computers. First I want to know what order they go in, south to north, and how big the gaps between them are."

"Leo, I tried to explain before, that would require (besides the presumption of authenticity) that they were all done at the same hour of the same day."

"Presume it all, Charley. They *were* all done at the same time, or we will assume that they were. We will work on that presumption."

"Leo, ah—I had hoped that you would fail in your collecting. I still believe we should drop it all."

"Me, I hoped I would succeed, Charley, and I hoped

harder. Why are you afraid of spooks? Me, I meet them every hour of my life. They're what keeps the air fresh."

"I'm afraid of it, Leo. All right, I'll get some equipment out here tomorrow, but I'm afraid of it. Damn it, Leo, *who was here?*"

"Wasn't anybody here," Ginger said. "I tell you like I tell Charley, I was only kidding, I don't really fool around with the fellows."

Charles Longbank got some equipment out there the next day. Charles himself was looking bad, maybe whiskeyed up a bit, jerky, and looking over his shoulder all the time as though he had an owl perched on the back of his neck. But he did work several days running the picture segments and got them all down on scan film. Then he would program his computer and feed the data from the scan films to it.

"There's like a shadow, like a thin cloud on several of the pictures," Leo Nation said. "You any idea what it is, Charley?"

"Leo, I got out of bed late last night and ran two miles up and down that rocky back road of yours to shake myself up. I was afraid I was *getting* an idea of what those thin clouds were. Lord, Leo, who was here?"

Charles Longbank took the data in to town and fed it to his computers.

He was back in several days with the answers.

"Leo, this spooks me more than ever," he said, and he looked as if the spooks had chewed him from end to end. "Let's drop the whole thing. I'll even give you back your retainer fee."

"No, man, no. You took the retainer fee and you are retained. Have you the order they go in, Charley, south to north?"

"Yes, here it is. But don't do it, Leo, don't do it."

"Charley, I only shuffle them around with my lift fork and put them in order. I'll have it done in an hour."

And in an hour he had it done.

"Now, let's look at the south one first, and then the north one, Charley."

"No, Leo, no, no! Don't do it."

"Why not?"

"Because it scares me. They really *do* fall into an order. They really could have been done all at the same hour of the same day. Who was here, Leo? Who is the giant looking over my shoulder?"

"Yeah, he's a big one, isn't he, Charley? But he was a good artist and artists have the right to be a little peculiar. He looks over my shoulder a lot too."

Leo Nation ran the southernmost segment of the Long Picture. It was mixed land and water, island, bayou and swamp, estuary and ocean mixed with muddy river.

"It's pretty, but it isn't the Mississippi," said Leo as it ran. "It's that other river down there. I'd know it after all these years too."

"Yes," Charles Longbank gulped. "It's the Atchafalaya River. By the comparative sun angle of the pieces that had been closely identified, the computer was able to give close bearings on all the segments. This is the mouth of the Atchafalaya River which has several times in the geological past been the main mouth of the Mississippi. But how did he know it if he wasn't here? Gah, the ogre is looking over my shoulder again. It scares me, Leo."

"Yeah, Charley, I say a man ought to be really scared at least once a day so he can sleep that night. Me, I'm scared for at least a week now, and I like the big guy. Well, that's one end of it, or mighty close to it. Now we take the north end.

"Yes, Charley, yes. The only thing that scares you is that they're real. I don't know why he has to look over our shoulders when we run them, though. If he's who I think he is he's already seen it all."

Leo Nation began to run the northernmost segment of the river that he had.

"How far north are we in this, Charley?" he asked.

"Along about where the Cedar River and the Iowa River later came in."

"That all the farther north? Then I don't have any segments of the north third of the river?"

"Yes, this is the farthest north it went, Leo. Oh God, this is the last one."

"A cloud on this segment too, Charley? What are they anyhow? Say, this is a pretty crisp scene for springtime on the Mississippi."

"You look sick, Long-Charley-Bank," Ginger Nation said.

"You think a little whiskey with possum's blood would help you?"

"Could I have the one without the other? Oh, yes, both together, that may be what I need. Hurry, Ginger."

"It bedevils me still how any painting could be so wonderful," Leo wondered.

"Haven't you caught on yet, Leo?" Charles shivered. "It isn't a painting."

"I tell you that at the beginning if you only listen to me," Ginger Nation said. "I tell you it isn't either one, canvas or paint, it is only picture. And Leo said the same thing once, but then he forgets. Drink this, old Charley."

Charles Longbank drank the healing mixture of good whiskey and possum's blood, and the northernmost segment of the river rolled on.

"Another cloud on the picture, Charley," Leo said. "It's like a big smudge in the air between us and the shore."

"Yes, and there will be another," Charles moaned. "It means we're getting near the end. Who were they, Leo? How long ago was it? Ah—I'm afraid I know that part pretty close—but they couldn't have been human then, could they? Leo, if this was just an inferior throwaway, why are they still hanging in the air?"

"Easy, old Charley, easy. Man, that river gets chalky and foamy! Charley, couldn't you transfer all this to microfilm and feed it into your computers for all sorts of answers?"

"Oh, God, Leo, it already is!"

"Already is what? Hey, what's the fog, what's the mist? What is it that bulks up behind the mist? Man, what kind of blue fog-mountain—?"

"The glacier, you dummy, the glacier," Charles Longbank groaned. And the northernmost segment of the river came to an end.

"Mix up a little more of that good whiskey and possum's blood, Ginger," Leo Nation said, "I think we're all going to need it."

"That old, is it?" Leo asked a little later as they were all strangling on the very strong stuff.

"Yes, that old," Charles Longbank jittered. "Oh, who was here, Leo?"

"And, Charley, it already is *what?*"

"It already *is* microfilm, Leo, to them. A rejected strip, I believe."

"Ah, I can understand why whiskey and possum's blood never caught on as a drink," Leo said. "Was old possum here then?"

"Old possum was, we weren't." Charles Longbank shivered. "But it seems to me that something older than possum is snuffing around again, and with a bigger snufter."

Charles Longbank was shaking badly. One more thing and he would crack.

"The clouds on the—ah—film, Charley, what are they?" Leo Nation asked.

And Charles Longbank cracked.

"God over my head," he moaned out of a shivering face, "I wish they *were* clouds on the film. Ah, Leo, Leo, who were they here, who were they?"

"I'm cold, Charley," said Leo Nation. "There's bone-chill draft from somewhere."

The marks . . . too exactly like something, and too big to be: the loops and whorls that were eighteen feet long. . . .

WE ALL DIE NAKED

James Blish

Of ecological-disaster stories there has been no shortage; in fact their prevalence in recent science fiction is fast becoming a species of literary pollution. Most of them bore s-f readers, who don't need to be told that the world is in a messy state. A story the entire content of which is a tract against environmental horrors is a mere sermon, and sermons are bores.

James Blish, whose distinguished science-fiction career is marked by such notable works as **A Case of Conscience** and the **Cities in Flight** series, is much too serious an artist and much too wily a craftsman to commit the sin of fictional sermon-mongering; and the precise, witty story that follows, although falling into the category of ecological s-f, is very much more than a dreary diatribe against the polluters.

[This story is dedicated to Philip K. Dick, who once suggested that something like it would be the logical successor to such novels as The Space Merchants, Gladiator at Law and Preferred Risk—to say nothing of If This Goes On. At the time, I thought he was kidding.—JB]

The good is oft interred with their bones;
So let it be with Caesar.

When Alexei-Aub Kehoe Salvia Sun-Moon-Lake Stewart,
San. D., went out for lunch, he found half a dozen men with
jackhammers tearing up the street in front of the building, the
chisel blades of their drills cutting the slowly bubbling asphalt
into sagging rectangular chunks. The din was fearsome, and a
sizable necklace of teen-agers was dancing to it, protected
from the traffic by the police barricades across both ends of
the block. In their gas masks they reminded him, after a
moment's assiduous mental groping, of some woodcut from
the *Totentanz* of Hans Holbein the Younger.

Not that he was any beauty himself, even out of a gas mask,
as he had long ago resigned himself. He was fair-haired, but no
Viking—in fact, he was on the short side even by modern
undernourished standards, and what was worse, chubby, which
caused strangers to look at him with that mixture of jealousy
and hatred the underfed reserve for people whom they suspect
of stuffing themselves at the public trough. In Alex's case, as
all his acquaintances knew, they were absolutely right: as the
head of a union under stringent government control, he was
even technically only one step removed from being a public
employee, *and* he could not blame his chubbiness on a meta-
bolic defect, either; the fact was that he felt about food the
way Shakespeare had felt about words. Nor, at forty, was he
about to undertake any vast program of dietary reform. As
for his face, it had been broad to begin with, and the accumulation of a faint double chin now made it look as though it
had been sat upon by some creature with gentle instincts but
heavy hindquarters. Oh well; since like everyone else he had
been born into an atmosphere, and an ecology in general,
which was a veritable sea of mutagens, he felt he had to think
himself lucky that his nose wasn't on upside down, or equipped
with an extra nostril.

As for the dancing teen-agers, they also made passage along
the sidewalk even more difficult than it usually was at this
hour, but Alex didn't mind. He watched them fondly. They
consumed, but did not produce. And it was a privilege to be
allowed to walk at all. In downtown Manhattan, you either
owned a canoe (if you were wealthy) or traveled by TA
barge, and left your office by a second-story window.

Twenty years ago, he liked to remember, Morningside Heights had consisted mostly of some (by modern standards) rather mild slums, completely surrounding the great university which had been their landlord. Today, like all other high ground in the city, the Heights was a vast skyscraper complex in which worked only the most powerful of the Earth. Lesser breeds had to paddle for it in the scummy, brackish canals of Times Square, Wall Street, Rockefeller Center, and other unimportant places, fending off lumps of offal and each other as best they could, or jamming over the interbuilding bridges, or trying to flag down an occasional blimp. Flatlands like Brooklyn—once all by itself one of the largest cities in the world—were of course completely flooded, which was probably just as well, for the earthquakes had been getting worse there lately.

The most powerful of the Earth. Alex liked the sound of the phrase. He was one of Them. As the General President of Local 802 of the International Brotherhood of Sanitation Engineers, he had in fact few peers, and not only in his own estimation. Doubtless such a figure as Everett Englebert Loosli Vladimir Bingovitch Felice de Tohil Vaca, by virtue of his higher lineage and his still higher post of U.S. Secretary of Health, Education, Welfare, and Resources (Disposal of), was the more honored; but it was doubtful that with all his hereditary advantages he could be the more cultured . . . and the next few weeks, Alex thought, would show which of them was truly the more powerful.

Adjusting his mask—no matter how new a mask was, it seemed to let in more free radicals from the ambient air every day—he put the thought resolutely aside and prepared to enjoy his stroll and his lunch. Today he was holding court with the writers, artists, and musicians in his circle—people of no importance whatsoever in the modern world, except to him; he was their patron. (*Patroon*, he corrected himself, with a nod toward the towers of Peter Stuyvesant's water-girdled village.) One, whom he might even consider making the next of his wives if she continued to shape up, he had even licensed to keep cats, creatures as useless as aesthetes in this hardening civilization, though a good deal less productive of solid wastes.

Nevertheless, he could not prevent himself—he was, after all, first and foremost a professional—from wondering how the masked men with the jackhammers were going to dispose of the asphalt they were cutting up. The project itself made sense: asphalt paving in a town where the noontime temperature rarely ran below eighty degrees ranged narrowly between being a nuisance and a trap. The dancers' shoes were already being slowed down by plaques and gobbets of the stuff. Nevertheless, it was virtually indigestible; once the men had dug it up and taken it away, where were they going to drop it? There was an underground tar pool in Riverdale in which such wastes were slowly—far too slowly—metabolized into carbon dioxide and water by an organism called *Bacillus aliphaticus,* but it was almost overflowing now and the sludge was being pushed up toward the top of the reservoir by the gas-trapping stickiness of the medium, like a beer with its head on the bottom. The time wasn't far off when the sewers of Riverdale would begin to ooze into its valleyed avenues not ordinary sewage, but stinking condensates so tacky and . . . indisposable . . . as to make hot asphalt seem as harmless as cold concrete. Nor was carbon dioxide a desirable end product any more. . . .

But never mind all that now. Alex knocked at the door of the *Brackette de Poisson,* was recognized, and was admitted. At his table his coterie was waiting, and hands were lifted solemnly to him. His glance had only just sought out Juliette Bronck in the dimness when Fantasia ad Parnassum rose ceremonially and said:

"*Ave,* garbage-man."

Alex was deeply offended—nobody used that word any more—and worse, he was afraid it showed. People ought to understand that it is difficult to be friends with friends who won't respect one's sensitivities. But there was worse to come.

"Listen," Fantasia said with quiet vehemence. "Sit down. Drop your shovel. You won't need it any more."

"Why not, Fan?"

"Why not?" Fantasia made a production of being astonished. At last he added, "God damn it, Alex, don't you know *yet* that the world is coming to an end?"

So here we go again; Fan has a new hobby. It didn't look, after all, like it was going to be a very pleasant lunch.

"All right," Alex said with a sudden accession of weariness. He sat down and looked around the table, trying to beam benevolently. It shouldn't have been difficult. After all, there was Juliette, a cameolike, 26-year-old, bikini-sized brunette who, in fact, at the moment was dressed in very little else; Will Emshredder, a tall, cadaverous, gentle-voiced man who had once produced a twelve-hour-long Experience called *The Junkpot Philosophy;* Rosasharn Ellisam, who was a cultural heroine of Alex's, since she made welded sculpture out of old bones which otherwise would have had to have been disposed of in some other way; Goldfarb Z, a white Muslim who for years had been writing, in invisible ink, a subliminal epic called *thus i marshal mcmoonahan;* Strynge Tighe, a desperate Irishman clad entirely in beads made of blue-dyed corn, who specialized in an unthinkably ancient Etruscan verse form called txckxrxsm; Beda Grindford, famous as the last man to get out of Los Angeles before the cyclone hit the Hyperion plant, but for nothing else; Arthur Lloyd Merlyn, a genuine, hereditary drip who was spending his life looking for somebody to put a plug in for him; Bang Jøhnsund, who wrote an interminable 3V serial named *The T.H.I.N.G. from O.U.T.B.A.C.K.;* Girlie Stonacher, a blond model who had been a hostess on the blimp limousine to the lunar orbital shuttle until all commercial lunar flights had been discontinued; Fantasia's wife, Gradus, possibly the most beautiful woman since Eleanor of Aquitaine, who went about totally naked and would cut you to ribbons if you gave the faintest sign of noticing it; Polar Pons, who by virtue of being nine feet tall was in great demand as a lecturer; and, of course, the usual youngsters, who didn't count.

And, also of course, the inevitable thorn in the side of any such group, in this case Fantasia himself; there was always one. He was a smallish but handsome man of about fifty who exacerbated Alex, first of all, by having the largest and most distinguished lineage of any man in America, so distinguished that a mere list of his names read like three pages of a hotel register from the heyday of the Austro-Hungarian Empire; secondly, by having become wealthy in a blamelessly social way by a number of useful inventions (for example, he had invented a container for beer which, when the bottle was empty, combined with smog and dissolved down to its base to leave behind a cup containing one more swallow of beer, after which the base itself turned into counter polish); third, by being willing to argue on any side of any question, without seeming to care which side he was on so long as he could make a case for it (that was, in this gathering of artists, his art); and last (or almost last), by turning out to be right nearly every time Alex had been sure he had caught him out in his facts.

Alex nevertheless rather loved him, and got along with him most of the time by refusing to believe that he took anything seriously. But this time, for the first time, Fantasia had genuinely insulted him; and—

"—the end of the world," Fantasia said grimly.

"Carry a sign," Alex said, picking up the menu with his very best indifference. He would have liked to have had Alaskan king crab, but it was extinct; the sea-level Guatemalan ship canal of 1980 had let the Atlantic's high tides flow rhythmically into the Pacific, with results similar to but much more drastic than the admission through the St. Lawrence canal of the lamprey eel into the Great Lakes. Today's Special was neon shrimp; knowing where they came from, Alex lost his appetite. He put the card down and looked at his sudden antagonist.

"Listen, dammit."

"Eri tu, Brute?"

"Alex," Fan said with a sort of disturbing tenderness, "you won't get out of this with dub macaronics, even with garbage sauce. Don't wince, it's time we called things by their right names. I've been doing some figuring, and no matter how I look at it, I think we're dead."

Juliette took Alex's elbow, in that gesture which said, *Don't listen, don't let him hurt you, I'll make it all up to you later;* but Alex had no choice. He said, snake to mongoose, "Go ahead."

After the last gasp, and the last plea not to tumble off just yet, Alex arranged his feet among the cats and was on the shimmering verge of oblivion when Juliette said: "Alex, are you asleep?"

He sighed, kneed away a cat with the demeaning name of Hausmaus, and propped himself up on one elbow. Beside him, Juliette exuded warmth and the mixed perfumes of spray deodorant and love, but her expression was that of a woman who now, at last, meant to get down to the real business of the evening. Thrusting a big toe vindictively into the ribs of the fat Siamese called Splat!, he said, "No, not lately. What is it?"

"Do you think Fan is right?"

"Of course not, he was just showing off. You know damned well that if I'd agreed with him, he'd have switched sides on the spot. Now let's get some sleep. School keeps tomorrow, for me at least."

"But Alex, he sounded so . . . *convinced*. He said, 'No matter how I look at it.' "

"He always sounds convinced. Look, Juli, of course we've got a junk problem. Everybody knows that. Who could know it better than I do? But we're coping. We always have coped. People have been predicting disaster for twenty years and there hasn't been any disaster. And there won't be."

"He did seem to have all the figures."

"And it wouldn't surprise me if he'd got them right. They sounded right, where I was familiar with them. But what Fan doesn't take into account is the sheer mass of the Earth—including the sea and the air, of which there's a hell of a lot. You can't create any major changes in a body that big just by a little litter. Making changes like that takes geological time."

"Are you sure?"

"Of course I'm sure. Go to sleep."

Go to sleep . . .

Some kinds of wastes—weather, rust, decay—are metabolized, or otherwise are returned to balance with the general order of nature. Others are not.

Among those which are not are aluminum cans, glass bottles, and jugs, and plastic containers of all kinds. The torrent began in 1938, when in the United States alone about 35 million tons of these indigestible, unreclaimable, nonburnable, or otherwise indefeasible objects were discarded. By 1969, the rate was three quarters of a ton per year for every man, woman, and child in the country, and was increasing by 4 percent per year. That year, Americans threw away 48 billion aluminum cans, 28 billion glass bottles and jars, and uncountable billions of plastic containers of every conceivable size and shape . . . 140 million tons of indestructible garbage.

By 1989, the total for the year had reached 311 million

tons. None of it had ever gone away. The accumulation—again, in the United States alone—was 7,141,950,000 tons.

Which is not to say that no attempts were made to cope with it. Cans that contained any iron at all were fished out by magnets. Some of the glass was pulverized to grains finer than sugar and fed into great cesspools like Lake Erie, where, since glass is slightly soluble in water, it would very slowly become a *dissolved* pollutant. But since glass had been broken and thrown away since the Phoenicians invented it, the pulverizing composters made no measurable difference in the world's rising burden of grit, slag, and ashes.

In the meantime, nylon "ghost nets" broke free from fishing vessels and were set floating as permanent fish destroyers. The composters tore up nylon stockings and socks into eight-inch fragments, which, however, refused to rot. Heavy concentrations of polyethylene continued to build in truck-garden soil, spread by compost plants which were supposed to be selling humus. Eventually, many of the polyethylene bags and plastic containers were screened out for burning, but almost nothing was known about what happens when plastics burn, and in fact most such polymerized substances simply evaporated, adding to the enormous load of air pollution, which by 1969 had reached the highest levels of the atmosphere from jet exhausts. By 1989, the air of the whole world—thanks to the law of the diffusion of gases, which no White House Office of Science and Technology had thought to repeal—was multiply ionized and loaded with poisons ranging from simple industrial gases like sulfur dioxide to constantly recomplexing hydrocarbons, and emphysema had become the principal cause of death, followed closely by lung cancer. Skin cancer, too, was rising in the actuarial tables, in incidence though not in mortality; the wide and beautiful sky had become a sea of carcinogens.

Masks were introduced, but of course nobody could stop breathing and emitting carbon dioxide. In 1980 there were 4,500 million human carbon dioxide emitters on the Earth—very few of other species—and so much of the world had been paved over, or turned into desert, that the green plants had long lost the battle to convert the gas into oxygen and water vapor. The burning of fossil fuels, begun in prehistory among the peat bogs, might have fallen off with the invention of nuclear power, but the discovery in 1968—when nuclear power was still expensive to exploit, and which produced wastes so long-lived and so poisonous that people had the rare good sense to be terrified of them while it was still early enough to cut down on their production—of the Alaskan oil field, the fourth largest in history, aborted the nuclear boom and produced a new spurt in burning. The breathers, in the meantime, continued to multiply; by 1989 nobody knew what the population of the world was—most of the statistics of the increase had been buried under the statistics for the increment of garbage.

Carbon dioxide is not a poisonous gas, but it is indefatigably heat-conservative, as are all the other heavy molecules that had been smoked into the air. In particular, all these gases and vapors conserved solar heat, like the roof of a greenhouse. In due course, the Arctic ice cap, which had been only a thin sheet over a small ocean, an ocean furthermore contained in a basin also heat-conservative, melted, followed by the Greenland cap. Now the much deeper Antarctic cap was dwindling, dumping great icebergs into the warming Antarctic Ocean. Great fog banks swept around the world, accelerating the process and chelating the heavier gas molecules as they moved, making them immune from attack by oxygen, ozone, or the activating effects of sunlight. The fogs stank richly of tars and arsenes, and were thicker and yellower than any London had seen in the worst years *before* the Clean Air Act had been passed.

And the ice continued to melt. Sea level in 1989 was twenty-one feet higher than it had been in 1938; every harbor in the world had been obliterated, every shoreline changed, and the brokers of lower Manhattan had been forced to learn to paddle. The worldwide temperature rose; more bergs fell into the Ross Sea; the last Ice Age was over.

Sleep, my child, and peace attend thee. . . .

For some reason, Alex awoke just before dawn. Disgruntled, he went to the head, had a long drink of water, took a tranquilizer, roughed up Splatl's fur along the back until he purred with contented indignation and bit him, peeked lubriciously at Juliette in her cocoon, constructed what replies he might have made to Fantasia at lunch had he not been taken so completely aback, and finally lay down again; but nothing served— he was completely alert.

Then he remembered: Today was the day of his appointment with Secretary de Tohil Vaca, and the beginning of their test of power. Suddenly Fan's irresponsible hypothesizing, and the poses, hobbies, crotchets, and vapors of the rest of the coterie, suddenly even Juliette herself, fell into perspective. He was back in the real world, where nothing ever changed unless you made it change, and never mind those who merely talked. Reality was what counted.

Swinging out of the warm bed with some reluctance, he sat on the edge until his hypotensive dizziness had passed, then washed, shaved, dressed, turned off the alarm—no point in having it wake Juli, since he had anticipated it—and kissed her on the end of the nose. She murmured disturbedly, "Lemonade," as though she were having some peculiarly private dream, and resettled herself. She still exuded that unpublic, compound, organic fragrance which was her gift to him, and for a moment he felt a desperate urgency to pull off all his clothes and other arrangements and lie beside her again; but at the same moment of the impulse, he happened to see the teddy bear on her dresser, which, though it made her seem more pathetic, and the room even tinier, also re-reminded him of the substantial world.

Well, but he would protect her. Part of protecting her was the matter of coping with the real world. He checked the contents of his briefcase carefully in the false dawn, and then left, closing the door very quietly.

Some forty-five seconds later he was fumbling with the key before her door and fuming with loveless indignation. He had forgotten to feed the goddam cats.

Juli's apartment was on the fifth and only habitable floor of what had once been a moderately expensive apartment building in the Chelsea district. Occasionally, the landlord managed to rent out a fourth-floor flat at reduced rates to some gullible and desperate family, on the showing that even high tide did not reach that far; but they seldom lasted a month, or until the first storm sent waves breaking over their windowsills.

Luckily, there was no wind today, nor even any rain. Alex

put on his mask, settled his stretch homburg carefully atop it, and went down the hallway. Rats scurried and squeaked ahead of him. Juli let the cats roam free in the building after she got up, but the rats always came back; unlike the cats, they could swim.

The canoe was lashed to the balcony of the fire escape, swung on davits, an arrangement kindly rigged by Fantasia; Alex himself could not so much as tie a knot without getting his forefinger caught in it. The tide was down today, and after settling himself in the canoe, he took a full five minutes lowering it gingerly to the greasy surface of the water. Once he had cast loose, however, he paddled up Eighth Avenue with fair skill and speed, an ability which was a by-product—not achieved without many spills—of the affair with Juli.

Thanks to the earliness of his awakening, there was not much traffic yet. Even the few barges he passed were half empty, the identical masked faces peering out of them looking as disconsolate as he felt to be up at this hour. At Thirty-Second, a street-sweeper went by him going the other way, sucking into its frontal maw everything that floated except the traffic, and discharging from its almost as capacious anus anything that did not clink, clank or crunch. The theory behind the monster, which had been designed over a decade ago, was that anything that did not make a noise as it passed through its innards could safely be left in the water for the fish and bacteria.

Actually, of course, there were no fish anywhere near this close to shore any more. There were not many even in the high seas. The Guatemalan canal had resulted in the destruction of about 23,000 Pacific species, through evolutionary competition, but the destruction in the Atlantic had not been that selective. It had begun with the poisoning of the Atlantic phytoplankton, the very beginning of the chain of nutrition for all marine life, by land effluents loaded with insecticides and herbicides. The population of the Atlantic from pole to pole, from brit to whales, was now only 10 percent of what it had been when the streetsweeper had been on the drawing boards. As for the bacteria, the number of species of molecules they could not digest now far outnumbered those that they could.

Nevertheless Alex waved to the monster as he went by.

Obsolete or not, it belonged to his own working force. The
men piloting it waved back. Though of course they did not
recognize him in his mask, it was known that the boss often
went to work this way: if somebody in a canoe waved to them,
it was safer to wave back. *Slllrrrrppp . . . Spprrrsttt,* said the
monster.

The city was waking up now. Outboard-powered car pools
of men in wet-suits, painted to look tailored, were beginning
to charge along the cross-streets, creating wakes and followed
by the muffled obscenities of people in canoes. Most of these
came across the Hudson from New Jersey, which had had a
beautifully planned new city built north of Newark, on what
had been the tidal swamp of the Meadows, only to have its
expensively filled and tended lawns become swamps again and
then go totally under water. Few of the commuters paid any
attention to the traffic semaphores, having learned from experience that the rare police launches were reluctant to chase
them—the wakes of the launches upset more canoes and row-
boats than the speeding outboards did. Lately, some of the
paddlers and rowers had taken to chucking sash weights over
the gunwales of speeders when possible. The police were prone
to ignore this, too, though they frowned at outright shooting.

Alex observed all the semaphores scrupulously and reached
Forty-Second Street without incident. There, before turning
starboard, he took off the homburg, stowed it in its plastic
bag, and put on his crash helmet.

Again, thanks to the relative earliness of the hour, he had
been able to thread his way through the jam of barges shipping produce into and out of what had once been Penn Station with considerable speed, but Times Square was another
matter. There was no time after dawn when it was not a mass
of boats of all sizes, many of them equipped with completely
illegal rams and spikes, many locked together willy-nilly in
raftlike complexes, the occupants swearing and flailing at each
other with oars, paddles, barge poles, whips, boarding hooks,
and specialized assegai-like weapons developed by the more
ingenious. There was no alternate route to where Alex was
going that was any better.

The police concentrated here as a matter of course, which
prevented individual acts of mayhem from fulminating into
outright riot, and often managing to keep some sort of narrow

canal open in one direction or another. Alex watched for these canals, and those that opened accidentally now and then, with the intensity of a mariner trying to pass through the mythical mazes of the Sargasso. He had learned long ago that picking fights with other boats was a waste of time. The only weapon that he carried was a table-tennis racquet sided with coarse sandpaper, with which he banged the knuckles of people in the water who tried to climb into his canoe. He did this completely impersonally and without malice; he knew, as the strugglers should have known, that it is impossible to get into a canoe from the water without upsetting it.

He took only two paddle blows elsewhere than directly on the helmet, which he thought must be a record for the course. Past Sixth Avenue, the furtive canals got wider and tempers tended to have cooled a little. By the time he reached the Public Library—whose books were now no more inaccessible to the public than they had been fifty years ago, though the reason had changed—he felt justified in removing the helmet and resuming the homburg. There was remarkably little water in the scuppers and he himself was only moderately splashed —the latter of no moment at all, since his clothing was entirely by Burberry and all he needed to do once he arrived was step into one of the Bell System's booths, deposit a quarter, and have the random garbage showered off with salt water.

All in all, he thought as he turned the canoe over to an Avis docker, it was a good thing that he hadn't been able to sleep. The trip had been an out-and-out snap.

Secretary de Tohil Vaca was a tall, fair, bearded man of almost insufferable elegance of manner. Ringed and ringleted, perfumed and pomaded, fringed and furbelowed, beaded and brocaded, he combined nature and nurture so overpoweringly, in fact in such an absolute assonance of synesthetic alliteration, that it became a positive pleasure to remind one's self that the underlying essence of his official cachet, like the musk of sex and the ambergris of the most ancient perfumes, was— Alex bit silently but savagely down on the word—garbage.

His office was on the top floor—in fact, *was* the top floor— of the old Pan Am building, which was itself one of the principal monuments to the ways junk had been piled up willy-nilly in the heyday of the Age of Waste. The building itself still sat over the vast septic tank which had once been Grand Central Station, a tank over which the tides gurgled semidaily without in any way slowing the accumulation of filth in those deep caverns and subway tubes. Most of the immense, ugly structure, which had always looked like the box some other building had been shipped in, was now occupied only by tax accountants, 3V producers, whores, mosquitoes, anthologists, brokers, blimp-race betting agencies, public-relations firms, travel agents, and other telephone-booth Indians, plus hordes and torrents of plague-bearing brown rats and their starving fleas.

Secretary de Tohil Vaca, however, reached his office, when he did, by private blimp, much accompanied by hostesses and secretaries rather like Girlie Stonacher; and he had been known, when he was in a rare hurry, to settle down upon the top of it by air-polluting helicopter. Rank had, as it is written, its privileges.

The office was flooded with sunlight from all sides when the smog let it through, and was hung alternately with Aztec tapestries and with modern collages of what was called the Reconstituted Findings school. The air was cool and almost odorless, and usually carried, as now, a discreet purring of music. In apparent—but only apparent—deference to Alex, the system was now playing a version of four exhaust-flutes of *Hector, the Garbage Collector,* the eighty-year-old anthem of Local 802.

It was all very well prepared, but Alex was not going to be seduced. He not only knew what he wanted, but knew that he had to get it; he was, after all, as much a creature of his constituency as de Tohil Vaca was of the administration.

"Sit down, Alex," he said affably. "I'm sorry this meeting has been postponed so frequently, but, you'll understand, I'm sure, there have been other pressing matters. . . ."

The Secretary waved vaguely and allowed the sentence to trail off. Alex thought he understood well enough: the Secretary had sought to convey the impression that the Administration did not regard the matter as serious and could, if it had to, get along very well without the services of Local 802. They both knew this to be nonsense, but the forms had to be gone through.

Now that he was actually in the presence, however, Alex found this diagnosis weakening a little. The Secretary's expression was that of a man rather grimly amused by some private piece of information, like that of a wife accepting flowers from a husband she knows is having an affair with the computer girl. Of course, de Tohil Vaca was a superb actor, but nevertheless Alex found the expression rather disquieting. He tried not to show it.

"Quite all right," he said automatically. "Of course you realize that having left so little time for negotiation means that you'll have to accept our terms as stated."

"Not at all, not at all. In the first place, my dear Alex, you know as well as I do that a strike by your men would be illegal. In our present society we could no more allow it than a wooden city could allow a fireman's strike."

"I'm quite prepared to go to jail if I have to. You can't jail the whole union." He did not go on to add that winning this strike would also win him de Tohil Vaca's office in the next administration. The Secretary knew well enough what the stakes were, which was the real reason why no negotiation would have been fruitful; the strike was absolutely inevitable.

"I'm not threatening you, I assure you. No, really, that issue has in reality become quite irrelevant. You see, Alex, there have been new developments of which you're not aware. They are of sufficient importance so that we no longer care if your men quit work and never go back."

"That," Alex said, "is pure nonsense. The only justification you could have for such a statement would be the development of machinery which made all my men obsolete. I know the technology at least as well as you do, and no such advance has occurred. And if such machines exist in theory, you can't possibly get them into production and on the job fast enough to prevent a disaster if we strike—not even if in theory they're capable of solving the entire problem."

"I imply no such thing," de Tohil Vaca said, with a calmness that seemed to conceal a certain relish. "We have not solved the problem. Quite the opposite. The problem has solved us."

"All right," Alex said. "You've produced your effect. Now, just what *are* we talking about?"

The Secretary leaned back in his chair and put his fingertips together. "Just this," he said. "We cannot 'dispose' of our wastes any longer. They have tipped the geological scales against us. The planet is breaking up. The process has already started, and the world will be effectively uninhabitable before the next ten years have passed."

The Secretary was watching Alex narrowly, and actor or no actor, could not prevent a faint shadow of disappointment from flitting over his face; Alex had only smiled.

"Good heavens, man," the Secretary said. "Do you hear an announcement like that every day? Or are you utterly without imagination?"

"Neither," Alex said. "But as it happens, I did hear a very similar statement less than twenty-four hours ago. It didn't come from quite so august a source, but I didn't believe it then, and I don't believe it now."

"What," de Tohil Vaca said, "would you think I stood to gain by making it?"

"I can't imagine. If you were another man, you might be hoping I'd carry this story back to the union and get the strike called off. Then, when the end of the world didn't come through on schedule, I'd be destroyed politically. But you know I'm not that credulous, and I know that you know you wouldn't dare to use such means; it'd destroy you, too."

"Well, at least we are now out in the open," de Tohil Vaca said. "But the fact is that I mean every word I say, and furthermore, I'm prepared to offer you a proposition, though not at all of the kind you thought you came here to discuss. To begin with, though, I had better offer you my documentation. You have, no doubt, noticed the Brooklyn earthquakes."

"Yes, and I know what caused them," Alex said, feeling suddenly, unexpectedly grateful for Fan's passionate lecture of the preceding day. "It's a residuum of deep-well disposal."

The Secretary looked openly astonished. "What on earth is that?" he said. "I've never heard of it."

"I'm not surprised. It hasn't been widely used in a long time. But back around 1950, some private firms began disposing of liquid wastes by injection into deep wells—mostly chemical companies and refineries. Most of the wells didn't go down more than six thousand feet and the drillers went to a lot of trouble not to get them involved with the water table. Everybody liked the idea at the time because it was an alternative to dumping into rivers and so on.

"But then the Army drilled one *twelve* thousand feet down, near Denver. They started pumping in 1962 and a month later, after only about four million gallons had gone down, Denver had its first earthquake in eighty years. After that, the tremors increased or decreased exactly in phase with the pumping volume. There's even a geological principal to explain it, called the Hubbert-Rubey Effect."

"My word," de Tohil Vaca said, taking notes rapidly. "What happened?"

"Well, nothing for a while. More than a hundred such wells were in operation by 1970, mostly in Louisiana and Texas. But by 1966 somebody had noticed the correlation—which was pretty sharp because the Denver area had never been subject to quakes before, and the quake zone was right underneath the Army's arsenal—so the Army stopped pumping. The quakes went on for another eighteen months—in fact, the biggest one of all was in 1970—but then they began to die back.

"And that's my point. The injection system was outlawed in most states, but there are still eight of them in operation in Pennsylvania, pumping into a strata system only marginally suited for them, and another right out here in Brookhaven, which is totally *un*suited for it. That brackets Brooklyn neatly —and unlike Denver, Brooklyn always has been subject to slight temblors. So there's your answer: cap those wells, and as soon as they get back into equilibrium again—which will take as long at it takes, eighteen months only applied to Denver—then, no earthquakes."

The Secretary dropped his stylus and stared at Alex in frank admiration.

"My word," he said again. "That's the most ingenious theory I've heard in years. I do seem to have underestimated you, after all."

"Well, it isn't entirely mine," Alex admitted. "The man I talked to yesterday thinks that once you trigger an earthquake, you can't untrigger it. But the Colorado experience shows you can."

"Even if you can," said de Tohil Vaca, "I regret to say that the theory, while elegant, is also irrelevant. The real process is something quite different, and absolutely irreversible. It's the greenhouse effect that's responsible—and I hope you'll pardon me if I read from notes here and there; I am no scientist."

"Go ahead."

The Secretary opened a folder. "You know the Arctic ice cap is gone. But that's minor; it was only pack ice. The real problem is down south. There are unthinkable billions of tons of ice over the Antarctic continent—which is volcanic, as Mount Erebus shows. Now the first effect of letting up the pressure of all that ice is that it changes the isostatic balance of the Earth's crust, which would be bad enough, but there's worse to follow.

"There's a thing called precession of the equinoxes, which means that not only does the Earth rotate on its axis, but the axis of rotation also moves around its own center, like the secondary motion of a top when it's slowing down."

"I know about that. It means the poles describe a small circle, so we don't always have the same pole star. But I also know just one of those circles takes twenty-five thousand years."

"Yes, but that's geologically a pretty short time. And bear in mind that swinging all that concentrated ice around and around represents an enormous amount of energy—of momentum. If you melt the ice and distribute its mass as water evenly all over the globe, where does the energy go?"

"I'm not a scientist either," Alex said. "But as an engineer, I'd predict that it'd show up as heat."

"And so some of it will—in *lots* of heat. Good-bye, fish, just for a starter. And the sea-level rise will total thirty-three feet when all the ice is gone. But there's still more, Alex. Besides the precession, the top wobbles. It used to be called the Drayson Effect, but I gather that everybody sneered so hard at poor old Drayson, whoever he was, for proposing it, that when they discovered the wobble was real, they gave it another name; it's called Chalmer's Wobble now. It shows up in a cyclical disturbance of the polar path, the equinoctial path."

"And how long is the cycle?"

"Fourteen months."

"Fourteen months! Are you sure you've got that right?"

"That's what it says here," de Tohil Vaca said grimly. "And

it's been known for twenty years that any major variation in the cycle is a signal that a *very* large strain release is about to occur somewhere in the crust. Lately, my dear fellow, the polar path has been wobbling irregularly all over northern Canada.

"The outcome is going to be vulcanism on a scale never seen before in the lifetime of man. I'm told that we are in for a new era of mountain-building, the first since the Rockies were thrust up. *That* will bury all our old cans and bottles and junked cars very nicely—but there'll be nobody left around to rejoice."

"My God," Alex said slowly. "And obviously it's irreversible —we can't take the carbon dioxide and the other heavy gases out of the air. We've changed the climate, and that's that. The ice is going to go right on melting. Faster and faster, in fact, as more energy's released."

"Precisely."

Irrationally, Alex felt a momentary flash of pleasure at being now able to tell Fan of a disaster that made Fan's hypothesis look like a mild attack of hiccups. The moment's elation vanished in a horrible nightmarish sinking of every recognizable human emotion except terror. He could not doubt his erstwhile antagonist; the whole sequence, even he could see, flowed inevitably from as fundamental a law as the conservation of energy. Trying to keep his voice from shaking, he said,

"And yet you said you had a proposition."

"I do. We are going to evacuate some people to the Moon. We still have the old commercial ships, as well as military vehicles, and we've been maintaining the bases, mostly because the Soviets have been maintaining theirs. Of course there's no hope of mankind's thriving on the Moon, but it's at least a tenable way-station until we can organize a further jump to Mars, which we just *might* make livable."

"And what about the Soviets themselves?"

"They'll just have to think of the idea for themselves," the Secretary said. "We certainly aren't going to propose it to them. Personally, I'd a lot rather outnumber them when it's all over; lunar bases are terribly vulnerable."

"Hmm. How are you going to choose our people?"

"Partly by need, partly at random. We want people of

proven ability and necessary skills; but we also want to mini-
mize genetic drift, which I'm told will be a real danger in so
small a population. Myself, I'm not even sure what it is. So
we're picking out a small group of technicians and known
leaders, and we're issuing each of them ten tickets, which they
can hand out to anyone they please."

"Without restrictions?"

"There are several restrictions. Secrecy is one, though of
course we know we can't maintain it for long. Another is baggage: twenty pounds per person, which has to pack into five
cubic feet. But the most important one is that in every group
of ten there must be six women. Under the circumstances, men
are almost unimportant. If they weren't our main repository of
technology, and of creative energy—and of course there's the
high possibility of accident—we'd make the ratio nine to one,
and still think it too high."

"No children, I suppose?"

"No children. We want skills plus genes. And potency. We'll
generate children later, when we're sure we can take care of
them. We can't ship them. So if any of your friends want to
give up their seats for bairns, you will have to tell them No."

"I can see myself doing that," Alex said.

"I hope you can. I'm sorry, Alex. It's ghastly, to be sure.
But it's the way it's going to have to go."

An easy policy for an obvious homosexual like de Tohill
Vaca to adapt to—or a childless man like Alex. But de Tohil
Vaca was not going to have to tell anybody No; he had passed
that obligation on. To, among other people, Alex.

"The system distributes the moral problem nicely, too,"
Alex said bitterly. "Every man a god to his friends."

"Would you rather have the Administration choose everybody?"

The answer to that was obvious. "What about livestock?"

"Oh, these vessels will be arks—animals, seeds, everything.
Why? Have you got pets?"

"Two cats."

"We're taking ten. If your cats are of opposite sexes and
haven't been altered, I'll issue you a ticket for your two; you're
the first to ask, and with cats we don't care about breeds—
they all reduce to alley cats in one crossing anyhow. Naturally
they'll have to pass a medical exam, and so will your friends.

These tickets, by the way, are being issued by commercial agencies with no connection—no *visible* connection—to the government. That cover won't last long, so don't fail to apply for yours *instanter*."

"I won't. But there must be a price for all this. There always is."

"My dear fellow," de Tohil Vaca said, "I told you we valued you. I do hope you'll call off the strike, as an obvious and complete irrelevancy now; just help us keep the garbage down to a dull roar until we get the ships off, and don't, if you'll pardon me the pun, rock the boat. No other price, except for the tickets, which are the same price the old spacelines used to sell them for to the Moon: a thousand dollars—ostensibly, round trip. That's a part of the cover."

"I see. Well, many thanks." Alex arose, hardly seeing his surroundings. The audio system was still playing that damned tune, which he had always hated. At the door, he turned and looked back.

"Mr. Secretary—you're going, of course."

"No, I am not," de Tohil Vaca said, his pleasantly vapid face suddenly turning to stone. "I am the man who failed to prevent this horror, as I was charged by my office to do. My presence on the Moon would dissolve the last chance of man in the bitterest kind of political strife. Under no circumstances would I introduce such a serpent into this rock garden." Then, suddenly, he smiled. "Besides, I want to see the end. When Ragnarök comes, there ought to be somebody on the spot who is capable of appreciating the spectacle."

When the door closed behind Alex, he felt, aside from all his other burdens, somewhat less than three inches high.

On the way back to his own office, Alex found himself wondering how Fan would take it. He had almost automatically decided that Fan would have to be one of "his" three men. There was nobody of his own sex that Alex loved better, and besides, the man was omni-competent—almost as much so as he made himself out to be. (Hmm . . . John Hillary, Alex's assistant, had better go, too. He was an expert on pressure systems, a good electronicist on the side, easy to get along with, and a vigorous forty *ae*.)

There was more than a little irony in Fan's being an obligatory survivor. He had lived an astonishingly full life, starting from the utmost poverty, leaving home at fourteen without a penny in his pocket, turning all kinds of odd jobs in a world where such jobs hardly existed any more, devouring the public library in every town he visited, eventually becoming a highly successful journalist until he got bored with the hours the job required him to keep, cranking out small but socially useful inventions at odd moments, and enjoying himself hugely every step of the way. The lives of most men, even when looked back at from the vantage point of half a century, by comparison resembled nothing so much as the slow growth of a forgotten turnip. Anything Fan accomplished from here on out would have to be regarded as a bonus.

And there was another side to the matter which might be even more important. Though Alex was nobody's adventurer, he had once faced death himself, but in retrospect it now seemed to have been very nearly a false alarm—an undifferentiated tumor of the mastoid process, of the same general class that struck many people these days, which had scared hell out of everybody concerned . . . and then turned out to be as easily operable as a hangnail, or almost.

Fan's experience had been quite different: he had been attacked by a mutated leukemia virus which had nearly cleaned out his bone marrow as thoroughly as if it had been sucked by a dog, leaving him virtually without any of the tissues necessary for generating blood cells. This had been followed, with utter inevitability, by a whole series of secondary infections for which it had been impossible to give him antibiotics—or, for that matter, even aspirin—because his natural immunity to any such foreign substances had been knocked out as well. And there was no treatment for the virus itself.

That siege had frightened nobody, for there was no doubt whatsoever that Fan was going to die. Fan's response was simply, "No thank you; not yet."

And so he hadn't. There was no explanation for that but Fan's own, which was preposterous: he claimed that he had directed his remaining blood-forming tissues to regenerate and get busy making antibodies against the virus, on pain of his extreme displeasure, and so of course they had. If you did not believe this analysis, Fan politely invited you to come up with one of your own.

It had become a moderately famous case history, and there were a good many medical research people who yearned for a few drops of Fan's blood to analyze for the antibodies. They had to go right on yearning, for any fooling around with Fan's blood was *verboten.* For nearly a year after his recovery, his attending physician had almost literally hovered over him night and day, waiting to slap a patch on him if he so much as cut himself shaving, until Fan tired of that too and told him to get out and go treat somebody who was *sick,* for God's sake.

That had all happened some years ago, but as a result Alex knew that few people in the world were as well equipped by temperament and by intelligence as Fan was to face the coming slaughter. If it had turned out that he had to stay behind, he would have watched the process with grave interest, and very likely some aesthetic pleasure. Rather like de Tohil Vaca, Alex thought; except that he had more confidence in Fan's ability to maintain his detachment to the end.

Maybe Fan ought to be left off the ship and asked to command the rock-tides to turn back. He would enjoy it so hugely if they did.

Now, who else? Juli, certainly; he would exercise that choice only because he had been given the power to do so and for no other reason, like an attorney's privilege for arbitrary challenge of a juror after all his challenges-for-cause had been used up. But the women were not the heart of the problem yet, for even with Juli ruled in, he had five more he could choose.

But since Fan had to go, and Hillary, he was left with only *one* more man. And very few of his male friends, he realized grimly, were really good for anything but amusing him . . . or, to put the matter more bluntly, flattering him and eating on his credit. Merlyn could be ruled out at once; he had no talents whatsoever, not even little ones, and besides had a vicious streak which would be dangerous in a small community. Grindford was a somewhat pleasanter person, with a demonstrated talent for survival; but what else could he do besides duck when he saw the egg approaching the fan? Not a damn thing, except brag about how irresistible he was to women. Even if the brags were true, which Alex gravely doubted, a great seducer would be nothing but a living fossil

on the Moon, under the conditions de Tohil Vaca had speci-
fied.

Those two eliminations were easy, but from there on out
the pain set in. All of the remaining men in the luncheon circle were creative in some slight degree—apparently equally
slight, and all utterly negligible, until you examined them each
on their merits under the new situation. Take Bang Jøhnsund,
for instance: who on the Moon could use a talent for writing
the most moronic and endless kind of 3V serial? The answer
might well be, *everybody;* surely, under such confined and
near-hopeless conditions, a talent for taking people's minds
off their troubles might turn out to be of tremendous value.
Much of the same kind of value might inhere in Polar Pons;
he entertained people, no, more, he told them things about
their world that they needed to know in such a way that they
thought they were being entertained while in fact they were
learning. The fact that he had to simplify the information he
imparted so well beyond the point of caricature—without
knowing that he was doing so—counted against him, but he
might shape up under pressure; almost everyone did.

Goldfarb Z and Tighe were only superficially easier cases.
To be sure, the subject of Goldfarb Z's Cantos was unknown
to everyone, including himself, since he had sworn not to
develop the invisible ink he had been writing it in until he
had finished the work. After that, he would read it, and probably change the title in the light of what he found; the present
title was only a sort of running head or slug. But he *was* a
poet, with a fair record of production behind him before he
had undertaken the completely hermetic opus. The same
could be said of Will Emshredder, though he worked in multi-
media and thus—if one could judge by Goldfarb Z's working
title—was of a completely opposite school. Obviously the
lunar colony could not afford to be without a poet, but did
Alex have to choose between schools as well, or was it only
the genes for creativity that mattered? And Tighe was a
scholar, and there again a propensity for scholarship might
be more important than the fact that Tighe's particular field
of study had no social utility on Earth even now, and would
completely cease to exist on the Moon.

Although he had never given the matter any thought before, Alex had the feeling that poets were scarce commodities,

whereas almost any other ten-man cadre might come up—literally—with a scholar. Which poet, then? Goldfarb Z, though gregarious, was also a man of almost impenetrable reserve; but even after all these years, Alex could not say he knew Emshredder any better, because the man was almost fumblingly inarticulate except when he was in front of his consoles. He thought he did not know which of the two he liked better, which was some small advantage, in that it made for at least a little impartiality. And sheerly on instinct, he felt that Will Emshredder had the larger talent. Very well; he should be the third man.

And promptly upon this decision, Alex found out what he had never known before: that it was in fact Goldfarb Z whom he liked better. It was astonishing how acutely painful the discovery was.

The pain became worse when he came to consider the women. Rosasharn had a limited talent—how limited, he had no way of assessing—but she was somewhat beyond her child-bearing years, and decidedly ugly to boot; taking her along would be a betrayal of one of the essential premises of the escape, if Alex had understood de Tohil Vaca on that point. By the same token, Girlie Stonacher was young, pretty, promiscuous and provenly fertile; she would fit into the proposed colonial society like a key into a slot, and furthermore enjoy it hugely. Count her in. The same terms, with some minor reservations as to what era one was thinking about, had been said—Alex did not know with how much truth—of Irene Pons; but how, how, how could he give Irene a ticket and refuse one to Polar? And would Irene go without him? And if she did, would she not feel the guilt of her husband's death all the rest of her life, regardless of the fact that it would be in no way her fault, and hate Alex for forcing the choice upon her?

Worse was to come. He realized that he had been assuming all along that Fan's wife Gradus would also be among the Chosen, not specifically because she was Fan's wife but because she was the quickest intelligence among all the women, as well as being the most beautiful. But in both these departments, Goldfarb Y was not far behind and should surely be included; and the one emotion Goldfarb Z had ever shown in public was a passionate devotion to her. Alex was therefore in the position of having to part them forever, while at the same time arbitrarily taking along his own Juli, who, though pretty and sweet and good in bed, had a brain about the size of a truffle, and no talent he had ever been able to discover.

This was a more painful case than that of Polar and Irene Pons—not to them, but to Alex. The numbers simply and inexorably ruled Polar out; Alex was entitled to only one man out of the group, and he was morally certain that, having included one administrator and one engineer, that third man should be a poet. But suddenly he thought he saw a way out. It was genes that counted, wasn't it? Wasn't it? And Will Emshredder had a daughter. . . .

Slowly, feeling as though he were dividing his own soul in two, he drew a line through Will Emshredder's name and wrote down that of Goldfarb Z.

It had never occurred to him before that the reason God demands love of everyone is that He must feel overwhelmingly guilty.

The basement warehouse was huge, but there were not many echoes in it; the Chosen were very subdued about their baggage-checking. Juli examined her two cartons for the umpteenth time. Twenty pounds and five cubic feet had not turned out to be much, and in the end, she had decided on taking almost nothing but keepsakes—and, of course, Splat! and Hausmaus, currently crouched in a carrier on the labeling table, from which occasionally issued low, hoarse cat-howls of protest. Presumably Alex's cartons, which had already gone out, had been more practical.

Of course her cartons were not *all* keepsakes, really. She had also put together the best approximation she could think of to a survival kit, consisting of small tools, a medicine chest, blankets, and a few other such items, including a nest of plastic containers—no matter where a woman went, she would find some use for those. She hoped the teddy bear wouldn't be discovered; it probably wouldn't show up on the fluoroscope, except for its eyes, and there were several dozen other buttons, all loose, in that box. She knew the stuffed animal had no business being in there at all, but it had been the only toy she had ever had.

Well, if she had forgotten anything important, it was too late to include it now. Reluctantly she shoved the cartons onto the moving belt, which would carry them to the blimp for Rockland Spaceport. The cats ought to go now, too, but suddenly, seeing nobody else around her that she knew, she decided not to part with them just yet.

Where, above all, was Alex? Juli already had her reservation, but Alex had to confirm his own, and it was getting close to the time for the helicopter shuttle for today's flight (only the baggage went by blimp), on which they were both booked. He and the other eight people he had chosen, not without much agony, had been holding some kind of farewell party to the Earth, which she had chosen not to attend as likely to be entirely too painful. Had they all gotten drunk and lost track of the time?

She did not dare to go looking for him; suppose he should show up at the last minute and find her gone? But time passed on the big warehouse clock, and passed, and passed. . . .

The elevator doors to the shuttle closed for the last time today. The endless belt stopped moving. There was nobody human left in the warehouse but herself.

They had missed the flight.

Halfway between panic and fury, she picked up the cat carrier, the contents of which had fallen asleep but now resumed its moans and squalls of despair, and marched off to a telephone booth, where she phoned, first of all, the ticket agent. For more than half an hour she got nothing but a recording telling her all the lines were busy, which she had fully expected. The secret was not yet out, at last reports, but all the same that office must be a madhouse; just the rumor (there had been no announcement) that commercial lunar flights were being resumed had generated a tidal wave of would-be tourists.

At last, she got through to a clerk. No. Dr. Stewart had not picked up his reservation. No, neither had Mr. ad Parnassum. Neither had any of the others.

Next, by citing the code formula which stood for (though the clerk did not know this) the real intent of the exodus, she reached the agent himself and made her plea.

"I'm-sorry-moddom, but you must understand that we have

many standbys for each flight. Your seats were doubtless filled long ago."

"You don't understand. I know we've missed *this* flight. What I want to do is transfer our reservations to the next flight."

"I'm-sorry-moddom, but our instructions are strict. We cannot under any circumstances issue alternative tickets to no-shows."

"Now that's just silly. We weren't entirely no-shows. After all, our baggage is already *on* today's flight. What's the point of shipping all that baggage and then not sending the people it belongs to?"

"I'm-sorry-moddom, but I'm sure the people who took your seats will find some use for it."

"No, they won't." Juli began to cry, and at least half the tears were real. "No, they won't; it's almost all just keepsakes. Things that w-won't be valuable to anybody b-but us."

The agent had doubtless had to slosh his way through gallons of previous tears. "I'm-sorry-moddom, but regulations do not permit us to issue a second set of tickets."

"Oh, damn your regulations! Now listen, my . . . husband is the head of one of these groups of ten people, a, a cadre leader."

"There are hundreds of those, moddom. We are not allowed to treat them any differently than anybody else."

"But he's not just an ordinary cadre leader. He's somebody that Secretary de Tohil Vaca *particularly* wanted to go. The Secretary told him so, personally."

"I'm-sorry-moddom, but surely any faceless person could claim that over the telephone." In the background, people were shouting at him to answer another phone.

"If I were just anybody, how would I know the project code?"

"These things leak, moddom. Now if you'll excuse me—"

"Wait a minute," Juli said desperately. "Why would just anybody be asking for tickets under these particular names? You should have some sort of list with the names on them."

"Yes, moddom, we do, but for today's flight only. We cannot issue second chances."

"If you called the Secretary—" And then, right in the middle of this sentence, which in fact she did not know how she was going to end, she remembered that Alex's priority number was different from the secret project code number. She said: "My husband has priority number FHGR-One."

There was a long silence, except for the dim pandemonium in the background. She could only pray that the agent was looking the number up.

At last he was back. "I have confirmed the priority, moddom. I am therefore issuing you two reservations for tomorrow's flight."

"Oh . . . thank God. And thank you, too."

"Please bear in mind, moddom, that this is the last chance. The last, the final, the ultimate chance. Are you sure you understand that?"

"Yes, I do," she said gratefully. Her relief was so great that instead of flipping the hang-up toggle, she hit the shower toggle instead, and was promptly drenched with salt water. She hardly noticed.

The panic ebbed, but she was still worried. They might have all been killed, or anyhow hospitalized, on the very eve of escape. Oh God. She called the *Brackette de Poisson*.

And God damn them, they were there. They were *all* there.

Now free to feel completely unadulaterated rage, she left a message for them with the management, put on her gas mask, snatched up the cats, and stamped out to flag down a water scooter.

The eight were still there when she arrived (after parking the grumbling cat carrier in the expensive supermarket next door, by polite but firm request of the restaurant's manager)— the eight who had survived Alex's playing God: three males (Fan, Goldfarb Z, and a man she placed vaguely as an engineer from Alex's office) and five females (Gradus, Girlie, Goldfarb Z's wife Y, Polar Pon's wife Irene, and Will Emshredder's divorced daughter Evadne).

Scanning this much constricted remnant of the old crew, and registering just exactly who remained of it here, Juli realized that more than the pains of choice and of partings had been involved here. There had also been a considerable spectrum of selfless sacrifice. With the realization, her righteous indignation began to simmer down toward the slightly more manageable level of simple resentment.

They all had indeed been drinking, but they did not look drunk. On the contrary, they were steady, quiet, and somber. As for Alex, he did not look guilty, or even contrite; only inexplicably sad.

"Why are you all just *sitting* here?" she demanded, but with much less vehemence than she would have believed possible only a few minutes ago. "Alex, I got us another reservation, I fought like mad for it, but you have to pick it up right *now* —we won't be able to get another!"

"I'm sorry, sweetheart," he said in a low voice. "You pick yours up if you want to. I wish you would. But we're leaving ours for the standbys."

"What?" she said, feeling dizzy. "Standbys? You're—you're not *going?*"

"No," he said, lower still. "We're staying here."

Juli felt as though she had been gored by two icicles. Then she at long last let the hysteria sweep through her. Blindly, she let them lead her to a chair. They all tried to comfort her, more or less clumsily—only the women thought to produce handkerchiefs—but the clouds had been gathering for too long to be checked now.

"And I, I p-packed everything so carefully—all the, all the things I loved—the things you g-gave me—"

"Sshh, dear," a woman's voice said. "It's all right."

"It's not all right, it's not all right! Now we'll not only die—we'll die without our things! Oh, Alex, I p-picked out a b-book for each of us—our tooth brushes—my t-t-t—"

The rest came out in a howl, about which she could do absolutely nothing. Pats rained gently on her from various angles, making her cringe and want to fight at the same time. She knew definitely that that last word was going to have been "teddy bear" and waited for them to laugh; but nobody did.

The woman's voice said:

"Juli, love, it doesn't matter . . . really it doesn't. No matter how else we die, we all die naked."

Perhaps—she would never know—this truism would have done Juli no good at all had it come from any other source; but she just at this point recognized the voice as that of Girlie Stonacher, the last person in the dying world from whom she would have expected the consolations of philosophy, even of the tritest sort. She got herself under partial control with a humiliatingly juicy sniffle, and allowed the woman to finish mopping her face.

Only then could she manage to look again around the circle, out of eyes she was sure were as red as her nose. After a pioneering hiccup, she said:

"Alex, why didn't you tell me? Instead of leaving me alone in that awful warehouse, getting scareder and scareder—while you sat here with all the friends we—"

"I did tell you, Juli," he said. "I remember telling you very distinctly. I even remember when, and where."

Juli still felt so frustrated and confused that under any ordinary circumstances she would have believed him gladly. After long suspicion of men in general, she had come to believe that Alex really did have an odd sort of trick memory, especially after drinking; where some of her previous lovers had had convenient blackouts, or at least blank spots where their promises had been lodged, he instead quite convincingly—to both of them—remembered things that hadn't happened at all, in particular things he hadn't told her but knew he should have, and hence readily admitted to. It had been a source of trust, though not one she would have felt comfortable explaining to anyone else, even a woman.

But these were not ordinary circumstances. "Alex," she said, "I don't believe you."

Clearly, this didn't surprise him. Instead, at last, he did look shamefaced.

"Well," he said, "Juli, the fact is, I *didn't* tell you. You see, I wanted you to go on that flight. I wanted you to have the chance, whatever I'd decided about myself. After all, we could still be wrong."

That did it. Juli's sorrow and hurt vanished; she was right back to being furious again.

"Wrong about what?" she fumed, clenching her fists until the nails bit into her palms. "Won't *somebody* in this high-and-mighty crew tell me *why* we're all committing suicide? I'd kind of like the chance to make up my own mind!"

"I told you so," Gradus said to Alex. "But you wouldn't listen to me."

"Juli," Alex said. "I can't explain it myself. I don't have the training, or the terms. And I couldn't quite face up to asking you to listen to hearing your life being explained away by Fan, with my consent. He's been wrong before."

"Do you believe him, Alex? Enough to stay behind?"

"Yes."

"Then I don't resent anything but your thinking that I'd
want to go without you. Fan, explain it, will you? I'd really
like to know. And somehow I'm not surprised to find you
pronouncing our funeral oration. It seems sort of comfortable.
Please speak, Fan, please."

"Thank you," Fan said. "I rise to the occasion."

But in fact he did not rise; he sat where he was, and
spoke very quietly.

The only thing that puzzled me at first (*Fan said*) about
our fairy friend de Tohil Vaca's theory—which made perfect
sense otherwise—was the fact that *he* wasn't going to the
Moon. That didn't seem to be in character with what I knew
about the man. I talked to Alex about it, since after all I
only know the Secretary by reputation, and Alex seemed surprised by it, too.

Alex gave the Secretary the benefit of being a more complex man than he had seemed. I never give any man such
credit until he's proved it by a lifetime of complex reactions.
The Secretary's history didn't deserve it; his public history, it
seemed to me, accurately reflected what little depths he had.
He certainly had never struck me as a natural martyr.

So I looked at the theory again. The Secretary had also told
Alex that he wasn't a scientist, and by God, on that second
look, I found out why he'd said so.

The theory *is* right, mind you. *But the Moon Project is
wrong.* The Moon is no safer now than the Earth is. As the
ice melts and the two processional movements of the Earth's
axis get more and more out of synch, the Earth's center of
gravity also is shifting. That will make the earthquakes even
more violent, but we don't have to worry about that now;
enough is enough; *es ist vollbracht.*

But in addition, the Earth-Moon system is a binary system
—a pair of twin planets, or at least close enough to being one
dynamically. Other plants have satellites bigger than the
Moon: for instance, there's Saturn's satellite Titan, which is
actually bigger than Mercury. But nowhere else in the solar
system can you find a satellite which is a quarter of the size
of its primary.

One result of this is something we've known about ever since Hershel's time. The Moon raises very large tides on the Earth —that is, it exerts a significant amount of gravitational energy on the sea, the atmosphere, and even on the crust. Now, every action has an equal and opposite reaction, as poor old Newton told us, and the reaction has to show up somewhere. And it does. It shows up in the Moon's angular momentum, so that the Moon has been gradually drawing away from the Earth for millennia. I forget the rate—something in the nature of a few hundred feet per year, but I could be wrong by several orders of magnitude.

Suddenly—very suddenly—there's going to be a lot more mobile water on the Earth for the Moon to affect. Result: the Moon's velocity in its orbit is going to increase, equally suddenly. Viewed on a geological time scale, it will be one hell of a lurch.

And at the same time, something *still* more drastic will be happening. Because the Moon is so big in proportion to the Earth, the Moon never has revolved around the exact center of the Earth. Instead, the two bodies revolved around a common center, which was inside the Earth, but not at the Earth's center.

Both these centers—the center of revolution of the twin planets, and the Earth's center of gravity—are now shifting, both independently and in relation to each other. This change will feed back to the Moon, too. And there is still some vulcanism on the Moon—enough to shake it up drastically, since compared to the Earth, the Moon is a low-density, rather fragile world. While new mountains are being built here at home, all the sheer escarpments of the Moon will be tumbling down on our colonies—those that great fissures in the surface haven't swallowed in advance.

I suspect that this process has already started, and that it's why the commercial flights to the Moon were cancelled so arbitrarily five or so years ago. Or maybe not; I'm just guessing. If it hasn't started, it will surely start soon.

I wish with all my heart that we'd had the sense to seed one of our planets—or the stars, it could have been done—a long time in the past. Did you know there was a starship in the planning stage in 1965? Well, there was. Even then it was clear to some people that the Earth was too small and too vulnerable for us to risk the whole future of our race on it alone. But instead, we killed off space-flight almost entirely—and that's that.

And so (*Fan continued*) in the end I agree with Juli. If I have to die, I too want to die with my *things*—under which I mean to subsume my world, my history, my heritage, my race. Not in some warren underneath a desert world that's fit for nothing but a quarry for tombstones. Naked we come into the world, but we do *not* all die naked; we have a choice. We can die naked on the Moon—or we can go to Hell with Shakespeare.

I don't find the choice very difficult.

There was a small color 3V in operation over the bar at the rear of the restaurant, which Juli had ignored from the beginning. If she had noticed it at all, she supposed she had assumed that it was tuned to a baseball game, the only channel 3V sets in bars ever seemed able to receive; and the audio volume was gratefully low.

But in the silence following Fan's peroration, she realized that the announcer was talking about the resumption of traffic to the Moon, and the imminent launching. Glancing up at the little hologram tank, she saw the ship that she and Alex were supposed to be on. It looked exactly like two raw onions, one white, one red, joined by a mutual sprout. It occurred to her that they would probably work better if they were boiled. The red sphere, the 3V announcer was overexplaining, was the power sphere, which had to be kept separated from the people, because of the radiation.

The vessel's immense size showed, however, by comparison with the crowd of spectators. There did seem to be a lot of them, held back only with difficulty by armed guards. The background murmur from them did not sound festive.

She felt tears beginning to come again.

"It seems so cruel," she said, almost to herself. "Luring all those people on such a hopeless journey. And so wasteful. Do you suppose the government really doesn't know? About the Moon?"

"Sure they know," Fan said. He reached for his beer bottle, but ten seconds earlier it had turned into counter polish. "They just don't care. Or maybe it's just that they've been lying to us for so long, they couldn't tell us the truth if they wanted to." Morosely, he mopped up his invention with his sleeve.

"Fan, that's a guess," Alex said. "And let me remind you, I do know de Tohil Vaca, and you don't except by reputation, just as you said. I still don't think he's the villain you make him out to be. He knows there's a risk, and he told me—I think he told all the potential trippers—that there's a risk. He didn't say exactly what it was, but if he had, nobody would have wanted to go at all."

"And maybe," Goldfarb Z said, "he hopes that at least a few of the bases will survive, after all. That would explain the effort, the expense, the deception, and so on. Otherwise, why bother?"

Fan snorted. "Impossible . . . *Herr Ober,* another beer here! . . . And even supposing that . . . no, damn it, I want a *glass* bottle, not one of those dissolving ones . . . even supposing a few bases do survive, they won't have the resources, or the population, or the spirit to put together a second jump to Mars. If there are any survivors on the Moon—and I insist, it's possible that there will be—they'll just die a little later of attrition. People can't hope if there aren't enough of them to keep each other hoping."

"Fan, as a psychologist you're a pain in the ass," Irene Pons said. "There's one thing you have to give de Tohil Vaca. He's given his passengers the chance to roll the dice. Which is more than we've got the courage to do. And I'll bet he knew exactly how many of us would chicken out, too."

"I do not play," Fan said stiffly, "with loaded dice. But since you insist, I'll give de Tohil Vaca one gold star: He did say, more or less vaguely, that the dice were loaded. It's a limited form of honesty, but honesty it is."

"And decency," Juli said. "Even pity."

"Pity? Juli, I love you, but sometimes you're rather hard to follow."

"I mean, here *I* am, with Alex, and people I love around me—and I've even still got Splat! and Hausmaus. So—I mean, oh well, that's not so bad, after all. But for most of the people who're going on the trip . . . do you think they'd be going if they had anyone to love? Someone to help them look death in the eye? And for them, isn't it better to have a little hope? Better than just to stand around, waiting for the end, like so many snowmen waiting for a thaw?"

"By God, Juli," Goldfarb Z said softly, "I love you too."

"It's a nice notion," Fan said, "but it's Juli's alone, I'm afraid. That kind of motive doesn't ordinarily move governments into spending billions of dollars on a foredoomed project."

"What good is a dollar now?" Alex demanded. "And what else would be worth spending it on instead? Now? Not sewage, I can tell you that, and the Secretary knows it. He told me so, and damn bluntly, too."

Fan shrugged. "I can't quite see them breaking the thinking habits of a century," he said. "But on the other hand, it doesn't cost *me* a cent to give them credit for compassion. Blessed be thee, de Tohil Vaca."

There was another silence, underlined by the rumbling of the crowd at the spaceport, now sounding somehow ominous. By unspoken assent, they turned their chairs to watch the tank.

Juli found herself calm, resigned, washed out. She was even interested in seeing the takeoff, though such things had never interested her before; and not entirely because her "things" were on board. Goldfarb Z ordered another round of drinks.

A moment later, the floor twitched under them, like the hide of a horse trying to dislodge persistent flies. Bottles fell from the bar. The 3V image flickered, and the crowd roar from it swelled suddenly. Most of the customers at the bar made for the door, at speed, and almost everyone around the table sprang up. Chairs fell over.

Fan shot out one hand and grabbed Gradus by a wrist. "Sit down," he said. "Where are you running to?"

"That was an earthquake," she said glacially, "in case you hadn't noticed."

From the 3V the roar grew louder. Juli saw that the crowd was rushing the ship. Evidently, the secret was finally out. Then there was a dull sound of sneeze-gas grenades going off.

"Really, Fan," Goldfarb Y said, "it's better to be out of doors in an earthquake. Everybody knows that."

"If that was ever true," Fan said, "it doesn't apply any more."

There was a second shock, and the 3V gave up entirely.

"Damn," Fan said. "I wanted to watch that. Alex, how tall is this building?"

"Seventeen stories, but the elevators only go up to the fifteenth. If they're still running at all."

"The lights are still on."

"But supposing the elevators quit on us while we're up there?" Girlie said.

"Suppose they do?" Fan said. There was silence. He went on:

"Girlie, do you really care what floor you die on? Wouldn't you rather see the first survival ship leave—or whether or not the quakes and the mob even let it leave—than run around in the street like a mouse? Let's be human beings to the end, goddam it. I'm going up. The rest of you can suit yourselves."

"Me too," Juli said. But she shook Alex's hand with great determination.

And there below them was the Earth, and its wide sky of islands; and the towers of the city to the south. It was a bright day; they could see the fugitive highlights of the sun glancing off the canals of lower Manhattan. It was all quite beautiful. Juli thought her heart ought to be breaking, but in fact she felt only a vast, free exhilaration. Soon it would all be gone; but she had never expected to outlive it. What filled her heart, instead, was something oddly like gratitude.

"There she goes!" Fan cried out suddenly, almost with joy. She felt his hand on her shoulder, turning her around to face toward the northwest. A thin, towering plume of pure white steam was rising slowly on the western horizon, rising, rising. . . . For an instant, just above its tip, there was a splintery flash of metal. Then the plume began to twist and drift.

There was a strange sound from the little party on the roof, a little like a sob, a little like a cheer.

"They made it," Goldfarb Y said, like a prayer.

Then the building jerked like a whip under their feet, and the sound turned to screams and hoarse yells. Asphalt and gravel ripped into Juli's knees and palms. A roar floated up from the city, laced with still fainter screams, like the glints of sunlight on the water.

"My God," the nameless engineer was saying mechanically. "My God. My God."

Alex's hands grasped her, helped her to her feet, steadied her. The building was still swaying a little. Once more, they were all looking south.

Not far away—perhaps ten or fifteen blocks—a few small, old buildings were toppling and sliding down into rubble and dust, unheard in a general uproar. Juli scarcely noticed them, nor did the others seem to be watching that. Much farther downtown, perhaps in what had once been the financial district, or else from the waters of Red Hook or Park Slope, a thick, dense column of black fumes was rising toward the risen half-Moon, like a Satanic mockery of the trail of the vanished ship. It made a sound like the full diapason of some gigantic organ.

"Fissure," Fan shouted, in an otherwise perfectly neutral voice. "I do hate to see my predictions jump the gun like that. It might make people think I lack influence in the proper quarters."

"*Your* predictions, Fan?" Alex said ironically.

"Certainly. That break's in Brooklyn Heights or thereabouts. That's where I said it would open if the injection wells were responsible. So you see the Secretary and I were both right."

"How nice for you both," Gradus said, but for once there was no malice in her voice. Of course she was all ready to die naked, having been dressing the part for many years; but no one else seemed at all alarmed any more. Irene and Evadne were weeping silently, but without even seeming to notice it.

The black fumes rose in the bright sky. Gradually, they parted at the top, and began to spread gently, parallel to the horizon, as if along some low air stratum. The striations fanned out a little to the west as they drifted; the hinge of that fan did seem to be focused somewhere over the near shore of Brooklyn.

"Temperature inversion," Fan said. "New York's last smog attack."

"Omniscient to the last," Gradus said.

"It's funny," Juli said. "I mean, it's odd. I never thought of it before."

"Of what?" Alex said, taking her hand.

"That everything means something special, no matter what it is, if you know it'll never happen again. Even smog."

The dark striations floated toward them, their shadows making broader stripes over the groaning city in the brilliant sunshine. Were they just parts of widening circles? Or had the prevailing winds also changed? Or—

The roof lurched again. Evadne, who had been standing closest to the parapet, would have gone over it had the unnamed engineer not grabbed her. A cornice fell off and went smashing down the setbacks toward the street.

"There won't be," Fan said gently, "any flight tomorrow. Good-bye, all."

The cats!

With a cry, Juli raced for the stairwell. Alex called after her, something about the danger and the power being off, but she did not care.

She was almost fainting with exhaustion by the time she reached the dust-choking, bombarded street, and another temblor threw her to her knees just in front of the smashed glass display windows of the expensive supermarket. Shaking her dirty hair out of her face, she got up again and staggered inside.

"Hausmaus! Splat!"

There was a dim cry. Inside, the cement and plaster dust was almost impenetrable, but she could see vaguely that the place had been looted before the last panic had struck. Not only were there cans, bottles, and packages lying where the shocks had thrown them, but there were also a number of half-filled string bags and two-wheeled pushcarts abandoned near the door.

"Here, kitty! Kitty, kitty!"

Three or four meows responded. Through her watering, gritty, gas-inflamed eyes she seemed to be seeing thousands of cats. And indeed there were a great many. The carrier was where she had left it, half buried under a pile of loose cornflakes, diet cookies, and other things that had burst out of fallen pasteboard packages; but the door had fallen open and it was empty.

Through the haze and the tears, she was able finally to make out that all those thousands of cats were actually only a store cat and four squealing, barely ambulatory kittens. Then she saw Splat!, who somehow had managed to scramble to the top tier of a display rack which still held a few canned goods. He was too fat to get back down by himself, or at least that seemed to be his theory, and Juli decided to leave him there for the moment. He would be no safer any-

where else, and as long as he was treed like that, she would
at least know where to find him.

"Hausmaus? Hausmaus?"

There was another violent earth shock. The entire front of
the store crunched down to about half its previous height, and
masonry roared into the street in front of it. Overhead, parallel
to the street, a beam burst through the plaster of the ceiling,
one end hanging free. Instantly changing her mind, Juli
grabbed Splat! and stuffed him back in the carrier, followed
by a kitten who happened to be in reach, and latched the door.

Was there another way out of the store? Yes, a door that
evidently gave into the lobby of the building. It was wooden
and had split at the top; its frame was twisted.

"Hausmaus! Here, puss!"

Another shock.

"Juli!"

It was Alex. He was pounding on the door, which evidently
was locked, jammed, or both. "Juli, Juli, where are you?"

There was the sound of a heavier blow, as if he had kicked
the door. Juli tugged frantically at the knob. It would not give.

He kicked the door again, and almost at the same time,
there was another tremor. Part of the bottom panel fell out
of the door. Juli dropped to her hands and knees, and found
Alex facing her on the other side in the same position. He
could not see her, however, for blood was streaming into his
eyes from a slash which ran diagonally across his forehead
and up over his scalp.

"Alex, here I am!"

She heard Splat!'s hoarse Siamese cry behind her, and then
he was clambering clumsily over her calves. Evidently the
door to the carrier had come open again.

"Juli—"

She reached out for Alex. As her hand touched his cheek,
there was still another shock, and the free end of the ceiling
began to fall, slowly at first. Juli felt the soft, familiar thump
of Hausmaus landing on his frequent perch between her
shoulder blades, and

CARCINOMA ANGELS

Norman Spinrad

A funny story about cancer? Why not? If any
phrase sums up the career of Norman Spinrad to
date, it's "Why not?"—for this gifted, irreverent
young author has made a specialty of tackling the
unlikely and the implausible. His controversial
novel, **Bug Jack Barron**, earned him the honor of
being the first science-fiction writer ever to be
denounced in Parliament as a "nameless degenerate"; his vigorous essays in the **Los Angeles
Free Press** and other underground journals have
won him a strong following in the counterculture;
his short stories, collected in a volume called **The
Last Hurrah of the Golden Horde**, demonstrate
versatility, energy, and fertility of invention. The
story that follows first appeared in Harlen Ellison's
anthology **Dangerous Visions**—and more than
amply fulfilled the theme implicit in that celebrated
collection's title.

At the age of nine Harrison Wintergreen first discovered
that the world was his oyster when he looked at it sidewise.
That was the year when baseball cards were *in*. The kid with
the biggest collection of baseball cards was *it*. Harry Wintergreen decided to become *it*.

Harry saved up a dollar and bought one hundred random
baseball cards. He was in luck—one of them was the very
rare Yogi Berra. In three separate transactions, he traded his

205

other ninety-nine cards for the only other three Yogi Berras in the neighborhood. Harry had reduced his holdings to four cards, but he had cornered the market in Yogi Berra. He forced the price of Yogi Berra up to an exorbitant eighty cards. With the slush fund thus accumulated, he successively cornered the market in Mickey Mantle, Willy Mays and Pee Wee Reese and became the J. P. Morgan of baseball cards.

Harry breezed through high school by the simple expedient of mastering only one subject—the art of taking tests. By his senior year, he could outthink any test writer with his gypsheet tied behind his back and won seven scholarships with foolish ease.

In college Harry discovered girls. Being reasonably good-looking and reasonably facile, he no doubt would've garnered his fair share of conquests in the normal course of events. But this was not the way the mind of Harrison Wintergreen worked.

Harry carefully cultivated a stutter, which he could turn on or off at will. Few girls could resist the lure of a good-looking, well-adjusted guy with a slick line who nevertheless carried with him some secret inner hurt that made him stutter. Many were the girls who tried to delve Harry's secret, while Harry delved *them*.

In his sophomore year Harry grew bored with college and reasoned that the thing to do was to become Filthy Rich. He assiduously studied sex novels for one month, wrote three of them in the next two which he immediately sold at $1000 a throw.

With the $3000 thus garnered, he bought a shiny new convertible. He drove the new car to the Mexican border and across into a notorious border town. He immediately contacted a disreputable shoeshine boy and bought a pound of marijuana. The shoeshine boy of course tipped off the border guards, and when Harry attempted to walk across the bridge to the States they stripped him naked. They found nothing and Harry crossed the border. He had smuggled nothing out of Mexico, and in fact had thrown the marijuana away as soon as he bought it.

However, he had taken advantage of the Mexican embargo on American cars and illegally sold the convertible in Mexico for $15,000.

Harry took his $15,000 to Las Vegas and spent the next six weeks buying people drinks, lending broke gamblers money, acting in general like a fuzzy-cheeked Santa Claus, gaining the confidence of the right drunks and blowing $5000.

At the end of six weeks he had three hot market tips which turned his remaining $10,000 into $40,000 in the next two months.

Harry bought four hundred crated government surplus jeeps in four one-hundred-jeep lots of $10,000 a lot and immediately sold them to a highly disreputable Central American government for $100,000.

He took the $100,000 and bought a tiny island in the Pacific, so worthless that no government had ever bothered to claim it. He set himself up as an independent government with no taxes and sold twenty one-acre plots to twenty millionaires seeking a tax haven at $100,000 a plot. He unloaded the last plot three weeks before the United States, with UN backing, claimed the island and brought it under the sway of the Internal Revenue Department.

Harry invested a small part of his $2,000,000 and rented a large computer for twelve hours. The computer constructed a betting scheme by which Harry parlayed his $2,000,000 into $20,000,000 by taking various British soccer pools to the tune of $18,000,000.

For $5,000,000 he bought a monstrous chunk of useless desert from an impoverished Arabian sultanate. With another $2,000,000 he created a huge rumor campaign to the effect that this patch of desert was literally floating on oil. With another $3,000,000 he set up a dummy corporation which made like a big oil company and publicly offered to buy this desert for $75,000,000. After some spirited bargaining, a large American oil company was allowed to outbid the dummy and bought a thousand square miles of sand for $100,000,000.

Harrison Wintergreen was, at the age of twenty-five, Filthy Rich by his own standards. He lost his interest in money.

He now decided that he wanted to Do Good. He Did Good. He toppled seven unpleasant Latin American governments and replaced them with six Social Democracies and a Benevolent Dictatorship. He converted a tribe of Borneo headhunters to Rosicrucianism. He set up twelve rest homes for overage whores and organized a birth control program which sterilized

twelve million fecund Indian women. He contrived to make
another $100,000,000 on the above enterprises.

At the age of thirty Harrison Wintergreen had had it with
Do-Gooding. He decided to Leave His Footprints in the
Sands of Time. He Left His Footprints in the Sands of Time.
He wrote an internationally acclaimed novel about King
Farouk. He invented the Wintergreen Filter, a membrane
through which fresh water passed freely, but which barred
salts. Once set up, a Wintergreen Desalinization Plant could
desalinate an unlimited supply of water at a per-gallon cost
approaching absolute zero. He painted one painting and was
instantly offered $200,000 for it. He donated it to the Museum
of Modern Art, gratis. He developed a mutated virus which
destroyed syphilis bacteria. Like syphilis, it spread by sexual
contact. It was a mild aphrodisiac. Syphilis was wiped out in
eighteen months. He bought an island off the coast of California, a five-hundred-foot crag jutting out of the Pacific. He
caused it to be carved into a five-hundred-foot statue of Harrison Wintergreen.

At the age of thirty-eight Harrison Wintergreen had Left
sufficient Footprints in the Sands of Time. He was bored. He
loked around greedily for new worlds to conquer.

This, then, was the man who, at the age of forty, was
informed that he had an advanced, well-spread and incurable
case of cancer and that he had one year to live.

Wintergreen spent the first month of his last year searching for an existing cure for terminal cancer. He visited lab-
oratories, medical schools, hospitals, clinics, Great Doctors,
quacks, people who had miraculously recovered from cancer,
faith healers and Little Old Ladies in Tennis Shoes. There was
no known cure for terminal cancer, reputable or otherwise.
It was as he suspected, as he more or less even hoped. He
would have to do it himself.

He proceeded to spend the next month setting things up to
do it himself. He caused to be erected in the middle of the
Arizona desert an air-conditioned walled villa. The villa had
a completely automatic kitchen and enough food for a year.
It had a $5,000,000 biological and biochemical laboratory. It
had a $3,000,000 microfilmed library which contained every
word ever written on the subject of cancer. It had the phar-

macy to end all pharmacies: a literal supply of quite literally every drug that existed—poisons, painkillers, hallucinogens, dandricides, antiseptics, antibiotics, vericides, headache remedies, heroin, quinine, curare, snake oil—everything. The pharmacy cost $20,000,000.

The villa also contained a one-way radiotelephone, a large stock of basic chemicals, including radioactives, copies of the *Koran*, the Bible, the *Torah*, the *Book of the Dead*, *Science and Health with Key to the Scriptures*, the *I Ching* and the complete works of Wilhelm Reich and Aldous Huxley. It also contained a very large and ultra-expensive computer. By the time the villa was ready, Wintergreen's petty cash fund was nearly exhausted.

With ten months to do that which the medical world considered impossible, Harison Wintergreen entered his citadel.

During the first two months he devoured the library, sleeping three hours out of each twenty-four and dosing himself regularly with Benzedrine. The library offered nothing but data. He digested the data and went on to the pharmacy.

During the next month he tried aureomycin, bacitracin, stannous fluoride, hexylresorcinol, cortisone, penicillin, hexachlorophene, shark-liver extract and 7312 assorted other miracles of modern medical science, all to no avail. He began to feel pain, which he immediately blotted out and continued to blot out with morphine. Morphine addiction was merely an annoyance.

He tried chemicals, radioactives, vericides, Christian Science, yoga, prayer, enemas, patent medicines, herb tea, witchcraft and yogurt diets. This consumed another month, during which Wintergreen continued to waste away, sleeping less and less and taking more Benzedrine and morphine. Nothing worked. He had six months left.

He was on the verge of becoming desperate. He tried a different tack. He sat in a comfortable chair and contemplated his navel for forty-eight consecutive hours.

His meditations produced a severe case of eyestrain and two significant words: "spontaneous remission."

In his two months of research, Wintergreen had come upon numbers of cases where a terminal cancer abruptly reversed itself and the patient, for whom all hope had been abandoned, had been cured. No one ever knew how or why. It could not be predicted, it could not be artificially produced, but it happened nevertheless. For want of an explanation, they call it spontaneous remission. "Remission," meaning cure. "Spontaneous," meaning no one knew what caused it.

Which was not to say that it did not have a cause.

Wintergreen was buoyed: he was even ebullient. He knew that some terminal cancer patients had been cured. Therefore terminal cancer could be cured. Therefore the problem was removed from the realm of the impossible and was now merely the domain of the highly improbable.

And doing the highly improbable was Wintergreen's specialty.

With six months of estimated life left, Wintergreen set jubilantly to work. From his complete cancer library he culled every known case of spontaneous remission. He coded every one of them into the computer—data on the medical histories of the patients, on the treatments employed, on their ages, sexes, religions, races, creeds, colors, national origins, temperaments, marital status, Dun and Bradstreet ratings, neuroses, psychoses and favorite beers. Complete profiles of every human being ever known to have survived terminal cancer were fed into Harrison Wintergreen's computer.

Wintergreen programed the computer to run a complete series of correlations between ten thousand separate and distinct factors and spontaneous remission. If even one factor— age, credit rating, favorite food—*anything* correlated with spontaneous remission, the spontaneity factor would be removed.

Wintergreen had shelled out $100,000,000 for the computer. It was the best damn computer in the world. In two minutes and 7.894 seconds it had performed its task. In one succinct word it gave Wintergreen his answer:

"Negative."

Spontaneous remission did not correlate with *any* external factor. It was still spontaneous; the cause was unknown.

A lesser man would've been crushed. A more conventional man would've been dumbfounded. Harrison Wintergreen was elated.

He had eliminated the entire external universe as a factor in spontaneous remission in one fell swoop. Therefore, in some mysterious way, the human body and/or psyche was capable of curing itself.

Wintergreen set out to explore and conquer his own internal universe. He repaired to the pharmacy and prepared a formidable potation. Into his largest syringe he decanted the following: Novocain; morphine, curare; *vlut,* a rare Central Asian poison which induced temporary blindness; olfactorcain, a top-secret smell-deadener used by skunk farmers; tympanoline, a drug which temporarily deadened the auditory nerves (used primarily by filibustering senators); a large dose of Benzedrine; lysergic acid; psilocybin; mescaline; peyote extract; seven other highly experimental and most illegal hallucinogens; eye of newt and toe of dog.

Wintergreen laid himself out on his most comfortable couch. He swabbed the vein in the pit of his left elbow with alcohol and injected himself with the witch's brew.

His heart pumped. His blood surged, carrying the arcane chemicals to every part of his body. The Novocain blanked out every sensory nerve in his body. The morphine eliminated all sensations of pain. The *vlut* blacked out his vision. The olfactorcain cut off all sense of smell. The tympanoline made him deaf as a traffic court judge. The curare paralyzed him.

Wintergreen was alone in his own body. No external stimuli reached him. He was in a state of total sensory deprivation. The urge to lapse into blessed unconsciousness was irresistible. Wintergreen, strong-willed though he was, could not have remained conscious unaided. But the massive dose of Benzedrine would not let him sleep.

He was awake, aware, alone in the universe of his own body with no external stimuli to occupy himself with.

Then, one and two, and then in combinations like the fists of a good fast heavyweight, the hallucinogens hit.

Wintergreen's sensory organs were blanked out, but the brain centers which received sensory data were still active. It was on these cerebral centers that the tremendous charge of assorted hallucinogens acted. He began to see phantom colors, shapes, things without name or form. He heard eldritch symphonies, ghost echoes, mad howling noises. A million impossible smells roiled through his brain. A thousand false pains and pressures tore at him, as if his whole body had been amputated. The sensory centers of Wintergreen's brain were like a mighty radio receiver tuned to an empty band— filled with meaningless visual, auditory, olfactory and sensual static.

The drugs kept his senses blank. The Benzedrine kept him conscious. Forty years of being Harrison Wintergreen kept him cold and sane.

For an indeterminate period of time he rolled with the punches, groping for the feel of this strange new non-environment. Then gradually, hesitantly at first but with ever growing confidence, Wintergreen reached for control. His mind constructed untrue but useful analogies for actions that were not actions, states of being that were not states of being, sensory data unlike any sensory data received by the human brain. The analogies, constructed in a kind of calculated madness by his subconscious for the brute task of making the incomprehensible palpable, also enabled him to deal with his non-environment as if it were an environment, translating mental changes into analogs of action.

He reached out an analogical hand and tuned a figurative radio, inward, away from the blank wave band of the outside side universe and towards the as yet unused wave band of his own body, the internal universe that was his mind's only possible escape from chaos.

He tuned, adjusted, forced, struggled, felt his mind pressing against an atom-thin interface. He battered against the interface, an analogical translucent membrane between his mind and his internal universe, a membrane that stretched, flexed, bulged inward, thinned . . . and finally broke. Like Alice through the Looking Glass, his analogical body stepped through and stood on the other side.

Harrison Wintergreen was inside his own body.

It was a world of wonder and loathsomeness, of the majestic and the ludicrous. Wintergreen's point of view, which his mind analogized as a body within his true body, was inside a vast network of pulsing arteries, like some monstrous freeway system. The analogy crystallized. It *was* a freeway, and Wintergreen was driving down it. Bloated sacs dumped things into the teeming traffic: harmones, wastes, nutrients. White blood cells careened by him like mad taxicabs. Red corpuscles drove steadily along like stolid burghers. The traf-

fic ebbed and congested like a crosstown rush hour. Wintergreen drove on, searching, searching.

He made a left, cut across three lanes and made a right
down toward a lymph node. And then he saw it—a pile of
white cells like a twelve-car collision, and speeding towards
him a leering motorcyclist.

Black the cycle. Black the riding leathers. Black, dull black,
the face of the rider save for two glowing blood-red eyes. And
emblazoned across the front and back of the black motor-
cycle jacket in shining scarlet studs the legend: "Carcinoma
Angels."

With a savage whoop, Wintergreen gunned his analogical
car down the hypothetical freeway straight for the imaginary
cyclist, the cancer cell.

Splat! Pop! Cuush! Wintergreen's car smashed the cycle
and the rider exploded in a cloud of fine black dust.

Up and down the freeways of his circulatory system Wintergreen ranged, barreling along arteries, careening down
veins, inching through narrow capillaries, seeking the black-
clad cyclists, the Carcinoma Angels, grinding them to dust
beneath his wheels. . . .

And he found himself in the dark moist wood of his lungs,
riding a snow-white analogical horse, an imaginary lance of
pure light in his hand. Savage black dragons with blood-red
eyes and flickering red tongues slithered from behind the
gnarled bolls of great air-sac trees. St. Wintergreen spurred
his horse, lowered his lance and impaled monster after hissing
monster till at last the holy lungwood was free of dragons. . . .

He was flying in some vast moist cavern, above him the
vague bulks of gigantic organs, below a limitless expanse of
shining slimy peritoneal plain.

From behind the cover of his huge beating heart a forma-
tion of black fighter planes, bearing the insignia of a scarlet
"C" on their wings and fusilages, roared down at him.

Wintergreen gunned his engine and rose to the fray, flying
up and over the bandits, blasting them with his machine guns,
and one by one and then in bunches they crashed in flames
to the peritoneum below. . . .

In a thousand shapes and guises, the black and red things
attacked. Black, the color of oblivion, red, the color of blood.
Dragons, cyclists, planes, sea things, soldiers, tanks and tigers

in blood vessels and lungs and spleen and thorax and bladder
—Carcinoma Angels, all.

And Wintergreen fought his analogical battles in an equal
number of incarnations, as driver, knight, pilot, diver, soldier,
mahout, with a grim and savage glee, littering the battlefields
of his body with the black dust of the fallen Carcinoma
Angels.

Fought and fought and killed and killed and finally. . . .

Finally found himself knee-deep in the sea of his digestive
juices lapping against the walls of the dank, moist cave that
was his stomach. And scuttling towards him on chitinous legs,
a monstrous black crab with blood-red eyes, gross, squat,
primeval.

Clicking, chittering, the crab scurried across his stomach
towards him. Wintergreen paused, grinned wolfishly, and
leaped high in the air, landing with both feet squarely on the
hard black carapace.

Like a sun-dried gourd, brittle, dry, hollow, the crab
crunched beneath his weight and splintered into a million
dusty fragments.

And Wintergreen was alone, at last alone and victorious,
the first and last of the Carcinoma Angels now banished and
gone and finally defeated.

Harrison Wintergreen, alone in his own body, victorious
and once again looking for new worlds to conquer, waiting
for the drugs to wear off, waiting to return to the world that
always was his oyster.

Waiting and waiting and waiting. . . .

Go to the finest sanitarium in the world, and there you
will find Harrison Wintergreen, who made himself Filthy Rich,
Harrison Wintergreen, who Did Good, Harrison Wintergreen,
who Left His Footprints in the Sands of Time, Harrison
Wintergreen, who stepped inside his own body to do battle
with Carcinoma's Angels, and won.

And can't get out.

MOTHER

Philip José Farmer

Philip Jose Farmer was a man well ahead of his proper time when he arrived on the science-fiction scene in 1952. Science fiction then had only just begun to emerge from its Boy Scout era, and, except for a few lonely pioneers like Theodore Sturgeon and Fritz Leiber, no one dared venture into the darker realms of psychology and psychopathology. Farmer's early stories—strange, disturbing, uninhibited, searching—unsettled and dismayed and ultimately antagonized many veteran s-f readers, and the reception he received probably contributed to his premature withdrawal from active writing. Fortunately, the world of science fiction has caught up with him at last; he is busy once more, productively mining the same veins of human experience he explored in his debut years, and this time receiving the acclaim he deserves. The story here is one of his first, dating from 1953 and demonstrating the skills and insights characteristic of his work from the start.

I

"Look, mother. The clock is running backwards."

Eddie Fetts pointed to the hands on the pilot room dial.

Dr. Paula Fetts said, "The crash must have reversed it."

"How could it do that?"

215

"I can't tell you. I don't know everything, son."

"Oh!"

"Well, don't look at me so disappointedly. I'm a pathologist, not an electronician."

"Don't be so cross, mother. I can't stand it. Not now."

He walked out of the pilot room. Anxiously, she followed him. The burial of the crew and her fellow scientists had been very trying for him. Spilled blood had always made him dizzy and sick; he could scarcely control his hands enough to help her sack the scattered bones and entrails.

He had wanted to put the corpses in the nuclear furnace, but she had forbidden that. The Geigers amidships were ticking loudly, warning that there was invisible death in the stern.

The meteor that struck the moment the ship came out of Translation into normal space had probably wrecked the engine-room. So she had understood from the incoherent high-pitched phrases of a colleague before he fled to the pilot room. She had hurried to find Eddie. She feared his cabin door would still be locked, as he had been making a tape of the aria "Heavy Hangs the Albatross" from Gianelli's *Ancient Mariner*.

Fortunately, the emergency system had automatically thrown out the locking circuits. Entering, she had called out his name in fear he'd been hurt. He was lying half-unconscious on the floor, but it was not the accident that had thrown him there. The reason lay in the corner, released from his lax hand; a quart free-fall thermos, rubber-nippled. From Eddie's open mouth charged a breath of rye that not even Nodor pills had been able to conceal.

Sharply she had commanded him to get up and onto the bed. Her voice, the first he had ever heard, pierced through the phalanx of Old Red Star. He struggled up, and she, though smaller, had thrown every ounce of her weight into getting him up and onto the bed.

There she had lain down with him and strapped them both in. She understood that the lifeboat had been wrecked also, and that it was up to the captain to bring the yacht down safely to the surface of this charted but unexplored planet, Baudelaire. Everybody else had gone to sit behind the captain, strapped in crashchairs, unable to help except with their silent backing.

Moral support had not been enough. The ship had come in

on a shallow slant. Too fast. The wounded motors had not been able to hold her up. The prow had taken the brunt of the punishment. So had those seated in the nose.

Dr. Fetts had held her son's head on her bosom and prayed out loud to her God. Eddie had snored and muttered. Then there was a sound like the clashing of the gates of doom—a tremendous bong as if the ship were a clapper in a gargantuan bell tolling the most frightening message human ears may hear—a binding blast of light—and darkness and silence.

A few moments later Eddie began crying out in a childish voice, "Don't leave me to die, mother! Come back! Come back!"

Mother was unconscious by his side, but he did not know that. He wept for a while, then he lapsed back into his rye-fogged stupor—if he had ever been out of it—and slept. Again, darkness and silence.

It was the second day since the crash, if "day" could describe that twilight state on Baudelaire. Dr. Fetts followed her son wherever he went. She knew he was very sensitive and easily upset. All his life she had known it and had tried to get between him and anything that would cause trouble. She had succeeded, she thought, fairly well until three months ago when Eddie had eloped.

The girl was Polina Fameux, the ash-blonde long-legged actress whose tridi image, taped, had been shipped to frontier stars where a small acting talent meant little and a large and shapely bosom much. Since Eddie was a well-known Metro tenor, the marriage made a big splash whose ripples ran around the civilized Galaxy.

Dr. Fetts had felt very bad about the elopement, but she had, she hoped, hidden her grief very well beneath a smiling mask. She didn't regret having to give him up; after all, he was a full-grown man, no longer her little boy. But, really, aside from the seasons at the Met and his tours, he had not been parted from her since he was eight.

That was when she went on a honeymoon with her second husband. And then she and Eddie had not been separated long, for Eddie had got very sick, and she'd had to hurry back and take care of him, as he had insisted she was the only one who could make him well.

Moreover, you couldn't count his days at the opera as a total loss, for he vised her every noon and they had a long talk—no matter how high the vise bills ran.

The ripples caused by her son's marriage were scarcely a week old before they were followed by even bigger ones. They bore the news of the separation of Eddie and his wife. A fortnight later, Polina applied for divorce on grounds of incompatibility. Eddie was handed the papers in his mother's apartment. He had come back to her the day he and Polina had agreed they "couldn't make a go of it," or, as he phrased it to his mother, "couldn't get together."

Dr. Fetts was, of course, very curious about the reason for their parting, but, as she explained to her friends, she "respected" his silence. What she didn't say was that she had told herself the time would come when he would tell her all.

Eddie's "nervous breakdown" started shortly afterwards. He had been very irritable, moody, and depressed, but he got worse the day a so-called friend told Eddie that whenever Polina heard his name mentioned, she laughed loud and long. The friend added that Polina had promised to tell someday the true story of their brief merger.

That night his mother had to call in a doctor.

In the days that followed, she thought of giving up her position as research pathologist at De Kruif and taking all her time to help him "get back on his feet". It was a sign of the struggle going on in her mind that she had not been able to decide within a week's time. Ordinarily given to swift consideration and resolution of a problem, she could not agree to surrender her beloved quest into tissue regeneration.

Just as she was on the verge of doing what was for her the incredible and the shameful, tossing a coin, she had been vised by her superior. He told her she had been chosen to go with a group of biologists on a research cruise to ten preselected planetary systems.

Joyfully, she had thrown away the papers that would turn Eddie over to a sanatorium. And, since he was quite famous, she had used her influence to get the government to allow him to go along. Ostensibly, he was to make a survey of the development of opera on planets colonized by Terrans. That the yacht was not visiting any colonized globes seemed to have been missed by the bureaus concerned. But it was not the first time in the history of a government that its left hand knew not what its right was doing.

Actually, he was to be "rebuilt" by his mother, who thought herself much more capable of curing him than any of the prevalent A, F, J, R, S, K, or H therapies. True, some of her friends reported amazing results with some of the symbol-chasing techniques. On the other hand, two of her close companions had tried them all and had got no benefits from any of them. She was his mother; she could do more for him than any of those "alphabatties"; he was flesh of her flesh, blood of her blood. Besides, he wasn't so sick. He just got awfully blue sometimes and made theatrical but insincere threats of suicide or else just sat and stared into space. But she could handle him.

II

So now it was that she followed him from the backward-running clock to his room. And saw him step inside, look for a second, and then turn to her with a twisted face.

"Neddie is ruined, mother. Absolutely ruined."

She glanced at the piano. It had torn loose from the wall-racks at the moment of impact and smashed itself against the opposite wall. To Eddie it wasn't just a piano; it was Neddie. He had a pet name for everything he contacted for more than a brief time. It was as if he hopped from one appellation to the next, like an ancient sailor who felt lost unless he was close to the familiar and designated points of the shoreline. Otherwise, Eddie seemed to be drifting helplessly in a chaotic ocean, one that was anonymous and amorphous.

Or, analogy more typical of him, he was like the night-clubber who feels submerged, drowning, unless he hops from table to table, going from one well-known group of faces to the next, avoiding the featureless and unnamed dummies at the strangers' tables.

He did not cry over Neddie. She wished he would. He had been so apathetic during the voyage. Nothing, not even the unparalled splendor of the naked stars nor the inexpressible alienness of strange planets had seemed to lift him very long. If he would only weep or laugh loudly or display some sign that he was reacting violently to what was happening. She would even have welcomed his striking her in anger or calling her "bad" names.

But no, not even during the gathering of the mangled corpses, when he looked for a while as if he were going to vomit, would he give way to his body's demand for expression. She understood that if he were to throw up, he would be much better for it, would have got rid of much of the psychic disturbance along with the physical.

He would not. He had kept on raking flesh and bones into the large plastic bags and kept a fixed look of resentment and sullenness.

She hoped now that the loss of his piano would bring tears and shaking shoulders. Then she could take him in her arms and give him sympathy. He would be her little boy again, afraid of the dark, afraid of the dog killed by a car, seeking her arms for the sure safety, the sure love.

"Never mind, baby," she said. "When we're rescued, we'll get you a new one."

"When—!"

He lifted his eyebrows and sat down on the bed's edge. "What do we do now?"

She became very brisk and efficient.

"The ultrad automatically started working the moment the meteor struck. If it's survived the crash, it's still sending SOS's. If not, then there's nothing we can do about it. Neither of us knows how to repair it.

"However, it's possible that in the last five years since this planet was located, other expeditions may have landed here. Not from Earth but from some of the colonies. Or from non-human globes. Who knows? It's worth taking a chance. Let's see."

A single glance was enough to wreck their hopes. The ultrad had been twisted and broken until it was no longer recognizable as the machine that sent swifter-than-light waves through the no-ether.

Dr. Fetts said with false cheeriness, "Well, that's that! So what? It makes things too easy. Let's go into the storeroom and see what we can see."

Eddie shrugged and followed her. There she insisted that each take a panrad. If they had to separate for any reason, they could always communicate and also, using the DF's—

the built-in direction finders—locate each other. Having used them before, they knew the instruments' capabilities and how essential they were on scouting or camping trips.

The panrads were lightweight cylinders about two feet high and eight inches in diameter. Crampacked, they held the mechanisms of two dozen different utilities. Their batteries lasted a year without recharging, they were practically indestructible and worked under almost any conditions.

Keeping away from the side of the ship that had the huge hole in it, they took the panrads outside. The long wave bands were searched by Eddie while his mother moved the dial that ranged up and down the shortwaves. Neither really expected to hear anything, but to search was better than doing nothing.

Finding the modulated wave-frequencies empty of any significant noises, he switched to the continuous waves. He was startled by a dot-dashing.

"Hey, mom! Something in the 1000 kilocycles! Unmodulated!"

"Naturally, son," she said with some exasperation in the midst of her elation. "What would you expect from a radiotelegraphic signal?"

She found the band on her own cylinder. He looked blankly at her. "I know nothing about radio, but that's not Morse."

"What? You must be mistaken!"

"I—I don't think so."

"Is it or isn't it? Good God, son, can't you be certain of *anything!*"

She turned the amplifier up. As both of them had learned Galacto-Morse through sleeplearn techniques, she checked him at once.

"You're right. What do you make of it?"

His quick ear sorted out the pulses.

"No simple dot and dash. Four different time-lengths."

He listened some more.

"They've got a certain rhythm, all right. I can make out definite groupings. Ah! That's the sixth time I've caught that particular one. And there's another. And another."

Dr. Fetts shook her ash-blonde head. She could make out nothing but a series of zzt-zzt-zzt's.

Eddie glanced at the DF needle.

"Coming from NE by E. Should we try to locate?"

"Naturally," she replied. "But we'd better eat first. We don't know how far away it is, or what we'll find there. While I fix a hot meal, you get our field trip stuff ready."

"O.K.," he said with more enthusiasm than he had shown for a long time.

When he came back he ate everything in the large dish his mother had prepared on the unwrecked galley stove.

"You always did make the best stew," he said.

"Thank you. I'm glad you're eating again, son. I am surprised. I thought you'd be sick about all this."

He waved vaguely but energetically.

"The challenge of the unknown. I have a sort of feeling this is going to turn out much better than we thought. Much better."

She came close and sniffed his breath. It was clean, innocent even of stew. That meant he'd taken Nodor, which probably meant he'd been sampling some hidden rye. Otherwise, how explain his reckless disregard of the possible dangers? It wasn't like him.

She said nothing, for she knew that if he tried to hide a bottle in his clothes or field sack while they were tracking down the radio signals, she would soon find it. And take it away. He wouldn't even protest, merely let her lift it from his limp hand while his lips swelled with resentment.

III

They set out. Both wore knapsacks and carried the panrads. He carried a gun over his shoulder, and she had snapped on to her sack her small black bag of medical and lab supplies.

High noon of late autumn was topped by a weak red sun that barely managed to make itself seen through the eternal double layer of clouds. Its companion, an even smaller blob of lilac, was setting on the northwestern horizon. They walked in a sort of bright twilight, the best that Baudelaire ever achieved. Yet, despite the lack of light, the air was warm. It was a phenomenon common to certain planets behind the Horsehead Nebula, one being investigated but as yet unexplained.

The country was hilly, with many deep ravines. Here and

there were prominences high enough and steep-sided enough to be called embryo mountains. Considering the roughness of the land, however, there was a surprising amount of vegetation. Pale green, red and yellow bushes, vines, and little trees clung to every bit of ground, horizontal or vertical. All had comparatively broad leaves that turned with the sun to catch the light.

From time to time, as the two Terrans strode noisily through the forest, small multicolored insect-like and mammal-like creatures scuttled from hiding place to hiding place. Eddie decided to carry his gun in the crook of his arm. Then, after they were forced to scramble up and down ravines and hills and fight their way through thickets that became unexpectedly tangled, he put it back over his shoulder, where it hung from a strap.

Despite their exertions, they did not tire quickly. They weighed about twenty pounds less than they would have on Earth and, though the air was thinner, it was richer in oxygen.

Dr. Fetts kept up with Eddie. Thirty years the senior of the twenty-three-year-old, she passed even at close inspection for his older sister. Longevity pills took care of that. However, he treated her with all the courtesy and chivalry that one gave one's mother and helped her up the steep inclines, even though the climbs did not appreciably cause her deep chest to demand more air.

They paused once by a creek bank to get their bearings.

"The signals have stopped," he said.

"Obviously," she replied.

At that moment the radar-detector built into the panrad began to ping. Both of them automatically looked upwards.

"There's no ship in the air."

"It can't be coming from either of those hills," she pointed out. "There's nothing but a boulder on top of each one. Tremendous rocks."

"Nevertheless, it's coming from there, I think. Oh! Oh! Did you see what I saw? Looked like a tall stalk of some kind being pulled down behind that big rock."

She peered through the dim light. "I think you were imagining things, son. I saw nothing."

Then, even as the pinging kept up, the zzting started again. But after a burst of noise, both stopped.

"Let's go up and see what we shall see," she said.

"Something screwy," he commented. She did not answer.

They forded the creek and began the ascent. Half-way up, they stopped to sniff in puzzlement at a gust of some heavy odor coming downwind.

"Smells like a cageful of monkeys," he said.

"In heat," she added. If his was the keener ear, hers was the sharper nose.

They went on up. The RD began sounding its tiny hysterical gonging. Nonplussed, Eddie stopped. The DF indicated the radar pulses were not coming from the top of the hill they were climbing, as formerly, but from the other hill across the valley. Abruptly, the panrad fell silent.

"What do we do now?"

"Finish what we started. This hill. Then we go to the other one."

He shrugged and then hastened after her tall slim body in its long-legged coveralls. She was hot on the scent, literally, and nothing could stop her. Just before she reached the bunga-low-sized boulder topping the hill, he caught up with her. She had stopped to gaze intently at the DF needle, which swung wildly before it stopped at neutral. The monkey-cage odor was very strong.

"Do you suppose it could be some sort of radio-generating mineral?" she asked, disappointedly.

"No. Those groupings were semantic. And that smell. . . ."

"Then what—"

He didn't know whether to feel pleased or not that she had so obviously and suddenly thrust the burden of responsibility and action on him. Both pride and a curious shrinking affected him. But he did feel exhilarated. Almost, he thought, he felt as if he were on the verge of discovering what he had been look-ing for for a long time. What the object of his search had been, he could not say. But he was excited and not very much afraid.

He unslung his weapon, a two-barrelled combination shot-gun and rifle. The panrad was still quiet.

"Maybe the boulder is camouflage for a spy outfit," he said. He sounded silly, even to himself.

Behind him, his mother gasped and screamed. He whirled

and raised his gun, but there was nothing to shoot. She was pointing at the hilltop across the valley, shaking, and saying something incoherent.

He could make out a long slim antenna seemingly projecting from the monstrous boulder crouched there. At the same time, two thoughts struggled for first place in his mind: one, that it was more than a coincidence that both hills had almost identical stone structures on their brows, and, two, that the antenna must have been recently stuck out, for he was sure he had not seen it the last time he looked.

He never got to tell her his conclusions, for something thin and flexible and irresistible seized him from behind. Lifted into the air, he was borne backwards. He dropped the gun and tried to grab the bands or tentacles around him and tear them off with his bare hands. No use.

He caught one last glimpse of his mother running off down the hillside. Then a curtain snapped down, and he was in total darkness.

IV

Eddie sensed himself, still suspended, twirled around. He could not know for sure, of course, but he thought he was facing in exactly the opposite direction. Simultaneously, the tentacles binding his legs and arms were released. Only his waist was still gripped. It was pressed so tightly that he cried out with pain.

Then, boot-toes bumping on some resilient substance, he was carried forward. Halted, facing he knew not what horrible monster, he was suddenly assailed—not by a sharp beak or tooth or knife or some other cutting or mangling instrument—but by a dense cloud of that same monkey perfume.

In other circumstances, he might have vomited. Now his stomach was not given the time to consider whether it should clean house or not. The tentacle lifted him higher and thrust him against something soft and yielding—something fleshlike and womanly—almost breastlike in texture and smoothness and warmth and in its hint of gentle curving.

He put his hands and feet out to brace himself, for he thought for a moment he was going to sink in and be covered up—enfolded—ingested. The idea of a gargantuan amoeba-thing hiding within a hollow rock—or a rocklike shell—made him writhe and yell and shove at the protoplasmic substance.

But nothing of the kind happened. He was not plunged into a smothering and slimy jelly that would strip him of his skin and then his flesh and then dissolve his bones. He was merely shoved repeatedly against the soft swelling. Each time, he pushed or kicked or struck at it. After a dozen of these seemingly purposeless acts, he was held away, as if whatever was doing it was puzzled by his behavior.

He had quit screaming. The only sounds were his harsh breathing and the zzts and pings from the panrad. Even as he became aware of them, the zzts changed tempo and settled into a recognizable pattern of bursts—three units that crackled out again and again.

"Who are you? Who are you?"

Of course, it could just as easily have been, "What are you?" or "What the hell!" or "Nov smoz ka pop?"

Or nothing—semantically speaking.

But he didn't think the latter. And when he was gently lowered to the floor, and the tentacle went off to only-God-knew-where in the dark, he was sure that the creature was communicating—or trying to—with him.

It was this thought that kept him from screaming and running around in the lightless and fetid chamber, brainlessly seeking an outlet. He mastered his panic and snapped open a little shutter in the panrad's side and thrust in his right-hand index finger. There he poised it above the key and in a moment, when the thing paused in transmitting, he sent back, as best he could, the pulses he had received. It was not necessary for him to turn on the light and spin the dial that would put him on the 1000 kc band. The instrument would automatically key that frequency in with the one he had just received.

The oddest part of the whole procedure was that his whole body was trembling almost uncontrollably—one part excepted. That was his index finger, his one unit that seemed to him to have a definite function in this otherwise meaningless situation. It was the section of him that was helping him to survive—the only part that knew how—at that moment. Even his brain seemed to have no connection with his finger. That digit was himself, and the rest just happened to be linked to it.

When he paused, the transmitter began again. This time the

units were unrecognizable. There was a certain rhythm to them, but he could not know what they meant. Meanwhile, the RD was pinging. Something somewhere in the dark hole had a beam held tightly on him.

He pressed a button on the panrad's top, and the built-in flashlight illuminated the area just in front of him. He saw a wall of reddish-grey rubbery substance. On the wall was a roughly circular, light grey swelling about four feet in diameter. Around it, giving it a Medusa appearance, were coiled twelve very long, very thin tentacles.

Though he was afraid that if he turned his back to them the tentacles would seize him once more, his curiosity forced him to wheel about and examine his surroundings with the bright beam. He was in an egg-shaped chamber about thirty feet long, twelve wide, and eight to ten high in the middle. It was formed of a reddish-grey material, smooth except for irregular intervals of blue or red pipes. Veins and arteries?

A door-sized portion of the wall had a vertical slit running down it. Tentacles fringed it. He guessed it was a sort of iris and that it had opened to drag him inside. Starfish-shaped groupings of tentacles were scattered on the walls or hung from the ceiling. On the wall opposite the iris was a long and flexible stalk with a cartilaginous ruff around its free end. When Eddie moved, it moved, its blind point following him as a radar antenna tracks the thing it is locating. That was what it was. And unless he was wrong, the stalk was also a C.W. transmitter-receiver.

He shot the light around. When it reached the end farthest from him, he gasped. Ten creatures were huddled together facing him! About the size of half-grown pigs, they looked like nothing so much as unshelled snails; they were eyeless, and the stalk growing from the forehead of each was a tiny duplicate of that on the wall. They didn't look dangerous. Their open mouths were little and toothless, and their rate of locomotion must be slow, for they moved like snails, on a large pedestal of flesh—a foot-muscle.

Nevertheless, if he were to fall asleep they could overcome him by force of numbers, and those mouths might drip an acid to digest him, or they might carry a concealed poisonous sting.

His speculations were interrupted violently. He was seized,

lifted, and passed on to another group of tentacles. He was carried beyond the antenna-stalk and towards the snail-beings. Just before he reached them, he was halted, facing the wall. An iris, hitherto invisible, opened. His light shone into it, but he could see nothing but convolutions of flesh.

His panrad gave off a new pattern of dit-dot-deet-dats. The iris widened until it was large enough to admit his body, if he were shoved in head first. Or feet first. It didn't matter. The convolutions straightened out and became a tunnel. Or a throat. From thousands of little pits emerged thousands of tiny, razor-sharp teeth. They flashed out and sank back in, and before they had disappeared thousands of other wicked little spears darted out and past the receding fangs.

Meat-grinder.

Beyond the murderous array, at the end of the throat, was a huge pouch of water. Steam came from it, and with it an odor like that of his mother's stew. Dark bits, presumably meat, and pieces of vegetables floated on the seething surface.

Then the iris closed, and he was turned around to face the slugs. Gently, but unmistakably, a tentacle spanked his buttocks. And the panrad zzted a warning.

Eddie was not stupid. He knew now that the ten creatures were not dangerous unless he molested them. In which case he had just seen where he would go if he did not behave.

Again he was lifted and carried along the wall until he was shoved against the light grey spot. The monkey-cage odor, which had died out, became strong again. Eddie identified its source with a very small hole which appeared in the wall.

When he did not respond—he had no idea yet how he was supposed to act—the tentacles dropped him so unexpectedly that he fell on his back. Unhurt by the yielding flesh, he rose.

What was the next step? Exploration of his resources. Itemization: The panrad. A sleeping-bag, which he wouldn't need as long as the present too-warm temperature kept up. A bottle of Old Red Star capsules. A free-fall thermos with attached nipple. A box of A-2-Z rations. A Foldstove. Cartridges for his double-barrel, now lying outside the creature's boulderish shell. A roll of toilet paper. Toothbrush. Paste. Soap. Towel. Pills: Nodor, hormone, vitamin, longevity, reflex, and sleeping. And a thread-thin wire, a hundred feet long when uncoiled, that held prisoner in its molecular structure a hundred symphonies, eighty operas, a thousand different types of musical pieces, and two thousand great books ranging from Sophocles and Dostoyevsky to the latest bestseller. It could be played inside the panrad.

He inserted it, pushed a button, and spoke. "Eddie Fetts's recording of Puccini's *Che gelida manina,* please."

And while he listened approvingly to his own magnificent voice, he zipped open a can he had found in the bottom of the sack. His mother had put into it the stew left over from their last meal in the ship.

Not knowing what was happening, yet for some reason sure he was for the present safe, he munched meat and vegetables with a contented jaw. Transition from abhorrence to appetite sometimes came easily for Eddie.

He cleaned out the can and finished with some crackers and a chocolate bar. Rationing was out. As long as the food lasted, he would eat well. Then, if nothing turned up, he would. . . . But then, he reassured himself as he licked his fingers, his mother, who was free, would find some way to get him out of his trouble.

She always had.

V

The panrad, silent for a while, began signalling. Eddie spotlighted the antenna and saw it was pointing at the snailbeings, which he had, in accordance with his custom, dubbed familiarly. Sluggos he called them.

The Sluggos crept towards the wall and stopped close to it. Their mouths, placed on the tops of their heads, gaped like so many hungry young birds. The iris opened, and two lips formed into a spout. Out of it streamed steaming-hot water and chunks of meat and vegetables. Stew! Stew that fell exactly into each waiting mouth.

That was how Eddie learned the second phrase of Mother Polyphema's language. The first message had been. "What are you?" This was, "Come and get it!"

He experimented. He tapped out a repetition of what he'd last heard. As one, the Sluggos—except the one then being fed—turned to him and crept a few feet before halting, puzzled.

Inasmuch as Eddie was broadcasting, the Sluggos must have had some sort of built-in DF. Otherwise they wouldn't have been able to distinguish between his pulses and their Mother's.

Immediately after, a tentacle smote Eddie across the shoulders and knocked him down. The panrad zzted its third intelligible message: "Don't ever do that!"

And then a fourth, to which the ten young obeyed by wheeling and resuming their former positions.

"This way, children."

Yes, they were the offspring, living, eating, sleeping, playing, and learning to communicate in the womb of their mother —the Mother. They were the mobile brood of this vast immobile entity that had scooped up Eddie as a frog scoops up a fly. This Mother. She who had once been just a Sluggo until she had grown hog-size and had been pushed out of her Mother's womb. And who, rolled into a tight ball, had freewheeled down her natal hill, straightened out at the bottom, inched her way up the next hill, rolled down, and so on. Until she found the empty shell of an adult who had died. Or, if she wanted to be a first class citizen in her society and not a prestigeless *occupée*, she found the bare top of a tall hill— any eminence that commanded a big sweep of territory—and there squatted.

And there she put out many thread-thin tendrils into the soil and into the cracks in the rocks, tendrils that drew sustenance from the fat of her body and grew and extended downwards and ramified into other tendrils. Deep underground the rootlets worked their instinctive chemistry; searched for and found the water, the calcium, the iron, the copper, the nitrogen, the carbons, fondled earthworms and grubs and larvae, teasing them for the secrets of their fats and proteins; broke down the wanted substance into shadowy colloidal particles; sucked them up the thready pipes of the tendrils and back to the pale and slimming body crouching on a flat space atop a ridge, a hill, a peak.

There, using the blueprints stored in the molecules of the cerebellum, her body took the building blocks of elements and fashioned them into a very thin shell of the most available material, a shield large enough so she could expand to fit it while her natural enemies—the keen and hungry predators that prowled twilighted Baudelaire—nosed and clawed it in vain.

Then, her evergrowing bulk cramped, she would resorb the hard covering. And if no sharp tooth found her during that process of a few days, she would cast another and a larger. And so on through a dozen or more

Until she had become the monstrous and much reformed body of an adult and virgin female. Outside would be the stuff that so much resembled a boulder, that was, actually, rock: either granite, diorite, marble, basalt, or maybe just plain limestone. Or sometimes iron, glass, or cellulose.

Within was the centrally located brain, probably as large as a man's. Surrounding it, the tons of organs: the nervous system, the mighty heart, or hearts, the four stomachs, the microwave and longwave generators, the kidneys, bowels, tracheae, scent and taste organs, the perfume factory which made odors to attract animals and birds close enough to be seized, and the huge womb. And the antennae—the small one inside for teaching and scanning the young, and a long and powerful stalk on the outside, projecting from the shelltop, retractable if danger came.

The next step was from virgin to Mother, lower case to uppercase as designated in her pulse-language by a longer pause before a word. Not until she was deflowered could she take a high place in her society. Immodest, unblushing, she herself made the advances, the proposals, and the surrender.

After which, she ate her mate.

The clock in the panrad told Eddie he was in his thirtieth day of imprisonment when he found out that little bit of information. He was shocked, not because it offended his ethics, but because he himself had been intended to be the mate. And the dinner.

His finger tapped, "Tell me, Mother, what you mean."

He had not wondered before how a species that lacked males could reproduce. Now he found that, to the Mothers, all creatures except themselves were male. Mothers were immobile and female. Mobiles were male. Eddie had been mobile. He was, therefore, a male.

He had approached this particular Mother during the mating season, that is, midway through raising a litter of young.

She had scanned him as he came along the creekbanks at the valley bottom. When he was at the foot of the hill, she had detected his odor. It was new to her. The closest she could come to it in her memorybanks was that of a beast similar to him. From her description, he guessed it to be an ape. So she had released from her repertoire its rut stench. When he seemingly fell into the trap, she had caught him.

He was supposed to attack the conception-spot, that light grey swelling on the wall. After he had ripped and torn it enough to begin the mysterious workings of pregnancy, he would have been popped into her stomach-iris.

Fortunately, he had lacked the sharp beak, the fang, the claw. And she had received her own signals back from the panrad.

Eddie did not understand why it was necessary to use a mobile for mating. A Mother was intelligent enough to pick up a sharp stone and mangle the spot herself.

He was given to understand that conception would not start unless it was accompanied by a certain titillation of the nerves—a frenzy and its satisfaction. Why this emotional state was needed, Mother did not know.

Eddie tried to explain about such things as genes and chromosomes and why they had to be present in highly-developed species.

Mother did not understand.

Eddie wondered if the number of slashes and rips in the spot corresponded to the number of young. Or if there were a large number of potentialities in the heredity-ribbons spread out under the conception-skin. And if the haphazard irritation and consequent stimulation of the genes paralleled the chance combining of genes in human male-female mating. Thus resulting in offspring with traits that were combinations of their parents.

Or did the inevitable devouring of the mobile after the act indicate more than an emotional and nutritional reflex? Did it hint that the mobile caught up scattered gene-nodes, like hard seeds, along with the torn skin, in its claws and tusks, that these genes survived the boiling in the stew-stomach, and were later passed out in the faeces? Where animals and birds picked them up in beak, tooth, or foot, and then, seized by other Mothers in this oblique rape, transmitted the heredity-carrying agents to the conception-spots while attacking them, the nodules being scraped off and implanted in the skin and blood of the swelling even as others were harvested? Later, the mobiles were eaten, digested, and ejected in the obscure but ingenious and never-ending cycle? Thus ensuring the continual, if haphazard, recombining of genes, chances for variations in offspring, opportunities for mutations, and so on?

Mother pulsed that she was nonplussed.

Eddie gave up. He'd never know. After all, did it matter?

He decided not, and rose from his prone position to request water. She pursed up her iris and spouted a tepid quartful into his thermos. He dropped in a pill, swished it around till it dissolved, and drank a reasonable facsimile of Old Red Star. He preferred the harsh and powerful rye, though he could have afforded the smoothest. Quick results were what he wanted. Taste didn't matter, as he disliked all liquor tastes. Thus he drank what the Skid Row bums drank and shuddered even as they did, renaming it Old Rotten Tar and cursing the fate that had brought them so low they had to gag such stuff down.

The rye glowed in his belly and spread quickly through his limbs and up to his head, chilled only by the increasing scarcity of the capsules. When he ran out—then what? It was at times like this that he most missed his mother.

Thinking about her brought a few large tears. He snuffled and drank some more and when the biggest of the Sluggos nudged him for a back-scratching, he gave it instead a shot of Old Red Star. A slug for Sluggo. Idly, he wondered what effect a taste of rye would have on the future of the race when these virgins became mothers.

At that moment he was shaken by what seemed a life-saving idea. These creatures could suck up the required elements from the earth and with them duplicate quite complex molecular structures. Provided, of course, they had a sample of the desired substance to brood over in some cryptic organ.

Well, what easier to do than give her one of the cherished capsules? One could become any number. Those, plus the abundance of water pumped up through hollow underground tendrils from the nearby creek, would give enough to make a master-distiller green!

He smacked his lips and was about to key her his request when what she was transmitting penetrated his mind.

Rather cattily, she remarked that her neighbor across the valley was putting on airs because she, too, held prisoner a communicating mobile.

VI

The Mothers had a society as hierarchical as table-protocol in Washington or peck-order in a barnyard. Prestige was what counted, and prestige was determined by the broadcasting power, the height of the eminence on which the Mother sat, which governed the extent of her radar-territory, and the abundance and novelty and wittiness of her gossip. The creature that had snapped Eddie up was a queen. She had precedence over thirty-odd of her kind; they all had to let her broadcast first, and none dared start pulsing until she quit. Then, the next in order began, and so on down the line. Any of them could be interrupted at any time by Number One, and if any of the lower echelon had something interesting to transmit, she could break in on the one then speaking and get permission from the queen to tell her tale.

Eddie knew this, but he could not listen in directly to the hilltop-gabble. The thick pseudo-granite shell barred him from that and made him dependent upon her womb-stalk for relayed information.

Now and then Mother opened the door and allowed her young to crawl out. There they practiced beaming and broadcasting at the Sluggos of the Mother across the valley. Occasionally that Mother deigned herself to pulse the young, and Eddie's keeper reciprocated to her offspring.

Turnabout.

The first time the children had inched through the exit-iris, Eddie had tried, Ulysses-like, to pass himself off as one of them and crawl out in the midst of the flock. Eyeless, but no Polyphemus, Mother had picked him out with her tentacles and hauled him back in.

It was following that incident that he had named her Polyphema.

He knew she had increased her own already powerful prestige tremendously by possession of that unique thing—a transmitting mobile. So much had her importance grown that the Mothers on the fringes of her area passed on the news to

others. Before he had learned her language, the entire continent was hooked-up. Polyphema had become a veritable gossip columnist; tens of thousands of hillcrouchers listened in
eagerly to her accounts of her dealings with the walking paradox: a semantic male.

That had been fine. Then, very recently, the Mother across
the valley had captured a similar creature. And in one bound
she had become Number Two in the area and would, at the
slightest weakness on Polyphema's part, wrest the top position
away.

Eddie became wildly excited at the news. He had often day-
dreamed about his mother and wondered what she was doing.
Curiously enough, he ended many of his fantasies with lip-
mutterings, reproaching her almost audibly for having left him
and for making no try to rescue him. When he became aware
of his attitude, he was ashamed. Nevertheless, the sense of
desertion colored his thoughts.

Now that he knew she was alive and had been caught, probably while trying to get him out, he rose from the lethargy
that had lately been making him doze the clock around. He
asked Polyphema if she would open the entrance so he could
talk directly with the other captive. She said yes. Eager to listen in on a conversation between two mobiles, she was very
cooperative. There would be a mountain of gossip in what
they would have to say. The only thing that dented her joy
was that the other Mother would also have access.

Then, remembering she was still Number One and would
broadcast the details first, she trembled so with pride and
ecstasy that Eddie felt the floor shaking.

Iris open, he walked through it and looked across the valley.
The hillsides were still green, red, and yellow, as the plants
on Baudelaire did not lose their leaves during winter. But a
few white patches showed that winter had begun. Eddie shivered from the bite of cold air on his naked skin. Long ago he
had taken off his clothes. The womb-warmth had made garments too uncomfortable; moreover, Eddie, being human, had
had to get rid of waste products. And Polyphema, being a
Mother, had had periodically to flush out the dirt with warm
water from one of her stomachs. Every time the tracheae-vents
exploded streams that swept the undesirable elements out
through her door-iris, Eddie had become soaked. When he

abandoned dress, his clothes had gone floating out. Only by sitting on his pack did he keep it from a like fate.

Afterwards, he and the Sluggos had been dried off by warm air pumped through the same vents and originating from the mighty battery of lungs. Eddie was comfortable enough—he'd always liked showers—but the loss of his garments had been one more thing that kept him from escaping. He would soon freeze to death outside unless he found the yacht quickly. And he wasn't sure he remembered the path back.

So now, when he stepped outside, he retreated a pace or two and let the warm air from Polyphema flow like a cloak from his shoulders.

Then he peered across the half-mile that separated him from his mother, but he could not see her. The twilight state and the dark of the unlit interior of her captor hid her.

He tapped in Morse, "Switch to the talkie, same frequency." Paula Fetts did so. She began asking him frantically if he were all right.

He replied he was fine.

"Have you missed me terribly, son?"

"Oh, very much."

Even as he said this he wondered vaguely why his voice sounded so hollow. Despair at never again being able to see her, probably.

"I've almost gone crazy, Eddie. When you were caught I ran away as fast as I could. I had no idea what horrible monster it was that was attacking us. And then, half-way down the hill, I fell and broke my leg. . . ."

"Oh, no, mother!"

"Yes. But I managed to crawl back to the ship. And there, after I'd set it myself, I gave myself B.K. shots. Only, my system didn't react like it's supposed to. There are people that way, you know, and the healing took twice as long.

"But when I was able to walk, I got a gun and a box of dynamite. I was going to blow up what I thought was a kind of rock-fortress, an outpost for some kind of extee. I'd no idea of the true nature of these beasts. First, though, I decided to reconnoitre. I was going to spy on the boulder from across the valley. But I was trapped by this thing.

"Listen, son. Before I'm cut off, let me tell you not to give up hope. I'll be out of here before long and over to rescue you."

"How?"

"If you remember, my lab kit holds a number of carcinogens for field work. Well, you know that sometimes a Mother's conception-spot when it is torn up during mating, instead of begetting young, goes into cancer—the opposite of pregnancy. I've injected a carcinogen into the spot and a beautiful carcinoma has developed. She'll be dead in a few days."

"Mom! You'll be buried in that rotting mass!"

"No. This creature has told me that when one of her species dies, a reflex opens the labia. That's to permit their young—if any—to escape. Listen, I'll—"

A tentacle coiled about him and pulled him back through the iris, which shut.

When he switched back to C.W., he heard, "Why didn't you communicate? What were you doing? Tell me! Tell me!"

Eddie told her. There was a silence that could only be interpreted as astonishment. After Mother had recovered her wits, she said, "From now on, you will talk to the other male through me."

Obviously, she envied and hated his ability to change wavebands, and, perhaps, had a struggle to accept the idea.

"Please," he persisted, not knowing how dangerous were the waters he was wading in, "please let me talk to my mother di—"

"Wha-wha-what? Your Mo-Mo-Mother?"

"Yes. Of course."

The floor heaved violently beneath his feet. He cried out and braced himself to keep from falling and then flashed on the light. The walls were pulsating like shaken jelly, and the vascular columns had turned from red and blue to grey. The entrance-iris sagged open, like a lax mouth, and the air cooled. He could feel the drop in temperature in her flesh with the soles of his feet.

It was some time before he caught on.

Polyphema was in a state of shock.

What might have happened had she stayed in it, he never knew. She might have died and thus forced him out into the winter before his mother could escape. If so, and he couldn't find the ship, he would die. Huddled in the warmest corner of the egg-shaped chamber, Eddie contemplated that idea and shivered to a degree for which the outside air couldn't account.

VII

However, Polyphema had her own method of recovery. It consisted of spewing out the contents of her stew-stomach, which had doubtless become filled with the poisons draining out of her system from the blow. Her ejection of the stuff was the physical manifestation of the psychical catharsis. So furious was the flood that her foster son was almost swept out in the hot tide, but she, reacting instinctively, had coiled tentacles about him and the Sluggos. Then she followed the first upchucking by emptying her other three waterpouches, the second hot and the third luke-warm and the fourth, just filled, cold.

Eddie yelped as the icy water doused him.

Polyphema's irises closed again. The floor and walls gradually quit quaking; the temperature rose; and her veins and arteries regained their red and blue. She was well again. Or so she seemed.

But when, after waiting twenty-four hours he cautiously approached the subject, he found she not only would not talk about it, she refused to acknowledge the existence of the other mobile.

Eddie, giving up hope of conversation, thought for quite a while. The only conclusion he could come to, and he was sure he'd grasped enough of her psychology to make it valid, was that the concept of a mobile female was utterly unacceptable.

Her world was split into two: mobile and her kind, the immobile. Mobile meant food and mating. Mobile meant—male. The Mothers were—female.

How the mobiles reproduced had probably never entered the hillcrouchers' minds. Their science and philosophy were on the instinctive body-level. Whether they had some notion of spontaneous generation or amoeba-like fission being responsible for the continued population of mobiles, or they'd just taken for granted they "growed," like Topsy, Eddie never found out. To them, they were female and the rest of the protoplasmic cosmos was male.

That was that. Any other idea was more than foul and obscene and blasphemous. It was—unthinkable.

Polyphema had received a deep trauma from his words. And though she seemed to have recovered, somewhere in those tons of unimaginably complicated flesh a bruise was buried. Like a hidden flower, dark purple, it bloomed, and the shadow it cast was one that cut off a certain memory, a certain tract, from the light of consciousness. That bruise-stained shadow covered that time and event which the Mother, for reasons unfathomable to the human being, found necessary to mark KEEP OFF.

Thus, though Eddie did not word it, he understood in the cells of his body, he felt and knew, as if his bones were prophesying and his brain did not hear, what came to pass.

Sixty-six hours later by the panrad clock, Polyphema's entrance-lips opened. Her tentacles darted out. They came back in, carrying his helpless and struggling mother.

Eddie, roused out of a doze, horrified, paralysed, saw her toss her lab kit at him and heard an inarticulate cry from her. And saw her plunged, headforemost, into the stomach-iris.

Polyphema had taken the one sure way of burying the evidence.

Eddie lay face down, nose mashed against the warm and faintly throbbing flesh of the floor. Now and then his hands clutched spasmodically as if he were reaching for something that someone kept putting just within his reach and then moving away.

How long he was there he didn't know, for he never again looked at the clock.

Finally, in the darkness, he sat up and giggled inanely, "Mother always did make good stew."

That set him off. He leaned back on his hands and threw his head back and howled like a wolf under a full moon.

Polyphema, of course, was dead-deaf, but she could radar his posture, and her keen nostrils deduced from his body-scent that he was in terrible fear and anguish.

A tentacle glided out and gently enfolded him.

"What is the matter?" zzted the panrad.

He stuck his finger in the keyhole.

"I have lost my mother!"

"?"

"She's gone away, and she'll never come back."

"I don't understand. *Here I am.*"

Eddie quit weeping and cocked his head as if he were listening to some inner voice. He snuffled a few times and wiped away the tears, slowly disengaged the tentacle, patted it, walked over to his pack in a corner, and took out the bottle of Old Red Star capsules. One he popped into the thermos; the other he gave to her with the request she duplicate it, if possible. Then he stretched out on his side, propped on one elbow like a Roman in his sensualities, sucked the rye through the nipple, and listened to a medley of Beethoven, Moussorgsky, Verdi, Strauss, Porter, Feinstein, and Waxworth.

So the time—if there were such a thing there—flowed around Eddie. When he was tired of music or plays or books, he listened in on the area hookup. Hungry, he rose and walked—or often just crawled—to the stew-iris. Cans of rations lay in his pack; he had planned to eat those until he was sure that—what was it he was forbidden to eat? Poison? Something had been devoured by Polyphema and the Sluggos. But sometime during the music-rye orgy, he had forgotten. He now ate quite hungrily and with thought for nothing but the satisfaction of his wants.

Sometimes the door-iris opened, and Billy Greengrocer hopped in. Billy looked like a cross between a cricket and a kangaroo. He was the size of a collie, and he bore in a marsupialian pouch vegetables and fruit and nuts. These he extracted with shiny green, chitinous claws and gave to Mother in return for meals of stew. Happy symbiote, he chirruped merrily while his many-faceted eyes, revolving independently of each other, looked one at the Sluggos and the other at Eddie.

Eddie, on impulse, abandoned the 100 kc. band and roved the frequencies until he found that both Polyphema and Billy were emitting a 108 wave. That, apparently, was their natural signal.

When Billy had his groceries to deliver, he broadcast. Polyphema, in turn, when she needed them, sent back to him. There was nothing intelligent on Billy's part; it was just his instinct to transmit. And the Mother was, aside from the 'semantic' frequency, limited to that one band. But it worked out fine.

VIII

Everything was fine. What more could a man want? Free food, unlimited liquor, soft bed, air-conditioning, shower-baths, music, intellectual works (on the tape), interesting conversation (much of it was about him), privacy, and security.

If he had not already named her, he would have called her Mother Gratis.

Nor were creature comforts all. She had given him the answers to all his questions, all. . . .

Except one.

That was never expressed vocally by him. Indeed, he would have been incapable of doing so. He was probably unaware that he had such a question.

But Polyphema voiced it one day when she asked him to do her a favor.

Eddie reacted as if outraged.

"One does not—! One does not—!"

He choked, and then he thought, how ridiculous! She is not—

And looked puzzled, and said, "But she is."

He rose and opened the lab kit. While he was looking for a scalpel, he came across the carcinogens. He threw them through the half-opened labia far out and down the hillside.

Then he turned and, scalpel in hand, leaped at the light grey swelling on the wall. And stopped, staring at it, while the instrument fell from his hand. And picked it up and stabbed feebly and did not even scratch the skin. And again let it drop.

"What is it? What is it?" crackled the panrad hanging from his wrist.

Suddenly, a heavy cloud of human odor—mansweat—was puffed in his face from a nearby vent.

"? ? ? ?"

And he stood, bent in a half-crouch, seemingly paralysed. Until tentacles seized him in fury and dragged him towards the stomach-iris, yawning man-sized.

Eddie screamed and writhed and plunged his finger in the panrad and tapped, "All right! All right!"

And once back before the spot, he lunged with a sudden and wild joy; he slashed savagely; he yelled. "Take that! And that, P . . ." and the rest was lost in a mindless shout.

He did not stop cutting, and he might have gone on and on until he had quite excised the spot had not Polyphema interferred by dragging him towards her stomach-iris again. For ten seconds he hung there, helpless and sobbing with a mixture of fear and glory.

Polyphema's reflexes had almost overcome her brain. Fortunately, a cold spark of reason lit up a corner of the vast, dark, and hot chapel of her frenzy.

The convolutions leading to the steaming, meat-laden pouch closed and the foldings of flesh rearranged themselves. Eddie was suddenly hosed with warm water from what he called the "sanitation" stomach. The iris closed. He was put down. The scalpel was put back in the bag.

For a long time Mother seemed to be shaken by the thought of what she might have done to Eddie. She did not trust herself to transmit until her nerves were settled. When they were, she did not refer to his narrow escape. Nor did he.

He was happy. He felt as if a spring, tight-coiled against his bowels since he and his wife had parted, was now, for some reason, released. The dull vague pain of loss and discontent, the slight fever and cramp in his entrails, and the apathy that sometimes afflicted him, were gone. He felt fine.

Meanwhile, something akin to deep affection had been lighted, like a tiny candle under the draughty and overtowering roof of a cathedral. Mother's shell housed more than Eddie; it now curved over an emotion new to her kind. This was evident by the next event that filled him with terror.

For the wounds in the spot healed and the swelling increased into a large bag. Then the bag burst and ten mouse-sized Sluggos struck the floor. The impact had the same effect as a doctor spanking a newborn baby's bottom; they drew in their first breath with shock and pain; their uncontrolled and feeble pulses filled the ether with shapeless SOS's.

When Eddie was not talking with Polyphema or listening in or drinking or sleeping or eating or bathing or running off the tape, he played with the Sluggos. He was, in a sense, their father. Indeed, as they grew to hog-size, it was hard for their female parent to distinguish him from her young. As he seldom walked any more, and was often to be found on hands and knees in their midst, she could not scan him too well. Moreover, something in the heavywet air or in the diet had caused every hair on his body to drop off. He grew very fat. Generally speaking, he was one with the pale, soft, round, and bald offspring. A family likeness.

There was one difference. When the time came for the virgins to be expelled, Eddie crept to one end, whimpering, and stayed there until he was sure Mother was not going to thrust him out into the cold, hard, and hungry world.

That final crisis over, he came back to the center of the floor. The panic in his breast had died out, but his nerves were still quivering. He filled his thermos and then listened for a while to his own tenor singing the "Sea Things" aria from his favorite opera, Gianelli's *Ancient Mariner*. Suddenly, he burst out and accompanied himself, finding himself thrilled as never before by the concluding words.

> And from my neck so free
> The Albatross fell off, and sank
> Like lead into the sea.

Afterwards, voice silent but heart singing, he switched off the wire and cut in on Polyphema's broadcast.

Mother was having trouble. She could not precisely describe to the continent-wide hook-up this new and almost inexpressible emotion she felt about the mobile. It was a concept her language was not prepared for. Nor was she helped any by the gallons of Old Red Star in her bloodstream.

Eddie sucked at the plastic nipple and nodded sympathetically and drowsily at her search for words. Presently, the thermos rolled out of his hand.

He slept on his side, curled in a ball, knees on his chest

and arms crossed, neck bent forward. Like the pilot room chronometer whose hands reversed after the crash, the clock of his body was ticking backwards, ticking backwards. . . .

In the darkness, in the moistness, safe and warm, well fed, much loved.

5,271,009

Alfred Bester

Alfred Bester began writing science fiction long
ago, when he was very young; he made his first
real impact in 1942 with a novella called "Hell is
Forever," in John W. Campbell's legendary fantasy
magazine Unknown Worlds, and then, a decade
later, let loose an earthquake of a novel called
The Demolished Man. The story reprinted here is
one of seven or eight brilliant shorter pieces that
followed that novel, like aftershocks, over the next
few years. Would that there were more.

Take two parts of Beelzebub, two of Israfel, one of Monte
Cristo, one of Cyrano, mix violently, season with mystery and
you have Mr. Solon Aquila. He is tall, gaunt, sprightly in
manner, bitter in expression, and when he laughs his dark
eyes turn into wounds. His occupation is unknown. He is
wealthy without visible means of support. He is seen everywhere and understood nowhere. There is something odd about
his life.

This is what's odd about Mr. Aquila, and you can make
what you will of it. When he walks he is never forced to wait
on a traffic signal. When he desires to ride there is always a
vacant taxi on hand. When he bustles into his hotel an elevator
always happens to be waiting. When he enters a store, a sales-
clerk is always free to serve him. There always happens to be
a table available for Mr. Aquila in restaurants. There are

245

always last-minute ticket returns when he craves entertainment at sold-out shows.

You can question waiters, hack drivers, elevator girls, salesmen, box-office men. There is no conspiracy. Mr. Aquila does not bribe or blackmail for these petty conveniences. In any case, it would not be possible for him to bribe or blackmail the automatic clock that governs the city traffic signal system. These things, which make life so convenient for him, simply happen. Mr. Solon Aquila is never disappointed. Presently we shall hear about his first disappointment and see what it led to.

Mr. Aquila has been seen fraternizing in low saloons, in middle saloons, in high saloons. He has been met in bagnois, at coronations, executions, circuses, magistrate's courts and handbook offices. He has been known to buy antique cars, historic jewels, incunabula, pornography, chemicals, porro prisms, polo ponies and full-choke shotguns.

"HimmelHerrGottSeiDank! I'm crazy, man, crazy. Eclectic, by God," he told a flabbergasted department store president. "The Weltmann type, nicht wahr? My ideal: Goethe. Tout le monde. God damn."

He spoke a spectacular tongue of mixed metaphors and meanings. Dozens of languages and dialects came out in machine-gun bursts. Apparently he also lied *ad libitum*.

"Sacré bleu, Jeez!" he was heard to say once. "Aquila from the Latin. Means aquiline. O tempora O mores. Speech by Cicero. My ancestor."

And another time: "My idol: Kipling. Took my name from him. Aquila, one of his heroes. God damn. Greatest Negro writer since *Uncle Tom's Cabin*."

On the morning that Mr. Solon Aquila was stunned by his first disappointment, he bustled into the atelier of Lagan & Derelict, dealers in paintings, sculpture and rare objects of art. It was his intention to buy a painting. Mr. James Derelict knew Aquila as a client. Aquila had already purchased a Frederic Remington and a Winslow Homer some time ago when, by another odd coincidence, he had bounced into the Madison Avenue shop one minute after the coveted painting went up for sale. Mr. Derelict had also seen Mr. Aquila boat a prize striper at Montauk.

"Bon soir, bel esprit, God damn, Jimmy," Mr. Aquila said.

He was on first name terms with everyone. "Here's a cool day for color, oui! Cool. Slang. I have in me to buy a picture."

"Good morning, Mr. Aquila," Derelict answered. He had the seamed face of a cardsharp, but his blue eyes were honest and his smile was disarming. However at this moment his smile seemed strained, as though the volatile appearance of Aquila had unnerved him.

"I'm in the mood for your man, by Jeez," Aquila said, rapidly opening cases, fingering ivories and tasting the porcelains. "What's his name, my old? Artist like Bosch. Like Heinrich Kley. You handle him, parbleu, exclusive. O si sic omnia, by Zeus!"

"Jeffrey Halsyon?" Derelict asked timidly.

"Oeil de boeuf!" Aquila cried. "What a memory. Chryselephantine. Exactly the artist I want. He is my favorite. A monochrome, preferably. A small Jeffrey Halsyon for Aquila, bitte. Wrap her up."

"I wouldn't have believed it," Derelict muttered.

"Ah! Ah-ha? This is not 100 proof guaranteed Ming," Mr. Aquila exclaimed brandishing an exquisite vase. "Caveat emptor, by damn. Well, Jimmy? I snap my fingers. No Halsyons in stock, old faithful?"

"It's extremely odd, Mr. Aquila," Derelict seemed to struggle with himself. "Your coming in like this. A Halsyon monochrome arrived not five minutes ago."

"You see? Tempo ist Richtung. Well?"

"I'd rather not show it to you. For personal reasons, Mr. Aquila."

"HimmelHerrGott! Pourquoi? She's bespoke?"

"N-no, sir. Not for *my* personal reasons. For *your* personal reasons."

"Oh? God damn. Explain myself to me."

"Anyway, it isn't for sale, Mr. Aquila. It can't be sold."

"For why not? Speak, old fish and chips."

"I can't say, Mr. Aquila."

"Zut alors! Must I judo your arm, Jimmy? You can't show. You can't sell. Me, internally, I have pressurized myself for a Jeffrey Halsyon. My favorite. God damn. Show me the Halsyon or sic transit gloria mundi. You hear me, Jimmy?"

Derelict hesitated, then shrugged. "Very well, Mr. Aquila. I'll show you."

Derelict led Aquila past cases of china and silver, past lac-
quer and bronzes and suits of shimmering armor to the gallery
in the rear of the shop where dozens of paintings hung on the
gray velour walls, glowing under warm spotlights. He opened
a drawer in a Goddard breakfront and took out an envelope.
On the envelope was printed BABLYLON INSTITUTE. From
the envelope Derelict withdrew a dollar bill and handed it to
Mr. Aquila.

"Jeffrey Halsyon's latest," he said.

With a fine pen and carbon ink, a cunning hand had drawn
another portrait over the face of George Washington on the
dollar bill. It was a hateful, diabolic face set in a hellish background. It was a face to strike terror, in a scene to inspire
loathing. The face was a portrait of Mr. Aquila.

"God damn," Mr. Aquila said.

"You see, sir? I didn't want to hurt your feelings."

"Now I must own him, big boy." Mr. Aquila appeared to
be fascinated by the portrait. "Is she accident or for purpose?
Does Halsyon know myself? Ergo sum."

"Not to my knowledge, Mr. Aquila. But in any event I can't
sell the drawing. It's evidence of a felony . . . mutilating
United States currency. It must be destroyed."

"Never!" Mr. Aquila returned the drawing as though he
feared the dealer would instantly set fire to it. "Never, Jimmy.
Nevermore quoth the raven. God damn. Why does he draw on
money, Halsyon? My picture, pfui. Criminal libels but n'importe. But pictures on money? Wasteful. Joci causa."

"He's insane," Mr. Aquila."

"No! Yes? Insane?" Aquila was shocked.

"Quite insane, sir. It's very sad. They've had to put him
away. He spends his time drawing these pictures on money."

"God damn, mon ami. Who gives him money?"

"I do, Mr. Aquila; and his friends. Whenever we visit him
he begs for money for his drawings."

"Le jour viendra, by Jeez! Why you don't give him paper
for drawings, eh, my ancient of days?"

Derelict smiled sadly. "We tried that, sir. When we gave
Jeff paper, he drew pictures of money."

"HimmelHerrGott! My favorite artist. In the looney bin.
Eh bien. How in the holy hell am I to buy paintings from same
if such be the case?"

"You won't, Mr. Aquila. I'm afraid no one will ever buy a Halsyon again. He's quite hopeless."

"Why does he jump his tracks, Jimmy?"

"They say its a withdrawal, Mr. Aquila. His success did it to him."

"Ah? Q.E.D. me, big boy. Translate."

"Well, sir, he's still a young man; in his thirties and very immature. When he became so very successful, he wasn't ready for it. He wasn't prepared for the responsibilities of his life and his career. That's what the doctors told me. So he turned his back on everything and withdrew into childhood."

"Ah? And the drawing on money?"

"They say that's his symbol of his return to childhood, Mr. Aquila. It proves he's too young to know what money is for."

"Ah? Oui. Ja. Astute, by crackey. And my portrait?"

"I can't explain that, Mr. Aquila, unless you have met him in the past and he remembers you somehow. Or it may be a coincidence."

"Hmmm. Perhaps. So. You know something, my attic of Greece? I am disappointed. Je n'oublierai jamais. I am most severely disappointed. God damn. No more Halsyons ever? Merde. My slogan. We must do something about Jeffrey Halsyon. I will not be disappointed. We must do something."

Mr. Solon Aquila nodded his head emphatically, took out a cigarette, took out a lighter, then paused, deep in thought. After a long moment, he nodded again, this time with decision, and did an astonishing thing. He returned the lighter to his pocket, took out another, glanced around quickly and lit it under Mr. Derelict's nose.

Mr. Derelict appeared not to notice. Mr. Derelict appeared, in one instant, to be frozen. Allowing the lighter to burn, Mr. Aquila placed it carefully on a ledge in front of the art dealer who stood before it without moving. The orange flame gleamed on his glassy eyeballs.

Aquila darted out into the shop, searched and found a rare Chinese crystal globe. He took it from its case, warmed it against his heart and peered into it. He mumbled. He nodded. He returned the globe to the case, went to the cashier's desk, took a pad and pencil and began ciphering in symbols that bore no relationship to any language or any graphology. He nodded again, tore up the sheet of paper and took out his wallet.

From the wallet he removed a dollar bill. He placed the bill on the glass counter, took an assortment of fountain pens from his vest pocket, selected one and unscrewed it. Carefully shielding his eyes, he allowed one drop to fall from the pen point onto the bill. There was a blinding flash of light. There was a humming vibration that slowly died.

Mr. Aquila returned the pens to his pocket, carefully picked up the bill by a corner and ran back into the picture gallery where the art dealer still stood staring glassily at the orange flame. Aquila fluttered the bill before the slightless eyes.

"Listen, my ancient," Aquila whispered. "You will visit Jeffrey Halsyon this afternoon. N'est-ce pas? You will give him this very own coin of the realm when he asks for drawing materials? Eh? God damn." He removed Mr. Derelict's wallet from his pocket, placed the bill inside and returned the wallet.

"And this is why you make the visit," Aquila continued. "It is because you have had an inspiration from le Diable Boiteux. Nolens volens, the lame devil has inspired you with a plan for healing Jeffrey Halsyon. God damn. You will show him samples of his great art of the past to bring him to his senses. Memory is the all-mother. HimmelHerrGott. You hear me, big boy? You do what I say. Go today and devil take the hindmost."

Mr. Aquila picked up the burning lighter, lit his cigarette and permitted the flame to go out. As he did so, he said: "No, my holy of holies! Jeffrey Halsyon is too great an artist to languish in durance vile. He must be returned to this world. He must be returned to me. È sempre l'ora. I will not be disappointed. You hear me, Jimmy? I will not!"

"Perhaps there's hope, Mr. Aquila," James Derelict said. "Something's just occurred to me while you were talking . . . a way to bring Jeff back to sanity. I'm going to try it this afternoon."

As he drew the face of the Faraway Fiend over George Washington's portrait on a bill, Jeffrey Halsyon dictated his autobiography to nobody.

"Like Cellini," he recited. "Line and literature simultane-

ously. Hand in hand, although all art is one art, holy brothers
in barbiturate, near ones and dear ones in nembutal. Very well.
I commence: I was born. I am dead. Baby wants a dollar.
No—"

He arose from the padded floor and raged from padded
wall to padded wall, envisioning anger as a deep purple fury
running into the pale lavenders of recrimination by the magic
of his brushwork, his chiaroscuro, by the clever blending of
oil, pigment, light and the stolen genius of Jeffrey Halsyon
torn from him by the Faraway Fiend whose hideous face—

"Begin anew," he muttered. "We darken the highlights.
Start with the underpainting...." He squatted on the floor
again, picked up the quill drawing pen whose point was warranted harmless, dipped it into carbon ink whose contents
were warranted poisonless, and applied himself to the monstrous face of the Faraway Fiend which was replacing the
first President on the dollar.

"I was born," he dictated to space while his cunning hand
wrought beauty and horror on the banknote paper. "I had
peace. I had hope. I had art. I had peace. Mama. Papa. Kin
I have a glass of water? Oooo! There was a big bad bogey
man who gave me a bad look; and now baby's afraid. Mama!
Baby wantsa make pretty pictures onna pretty paper for
Mama and Papa. Look, Mama. Baby makin' a picture of the
bad bogey man with a mean look, a black look with his black
eyes like pools of hell, like cold fires of terror, like faraway
fiends from faraway fears— Who's that!"

The cell door unbolted. Halsyon leaped into a corner and
cowered, naked and squalling, as the door was opened for the
Faraway Fiend to enter. But it was only the medicine man in
his white jacket and a stranger man in black suit, black homburg, carrying a black portfolio with the initials J.D. lettered
on it in a bastard gold Gothic with ludicrous overtones of
Goudy and Baskerville.

"Well, Jeffrey?" the medicine man inquired heartily.

"Dollar?" Halsyon whined. "Kin baby have a dollar?"

"I've brought an old friend, Jeffrey. You remember Mr.
Derelict?"

"Dollar," Halsyon whined. "Baby wants a dollar."

"What happened to the last one, Jeffrey? You haven't finished it yet, have you?"

Halsyon sat on the bill to conceal it, but the medicine man was too quick for him. He snatched it up and he and the stranger-man examined it.

"As great as all the rest," Derelict sighed. "Greater! What a magnificent talent wasting away. . . ."

Halsyon began to weep. "Baby wants a dollar!" he cried.

The stranger man took out his wallet, selected a dollar bill and handed it to Halsyon. As soon as Halsyon touched it, he heard it sing and he tried to sing with it, but it was singing him a private song so he had to listen.

It was a lovely dollar; smooth but not too new, with a faintly matte surface that would take ink like kisses. George Washington looked reproachful but resigned, as though he was used to the treatment in store for him. And indeed he might well be, for he was much older on this dollar. Much older than on any other for his serial number was 5,271,009 which made him 5,000,000 years old and more, and the oldest he had ever been before was 2,000,000.

As Halsyon squatted contently on the floor and dipped his pen in the ink as the dollar told him to, he heard the medicine may say, "I don't think I should leave you alone with him, Mr. Derelict."

"No, we must be alone together, doctor. Jeff always was shy about his work. He could only discuss it with me privately."

"How much time would you need?"

"Give me an hour."

"I doubt very much whether it'll do any good."

"But there's no harm trying?"

"I suppose not. All right, Mr. Derelict. Call the nurse when you're through."

The door opened; the door closed. The stranger-man named Derelict put his hand on Halsyon's shoulder in a friendly, intimate way. Halsyon looked up at him and grinned cleverly, meanwhile waiting for the sound of the bolt in the door. It came; like a shot, like a final nail in a coffin.

"Jeff, I've brought some of your old work with me," Derelict said in a voice that was only approximately casual. "I thought you might like to look it over with me."

"Have you got a watch on you?" Halsyon asked.

Restraining his start of surprise at Halsyon's normal tone, the art dealer took out his pocket watch and displayed it.

"Lend it to me for a minute."

Derelict unchained the watch and handed it over. Halsyon took it carefully and said, "All right. Go ahead with the pictures."

"Jeff!" Derelict exclaimed. "This is you again, isn't it? This is the way you always—"

"Thirty," Halsyon interrupted. "Thirty-five, forty, forty-five, fifty, fifty-five, ONE." He concentrated on the flicking second hand with rapt expectation.

"No, I guess it isn't," the dealer muttered. "I only imagined you sounded—Oh well." He opened the portfolio and began sorting mounted drawings.

"Forty, forty-five, fifty-five, TWO."

"Here's one of your earliest, Jeff. Remember when you came into the gallery with the roughs and we thought you were the new polisher from the agency? Took you months to forgive us. You always claimed we bought your first picture just to apologize. Do you still think so?"

"Forty, forty-five, fifty, fifty-five, THREE."

"Here's that tempera that gave you so many heartaches. I was wondering if you'd care to try another? I really don't think tempera is as inflexible as you claim and I'd be interested to have you try again now that your technique's so much more matured. What do you say?"

"Forty, forty-five, fifty, fifty-five, FOUR."

"Jeff, put down that watch."

"Ten, fifteen, twenty, twenty-five . . ."

"What the devil's the point of counting minutes?"

"Well," Halsyon said reasonably, "sometimes they lock the door and go away. Other times they lock up and stay and spy on you. But they never spy longer than three minutes so I'm giving them five just to make sure. FIVE."

Halsyon gripped the pocket watch in his big fist and drove the fist cleanly into Derelict's jaw. The dealer dropped without a sound. Halsyon dragged him to the wall, stripped him naked, dressed himself in his clothes, repacked the portfolio and closed it. He picked up the dollar bill and pocketed it. He picked up the bottle of carbon ink warranted nonpoisonous and smeared the contents over his face.

Choking and shouting, he brought the nurse to the door.

"Let me out of here," Halsyon cried in a muffled voice.

"That maniac tried to drown me. Threw ink in my face. I want out!"

The door was unbolted and opened. Halsyon shoved past the nurse-man, cunningly mopping his blackened face with a hand that only masked it more. As the nurse-man started to enter the cell, Halsyon said, "Never mind Halsyon. He's all right. Get me a towel or something. Hurry!"

The nurse-man locked the door again, turned and ran down the corridor. Halsyon waited until he disappeared into a supply room, then turned and ran in the opposite direction. He went through the heavy doors to the main wing corridor, still cleverly mopping, still sputtering with cunning indignation. He reached the main building. He was halfway out and still no alarm. He knew those brazen bells. They tested them every Wednesday noon.

It's like a game, he told himself. It's fun. It's nothing to be scared of. It's being safely, sanely, joyously a kid again and when we quit playing, I'm going home to mama and dinner and papa reading me the funnies and I'm a kid again, really a kid again, forever.

There still was no hue and cry when he reached the main floor. He complained about his indignity to the receptionist. He complained to the protection guards as he forged James Derelict's name in the visitors' book, and his inky hand smeared such a mess on the page that the forgery was undetected. The guard buzzed the final gate open. Halsyon passed through into the street, and as he started away he heard the brass of the bells begin a clattering that terrified him.

He ran. He stopped. He tried to stroll. He could not. He lurched down the street until he heard the guards shouting. He darted around a corner, and another, tore up endless streets, heard cars behind him, sirens, bells, shouts, commands. It was a ghastly Catherine Wheel of flight. Searching desperately for a hiding place, Halsyon darted into the hallway of a desolate tenement.

Halsyon began to climb the stairs. He went up three at a clip, then two, then struggled step by step as his strength failed and panic paralyzed him. He stumbled at a landing and fell against a door. The door opened. The Faraway Fiend stood within, smiling briskly, rubbing his hands.

"Glückliche Reise," he said. "On the dot. God damn. You

twenty-three skidooed, eh? Enter, my old. I'm expecting you. Be it never so humble . . ."

Halsyon screamed.

"No, no, no! No Sturm und Drang, my beauty," Mr. Aquila clapped a hand over Halsyon's mouth, heaved him up, dragged him through the doorway and slammed the door.

"Presto-changeo," he laughed. "Exit Jeffrey Halsyon from mortal ken. Dieu vous garde."

Halsyon freed his mouth, screamed again and fought hysterically, biting and kicking. Mr. Aquila made a clucking noise, dipped into his pocket and brought out a package of cigarettes. He flipped one out of the pack expertly and broke it under Halsyon's nose. The artist at once subsided and suffered himself to be led to a couch, where Aquila cleansed the ink from his face and hands.

"Better, eh?" Mr. Aquila chuckled. "Non habit-forming. God damn. Drinks now called for."

He filled a shot glass from a decanter, added a tiny cube of purple ice from a fuming bucket, and placed the drink in Halsyon's hand. Compelled by a gesture from Aquila, the artist drank it off. It made his brain buzz. He stared around, breathing heavily. He was in what appeared to be the luxurious waiting room of a Park Avenue physician. Queen Anne furniture. Axminster rug. Two Hogarths and a Copley on the wall in gilt frames. They were genuine, Halsyon realized with amazement. Then, with even more amazement, he realized that he was thinking with coherence, with continuity. His mind was quite clear.

He passed a heavy hand over his forehead. "What's happened?" he asked faintly. "There's like . . . Something like a fever behind me. Nightmares."

"You have been sick," Aquila replied. "I am blunt, my old. This is a temporary return to sanity. It is no feat, God damn. Any doctor can do it. Niacin plus carbon dioxide. Id genus omne. Only temporary. We must search for something more permanent."

"What's this place?"

"Here? My office. Anteroom without. Consultation room within. Laboratory to left. In God we trust."

"I know you," Halsyon mumbled. "I know you from somewhere. I know your face."

"Oui. You have drawn and redrawn me in your fever. Ecce homo. But you have the advantage, Halsyon. Where have we met? I ask myself." Aquila put on a brilliant speculum, tilted it over his left eye and let it shine into Halsyon's face. "Now I ask you. Where have we met?"

Hypnotized by the light, Halsyon answered dreamily. "At the Beaux Arts Ball. . . . A long time ago. . . . Before the fever. . . ."

"Ah? Si. It was one half year ago. I was there. An unfortunate night."

"No. A glorious night. . . . Gay, happy fun. . . . Like a school dance. . . . Like a prom in costume. . . ."

"Always back to the childhood, eh?" Mr. Aquila murmured. "We must attend to that. Cetera desunt, young Lochinvar. Continue."

"I was with Judy. . . . We realized we were in love that night. We realized how wonderful life was going to be. And then you passed and looked at me. . . . Just once. You looked at me. It was horrible."

"Tch!" Mr. Aquila clicked his tongue in vexation. "Now I remember said incident. I was unguarded. Bad news from home. A pox on both my houses."

"You passed in red and black. . . . Satanic. Wearing no mask. You looked at me. . . . A red and black look I never forgot. A look from black eyes like pools of hell, like cold fires of terror. And with that look you robbed me of everything . . . of joy, of hope, of love, of life. . . ."

"No, no!" Mr. Aquila said sharply. "Let us understand ourselves. My carelessness was the key that unlocked the door. But you fell into a chasm of your own making. Nevertheless, old beer and skittles, we must alter same." He removed the speculum and shook his finger at Halsyon. "We must bring you back to the land of the living. Auxilium ab alto. Jeez. That is for why I have arranged this meeting. What I have done I will undone, eh? But you must climb out of your own chasm. Knit up the ravelled sleave of care. Come inside."

He took Halsyon's arm, led him down a panelled hall, past a neat office and into a spanking white laboratory. It was all tile and glass with shelves of reagent bottles, porcelain filters, an electric oven, stock jars of acids, bins of raw materials. There was a small round elevation in the center of the floor, a sort of dais. Mr. Aquila placed a stool on the dais, placed Halsyon on the stool, got into a white lab coat and began to assemble apparatus.

"You," he chatted, "are an artist of the utmost. I do not dorer la pilule. When Jimmy Derelict told me you were no longer at work, God damn! We must return him to his muttons, I said. Solon Aquila must own many canvases of Jeffrey Halsyon. We shall cure him. Hoc age."

"You're a doctor?" Halsyon asked.

"No. Let us say, a warlock. Strictly speaking a witch-pathologist. Very high class. No nostrums. Strictly modern magic. Black magic and white magic are passé, n'est-ce pas? I cover entire spectrums, specializing mostly in the 15,000 angstrom band."

"You're a witch-doctor? Never!"

"Oh yes."

"In this kind of place?"

"Ah-ha? You too are deceived, eh? It is our camouflage. Many a modern laboratory you think concerns itself with tooth paste is devoted to magic. But we are scientific too. Parbleu! We move with the times, we warlocks. Witch's Brew now complies with Pure Food and Drug Act. Familiars 100 per cent sterile. Sanitary brooms. Cellophane-wrapped curses. Father Satan in rubber gloves. Thanks to Lord Lister; or is it Pasteur? My idol."

The witch-pathologist gathered raw materials, consulted an ephemeris, ran off some calculations on an electronic computer and continued to chat.

"Fugit hora," Aquila said. "Your trouble, my old, is loss of sanity. Oui? Lost in one damn flight from reality and one damn desperate search for peace brought on by one unguarded look from me to you. Hélas! I apologize for that, R.S.V.P." With what looked like a miniature tennis line-marker, he rolled a circle around Halsyon on the dais. "But your trouble is, to wit: You search for the peace of infancy. You should be fighting to acquire the peace of maturity, n'est-ce pas? Jeez."

Aquila drew circles and pentagons with a glittering compass and rule, weighed out powders on a micro-beam balance, dropped various liquids into crucibles from calibrated burettes, and continued: "Many warlocks do brisk trade in potions from

Fountains of Youths. Oh yes. Are many youths and many fountains; but none for you. No. Youth is not for artists. Age is the cure. We must purge your youth and grow you up, nicht wahr?"

"No," Halsyon argued. "No. Youth is the art. Youth is the dream. Youth is the blessing."

"For some, yes. For many, not. Not for you. You are cursed, my adolescent. We must purge you. Lust for power. Lust for sex. Injustice collecting. Escape from reality. Passion for revenges. Oh yes, Father Freud is also my idol. We wipe your slate clean at very small price."

"What price?"

"You will see when we are finished."

Mr. Aquila deposited liquids and powders around the helpless artist in crucibles and petri dishes. He measured and cut fuses, set up a train from the circle to an electric timer which he carefully adjusted. He went to a shelf of serum bottles, took down a small Woulff vial numbered 5-271-009, filled a syringe and meticulously injected Halsyon.

"We begin," he said, "the purge of your dreams. Voilá."

He tripped the electric timer and stepped behind a lead shield. There was a moment of silence. Suddenly black music crashed from a concealed loudspeaker and a recorded voice began an intolerable chant. In quick succession the powders and liquids around Halsyon burst into flame. He was engulfed in music and fire. The world began to spin around him in a roaring confusion. . . .

The president of the United Nations came to him. He was tall and gaunt, sprightly but bitter. He was wringing his hands in dismay.

"Mr. Halsyon! Mr. Halsyon!" he cried. "Where you been, my cupcake? God damn. Hoc tempore. Do you know what has happened?"

"No," Halsyon answered. "What's happened?"

"After your escape from the looney bin. Bango! Atom bombs everywhere. The two-hour war. It is over. Hora fugit, old faithful. Virility is over."

"What!"

"Hard radiation, Mr Halsyon, has destroyed the virility of the world. God damn. You are the only man left capable of

engendering children. No doubt on account of a mysterious
mutant strain in your makeup which it makes you different.
Jeez."

"No."

"Oui. It is your responsibility to repopulate the world. We
have taken for you a suite at the Odeon. It has three bed-
rooms. Three; my favorite. A prime number."

"Hot dog!" Halsyon said. "This is my big dream."

His progress to the Odeon was a triumph. He was garlanded
with flowers, serenaded, hailed and cheered. Ecstatic women
displayed themselves wickedly before him, begging for his
attention. In his suite, Halsyon was wined and dined. A tall,
gaunt man entered subserviently. He was sprightly but bitter.
He had a list in his hand.

"I am World Procurer at your service, My Halsyon," he
said. He consulted his list. "God damn. Are 5,271,009 virgins
clamoring for your attention. All guaranteed beautiful. Ewig-
Weibliche. Pick a number from one to 5,000,000."

"We'll start with a redhead," Halsyon said.

They brought him a redhead. She was slender and boyish,
with a small hard bosom. The next was fuller with a rollicking
rump. The fifth was Junoesque and her breasts were like African pears. The tenth was a voluptuous Rembrandt. The twentieth was slender and boyish with a small hard bosom.

"Haven't we met before?" Halsyon inquired.

"No," she said.

The next was fuller with a rollicking rump.

"The body is familiar," Halsyon said.

"No," she answered.

The fiftieth was Junoesque with breasts like African pears.

"Surely?" Halsyon said.

"Never," she answered.

The World Procurer entered with Halsyon's morning aphrodisiac.

"Never touch the stuff," Halsyon said.

"God damn," the Procurer exclaimed. "You are a veritable
giant. An elephant. No wonder you are the beloved Adam.
Tant soit peu. No wonder they all weep for love of you." He
drank off the aphrodisiac himself.

"Have you noticed they're all getting to look alike?" Halsyon complained.

"But no! Are all different. Parbleu! This is an insult to my office."

"Oh, they're different from one to another, but the types keep repeating."

"Ah? This is life, my old. All life is cyclic. Have you not, as an artist, noticed?"

"I didn't think it applied to love."

"To all things. Wahrheit und Dichtung."

"What was that you said about them weeping?"

"Oui. They all weep."

"Why?"

"For ecstatic love of you. God damn."

Halsyon thought over the succession of boyish, rollicking, Junoesque, Rembrandtesque, wiry, red, blonde, brunette, white, black and brown women.

"I hadn't noticed," he said.

"Observe today, my world father. Shall we commence?"

It was true. Halsyon hadn't noticed. They all wept. He was flattered but depressed.

"Why don't you laugh a little?" he asked.

They would not or could not.

Upstairs on the Odeon roof where Halsyon took his afternoon exercise, he questioned his trainer who was a tall, gaunt man with a sprightly but bitter expression.

"Ah?" said the trainer. "God damn. I don't know, old scotch and soda. Perhaps because it is a traumatic experience for them."

"Traumatic?" Hansyon puffed. "Why? What do I do to them?"

"Ah-ha? You joke, eh? All the world knows what you do to them."

"No, I mean . . . How can it be traumatic? They're all fighting to get to me, aren't they? Don't I come up to expectations?"

"A mystery. Tripotage. Now, beloved father of the world, we practice the push-ups. Ready? Begin."

Downstairs, in the Odeon restaurant, Halsyon questioned the headwaiter, a tall, gaunt man with a sprightly manner but bitter expression.

"We are men of the world, Mr. Halsyon. Suo jure. Surely

you understand. These women love you and can expect no more than one night of love. God damn. Naturally they are disappointed."

"What do they want?"

What every women wants, my gateway to the west. A permanent relationship. Marriage."

"Marriage!"

"Oui."

"All of them?"

"Oui."

"All right. I'll marry all 5,271,009."

But the World Procurer objected. "No, no, no, young Lochinvar. God damn. Impossible. Aside from religious difficulties there are human also. Who could manage such a harem?"

"Then I'll marry one."

"No, no, no. Pensez à moi. How could you make the choice? How could you select? By lottery, drawing straws, tossing coins?"

"I've already selected one."

"Ah? Which?"

"My girl," Halsyon said slowly. "Judith Field."

"So. Your sweetheart?"

"Yes."

"She is far down on the list of 5,000,000."

"She's always been number one on my list. I want Judith." Halsyon sighed. "I remember how she looked at the Beaux Arts Ball. . . . There was a full moon. . . ."

"But there will be no full moon until the twenty-sixth."

"I want Judith."

"The others will tear her apart out of jealousy. No, no, no, Mr. Halsyon, we must stick to the schedule. One night for all, no more for any."

"I want Judith . . . or else."

"It will have to be discussed in council. God damn."

It was discussed in the U. N. council by a dozen delegates, all tall, gaunt, sprightly but bitter. It was decided to permit Jeffrey Halsyon one secret marriage.

"But no domestic ties," the World Procurer warned. "No faithfulness to your wife. That must be understood. We cannot spare you from our program. You are indispensable."

They brought the lucky Judith Field to the Odeon. She was a tall, dark girl with cropped curly hair and lovely tennis legs. Halsyon took her hand. The World Procurer tip-toed out.

"Hello, darling," Halsyon murmured.

Judith looked at him with loathing. Her eyes were wet, her face was bruised from weeping.

"Hello, darling," Halsyon repeated.

"If you touch me, Jeff," Judith said in a strangled voice, "I'll kill you."

"Judy!"

"That disgusting man explained everything to me. He didn't seem to understand when I tried to explain to him. . . . I was praying you'd be dead before it was my turn."

"But this is marriage, Judy."

"I'd rather die than be married to you."

"I don't believe you. We've been in love for—"

"For God's sake, Jeff, love's over for you. Don't you understand? Those women cry because they hate you. I hate you. The world loathes you. You're disgusting."

Halsyon stared at the girl and saw the truth in her face. In an excess of rage he tried to seize her. She fought him bitterly. They careened around the huge living room of the suite, overturning furniture, their breath hissing, their fury mounting. Halsyon struck Judith Field with his big fist to end the struggle once and for all. She reeled back, clutched at a drape, smashed through a french window and fell fourteen floors to the street like a gyrating doll.

Halsyon looked down in horror. A crowd gathered around the smashed body. Faces upturned. Fists shook. An ominous growl began. The World Procurer dashed into the suite.

"My old! My blue!" he cried. "What have you done? Per conto. It is a spark that will ignite savagery. You are in very grave danger. God damn."

"Is it true they all hate me?"

"Hélas, then you have discovered the truth? That indiscreet girl. I warned her. Oui. You are loathed."

"But you told me I was loved. The new Adam. Father of the new world."

"Oui. You are the father, but what child does not hate its father? You are also a legal rapist. What woman does not hate being forced to embrace a man . . . even by necessity for survival? Come quickly, my rock and rye. Passim. You are in great danger."

He dragged Halsyon to a back elevator and took him down to the Odeon cellar.

"The army will get you out. We take you to Turkey at once and effect a compromise."

Halsyon was transferred to the custody of a tall, gaunt, bitter army colonel who rushed him through underground passages to a side street, where a staff car was waiting. The colonel thrust Halsyon inside.

"Jacta alea est," he said to the driver. "Speed, my corporal. Protect old faithful. To the airport. Alors!"

"God damn, sir," the corporal replied. He saluted and started the car. As it twisted through the streets at breakneck speed, Halsyon glanced at him. He was a tall, gaunt man, sprightly but bitter.

"Kulturkampf der Menscheit," the corporal muttered. "Jeez!"

A giant barricade had been built across the street, improvised of ash barrels, furniture, overturned cars, traffic stanchions. The corporal was forced to brake the car. As he slowed for a U-turn, a mob of women appeared from doorways, cellars, stores. They were screaming. Some of them brandished improvised clubs.

"Excelsior!" the corporal cried. "God damn." He tried to pull his service gun out of its holster. The women yanked open the car doors and tore Halsyon and the corporal out. Halsyon broke free, struggled through the wild clubbing mob, dashed to the sidewalk, stumbled and dropped with a sickening yaw through an open coal chute. He shot down and spilled out into an endless black space. His head whirled. A stream of stars sailed before his eyes. . . .

And he drifted alone in space, a martyr, misunderstood, a victim of cruel injustice.

He was still chained to what had once been the wall of Cell 5, Block 27, Tier 100, Wing 9 of the Callisto Penitentiary until that unexpected gamma explosion had torn the vast fortress dungeon—vaster than the Chateau d' If—apart. That explosion, he realized, had been detonated by the Grssh.

His assets were his convict clothes, a helmet, one cylinder

of O₂, his grim fury at the injustice that had been done him, and his knowledge of the secret of how the Grssh could be defeated in their maniacal quest for solar domination.

The Grssh, ghastly marauders from Omicron Cei, space-degenerates, space-imperialists, cold-blooded, roachlike, depending for their food upon the psychotic horrors which they engendered in man through mental control and upon which they fed, were rapidly conquering the galaxy. They were irrestible, for they possessed the power of simul-kinesis—the ability to be in two places at the same time.

Against the vault of space, a dot of light moved, slowly, like a stricken meteor. It was a rescue ship, Halsyon realized, combing space for survivors of the explosion. He wondered whether the light of Jupiter, flooding him with rusty radiation, would make him visible to the rescuers. He wondered whether he wanted to be rescued at all.

"It will be the same thing again," Halsyon grated. "Falsely accused by Balorsen's robot. . . . Falsely convicted by Judith's father. . . . Repudiated by Judith herself. . . . Jailed again . . . and finally destroyed by the Grssh as they destroy the last strongholds of Terra. Why not die now?"

But even as he spoke he realized he lied. He was the one man with the one secret that could save the earth and the very galaxy itself. He must survive. He must fight.

With indomitable will, Halsyon struggled to his feet, fighting the constricting chains. With the steely strength he had developed as a penal laborer in the Grssh mines, he waved and shouted. The spot of light did not alter its slow course away from him. Then he saw the metal link of one of his chains strike a brilliant spark from the flinty rock. He resolved on a desperate expedient to signal the rescue ship.

He detached the plasti-hose of the O₂ tank from his plasti-helmet, and permitted the stream of life-giving oxygen to spurt into space. With trembling hands, he gathered the links of his leg chain and dashed them against the rock under the oxygen. A spark glowed. The oxygen caught fire. A brilliant geyser of white flame spurted for half a mile into space.

Husbanding the last oxygen in his plasti-helmet, Halsyon twisted the cylinder slowly, sweeping the fan of flame back and forth in a last desperate bid for rescue. The atmosphere in his plasti-helmet grew foul and acrid. His ears roared. His sight flickered. At last his senses failed. . . .

When he recovered consciousness he was in a plasti-cot in the cabin of a starship. The high frequency whine told him they were in overdrive. He opened his eyes. Balorsen stood before the plasti-cot, and Balorsen's robot and High Judge Field, and his daughter Judith. Judith was weeping. The robot was in magnetic plasti-clamps and winced as General Balorsen lashed him again and again with a nuclear plasti-whip.

"Parbleu! God damn!" the robot grated. "It is true I framed Jeff Halsyon. Ouch! Flux de bouche. I was the space-pirate who space-hijacked the space-freighter. God damn. Ouch! The space-bartender in the Spaceman's Saloon was my accomplice. When Jackson wrecked the space-cab I went to the space-garage and X-beamed the sonic *before* Tantial murdered O'Leary. Aux armes. Jeez. Ouch!"

"There you have the confession, Halsyon," General Balorsen grated. He was tall, gaunt, bitter. "By God. Ars est celare artem. You are innocent."

"I falsely condemned you, old faithful," Judge Field grated. He was tall, gaunt, bitter. "Can you forgive this God damn fool? We apologize."

"We wronged you, Jeff," Judith whispered. "How can you ever forgive us? Say you forgive us."

"You're sorry for the way you treated me," Halsyon grated. "But it's only because on account of a mysterious mutant strain in my makeup which it makes me different, I'm the one man with the one secret that can save the galaxy from the Grssh."

"No, no, no, old gin and tonic," General Balorsen pleaded. "God damn. Don't hold grudges. Save us from the Grssh."

"Save us, faute de mieux, save us, Jeff," Judge Field put in.

"Oh please, Jeff, please," Judith whispered. "The Grssh are everywhere and coming closer. We're taking you to the U. N. You must tell the council how to stop the Grssh from being in two places at the same time."

The starship came out of overdrive and landed on Governor's Island where a delegation of world dignitaries met the ship and rushed Halsyon to the General Assembly room of the U. N. They drove down the strangely rounded streets lined with strangely rounded buildings which had all been altered when it was discovered that the Grssh always appeared in corners. There was not a corner or an angle left on all Terra.

The General Assembly was filled when Halsyon entered. Hundreds of tall, gaunt, bitter diplomats applauded as he made his way to the podium, still dressed in convict plasti-clothes. Halsyon looked around resentfully.

"Yes," he grated. "You all applaud. You all revere me now; but where were you when I was framed, convicted and jailed ... an innocent man? Where were you then?"

"Halsyon, forgive us. God damn!" they shouted.

"I will not forgive you, I suffered for seventeen years in the Grssh mines. Now it's your turn to suffer."

"Please, Halsyon!"

"Where are your experts? Your professors? Your specialists? Where are your electronic calculators? Your super thinking machines? Let them solve the mystery of the Grssh."

"They can't, old whiskey and soda. Entre nous. They're stopped cold. Save us, Halsyon. Auf wiedersehen."

Judith took his arm. "Not for my sake, Jeff," she whispered. "I know you'll never forgive me for the injustice I did you. But for the sake of all the other girls in the galaxy who love and are loved."

"I still love you, Judy."

"I've always loved you, Jeff."

"Okay. I didn't want to tell them but you talked me into it." Halsyon raised his hand for silence. In the ensuing hush he spoke softly. "The secret is this, gentlemen. Your calculators have assembled data to ferret out the secret weakness of the Grssh. They have not been able to find any. Consequently you have assumed that the Grssh have no secret weakness. *That was a wrong assumption.*"

The General Assembly held its breath.

"Here is the secret. *You should have assumed there was something wrong with the calculators.*"

"God damn!" the General Assembly cried. "Why didn't we think of that? God damn!"

"And I know what's wrong!"

There was a deathlike hush.

The door of the General Assembly burst open. Professor Deathhush, tall, gaunt, bitter, tottered in. "Eureka!" he cried.

"I've found it. God damn. Something wrong with the thinking machines. Three comes *after* two, not before."

The General Assembly broke into cheers. Professor Death-hush was seized and pummeled happily. Bottles were opened. His health was drunk. Several medals were pinned on him. He beamed.

"Hey!" Halsyon called. "That was my secret. I'm the one man who on account of a mysterious mutant strain in my—"

The ticker-tape began pounding: ATTENTION. ATTENTION. HUSHENKOV IN MOSCOW REPORTS DEFECT IN CALCULATORS. 3 COMES AFTER 2 AND NOT BEFORE. REPEAT: AFTER (UNDERSCORE) NOT BEFORE.

A postman ran in. "Special delivery from Doctor Lifehush at Caltech. Says something's wrong with the thinking machines. Three comes after two, not before."

A telegraph boy delivered a wire: THINKING MACHINE WRONG STOP TWO COMES BEFORE THREE STOP NOT AFTER STOP. VON DREAMHUSH, HEIDELBERG.

A bottle was thrown through the window. It crashed on the floor revealing a bit of paper on which was scrawled: *Did you ever stop to thinc that maibe the number 3 comes after 2 insted of in front? Down with the Grish. Mr. Hush-Hush.*

Halsyon buttonholed Judge Field. "What the hell is this?" he demanded. "I thought I was the one man in the world with that secret."

"HimmelHerrGott!" Judge Field replied impatiently. "You are all alike. You dream you are the one men with a secret, the one men with a wrong, the one men with an injustice, with a girl, without a girl, with or without anything. God damn. You bore me, you one-man dreamers. Get lost."

Judge Field shouldered him aside. General Balorsen shoved him back. Judith Field ignored him. Balorsen's robot sneakily tripped him into a corner of the crowd where a Grssh, also in a crowded corner on Neptune, appeared, did something unspeakable to Halsyon and disappeared with him, screaming, jerking and sobbing into a horror that was a delicious meal for the Grssh but a plasti-nightmare for Halsyon. . . .

From which his mother awakened him and said, "This'll

teach you not to sneak peanut-butter sandwiches in the middle of the night, Jeffrey."

"Mama?"

"Yes. It's time to get up, dear. You'll be late for school."

She left the room. He looked around. He looked at himself. It was true. True! The glorious realization came upon him. His dream had come true. He was ten years old again, in the flesh that was his ten-year-old body, in the home that was his boyhood home, in the life that had been his life in the nineteen thirties. And within his head was the knowledge, the experience, the sophistication of a man of thirty-three.

"Oh joy!" he cried. "It'll be a triumph. A triumph!"

He would be the school genius. He would astonish his parents, amaze his teachers, confound the experts. He would win scholarships. He would settle the hash of that kid Rennahan who used to bully him. He would hire a typewriter and write all the successful plays and stories and novels he remembered. He would cash in on that lost opportunity with Judy Field behind the memorial in Isham Park. He would steal inventions and discoveries, get in on the ground floor of new industries, make bets, play the stockmarket. He would own the world by the time he caught up with himself.

He dressed with difficulty. He had forgotten where his clothes were kept. He ate breakfast with difficulty. This was no time to explain to his mother that he'd gotten into the habit of starting the day with Irish coffee. He missed his morning cigarette. He had no idea where his schoolbooks were. His mother had trouble starting him out.

"Jeff's in one of his moods," he heard her mutter. "I hope he gets through the day."

The day started with Rennahan ambushing him at the Boy's Entrance. Halsyon remembered him as a big tough kid with a vicious expression. He was astonished to discover that Rennahan was skinny and harassed, and obviously compelled by some bedevilments to be omnivorously aggressive.

"Why, you're not hostile to me," Halsyon exclaimed. "You're just a mixed-up kid who's trying to prove something."

Rennahan punched him.

"Look, kid," Halsyon said kindly. "You really want to be friends with the world. You're just insecure. That's why you're compelled to fight."

Rennahan was deaf to spot analysis. He punched Halsyon harder. It hurt.

"Oh leave me alone," Halsyon said. "Go prove yourself on somebody else."

Rennahan, with two swift motions, knocked Halsyon's books from under his arm and ripped his fly open. There was nothing for it but to fight. Twenty years of watching films of the future Joe Louis did nothing for Halsyon. He was thoroughly licked. He was also late for school. Now was his chance to amaze his teachers.

"The fact is," he explained to Miss Ralph of the fifth grade, "I had a run-in with a neurotic. I can speak for his left hook but I won't answer for his compulsions."

Miss Ralph slapped him and sent him to the principal with a note, reporting unheard-of insolence.

"The only thing unheard of in this school," Halsyon told Mr. Snider, "is psychoanalysis. How can you pretend to be competent teachers if you don't—"

"Dirty little boy!" Mr. Snider interrupted angrily. He was tall, gaunt, bitter. "So you've been reading dirty books, eh?"

"What the hell's dirty about Freud?"

"And using profane language, eh? You need a lesson, you filthy little animal."

He was sent home with a note requesting an immediate consultation with his parents regarding the withdrawal of Jeffrey Halsyon from school as a degenerate in desperate need of correction and vocational guidance.

Instead of going home he went to a newsstand to check the papers for events on which to get a bet down. The headlines were full of the pennant race. But who the hell won the pennant in 1931? And the series? He couldn't for the life of him remember. And the stock market? He couldn't remember anything about that either. He'd never been particularly interested in such matters as a boy. There was nothing planted in his memory to call upon.

He tried to get into the library for further checks. The librarian, tall, gaunt, and bitter, would not permit him to enter until children's hour in the afternoon. He loafed on the streets. Wherever he loafed he was chased by gaunt and bitter adults. He was beginning to realize that ten-year-old boys had limited opportunities to amaze the world.

At lunch hour he met Judy Field and accompanied her home from school. He was appalled by her knobby knees and black corkscrew curls. He didn't like the way she smelled either. But he was rather taken with her mother who was the image of the Judy he remembered. He forgot himself with Mrs. Field and did one or two things that indeed confounded her. She drove him out of the house and then telephoned his mother, her voice shaking with indignation.

Halsyon went down to the Hudson River and hung around the ferry docks until he was chased. He went to a stationery store to inquire about typewriter rentals and was chased. He searched for a quiet place to sit, think, plan, perhaps begin the recall of a successful story. There was no quiet place to which a small boy would be admitted.

He slipped into his house at 4:30, dropped his books in his room, stole into the living room, sneaked a cigarette and was on his way out when he discovered his mother and father inspecting him. His mother looked shocked. His father was gaunt and bitter.

"Oh," Halsyon said. "I suppose Snider phoned. I'd forgotten about that."

"*Mister* Snider," his mother said.

"And Mrs. Field," his father said.

"Look," Halsyon began. "We'd better get this straightened out. Will you listen to me for a few minutes? I have something startling to tell you and we've got to plan what to do about it. I—"

He yelped. His father had taken him by the ear and was marching him down the hall. Parents did not listen to children for a few minutes. They did not listen at all.

"Pop. . . . Just a minute. . . . Please! I'm trying to explain. I'm not really ten years old. I'm thirty-three. There's been a freak in time, see? On account of a mysterious mutant strain in my makeup which—"

"Damn you! Be quiet!" his father shouted. The pain of his big hands, the suppressed fury in his voice silenced Halsyon. He suffered himself to be led out of the house, down four blocks back to the school, and up one flight to Mr. Snider's office where a public school psychologist was waiting with the principal. He was a tall man, gaunt, bitter, but sprightly.

"Ah yes, yes," he said. "So this is our little degenerate. Our

Scarface Al Capone, eh? Come, we take him to the clinic and there I shall take his journal intime. We will hope for the best. Nisi prius. He cannot be all bad."

He took Halsyon's arm. Halsyon pulled his arm away and said, "Listen, you're an adult, intelligent man. You'll listen to me. My father's got emotional problems that blind him to the—"

His father gave him a tremendous box on the ear, grabbed his arm and thrust it back into the psychologist's grasp. Halsyon burst into tears. The psychologist led him out of the office and into the tiny school infirmary. Halsyon was hysterical. He was trembling with frustration and terror.

"Won't anybody listen to me?" he sobbed. "Won't anybody try to understand? Is this what we're all like to kids? Is this what all kids go through?"

"Gently, my sausage," the psychologist murmured. He popped a pill into Halsyon's mouth and forced him to drink some water.

"You're all so damned inhuman," Halsyon wept. "You keep us out of your world, but you keep barging into ours. If you don't respect us, why don't you leave us alone?"

"You begin to understand, eh?" the psychologist said. "We are two different breeds of animal, childrens and adults. God damn. I speak to you with frankness. Les absents ont toujours tort. There is no meetings of the minds. Jeez. There is nothing but war. It is why all childrens grow up hating their childhoods and searching for revenges. But there is never revenges. Pari mutuel. How can there be? Can a cat insult a king?"

"It's . . . s'hateful," Halsyon mumbled. The pill was taking effect rapidly. "Whole world's hateful. Full of conflicts'n'insults 'at can't be r'solved . . . or paid back. . . . S'like a joke somebody's playin' on us. Silly jokes without point. Isn't?"

As he slid down into darkness, he could hear the psychologist chuckle, but couldn't for the life of him understand what he was laughing at. . . .

He picked up his spade and followed the first clown into the cemetery. The first clown was a tall man, gaunt, bitter, but sprightly.

"Is she to be buried in Christian burial that wilfully seeks her own salvation?" the first clown asked.

"I tell thee she is," Halsyon answered. "And therefore make her grave straight: the crowner hath sat on her, and finds it Christian burial."

"How can that be, unless she drowned herself in her own defense?"

"Why, 'tis found so."

They began to dig the grave. The first clown thought the matter over, then said, "It must be *se offendendo;* it cannot be else. For here lies the point: if I drown myself wittingly, it argues an act: and an act hath three branches; it is, to act, to do, to perform: argal, she drowned herself wittingly."

"Nay, but hear you, goodman delver—" Halsyon began.

"Give me leave," the first clown interrupted and went on with a tiresome discourse on quest-law. Then he turned sprightly and cracked a few professional jokes. At last Halsyon got away and went down to Yaughan's for a drink. When he returned, the first clown was cracking jokes with a couple of gentlemen who had wandered into the graveyard. One of them made quite a fuss about a skull.

The burial procession arrived; the coffin, the dead girl's brother, the king and queen, the priests and lords. They buried her, and the brother and one of the gentlemen began to quarrel over her grave. Halsyon paid no attention. There was a pretty girl in the procession, dark, with cropped curly hair and lovely long legs. He winked at her. She winked back. Halsyon edged over toward her, speaking with his eyes and she answered him saucily the same way.

Then he picked up his spade and followed the first clown into the cemetery. The first clown was a tall man, gaunt, with a bitter expression but a sprightly manner.

"Is she to be buried in Christian burial that wilfully seeks her own salvation?" the first clown asked.

"I tell thee she is," Halsyon answered. "And therefore make her grave straight: the crowner hath sat on her, and finds it Christian burial."

"How can that be, unless she drowned herself in her own defense?"

"Didn't you ask me that before?" Halsyon inquired.

"Shut up, old faithful. Answer the question."

"I could swear this happened before."

"God damn. Will you answer? Jeez."

"Why, 'tis found so."

They began to dig the grave. The first clown thought the matter over and began a long discourse on quest-law. After that he turned sprightly and cracked trade jokes. At last Halsyon got away and went down to Yaughan's for a drink. When he returned there were a couple of strangers at the grave and then the burial procession arrived.

There was a pretty girl in the procession, dark, with cropped curly hair and lovely long legs. Halsyon winked at her. She winked back. Halsyon edged over toward her, speaking with his eyes and she answering him the same way.

"What's your name?" he whispered.

"Judith," she answered.

"I have your name tattooed on me, Judith."

"You're lying, sir."

"I can prove it, Madam. I'll show you where I was tattooed."

"And where is that?"

"In Yaughan's tavern. It was done by a sailor off the Golden Hind. Will you see it with me tonight?"

Before she could answer, he picked up his spade and followed the first clown into the cemetery. The first clown was a tall man, gaunt, with a bitter expression but a sprightly manner.

"For God's sake!" Halsyon complained. "I could swear this happened before."

"Is she to be buried in Christian burial that wilfully seeks her own salvation?" the first clown asked

"I just know we've been through all this."

"Will you answer the question!"

"Listen," Halsyon said doggedly. "Maybe I'm crazy; maybe not. But I've got a spooky feeling that all this happened before. It seems unreal. Life seems unreal."

The first clown shook his head. "HimmelHerrGott," he muttered. "It is as I feared. Lux et veritas. On account of a mysterious mutant strain in your makeup which it makes you different, you are treading on thin water. Ewigkeit! Answer the question."

"If I've answered it once, I've answered it a hundred times."

"Old ham and eggs," the first clown burst out, "you have answered it 5,271,009 times. God damn. Answer again."

"Why?"

"Because you must. Pot au feu. It is the life we must live."

"You call this life? Doing the same things over and over again? Saying the same things? Winking at girls and never getting any further?"

"No, no, no, my Donner and Blitzen. Do not question. It is a conspiracy we dare not fight. This is the life every man lives. Every man does the same things over and over. There is no escape."

"Why is there no escape?"

"I dare not say; I dare not. Vox populi. Others have questioned and disappeared. It is a conspiracy. I'm afraid."

"Afraid of what?"

"Of our owners."

"What? We are owned?"

"Si. Ach, ja! All of us, young mutant. There is no reality. There is no life, no freedom, no will. God damn. Don't you realize? We are. . . . We are all characters in a book. As the book is read, we dance our dances; when the book is read again, we dance again. E pluribus unum. Is she to be buried in Christian burial that wilfully seeks her own salvation?"

"What are you saying?" Halsyon cried in horror. "We're puppets?"

"Answer the question."

"If there's no freedom, no free will, how can we be talking like this?"

"Whoever's reading our book is day-dreaming, my capital of Dakota. Idem est. Answer the question."

"I will not. I'm going to revolt. I'll dance for our owners no longer. I'll find a better life. . . . I'll find reality."

"No, no! It's madness, Jeffrey! Cul-de-sac!"

"All we need is one brave leader. The rest will follow. We'll smash the conspiracy that chains us!"

"It cannot be done. Play it safe. Answer the question."

Halsyon answered the question by picking up his spade and bashing in the head of the first clown who appeared not to notice. "Is she to be buried in Christian burial that wilfully seeks her own salvation?" he asked.

"Revolt!" Halsyon cried and bashed him again. The clown

started to sing. The two gentlemen appeared. One said: "Has this fellow no feeling of business that he sings at grave-making?"

"Revolt! Follow me!" Halsyon shouted and swung his spade against the gentleman's melancholy head. He paid no attention. He chatted with his friend and the first clown. Halsyon whirled like a dervish, laying about him with his spade. The gentleman picked up a skull and philosophized over some person or persons named Yorick.

The funeral procession approached. Halsyon attacked it, whirling and turning, around and around with the clotted frenzy of a man in a dream.

"Stop reading the book," he shouted. "Let me out of the pages. Can you hear me? Stop reading the book! I'd rather be in a world of my own making. Let me go!"

There was a mighty clap of thunder, as of the covers of a mighty book slamming shut. In an instant Halsyon was swept spinning into the third compartment of the seventh circle of the Inferno in the fourteenth Canto of the Divine Comedy where they who have sinned against art are tormented by flakes of fire which are eternally showered down upon them. There he shrieked until he had provided sufficient amusement. Only then was he permitted to devise a text of his own . . . and he formed a new world, a romantic world, a world of his fondest dreams. . . .

He was the last man on earth.

He was the last man on earth and he howled.

The hills, the valleys, the mountains and streams were his, his alone, and he howled.

Five million two hundred and seventy-one thousand and nine houses were his for shelter, 5,271,009 beds were his for sleeping. The shops were his for the breaking and entering. The jewels of the world were his; the toys, the tools, the play-things, the necessities, the luxuries . . . all belonged to the last man on earth, and he howled.

He left the country mansion in the fields of Connecticut where he had taken up residence; he crossed into Westchester, howling; he ran south along what had once been the Hendrick Hudson Highway, howling; he crossed the bridge into Man-hattan, howling; he ran downtown past lonely skyscrapers, department stores, amusement palaces, howling. He howled down Fifth Avenue, and at the corner of Fiftieth Street he saw a human being.

She was alive, breathing; a beautiful woman. She was tall and dark with cropped curly hair and lovely long legs. She wore a white blouse, tiger-skin riding breeches and patent leather boots. She carried a rifle. She wore a revolver on her hip. She was eating stewed tomatoes from a can and she stared at Halsyon in unbelief. He ran up to her.

"I thought I was the last human on earth," she said.

"You're the last woman," Halsyon howled. "I'm the last man. Are you a dentist?"

"No," she said. "I'm the daughter of the unfortunate Professor Field whose well-intentioned but ill-advised experiment in nuclear fission has wiped mankind off the face of the earth with the exception of you and me who, no doubt on account of some mysterious mutant strain in our makeup which it make us different, are the last of the old civilization and the first of the new."

"Didn't your father teach you anything about dentistry?"

"No," she said.

"Then lend me your gun for a minute."

She unholstered the revolver and handed it to Halsyon, meanwhile keeping her rifle ready. Halsyon cocked the gun.

"I wish you'd been a dentist," he said.

"I'm a beautiful woman with an I.Q. of 141 which is more important for the propagation of a brave new beautiful race of men to inherit the good green earth," she said.

"Not with my teeth it isn't," Halsyon howled.

He clapped the revolver to his temple and blew his brains out.

He awoke with a splitting headache. He was lying on the tile dais alongside the stool, his bruised temple pressed against the cold floor. Mr. Aquila had emerged from the lead shield and was turning on an exhaust fan to clear the air.

"Bravo, my liver and onions," he chuckled. "The last one you did by yourself, eh? No assistance from yours truly required. Meglio tarde che mai. But you went over with a crack before I could catch you. God damn."

He helped Halsyon to his feet and led him into the consultation room where he seated him on a velvet chaise lounge and gave him a glass of brandy.

"Guaranteed free of drugs," he said. "Noblesse oblige. Only the best spiritus frumenti. Now we discuss what we have done, eh? Jeez."

He sat down behind the desk, still sprightly, still bitter, and regarded Halsyon with kindliness. "Man lives by his decisions, n'est-ce pas?" he began. "We agree, oui? A man has some five million two hundred seventy-one thousand and nine decisions to make in the course of his life. Peste! It is a prime number? N'importe. Do you agree?"

Halsyon nodded.

"So, my coffee and doughnuts, it is the maturity of these decisions that decides whether a man is a man or a child. Nicht wahr? Malgré nous. A man cannot start making adult decisions until he has purged himself of the dreams of childhood. God damn. Such fantasies. They must go."

"No," Halsyon said slowly. "It's the dreams that make my art . . . the dreams and fantasies that I translate into line and color. . . ."

"God damn! Yes. Agreed. Maître d'hôtel! But adult dreams, not baby dreams. Baby dreams. Pfui! All men have them. . . . To be the last man on earth and own the earth. . . . To be the last fertile man on earth and own the women. . . . To go back in time with the advantage of adult knowledge and win victories. . . . To escape reality with the dream that life is make-believe. . . . To escape responsibility with a fantasy of heroic injustice, of martyrdom with a happy ending. . . . And there are hundreds more, equally popular, equally empty. God bless Father Freud and his merry men. He applies the quietus to such nonsense. Sic semper tyrannis. Avaunt!"

"But if everybody has those dreams, they can't be bad, can they?"

"God damn. Everybody in fourteenth century had lice. Did that make it good? No, my young, such dreams are for childrens. Too many adults are still childrens. It is you, the artists, who must lead them out as I have led you. I purge you; now you purge them."

"Why did you do this?"

"Because I have faith in you. Sic vos non vobis. It will not be easy for you. A long hard road and lonely."

"I suppose I ought to feel grateful," Halsyon muttered, "but I feel . . . well . . . empty. Cheated."

"Oh yes, God damn. If you live with one Jeez big ulcer long enough you miss him when he's cut out. You were hiding in an ulcer. I have robbed you of said refuge. Ergo: you feel cheated. Wait! You will feel even more cheated. There was a price to pay, I told you. You have paid it. Look."

Mr. Aquila held up a hand mirror. Halsyon glanced into it, then started and stared. A fifty-year-old face stared back at him: lined, hardened, solid, determined. Halsyon leaped to his feet.

"Gently, gently," Mr. Aquila admonished. "It is not so bad. It is damned good. You are still thirty-three in age of physique. You have lost none of your life . . . only all of your youth. What have you lost? A pretty face to lure young girls? Is that why you are wild?"

"Christ!" Halsyon cried.

"All right. Still gently, my child. Here you are, purged, disillusioned, unhappy, bewildered, one foot on the hard road to maturity. Would you like this to have happened or not have happened? Si. I can do. This can never have happened. Spurlos versenkt. It is ten seconds from your escape. You can have your pretty young face back. You can be recaptured. You can return to the safe ulcer of the womb . . . a child again. Would you like same?"

"You can't."

"Sauve qui peut, my Pike's Peak. I can. There is no end to the 15,000 angstrom band."

"Damn you! Are you Satan? Lucifer? Only the devil could have such powers."

"Or angels, my old."

"You don't look like an angel. You look like Satan."

"Ah? Ha? But Satan was an angel before he fell. He has many relations on high. Surely there are family resemblances. God damn." Mr. Aquila stopped laughing. He leaned across the desk and the sprightliness was gone from his face. Only the bitterness remained. "Shall I tell you who I am, my chicken? Shall I explain why one unguarded look from this phizz toppled you over the brink?"

Halsyon nodded, unable to speak.

"I am a scoundrel, a black sheep, a scapegrace, a blackguard. I am a remittance man. Yes. God damn! I am a remittance man." Mr. Aquila's eyes turned into wounds. "By your standards I am the great man of infinite power and variety. So was the remittance man from Europe to naive natives on the beaches of Tahiti. Eh? And so am I to you as I comb the beaches of the stars for a little amusement, a little hope, a little joy to while away the lonely years of my exile. . . .

"I am bad," Mr. Aquila said in a voice of chilling desperation. "I am rotten. There is no place in my home that can tolerate me. They pay me to stay away. And there are moments, unguarded, when my sickness and my despair fill my eyes and strike terror into your innocent souls. As I strike terror into you now. Yes?"

Halsyon nodded again.

"Be guided by me. It was the child in Solon Aquila that destroyed him and led him into the sickness that destroyed his life. Oui. I too suffer from baby fantasies from which I cannot escape. Do not make the same mistake. I beg of you. . . ." Mr. Aquila glanced at his wristwatch and leaped up. The sprightly returned to his manner. "Jeez. It's late. Time to make up your mind, old bourbon and soda. Which will it be? Old face or pretty face? The reality of dreams or the dream of reality?"

"How many decisions did you say we have to make in a lifetime?"

"Five million two hundred and seventy-one thousand and nine. Give or take a thousand. God damn."

"And which one is this for me?"

"Ah? Vérité sans peur. The two million six hundred and thirty-five thousand five hundred and fourth . . . off hand."

"But it's the big one."

"They are all big." Mr. Aquila stepped to the door, placed his hand on the buttons of a rather complicated switch and cocked an eye at Halsyon.

"Voilà tout," he said. "It rests with you."

"I'll take it the hard way," Halsyon decided.

There was a silver chime from the switch, a fizzing aura, a soundless explosion, and Jeffrey Halsyon was ready for his 2,635,505th decision.

About the Author

ROBERT SILVERBERG is the author of many science fiction novels, including *The Masks of Time, Son of Man, A Time of Changes,* and *Tower of Glass,* and others, as well as numerous short stories. He has won two Hugo Awards and two Nebulas for novel and short story. He is a Past-President of the Science Fiction Writers of America.

Mr. Silverberg has also written several nonfiction books on historical and archaeological subjects, including *The Pueblo Revolt, Mound Builders of Ancient America, The Challenge of Climate, Lost Cities and Vanished Civilizations* and *The Realm of Prester John.*

Born and educated in New York City, the author now lives in California with his wife, Barbara.

And don't miss

DYING INSIDE

Robert Silverberg

". . . A fascinating speculative novel on the theme of telepathy."

—Chicago Daily News

"A chilling, realistic novel that explores the psychology of man today, the uninvolved man. A novel that shows the new paths of science fiction."

—Dallas Morning News